# BAD ACTORS

The sequel to *Man Down*.
And a sequel to *Veteran Avenue*.

## By Mark Pepper

First published in Great Britain in 2024 by Ballistic Books

Copyright © Mark Pepper 2024

Mark Pepper has asserted his right under the
Copyright, Designs and Patents Act, 1988,
to be identified as the author of this work.

All rights reserved. No part of this publication may be reproduced, stored in a retrieval system, or transmitted in any form or by any means, electronic, mechanical, photocopying, recording, or otherwise, without the prior permission of both the copyright owner and the above publisher – except for brief quotations for the purpose of book reviews.
All characters in this book are fictional, and any resemblance to actual persons living or dead is purely coincidental.

No content in this work of fiction has been
produced or inspired by artificial intelligence.

Cover design and execution by Simon Churton

Other novels by Mark Pepper:

*Man Down*
*Veteran Avenue*
*Man on a Murder Cycle*
*The Short Cut*

All soon to be republished by Ballistic Books

**www.markpepper.com**

For Killian, Clem, and Eliza,
and those yet to make an appearance.
With much love.

**2022**

## ONE

THE ENGLISH ACTOR had been in Los Angeles for more than twenty years. He was well-regarded within the industry, being a nice enough chap who never ruffled any feathers, but he wasn't what anyone would call naturally gifted, so his swift ascent had never made much sense. Except to Hollywood insiders, who knew the truth. Straight out of a mediocre drama school, his rise had been stratospheric. A single stint in repertory theatre, then straight over to LA. Like many pond-jumpers, he had carved a niche for himself as a bad guy, mostly being cast as the nemesis of heroic characters who weren't half as much fun for the audience to watch. He had once totted up his personal body-count across all his movies, which had averaged out at thirteen. If ever his rapid fame was questioned, he would just say he'd been lucky, but he never attempted to qualify the nature of that good fortune: that a distant aunt – his father's sister-in-law – had been a minor member of Hollywood royalty back in the day. Minor, but with sufficient clout to pave a golden path across the Atlantic for a nephew she had never even met. By local standards, he maintained a quaint humility, but few knew it was derived from an enduring and childlike wonderment, undimmed after two decades, that he had been able to get where he was and stay there. He still lived in the same house he'd bought twenty years earlier, overlooking Stone Canyon Reservoir. It was a Bel-Air mansion, but considering the money he'd put by over the years, it was a relatively modest home, which he shared with the latest in a long line of paramours since his wife had abandoned hope of mended ways and had moved to Arizona with his three children.

It was a short walk to the local store. He loved to be in the open when the July sun was sliding out of sight above Encino, cresting the hills. It was a magical time. The color in the sky, LA's never-ending promise of a bright tomorrow; the wild aromas of the hills mixed with the grass of the manicured lawns, made pungent by the sprinklers; the dissonance of the insects against the hum of the I-405 down Mulholland Drive to the west, marred only by a distant siren.

He was especially happy that evening. For the first time since he'd arrived in LA, he felt he was on the cusp of realizing his potential, of finally busting out of his violent cinematic pigeon-hole, seizing a part that was made for him, and proving to the world he had more than a snarling face to offer.

His hair was already dry from his evening swim, and he smiled as he sauntered across the small parking lot. The businesses that circled it were closed, except for the general store on the other side. He laughed; he wasn't even sure what he wanted to buy. His joy at being in that place at that time was unyielding, but sometimes its power surprised even him, pouncing as though it never wanted him to forget how lucky he was.

Rushed footsteps behind him. Then another sound, one he recognized from his movies, and a simultaneous thud in his back. His smile twitched on and off, like a failing bulb trying to figure out if its time was up. He slowed his pace; maybe out of choice, he couldn't tell. His palm went to his flank, to his singlet above his right kidney, and came away wet. He stopped, looked down at the exit wound through his abs. He slipped a hand into his shorts pocket, pulled out his wallet, although it didn't feel like anyone wanted to rob him.

Another thud – higher this time. Maybe his shoulder blade. No exit wound.

Scripted options flooded his head. Every death-scene, every desperate move his characters had made, reeled across his vision like the fondest memories of a drowning man. He felt the need to turn around, to face the source, to fight, to run.

Perversely, he carried on walking, his gait now twisted, as though the event was a mistake that he could leave behind him if he feigned plausible ignorance of its import. Perhaps if he could get inside the store.

The third shot caught something vital, and his legs collapsed under him. He pitched forward, face-planting the concrete, feeling his nose flatten. Of all the physical insults, he squealed at that. Then he held his breath, froze, played dead like all those times before, praying to hear his assailant scurry away.

Instead, the footsteps drew near. His wallet had landed a few feet in front of his face, standing open like a small leather-backed frame, showing his cards on one side and a picture of his estranged, laughing children on the other. The footsteps halted. He closed his eyes, thought of the amazing life he was losing, then felt nothing more.

MATT SPILLER WAS pouring sweat as he finally managed to locate his house. He'd spent the first few months renting in Toluca Lake, near the studios. It had seemed like an awful waste of money considering the square footage he never stepped in. He'd been one person in a grand, four-bedroom house. Having left England at the end of January as a poor taxi driver with big bills and a wife and two daughters to support, he had baulked at the idea of handing over a single penny of his new-found wealth, even when that wealth amounted to six million dollars, pre-tax, but post-agent's commission. The house had been forced on him by the production company, who wanted him close by. Understanding his financial situation, they had offered to front the fifteen-thousand-dollar monthly rental for the duration of the shoot, then reclaim fifty percent when he got paid. It was perhaps a sweet deal – he didn't know – but it was still too much money. His initial delirium at landing the role had spawned a hell-with-it attitude that had him thinking no house would be too big, and no driveway long enough to accommodate all the cars he thought he'd buy. Then doubt had set in. He was coming forty-four. Perhaps this would not be the glorious late start to a long overdue Hollywood career; perhaps this was just a cruel anomaly. Maybe this was all the money he'd ever see, and this time next year he'd be back in England, desperate for one line on *Emmerdale*. So, he'd informed the production people that he'd rent an apartment somewhere cheap. Their blinding LA smiles had barely concealed their horror. He didn't know the city. They knew he didn't know the city. What if he chose a dangerous locale? What if, one evening, he went for a stroll down the wrong street and wound up in a body bag? It would be a tragedy; they would have to recast and start over. And obviously he'd be dead, so… that would be kinda sad, too. But Spiller suspected it wasn't the production coordinator who had clinched the Toluca Lake house for him totally *gratis*, but the director himself. Far from being afeared for Spiller's safety, Brett Stutz must have been picturing what might happen if his star woke up one day in a bad mood and decided to make his own way into work, cutting a bloody swathe across the city *à la* Michael Douglas in *Falling Down*.

He had stayed on in the Toluca Lake house beyond the shoot, through the rest of April, May, and into June, while he looked around for somewhere more permanent, and popped into the studio for some post-production tweaks. The rent continued to be paid, right up to the point that he informed the studio he'd found a place of his own and it wasn't in Compton.

Spiller stripped naked and jumped in his private pool behind the home he'd owned for the past month, tucked out of sight at the end of a narrow lane off North Beverly Glen Boulevard. He still found it to be a wondrous area to live in. The lanes, winding through the wild and wooded hills, adhering to their dips and contours, dotted by strange edifices, no two alike, some grand, some barely more than shacks, variously built of wood, brick, concrete, stone, or clad in granite slabs. It was all so twee and eclectic and *mellow*. Yet, there was also something menacing about its isolation. Almost smack at the epicenter of a sprawling city of four million people, it felt like something awful could happen there and no one would know for months. Perhaps it was the proximity of the Sharon Tate house in Benedict Canyon, or perhaps it was just the exhausted mind of a man who had seen and done too much too quickly.

The house was relatively new, constructed of white-washed concrete, built to the confines of the land on which it sat. Double garage, small pool, three bedrooms, two bathrooms, one-point-eight million dollars. Spiller had snapped it up on the advice of the realtor who had assured him such "reasonably priced" properties rarely appeared on the market. His O1 visa gave him an initial three years to enjoy the place. Beyond that, he wasn't worried. He'd be fully established with a Green Card by then, or he'd be long gone.

He thought he'd probably continue sweating if he got out, so he floated on his back, looking up at the sky, twinkling with the first stars of the night, feeling his short hair splay out on the surface. He'd shaved his head after filming. Not a great blow to his crowning glory, given he'd been sporting a white Mohawk throughout the role. Now it was back to the length he usually preferred. It seemed to grow quicker in the heat, although he doubted there was any science to that.

As the water lapped into his ears, he smiled at his general good fortune, but especially his luck in finding his way back that evening. That evening, he had got thoroughly lost. While he knew the surrounding lanes by now, his daily jogs too frequently had him blindly following his nose, venturing into the hills or down onto the twisting trails around Stone Canyon Reservoir. On those occasions, he would often stop and look across to the Bel-Air side – but not with any feeling of jealousy at the more expensive zip code; merely with a sense of bafflement, that he had managed to go from a deadbeat provincial English taxi driver to a person who could gaze upon such wealth from a resident's point of view. He guessed he'd have felt the same looking from Bel-Air to Beverly Glen. To him, it was all the same. It was LA, and he lived there.

AS THE LAST of the lingering sun left the sky, and the aurora of the city bloomed above him, Spiller decided he had better get ready. His fingers and toes had crinkled. He collected his running gear from the poolside and went into the house. The recessed spots were bright, but they provided scant comfort. His mood was spiraling again. It was a nightly occurrence. Every nightfall felt like the drawing-in of a long, sunless Lapland winter. Too many bad things had happened in the dark. The sun would be back in a few hours and his mood would dissipate like a nightmare he couldn't recall, but right now he craved its return like a junkie hungering for his fix.

An hour later, he was dressed and waiting for his ride. He'd sunk a couple of beers to calm his nerves, but they had sent him scampering for the toilet. His stomach had been out of sorts for days in anticipation of this evening. It was precisely the event he had hankered after for twenty years. Now it had arrived, he was in a maelstrom of fear and self-doubt. Soon, he would be heading to one of the studios at Burbank, just beyond his old digs at Toluca Lake, for the opening salvo in what would be a month-long round of publicity prior to the release of his movie. A month. Damn. He just wanted to stay home.

The black Chevy Suburban that pulled onto his short driveway fifteen minutes later made him smile. He loved the vehicles the studio sent for him. Probably it was immature, but they always made him feel like he was in the CIA. He watched unseen from the sundeck above his garage as his publicist emerged from the darkened windows, then he lost sight of her as she approached the front door. He heard the bell ring below him.

He wasn't keen on his publicist. Then again, he wasn't keen on human beings generally, and she almost qualified. She looked like an alien replica of a real person; as though, for all their advanced ways, they couldn't quite get the look right; they couldn't instill any *character* in their creations. Spiller could only guess at her age. Perhaps somewhere between forty-five and seventy. Scalpels and fillers had irrevocably erased her identity, like a finger without a print. Pre-surgery, she had possibly been an attractive woman. Her manner with him suggested his presence in LA was an aberration; that the studio had screwed up at a level so far above her pay grade that she didn't feel able to say anything out loud.

She looked him up and down when he opened the door.

"Hey, Cathy. What's up?"

"Evening, Matthew. Are you wearing that outfit?"

"No, it's an optical illusion. Sorry, are you pleased or pissed off – I can never tell."

She placed her hands on her bony hips as if to clarify the point.

"No, you need to give me more. I'm still not getting anything. Are you trying to frown?"

"Matthew, you look like an undertaker, or like you're auditioning for a remake of *Reservoir Dogs*."

"What would you have had me wear?"

"I said: smart casual."

"I have smart *or* I have casual. And you really don't want me in my casual."

"You know, if you'd told me earlier, I'd have taken you shopping."

"Aww, thanks, *mom*."

"Just get in the car."

He stood his ground, a king on his own porch. "Anyway, it's not like anyone's going to see me. It goes out live at midnight. Everyone's going to be in bed."

"Jesus, Matthew, have you not at least googled this guy? He averages nearly five million viewers each episode, and that's not including the three repeats during the week."

"And that's a lot? For a country of over three hundred million people?"

She went squeaky. *"It's the top-rated talk show in America!"*

"Okay – what's his name again?"

"You're kidding me, right? Is that English humor?"

Spiller smirked. "He's Mel Banaghan. He went from stand-up to sit-down. People love him."

"Yeah, so this is a real fucking coup, Matthew."

"I'm sorry – remind me again: do I pay you to swear at me?"

"You don't pay me – the studio does. Now, can you and your thrift-shop suit please get in the car?"

Spiller obliged, ignoring Cathy's protestation as he climbed in the front alongside the blonde female driver, who looked at him askance.

"Am I okay here?" Spiller asked.

The driver appeared to be around thirty years old. She shrugged amiably at Spiller's question.

Cathy got in the back, diagonally opposite. "Matthew, I need you sitting next to me. I need to talk ground-rules – for tonight."

"I can hear you. It's not like your expression's going to add anything to the conversation."

Spiller caught a subtle grin on the driver's face and offered his hand. "I'm Matt."

"Sadie."

"Matthew! Get back here so we can talk!"

"How long have you been driving Miss Crazy?" Spiller asked Sadie, who burst out laughing.

"*Matthew!*"

"Let's get going," Spiller said.

The radio came on low as Sadie started the engine and reversed off the driveway.

Cathy raised her voice. "*Matthew!* You need to listen to me. This is very important."

"All ears."

"Mel Banaghan is a jerk. Bear that in mind. He built his career on saying things other people won't say. How he hasn't been canceled by now... Anyway, he's gonna ask you questions you might not wanna answer. Things you probably shouldn't answer."

"Such as?"

"I don't know."

"Exactly. You're my publicist and you know nothing about me. So, how could he? My life before I came here is a closed book. A failed actor who drove a cab – that's it."

"Everyone has skeletons in their closet, Matthew."

"Well, mine were in the hills and they never managed to pin them on me, so..."

A brief lull ensued. Spiller felt the need to laugh at his silly joke – which wasn't a joke – but it came out as a hoot, which sounded even worse.

"Joking!" he said. "Jesus..."

"Don't joke," Cathy told him. "Really. Leave the jokes to Mel Banaghan. You say something off, it could majorly hurt the movie. Okay?"

"I thought there was no such thing as bad publicity."

"In this town, these days, there sure as hell is. Careers are wrecked by it. You need me to name names?"

Spiller thought about it. "No. Oh, stick this up, would you?" He pointed at the media screen.

As Sadie turned the SUV onto North Beverly Glen Boulevard, she hit the wheel-mounted volume, and Spiller began to croon along to Keane, raising his voice whenever Cathy began to speak.

Eventually, she gave up.

## TWO

THE DISPLACED NEW Yorker stood in the garden of the Bel-Air mansion, looking out across Stone Canyon Reservoir toward the sprawling lights of downtown Los Angeles. Such potential for heartache out there. Not so much up here, but tonight was different.

Next to him, the infinity pool turned dark as the timer clicked off, just as the last of the TV-station choppers performed one final pass, then it dipped its nose and headed off back to its rooftop nest. Vultures, circling until the coroner had removed the carcass and there was nothing left to pick over. He raised a middle finger to its departing taillight, then followed its path until it descended over the city, and its winking was swamped by the luminosity. So nice for his ears to be rid of the rotor blades.

He was alone in the garden. It hadn't happened there, but killers sometimes stalked their victims, and this area was easily accessed by anyone sufficiently determined to traipse around the reservoir and climb up through the scrub. The perfect vantage-point to spy on the huge expanse of glass at the rear, the entire edifice seemingly open to the elements, like a doll's house without its façade.

Now the choppers had disappeared, the girlfriend was still audible, even from that distance. Distraught, she had earlier struggled through her tears to deny any knowledge of why anyone would want to kill her lover. She was being comforted by a friend now, but not enough to prevent her rending the night air. The detective didn't see her as a suspect. Her ulterior concerns were too obvious. *"What am I gonna do now?"* she'd kept wailing mournfully, as though she needed a housing officer more than a police officer.

He grabbed the trunk of a palm tree as he clambered down five feet from the lawn to the scrubland of the hill. Using a small tac-light, he scanned around for signs of a fresh trail, footprints in the dirt, a cigarette butt, or a gum wrapper. It was unlikely, but you could never discount such idiocy. With nothing close to the garden, he made his way down, shuffling his sensible detective shoes gingerly in the slick dust, searching with his beam.

Just one clue, that's all he wanted. In the three months he'd been attached to West Bureau, he'd not managed to get his teeth into anything meaty. Tonight bucked the trend. Considering the rich pickings in this hilly enclave, it seemed there was an invisible boundary that ran around it, repelling the serious ne'er-do-wells; a zone bordered by Ventura Boulevard to the north, Cahuenga to the east, Sunset to the south, and the wilderness to the west, inside of which nothing very terrible happened. You needed to add burglary to really get any markers appearing on the crime map for this privileged neighborhood. So, tonight was an oddity, and his juices were flowing.

No one knew it, but he had something to prove. He'd left his last city lauded as a hero. A single case that had seen a gang leader taken down and several murders solved. Only, he had been clueless throughout, thwarted at every turn by an asshole he knew was involved, but who kept wriggling off the hook. But the real affront had been his final acquiescence to that asshole, agreeing to back off in exchange for a pretty bow that *apparently* tied the whole thing together.

The detective forced his mind back to the present. He stood still, killed the light, closed his eyes, listened to the sounds of the night. Christ. Three in the back, one in the base of the skull. All for what? A few bucks? He opened his eyes, peered at the distant city. Where was the callous son-of-a-bitch? Where in this heartless metropolis?

"Police Officer!" A stern female voice from the garden. "Stay right there! Show me your hands!"

He raised his hands high, far from his holstered Kimber .45. "Don't shoot, I'm a cop."

"Turn around slowly; keep your hands in the air."

He shuffled round into the bright gaze of the officer's tac-light, which caused the detective's shield on his belt to gleam back at her.

"Can you get that out of my eyes, please?"

The officer cut the light and holstered her 9mm FN 509. "Sorry, sir."

The detective made his way back up to the garden, smiled crookedly. "Blue-on-blue. Not the best way to end a thirty-year career."

"Sorry," she said again.

"No problem – all by the book. Officer...?"

"Gabriela Contreras."

"Good to meet you." He extended his hand, and they shook. "What are you doing here, Contreras?"

"Sorry, I thought everyone had left."

"Hey, stop apologizing for doing your job. I left my car at the scene, walked. I meant, why are you *still* here?"

"Oh. I wanted to check around. I was here a couple of months back. Report of a possible prowler. Nothing, though."

"And you thought... some connection?"

Contreras shrugged. "You find anything down there?"

He shook his head, smiled. "Good for you, Contreras."

"Good for me? Sir?"

"You're keen." He nodded at the two chevrons on her upper sleeve. "Grade three already. What are you, twenty-five?"

She smiled. "Thank you, I'm twenty-nine."

"So, your next step toward Chief of Police is what? Detective Trainee?"

"Considering it. Open to all options."

"Well..." he dipped two fingers in his breast pocket, offered her a card "...look me up if you think I can help."

"Thanks." Contreras perused the information. "Lieutenant. You're the lead on this?"

He nodded. "See you around, Contreras." He was about to walk away, but noticed she was suddenly transfixed by the pool, her eyes pinched in puzzlement as though she'd never seen such a thing.

"Contreras?"

She looked at him. "Uh, something just... can I run something by you?"

"Sure."

She sat on a pool chair, so he claimed one for himself.

"This may be really left field, but…"

"Go on," he said.

"Aiden Powers. Major Hollywood tough guy, found dead in his pool at the end of March."

"Just before I got here, but I recall the news."

"Head trauma, blood found on a coping stone. High blood-alcohol level, drugs in his system, no evidence of foul play, so the coroner ruled it an accident. Likely scenario being he tripped, fell across the corner of the pool, knocked himself out on the edge, drowned."

"Okay."

"Powers lived on Blue Sail Drive, backing onto the hills. Near the Getty Villa. If you left a vehicle on Palisades Drive, you could walk in and out. Drop down on the house, no chance of being tracked."

He nodded thoughtfully. "Go on."

"Early May, John Frears, major Hollywood tough guy, drives his Ferrari into a ravine off of Mulholland. Crashed and burned. Nothing much left of anything. No witnesses. Well, no eyewitnesses. Local homeowner heard some collision immediately prior to the crash and explosion. Metal on metal, like two cars bumping each other."

"Anything from nearby traffic cams, CCTV?"

"Drew a blank. Case is still open, given the witness statement, but…" She shrugged.

"So, you're saying the three incidents could be connected?"

"I'm saying three big Hollywood tough guys are dead within the past five months. First two look like accidents, and the third is clearly a homicide, but it could easily be construed as a random street robbery. Guy gets shot in the back, goes down face-first. Easy to assume the assailant had no clue who he was. Just wrong place, wrong time. Only, this is not the usual area for crimes of this nature. You know that."

The detective scratched his chin, ran a clawing hand back through his abundant silver hair, restoring its Mafia-like coif. He smiled crookedly at her.

"Am I being stupid?" she asked.

"Only stupid theory is the one you keep to yourself. I'm gonna put a heavy pencil on this."

She smiled, relieved. "Really? What? Two-B? Three-B?"

"I'll go with a Four-B — for now." He wasn't sure if he was humoring her because he liked the intrigue behind the idea, or he liked the person who just proposed it. Probably both. "But if you're right, it means there's a serial killer out there targeting Hollywood tough guys, and doing it surreptitiously to keep us off the scent."

He stood up, and she followed suit.

"Do we say anything?" Contreras asked. "I mean, to the studios? So they can warn their stars? Or do we just wait to see if it happens again?"

"I don't think we should start a panic at this point."

She nodded. "Yeah. More of an HB, then, huh?"

"Listen, once this news gets out there, people are gonna hypothesize. You thought it; other people will. I just don't want the LAPD to be the source. Okay?"

"Sure."

He offered a grin he hoped wouldn't appear too lecherous. "Take care, Contreras. You got my number."

"In case I think of anything pertinent to the investigation?" She smirked.

"Sure. That, too."

SADIE PARKED AT the rear of the studio in one of the six spots marked *Reserved – Guests*. Sandwiched between the Suburban and a silver Lincoln Navigator was a vintage, bright green Ford Bronco, which Spiller recognized as the director's car.

With the music now absent, Cathy spoke up. "Matthew, you need to be on your game tonight, got it? You are a major face of this movie."

"I know," Spiller said, then twisted around. "So, what happens now? Do I meet Mel, tell him a few amusing anecdotes so he can ask me about them on the show?"

"We could have spoken about this on the way, except you wouldn't shut the hell up singing. No, Matthew, you do not get to meet Mel Banaghan before the show. You don't get to prepare. That's every other chat show. This one, you walk out there and he asks you whatever he wants. Which means you need to take a moment before answering. And if you don't like the question, just say 'no comment' and smile."

"I was warned not so long ago by, uh... someone in the know, that *no comment* makes a person look guilty as hell."

Cathy raised a tattooed eyebrow. "*Someone in the know?* Jeepers, is there something about your past you haven't told me? Doesn't matter – I don't wanna hear. And the studio doesn't want five million people to be the *first* to hear. Just... you can't be hung for something you don't say. Remember that."

She hopped out and went around to the front passenger door. Spiller could see her through the privacy glass, but he waited for her to tap before he lowered the window.

"Are you coming?" she asked. "They'll need you in makeup."

"Two minutes."

She exhaled sharply. "Sadie, you know where to bring him?"

"I do, Miss Zengler."

"Two minutes, Sadie. Make sure."

"No problem," Sadie replied through an ever-shrinking window gap.

Spiller watched Cathy enter the building, then looked at Sadie with a kind of awkward pleading.

"What's up, Matt?"

"Sadie, I don't know you, so please don't be offended, but... would you have anything to calm me down? I have a social anxiety thing. I don't even want to go in the greenroom with the other guests. But, holy crap, five million people?"

"What are you after?"

"I have no idea; I don't do that stuff."

"And you wanna start *now?*" She laughed.

"Do you have anything?"

"No. But you see Miss Crazy's tote bag in the back?" Sadie gave a couple of deliberate sniffs.

"Oh, really?"

Sadie nodded. "You sure you wanna do this?"

"Right now, I have a choice: take something, or run screaming into the night."

"Do it, then. Quick."

Spiller was in the rear of the vehicle in five seconds.

"Zip pocket inside," Sadie said, watching the studio entrance.

Spiller found a small vial of white powder and unscrewed the cap. "Is this cocaine?"

"I'm not a pharmacist, but…"

Spiller tapped some powder out and stared at the little mound nestled on the skin between his thumb and forefinger. "Just…?"

"Snort like they do in the movies."

BY THE TIME Spiller's face had been caked in a wholly less interesting powder, he felt euphoric. Five million people? Bring it on. The makeup woman peered oddly at his grinning face, but he reckoned she'd just possibly suffered a coked-up star in her chair once or twice before. He tried to flatten his mouth, but he sensed it only made his eyes go bigger to compensate. In the corner of the room, Sadie looked on with an expression that was half-amusement, half-concern.

"Okay, Mr Spiller, you are done," said the woman, removing the bib from his neck. Then, under her breath: "*So* done."

"What?"

Sadie beckoned. "Matt, greenroom." Out in the corridor, which was lined with photographs of the visiting celebrities, and far too many of the host himself, Sadie stopped Spiller and handed him a pair of black Ray-Bans. "You need these. Whatever anyone says, you don't take them off. Okay? You got frigging shark-eyes."

"Cool."

The greenroom was buzzing. Huddled on a sofa in one corner was a rock band, four adolescent white dudes, laughing among themselves. One of them offered him a strange splay-fingered hand-gesture. In the opposite corner was a black female comedian he vaguely recognized, and along the left wall was seated an ex-wrestling star, whose name also wouldn't come to mind, who had taken a sideways leap into wrestling with dialog and directions and acting in general.

To his right, Cathy was chatting to Brett Stutz. Stutz broke from the conversation and looked Spiller up and down. "Elwood Blues, as I live and breathe."

"Whatever."

"Joliet Jake joining us later?"

"Yeah, *Brat*, I got the reference."

From the corner, one of the band piped up with, *"Rolling rolling rolling, keep those dogies rolling…"* which made everyone laugh.

At that moment, a production assistant entered the room, and everyone quietened. "Okay, order of business," she said. "Bobby, you're up first."

The ex-wrestler grunted.

"Then Toni."

The comedian nodded.

"Then, Brett, we'll bring you on, you talk about your new movie, then Mel will introduce Matthew, so we'll have the two of you on together. Then a musical finale with you guys."

The band barked and howled like dogs until they realized it all sounded a bit lame.

"Keep watching the monitor, please. Someone will come get you, but we will occasionally cut to this room, so I need you all to be paying attention." She paused and pointed at Spiller's suit. "Do you need to get changed?"

"No! Bloody hell, really? This is worse than that, is it?" He indicated Stutz's trademark black leather pants over winklepickers.

"Okay, five minutes, everyone!"

Spiller looked at his driver. "Sadie, walk with me."

He found an unoccupied canteen along the corridor and rifled through the drawers next to the sink as she looked on.

"Ah-ha!" He held up a pair of scissors, then laid them against one knee. "Above or below?"

"Matt…"

"They don't like my suit? It can get a whole lot worse. Above or below?"

"Depends what vibe you're going for. Naughty schoolboy or executive surf dude."

"Defo the naughty schoolboy."

"Gotta be above."

Spiller jabbed the sharper prong through his right pants leg and proceeded to snip around the circumference, then did the same with his left leg. He removed his shoes and pulled the extraneous material off his feet, then put his shoes back on.

"Nailed it, right?" he asked.

"You know Miss Crazy won't let you walk out there like that."

"She's not going to see me." Spiller grabbed a remote and zapped a wall-hung TV into life. It was already tuned into the right channel. "We'll watch from here, then pounce when the moment comes."

"You're insane, you know that?"

AS BRETT STUTZ walked onto the set of *The Mel Banaghan Show*, Matt Spiller was starting to come down. It had been thirty minutes. Perhaps he hadn't taken enough. He and Sadie watched as the resident quartet struck up Mel's theme tune, and the audience hollered for the man who had brought them so much cinematic bloodshed over the years. Stutz strolled onto the set, waving at the faces in the dark, then sank into the guest chair. The previous guests had been removed from the stage. From behind his desk, Mel calmed the audience, then ran through a few digs and in-jokes, stopping just short of a full-blown roast. For the next five minutes, they chatted about Hollywood, the state of the industry, and much to Stutz's chagrin, his failed marriages. Then as time was short, Mel asked Stutz to explain his latest movie.

Stutz crossed his long legs, creaking his pants. "Well, Mel, it's titled *Man on a Murder Cycle*. Great plot—"

"Oh, so a big departure from your previous work."

The audience hooted.

Stutz offered a facetious grin. "I make movies that these lovely people pay to see. Am I right?"

The audience hooted more loudly.

Mel smiled. "Continue."

"So, the movie's based on a novel that was out some years back, called *The Madness of Milton*. It's a horror treatment of the circumstances surrounding the publication of that novel. It all took place in the UK, so people may not know much about it, but what everyone will recall is the mid-air collision of flights Western Air five-one-two and Albion Atlantic six-three-nine. The author – Tom Roker – his family was on that flight, but that wasn't the start of this guy's problems, which began just after publication, when some maniac on a motorcycle decided to act out every grisly murder in the book. Not only that, but Roker's agent was murdered, the two lead detectives on the case, and, well... I don't wanna spoil the plot, but a lot of people got killed."

"Who wrote the script?" Mel asked.

"This is where it gets weird, because the screenplay was written by the ex-husband of Roker's agent, and he says he could only write it because he got the whole story from his second wife, who claims Roker didn't even write the book; it was her brother wrote the book, just before he died in a motorcycle accident at the Isle of Man TT."

Mel laughed. "So, Roker stole the plot?"

"Stole everything. Word-for-word."

"Unbelievable. And when's the movie out?"

"End of next month. Cinema only, people."

At the side of the stage, a man with a sign needlessly encouraged the pliable audience to applaud, and they obliged.

"Coming up next..." Mel pointed to his band, and the drummer began a roll "...a world exclusive here on *The Mel Banaghan Show*. Introducing for the first time, all the way from little old England... one of the stars of *Man on a Murder Cycle*... Matt Spiller! Don't go away. Back in two."

Spiller stared at the screen, heard the drum roll morph into Mel's theme tune, and watched the commercials begin. He could hear his name interspersed with the distraught pleas of the production assistant and the profanities of Cathy Zengler out in the corridor. He waited for the ads to end, then grinned at Sadie.

"Guess that's me. Wish me luck."

"Knock 'em dead."

Spiller emerged into the corridor, and Cathy squealed and pointed at his pants. "Matthew, what the fuck?"

"I was hot."

The production assistant tutted at his tailoring skills, grabbed his arm, and pulled him down the corridor to the door that led onto the set. She opened it, and Spiller heard a momentary burst of Mel's theme tune before the host welcomed back the audience.

"Come on out here, Matt, don't be shy! Matt Spiller, everyone!"

Spiller looked down at his legs and wondered if he'd been stupid. Then he suddenly felt quite irritated and wondered if his high was beginning to cede control to its after-effects rather too soon.

"Bollocks," he said, and walked on anyway.

## THREE

BEHIND HIS BORROWED Wayfarers, Spiller kept his eyes fixed on Brett Stutz. He wasn't disappointed. The lapse in the director's sunny countenance was momentary, and anyone not concentrating would have missed it, but Stutz was mortified. From his chair, which was now one away from Mel Banaghan's desk, his smile resumed, morphing into a grin that said: *this guy, huh? Brits, what are they like?*

The host himself was smiling bemusedly and shaking his head in front of a large digital image of LA's night-time cityscape. The audience applause quickly gave way to laughter. Spiller gave them a double thumbs-up and extended his arm to the host. Mel stood up as he grasped the proffered hand, leaning forward to confide something the audience wouldn't hear.

"Dude, you are out to lunch."

"That would be the consensus."

"Take a seat," the host said loudly, including the audience again.

Spiller claimed the empty chair Stutz had just vacated, and greeted his director by slapping him unnecessarily hard on a leather thigh. The audience began to calm down, ripples of amusement rising and falling until the sign-man flapped his arms to indicate quiet.

Mel shook his head again. "So, you're making me ask…"

"Well, my mum always told me: stop crying or I'll give you something to cry about."

"Did someone not like your suit?"

"This old fart in the leather pants, for one."

Stutz forced a laugh. "I like your suit."

"Really?" Spiller moved to kneel in front of him and produced the scissors from his pocket.

"Don't you dare!" Stutz said, tittering at the audience, which was roaring with laughter.

Spiller shoved one blade inside the material that was tight against the director's winklepickers and began snipping up his leg to above his calf, then circled around beneath his knee to complete the cut. Spiller stood up and offered Stutz the scissors. "Here you go; you can do the other one yourself."

Stutz waved him away, clearly struggling to sustain his veneer of conviviality. Spiller resumed his seat and put the scissors on Mel Banaghan's desk, then beamed at the audience.

Mel nodded. "Okay, I'm beginning to see why you might have been cast as the psychopath in this movie. Speaking of, here's an exclusive peek at Matt's character. And keep in mind, this is based on CCTV and eyewitness accounts of what the guy actually looked like."

Behind the host, four of the screens depicting the cityscape yielded to a physiognomy that made the audience audibly wince. It was Spiller's face, heavily made-up to appear as though it had been ripped apart and stitched back together, topped by a white Mohawk.

"And that's Milton, right?" Mel asked.

Spiller nodded. "The mental motorcyclist. The barking biker."

"Was it a fun part to play?"

Stutz cut in: "How the hell would he know? He's got zilch to compare it to. I plucked this loser from obscurity."

Spiller smiled at him. "Aw, someone's missing his trouser leg. To answer your question, Mel, it was enormous fun, and the best part was I got to keep the bike. And just so people know, I was an actor before this prat turned up. I was in a big British movie."

"Then he spent fifteen years driving a cab," Stutz said. "Until I rode in like the cavalry to save him."

Mel smacked his palms repeatedly on his desk, then formed a time-out symbol with his hands. "Okay, so... this is not the sycophantic, mutual actor-director hug-fest we normally get on this show. Just a hunch, but I'm sensing bad blood here. Care to share?"

Spiller shrugged. He couldn't explain the tension without confessing to a past that would end his career and send him to prison.

Stutz spoke: "Artistic differences."

Spiller heaved an internal sigh and wished he could re-do the evening with full-length trouser legs and without cocaine. He was just about to apologize to Stutz when the director came out with it.

"Matt, should I tell them all about your first audition? That's a fun story, huh?"

"No."

"So, I visit the UK looking for a couple of British actors. Matt here picks me up from the airport in his cab. I didn't even know he was an actor. We chat a little on the way, he tells me he is an actor, then we get to the hotel and he won't open the trunk so I can get my case. Then—"

Spiller grabbed the scissors off the desk and launched at Stutz. The director squeaked as Spiller straddled his legs like a dominant lover. Spiller pulled the mic from Stutz's collar and snipped the wire, then cut his own and held the tips of the open blades against Stutz's neck. He swiveled as he sensed a back-up mic boom lowering toward his head.

"Get that thing away from me!"

The boom rose upward out of sight. Mel Banaghan wheeled his chair back a little, signaling to some off-stage security personnel to hold back, and indicating with a rotating finger that the cameras keep rolling and that they shouldn't go to a commercial break. The audience fell silent.

Spiller whispered in Stutz's ear. "You say one more word and the next thing that gets snipped is your carotid."

Clandestinely, Stutz said, "I know what you did."

"I know you know. Didn't stop you taking me on, though, did it."

"*Both* auditions. Both *executions*."

"You don't know the backstory. If you'd asked, I'd have told you."

"Millions of people are watching this, Matt. This is great TV, and you're awesome as Milton, but you better sit back down right now so I can rescue this."

Spiller pulled back and stared into his eyes.

"Follow my lead," Stutz whispered.

Spiller removed himself from Stutz's lap and reclaimed his seat. He set the scissors on the desk again, but this time Mel made a point of picking them up and stowing them in a drawer on his side. He simpered at the audience, pretending to wipe some sweat from his brow, but they remained quiet, still unsure.

Stutz rose to his feet and offered a hand to Spiller in a theatrical gesture he knew from his repertory days. It was time to take a bow. He joined his director and they both burst out laughing and offered their obeisance to the seated rabble. Slowly, people started clapping, then howling in appreciation.

"I need a drink!" Mel said, when the studio had calmed down. "No, I mean it, someone get me a fucking drink!"

Shortly, a studio-hand dressed in black ran on with a bottle of Jack Daniels. Mel threw the water from his glass over his right shoulder, like salt for good luck, prompting more audience hilarity, then refilled with a full dose of amber liquid and downed it.

Grinning, Stutz pointed at Spiller. "Now, *that* is why I picked Mr Matt Spiller over everyone else. What you just saw; that was pretty much his audition. I tell you, I nearly had a frigging heart attack. I instantly knew this guy was the real deal."

Mel topped up and glugged some more. "So, Matt, you got any projects lined up?"

Spiller smiled and nearly removed his sunglasses, before remembering why they were on his face. "Not yet. Maybe I'm not in a position to pick and choose yet, but—"

He was halted mid-sentence by a hand rudely thrust toward his face. Mel cocked his head and put a finger to his ear to indicate he was receiving some information. There was another lull in the studio. Twenty seconds later, the host lowered his finger and gave the audience a somber look.

"Okay, I've just heard some terrible breaking news, which I'd like to share with you. In the last few minutes, police have confirmed that the actor Harry Sullivan was found shot dead near his Bel-Air home this evening."

The audience gasped and began chattering.

"Sorry, I know I'm not a news anchor, but we had Harry on the show only a couple of weeks back, and I wanted to offer our condolences – the whole team here at *The Mel Banaghan Show* – to Harry's family and friends."

Spiller bowed his head at the news, stared down at his bare legs. He ruffled his knee hairs and thought they needed a trim, which he'd never thought before. No more drugs for Matt Spiller. He looked at the empty musical set across the studio, and prayed the white-boy band in the greenroom was about to get their skinny arses on stage to lighten the mood.

"Before we go to the break," Mel said. "Matt…"

Spiller looked up. "Still here."

"Anything you'd like to share about Harry Sullivan?"

"What?"

"A fond remembrance."

"Huh?"

Mel tapped his earpiece. "My researcher tells me you worked with him."

"Oh… right… uh… long time ago. I think it was his first gig out of drama school. Before he came over here. Gotta be twenty years ago."

"Anything you'd like to say?"

"Well… just… obviously, very sad to hear the news. To be honest, I don't recall much about the play, I had other stuff on my mind back then. But, um… he did what every young actor strives for, you know? He got here. Made a career. Famous aunt didn't do him any harm, but… hats off to him. Condolences."

Mel nodded solemnly. "Absolutely. Okay, coming up, here to perform their latest hit single… it's The Dingo Dudes!" Mel gave a doggy howl. "Stay tuned. We'll be right back."

Spiller waited for the red lights to wink out on the cameras. "Murdered actor, but the show must go on, eh?" he said to Mel Banaghan.

"Give me a break. This is meant to be light entertainment. I'm a comedian, okay?"

"Allegedly. I mean, you've not made me laugh once."

Mel laughed at that. "You know, I shouldn't like you but I kinda do."

"You check your ratings at the end of the week, mate. You'll love me then."

"Reckon you might be right."

As The Dingo Dudes moved into position, Spiller got up and left the stage, waving at the appreciative crowd as he went. Behind him, Stutz debated, then quickly followed, his severed pants leg crumpled on his winklepicker like a forlorn 1980s legwarmer.

THEY CORNERED HIM in the greenroom. Cathy blocked the corridor, waving him into the empty space like a cop flagging a detour, while Stutz corraled him from the rear.

"What?" he said, as he turned to face them.

Sadie hovered in the corridor, waiting, grinning over their shoulders at him.

"Matthew…" Cathy began, her utter bewilderment stealing whatever else she might have rehearsed.

"What the fuck was that?" Stutz asked, pulling the plug on the wall display to mute Mel Banaghan's intermission banter with the audience.

"I could ask you the same. My audition? You wanted to talk about my audition on national television?"

Cathy's unlined features tried to crease. "What's the big deal about your audition?"

"Doesn't matter," Spiller said. "Just know that this tosser was on the verge of wrecking everything."

"I wouldn't have. You think I'd have destroyed my movie for a stupid anecdote."

Cathy's gnarly fingers clawed into Stutz's shirt. "What is this about Matthew's audition? I need to know. I'm gonna be asked. Twitter's already lighting up like a Christmas tree."

Stutz stared down at his ankle. "You cut my pants."

"Man, buy some blue jeans. What are you, sixty?"

"Matthew!" Cathy stared at him. "You… Christ, do you even want a career in this town?"

Spiller chuckled. "Oh, chill out. I just *made* your movie for you. Who's not going to want to see it now?"

Cathy considered. "You better be right. Or I'll make sure the studio sues your ass. It's called a morals clause. It's in your contract, *dumbo*."

A bass thud permeated the room as The Dingo Dudes got going several walls away.

"Are you two done with me?"

"I'm not," Stutz said. "We are gonna have serious words about tonight."

"You're damn right we are. You know where I live. Sadie, we good to go?"

Sadie adopted a serious attitude as Cathy turned to her.

"Miss Zengler?"

"Get him out of my sight."

"You need a ride, too, Miss Zengler?"

Spiller answered. "She can get back on her own; I saw a broomstick in the kitchen."

Cathy ignored him. "Just go grab my bag from the car, please, Sadie. Then take this Limey prick home."

"Limey prick," Spiller mused. "I guess this is what's known as the Special Relationship." He grabbed a complimentary Mel Banaghan tote bag from beside a table piled with pastries and drinks, and swiped several snacks into the bag, then picked up a can of Coca-Cola and offered it to Cathy. "Here, I owe you some coke."

Sadie coughed to cover a splutter of amusement, and quickly headed out to the Suburban. Cathy narrowed her eyes at her wayward charge, refusing the drink with a waft of her skeletal hand.

Spiller opened the can, spraying her slightly. He took a gulp and grinned. "Okie-dokie-cokie, then."

SADIE RETURNED FROM delivering Cathy's bag to her and hopped in behind the wheel. She gave her front-seat passenger a look. "Dare I ask what that was all about?"

Spiller reached into his bag for a pastry. "What?"

"Don't drop crumbs. You and Stutz. The scissors thing. That act that wasn't an act."

"That is on a strictly need-to-know basis."

"Ha, you sound like my old sergeant."

"You were in the military?" He pulled the bag wide, and bit into a cinnamon roll over the opening.

"Army. First Brigade Combat Team, Tenth Mountain Division. Fort Drum, New York."

"Were you deployed?"

"Iraq, twenty-sixteen. Afghanistan, twenty-twenty. Got out a few months back."

Spiller carried on chomping.

"What?" Sadie said. "You look doubtful."

"No, not at all," Spiller said through his food. "Thank you for your service."

Sadie scrutinized him. "What? Something's on your mind."

Spiller smiled. "It just sparked a memory."

"How so?"

"I've been where you are. Driving people around. And one time – this is going to sound really bad – but when I was really bored, I'd make up crap about my past. I'd tell my passengers I'd done all sorts of stuff, just pushing the boundaries to see what they'd swallow."

"And?"

"I told one person I'd been in the army."

Unimpressed, Sadie tutted. "That's stolen valor."

"I know. That wasn't my intention. And if it makes you feel any better, it royally backfired. I ended up in a world of hurt that would have made a year in Afghanistan feel like a walk in the park."

"Not true. You can't say that. You don't know."

Spiller slumped in his seat. "Sorry. It really was a very bad time. You wouldn't believe me if I told you."

"That have anything to do with tonight? You and Stutz?"

After a moment, Spiller nodded. "Weird thing is, I'm only here now because of it. I told a lie, my life collapsed around me, then somehow it put itself back together in glorious fashion. I got the career I'd been after for twenty years."

Sadie regarded Spiller's expression, all out of whack with his words. "Yet you're not feeling the glory, huh?"

"How could you tell?" Spiller laughed.

"Matt, take it from someone who knows: your life ain't that shabby."

"I know. I mean, my head knows. It's just... something feels unplugged. Like none of this good fortune is getting through."

"Was it *ever* plugged in?"

Spiller waved a finger at Sadie, smiling. "You, young lady, are pretty astute."

"Matt, you just need to cheer up."

"Spoken like someone who doesn't understand."

"Depression? Really? Tours in Iraq and Afghanistan? You think I wasn't affected? You deal with it. You look at the bright side and you never take your eyes off it. It's the only way. You really think your life stinks..." She reached inside her jacket and produced a black handgun. "Here."

"I'm okay, thanks."

"No? You don't wanna kill yourself?"

"No, but thanks for the offer."

"Then – with respect – get over yourself." Sadie re-holstered the weapon.

"Anyway, why are you armed?" Spiller asked.

"I work for a security company. We drive all kinds of high-profile individuals, not just studio people."

"Oh. Looked like a Heckler and Koch."

"Good spot. USP forty-five ACP Compact. Ten in the mag, one in the pipe."

"Big caliber."

"Stopping power. All there is."

"You wouldn't prefer more rounds?"

"Then the frame's bigger and people notice. Plus, after my training, if I need more than eleven rounds to put someone down, I deserve to get shot."

At that moment, Stutz and Cathy emerged from the building and passed the Suburban. Both made a point of ignoring its occupants. Stutz opened the door of his Bronco for his passenger.

Sadie began gently swaying in her seat. *"Let's get it oooooon, woo hoo. C'mon, c'mon, c'mon, c'mon, c'mon, darlin'... start beatin' round my bush."*

Spiller cackled loudly enough that Cathy heard and shot him an acid stare. He watched as she slammed the door of the garish green Bronco, and Stutz reversed and headed out of the lot.

Spiller licked his fingers and dipped in for another pastry. "I am so hungry."

Sadie started the engine and reversed.

"What's the plan, then, Sadie? Your life. You got a plan or are you just winging it?"

The Suburban left the lot, heading for the Ventura Freeway.

"Sure, I got a plan. Build up some cash, buy a Caddy Escalade, go freelance. Few years, couple more vehicles, who knows?"

*"Who knows?"* Spiller echoed. "Is that not winging it?"

"Nope. That's called staying liquid. Can't predict five years from now. Did you have a plan?"

"Me? Always. Ever since drama school."

"And twenty years later it worked out, only you still ain't happy."

Spiller munched on a croissant, contemplating. He laughed at his naivety. "Point taken. Plans do indeed go to shit."

Sadie turned the SUV onto the on-ramp and picked up speed. Spiller looked to his right at the sand-colored stone wall that obscured his view of Johnny Carson Park. Then the lights of the freeway, and soon they were passing Toluca Lake, a place that seemed to belong to a past life, one that directly preceded the notoriety of this one, but so completely dissimilar. If he'd needed corroboration, tonight had been it.

"You want some music?" Sadie asked.

"Not fussed." Then a thought struck him. "Have you considered acting as a career?"

"Why would I?"

"If you're looking for easy money. You're very attractive, tough, smart, military background. You're cool. And it's not like you don't have access to people who can pull a few strings."

Sadie huffed. "Why do you people think everyone wants to do what you do? Like you're something special. I've met the most screwed-up people on the planet right here in Hollywood. And you know why they're screwed up? Because, just like you, they got what they wanted, and they don't know why it didn't make everything better. Only, now they got nothing to strive for. The chase was everything. They got nowhere to go anymore. No hope. They got as good as it gets, and it ain't all that. They caught up with the carrot and it tastes like shit."

"Wow, I hope you didn't get all that from me."

"Besides, I detest what you do. I wish you'd all just stop."

Spiller glanced at the speedometer, the needle that had shifted through 70, 80, 90, in synch with Sadie's growing bile. "I'd be happy if you just slowed down a bit."

Sadie eased back to the limit.

"Anyway, what's wrong with what I do? You may not like actors, but we give people what they want. Everyone wants to be entertained."

Sadie thought for a moment. "It's not all actors."

"Oh, great. You've made me feel very special."

"It's the bloodshed, Matt. Glorifying the bloodshed. It's all about death. There's a disconnect in people. They hate violence when it affects them, but they love it when it's up there on the big screen. Can you imagine one of the *Gone with the Wind* generation, what they'd make of the gory crap that comes out of those studios we just left? *Hostel* or *Saw*? It's disgusting. They'd think the whole world needs a check-up from the neck up. Your new movie – how many people you kill in it?"

"Uh…"

"You don't know. Because it's meaningless. It's not real to you." Sadie indicated to join the off-ramp, then took a left under the freeway onto Van Nuys Boulevard.

Spiller wasn't certain if he should share what was in his head, but he felt compelled to.

"I do know about death. It's that need-to-know thing I mentioned. And you don't need to know, but I did some really bad stuff back in the UK."

Sadie drove a little further, then pulled into the curb next to an apartment building. She looked at her passenger.

"I don't like what I do, either, Sadie. I don't want to do another film like that. I want to do something meaningful, something people will remember for all the right reasons. But I have to take what they give me. I can't deny what's happening now. I've been trying to get here all my adult life. What? I'm just going to pack it in, so it's all been for nothing? Where the hell am I meant to go? I sacrificed a beautiful family for this. Messed them up for years, then came here, which pretty much shut them out completely. And deep down, I think I always knew that would happen. There's no going back. So, you want to look down on me, what I do… go for it. I don't care anymore."

She regarded him with pity. "You really like LA? Man, the city you wanted to get to all those years ago is long gone. There are parts of this city that would gag a maggot. It's third world in places. The inequity would make you weep. Just go home to your family, Matt, sort it out with them. You got a Hollywood movie under your belt. You'd get work back in England."

He shook his head. "Bridges have been burnt."

A FLASH OF red and blue illuminated the Suburban's interior. Sadie glanced in the rearview at the police cruiser pulled up behind them. Her hand touched her jacket above the HK under her arm.

"You're licensed, right?" Spiller asked.

"Carry permit, everything. But if they spot I got a weapon on me, a lot can go wrong before I get to show any paperwork."

In his door mirror, Spiller watched a male cop approach, as Sadie peered at the same reflection on her side, keeping her hands on the wheel at the top.

"Get your hands on the dash," she told him.

But Spiller had other ideas. Before Sadie could grab him, he was out onto the sidewalk and facing the patrol cop, who pulled his sidearm.

"Don't move!" the cop shouted. "Did I tell you to exit the vehicle? You looking to get shot?"

Through the two walls of the Suburban's darkened glass, Spiller could see the cop on the road had his weapon drawn, directed at Sadie's door.

"Just going home, officer," Spiller said. "Been at the Burbank Studios doing a bit of late-night TV. Just chatting with my friend, that's all."

The cop cocked his head, squinted, then barked a laugh, holstered his gun, and pointed at Spiller's scissored pants. "You're Matt Spiller! We just watched you on Mel Banaghan! We always try and grab a coffee when Mel's on. Cal! Cal! We just pulled over Matt Spiller!"

A grinning Cal appeared at the rear of the Suburban, his weapon now harmless on his hip again. "Matt Spiller? Holy moly, you were crazy tonight. Can we get a photo? Would you mind?"

Spiller shook his head. Laughing, they approached, fiddling with the settings on their cells. They flanked him, draping him in their aftershaves, two heavy arms around his shoulders, two outstretched for a series of selfies, as Spiller offered suitably insane expressions under a streetlight. All done, Cal offered his hand.

"Thanks, Matt, really appreciate it."

"No worries."

The other cop extended his arm. "I'm Ethan. Officer Ethan King – you ever need help with anything. In fact, let's seal the deal. Can I get those pants?"

"Pardon?"

Cal said, "Come on, Ethan, leave the guy to get home."

"Can I?"

"You want my pants?" Spiller asked.

"Uh-huh."

"That's American pants, right? You don't want my undies."

Ethan smiled. "Your, uh… trousers. I'm guessing you're only gonna throw them in the trash."

"Why would you want them?"

"Those are gonna be famous. Few years from now, I put those bad boys on eBay, I got provenance with the photos, I could put a kid through college."

Spiller laughed. "I think you're overestimating my worth."

Cal chipped in. "You could die. That would really up the price. Including Harry Sullivan tonight, that's three tough guys gone already this year."

"We should start a dead pool," an eager Ethan told his partner.

Spiller gave a counterfeit grin. "Yeah, you may get lucky – I could die horribly in the next few days."

Ethan pointed at Spiller's legs. "So?"

"Good God," Spiller said, unbuckling his belt and dropping his home-made shorts. "This isn't at all weird." He handed them to Ethan as Cal returned to the patrol car.

Ethan received his gift. "Thanks, buddy."

"Yeah, no problem. I'm sure this is no different to signing an autograph."

Ethan laughed.

"Officer Ethan King, you owe me. And trust me, I always pull in my markers. In fact, do you have a card?"

"Sure." Ethan pulled a card from his breast pocket but held it back. "Promise me we'll grab a cold one sometime."

"Why not? We all need a friend, right?"

Ethan gave Spiller the card and shook his hand, then returned to his vehicle, muttering how the guys back at the station wouldn't believe it. Spiller waited for them to drive past, waving at them as they went.

Back inside the Suburban, Sadie looked at him. "Why did you do that? You know how squirly that looked? You could have got shot for getting out."

"Yeah, but you could have got shot just for sitting there, so…"

Sadie nodded. "Thanks."

"No worries."

"Nice legs, by the way." She winked as she pulled away from the curb. "Sorry. What I said about stolen valor; looks like you got some of your own."

Spiller shrugged. "Brave or stupid. It's a fine line."

"And sorry I offered you my piece back at the studios. That was dumb."

"Yeah, not the best start to your limo career if I'd taken you up on it. Give me your cell."

She handed over her phone without question, and he input his number and gave it back.

"What's that for?" she asked.

"In case you get a yearning to see my beautiful legs again."

Through Sherman Oaks, Van Nuys wound its way onto Beverly Glen Boulevard. They rode in silence. Crossing Mulholland Drive to join North Beverly Glen and the final stretch, Sadie piped up.

"Earlier… why did you tell me all that?"

Spiller answered immediately, because he'd been wondering the same thing. "It's been on my mind. Some days, it's all I ever think about. Maybe I just needed to share."

"Okay. But I don't get what you said about your family. You said you shut them out. Why would you do that? You got kids, right?"

"Two daughters. One won't talk to me."

"So, you shut them *all* out?"

"I'm better off without them."

"Sorry, *you're* better off without *them?* You mean they're better off without you, right? Right? That's what people normally say."

"At what point this evening did you get the impression I'm normal?"

## FOUR

THE HOUSE FELT particularly dark and empty. Even with all the lights on, the night seemed to permeate its every cubed inch, sapping the building of life. Spiller was still waiting for his house to become a home, with all the good stuff that label brought, but it hadn't happened yet, and he was beginning to think it never would. It was nothing to do with ownership, or fancy possessions, or location; it was about people. The house he'd shared with his family had been a home. Mortgaged to the hilt, battered by monthly bills they could barely afford, and crammed with cheap trinkets. But those cheap trinkets belonged to people he loved.

He felt bad when he thought of his final conversation with Sadie. Apart from thanking his driver, the two of them hadn't exchanged any more words. He was in no doubt he'd left her with the impression that he disliked his family, that something about them was somehow unsavory. It was difficult to explain. Without being party to recent intimate husband-wife conversations that bordered patient-shrink status, Sadie could never understand the nuances that had caused him to apparently blame his family for their estrangement.

Spiller changed into some joggers and a singlet and went out to the pool, activating the submerged lights for company. Somewhere nearby, someone was playing Elvis with the windows open. As he checked the time on his cell, he hummed along to *You're the Devil in Disguise*. Eight hours difference, so 10.15 in the UK, Saturday morning.

He pressed to call his wife.

A man answered. "Hello, Helen's phone."

"I bloody know it is! Who the hell are you?"

"Oh, hi, Matt. How's LA treating you?"

Spiller placed the voice. "David?"

"She's here. Take it easy. It's Matt!"

Spiller tapped to switch to a video call.

"Hello, Matt. How are you?"

"Helen, go to video."

"No."

"Why not?"

"Because then you'd see I'm only wearing a pair of knickers."

"Oh, come on… you're not shagging David."

"Not at this precise moment."

"Where are the kids? Tell me they're staying with friends."

"Okay, they're staying with friends."

"Are they?"

"No. They're asleep. Matt, before you kick off, David and I have been together for weeks. The kids are fine about it. We all get on very well."

Spiller was at least grateful she hadn't said, *like a proper family*. But there was still a knife she could twist.

"And if you called more often, you'd know these things."

"Ha! Sure. Why would I call, Helen? You don't want to talk to me. Sammy won't talk to me. And FYI, I WhatsApp Soph all the time. At least I'm not in the doghouse with her."

At that moment, an impeccably timed, high-pitched canine yelp came from her end.

"Helen? Do you have a dog?"

"David bought Sophie a puppy," she said defiantly.

"Oh, of course. When I wanted to, you said no. But David can waltz in with one and that's fine."

"Our situation is very different now, Matt. Back then, we couldn't afford a dog. Food, vets' bills, kennels – not that we ever went on holiday."

Spiller fumed. He went to his poolside bar and grabbed a cold one from the cooler.

"Matt? You there?"

He twisted the cap off and took a glug. "And *why* is your situation very different, Helen? Huh? Because I'm here earning the big bucks. I bought that house for you and the kids, Helen. Okay? I paid off the mortgage, gave you a load of money. I pay you every month, and I pay you very well. No nastiness, no lawyers. I do it because it's the right thing to do, but I am not—"

"Supporting David. I know. You're not. He still has his house next door. Still has his job. If you think I'd jeopardize the girls' financial future after what we've been through. Everything that happened with my dad – squandering all those savings. The money you send to me is set aside for the girls. I have a job. I work to pay the household bills. David doesn't want my money and he's not getting it. And he's listening right now, so you can be sure I mean it."

"Bugger," David said in the background, then laughed.

"Helen, can we have a private conversation, please?"

"Shoo," Helen said. "Okay, all alone. Now, what do we have to talk about, husband-of-mine?"

Spiller didn't know. Then he did. "You remember that conversation we had about the squash court?"

"Squash court?"

"Ages ago. You said I hit you with my moods and they came right back at me. So, they're self-perpetuating; as long as I'm with you. Or anyone. Remember?" He took a swig.

"Yes."

"You said you felt better not being emotionally battered by me all the time. And you thought I was better off, because without you, my moods didn't rebound on me, and so I didn't feel guilty about always upsetting you."

"I remember. Is it true? Now you've had all this time on your own?"

Spiller was walloped by a revelation, a sudden consolidation of long-held thoughts – up to now suppressed, indistinct and unpalatable – into a blinding fact. "Yes. Hundred percent. I miss the kids, but I don't miss you. Jesus, why would I miss a brick wall?"

"Then why were we so lovey-dovey before you went to LA? We got back together, didn't we? It certainly felt like we got back together. The *girls* certainly thought we did."

Spiller felt winded – as he was meant to. "You didn't want to talk to me for a whole month after I landed here. Sammy still won't."

"After what happened at the airport? Are you surprised?"

Spiller miraculously managed not to throw his bottle through his bi-fold doors. "You waved me away, Helen! You told me to go! I was looking straight into your eyes. You shook your head, you waved me away."

Helen fell quiet for a few seconds. She spoke softly. "I wanted you to go. But I didn't think you would."

Spiller sank onto a pool chair. "So... you're disappointed because I did what you wanted me to do?"

She didn't reply.

"Helen, if I'd stayed behind, spoken to the police, it could have blown everything out of the water. I'd just settled everything. Against all the odds. Bartoli had given up because he couldn't piece it all together. We were free and clear. I couldn't get myself involved in another bloody shooting."

"I saved your life that day."

Spiller got up and wandered to the gate that led to the reservoir. He went through and stood in the scrub, staring at the dark outlines of the big houses across the water. She was right. The vista before him was thanks to her. She didn't chivvy him for a response.

"I know," he said finally.

"I felt that bullet whizz by my ear."

"I know." He hurled his bottle into the darkness.

"I was on the floor, Matt. For all you knew, I'd been shot."

"Everyone in that terminal was on the floor. Me included."

"And you scurried away, like a rat. While no one was watching."

"You told me to go."

She was quiet.

"Oh – but you didn't *want* me to go. Yeah, great logic. Helen, have you ever told Sammy that? That you told me to go?"

"I... I must have done. Would it make a difference?"

He requested video again. Helen accepted, and Spiller found himself looking at his wife's face and too much, but not quite enough, of her cleavage. He took a screenshot.

"It would be nice to find out," he said. "Seeing as I seem to have lost a daughter. The full facts might be useful."

She nodded. "Where are you?"

"By the reservoir. Beyond my perimeter wall." He turned the phone so she could see the view, then returned to the pool area.

"Soph would love that," Helen said. "You'd never get her out of it."

He turned the phone back to his face and took a couple more screenshots. "Well, maybe one day you'll bring her."

Helen nodded unconvincingly. "Terrible about Harry Sullivan. You saw the news?"

"Yep. Happened just across the water from me."

"Life, eh? One minute the world's at your feet…"

"I don't dwell on it," he fibbed.

"Okay, Matt, I'll let you get to sleep. You take care. I'll pass on your regards to David."

"Funny. Helen…"

"What?"

"Are you happy with David?"

"Yes."

"Happier than when you were with me?"

"It's different."

"Every relationship's different, but happy is happy. You must know if you're more or less happy."

"I'm more at peace."

He let it sink in. "That's more important."

"I think so. Night, Matt."

"Night."

"And here – if you really want a good shot." She pulled the phone away, so her breasts entered the frame.

He managed one capture before the screen blacked as she cut the connection. Elvis was still out there, asking some woman to wear his ring around her neck. Spiller took his phone and its media content up to bed.

THE DISPLACED NEW York detective couldn't sleep. He was at the same time elated and terrified about the events of the previous evening. Finally, a case he could sink his teeth into. And a case that could end his career if it went cold on his watch. Because the world was now watching him. As a standalone case, the murder of Harry Sullivan was headline news. As the lead detective, he would be interviewed on TV, and he knew from previous bitter experience that no one was fooled by a prevaricating cop. But a far worse scenario existed. Officer Contreras would likely not be the only person to draw a tenuous line between the sudden exits of three Hollywood hard men in a few short months. And it wouldn't matter if there were no substance to the theory, it would spread and be believed, and the evidentiary burden on him would mushroom.

He grabbed some cold pizza from the fridge and microwaved it back to a semblance of its former glory. Dumping himself on the sofa, he scratched his sweaty crotch through his boxer shorts. The ceiling fan wasn't cutting it tonight. He'd have to get the AC fixed. He laid the open box on his distended abdomen and realized that was another thing that needed fixing. His diet had gone wrong since getting to LA, and he dimly wondered if he hadn't been comfort-eating to assuage the humiliation he felt over the sham of his last big case. He took a mouthful of floppy pizza and zapped the TV, going to his recordings. There wasn't much he liked on TV anymore, but there were some shows that offered a welcome distraction, mixing equal amounts of comedy and tragedy, such as *The Mel Banaghan Show*; Mel providing the laughter, with the misfortune provided by a parade of illustrious douchebags, so utterly deluded by the adulation of the moron that was John Q Public. He didn't have much time for famous folk, or even the anonymous rich. They all ended up in the ground, their baubles rudely wrenched from their grasp to be divided among the fleetingly bereaved.

Into his second bite, his jaw went slack, and he used his tongue to push the masticated lump back out into the box like a splat of bird crap. At that moment, his throat was so tight he couldn't have swallowed his own spit. Plus, he needed his mouth vacant to utter a whispered curse.

"Mother*fucker*."

He paused the show. He stared at the visage of Mel Banaghan; Mel's mouth frozen several syllables beyond the utterance of a name he'd hoped would never again insult his ears. He slowly set the pizza box to one side, stared at his holstered .45, waiting on the table next to the hallway that led to his bedroom, where it would, as usual, spend the night within easy reach. This evening, though, he sorely wanted to empty its magazine into someone before bed.

He whizzed the show forward and watched the relevant segment with mounting disbelief. It would have been distasteful under normal circumstances, seeing that cursed face again, but the inappropriate attire and the errant behavior raised his hackles like a mane of broken glass down his spine. He watched the segment again, vainly hoping to lip-read the inaudible exchange between the two men.

Never mind, because there was so much else to be gleaned from the altercation – so much that their faux rapprochement at the end could do nothing to negate.

Then he grinned. And soon he was laughing, hooting like a lunatic who'd just spotted the door to the asylum was ever so slightly ajar.

Tomorrow, someone was going to receive a visit.

## FIVE

SPILLER'S WARY SMILE and friendly, questioning eyes were met with a cold smirk. The recognition was briefly one-way, then the penny dropped, and Spiller knew full-well who was blocking his path and what he'd come for. The man's hand disappeared inside his jacket and appeared again clutching a silver semi-automatic. The cacophony seemed to dim, as though the incident had hushed everyone, curtailing their conversations and halting their footsteps, but Spiller knew he was the only one aware of the danger. He thought he heard the double snick of the hammer being primed, then the din of the terminal building resumed like a crashing wave. He turned his head toward a couple of armed police, twenty feet away, opened his mouth to shout, then decided that this was his time and he had to accept it. He closed his eyes.

A desperate ululation tore through the mellow airport soundtrack, like a needle dragged hard across an easy-listening LP. *"Guuuuuuuuuuuuuuun!"*

Spiller opened his eyes to see the man with the pistol swivel to face the source, and found himself gawking at his wife, standing near the armed police. The cops reacted, following Helen's gaze to target the location of the threat. The man loosed off several haphazard rounds toward the officers, as the whole of the terminal dropped, ducked, or dispersed. Spiller did a stooping sprint toward a bench, dragging his case behind him, as a return volley of lethal force shattered the lull. He settled behind his makeshift shield and just caught the final stilling of the gunman's ruined body on the floor. His focus darted back to his wife. Helen was spread-eagled and he wondered at first if she'd been hit. Then her hand moved to her ear, and she felt around frantically as though she feared the same thing.

Then their eyes met. His expression pleaded for guidance. She waved him away. *Get lost.* He frowned, made a slight move in her direction. And she did it again. *Get out of here. Go. Now!*

The cops were standing over the body, carbines raised, targeting the corpse as though it might reanimate and come for them. More armed cops were rushing over. Spiller shuffled away from them, wriggling out of his jacket as he dragged his case. Behind a bag-wrapping machine, he shoved his jacket into his case and put on a black baseball cap. With the crime scene secured by multiple uniforms, the first two officers were now scanning the area, as though they vaguely recalled someone else had been near the shooter – possibly an accomplice.

People were getting up now, a crouched exodus. Passengers hurrying toward passport control, non-passengers dashing back to their cars. The police looked on, eyeing everyone, but their numbers were insufficient to stem the scattering of potential witnesses. Spiller joined the airside crowd. As he was about to leave the concourse, he looked back at Helen. Her face was now ashen, and she was peering down at her chest at two expanding circles of blood.

Spiller awoke from his nightmare with a yelp. Helen had always said he whimpered for a while before yelping and waking. This time he heard his own cry as he came to. He swore at the awful authenticity of his dream.

The clock told him it was two p.m. The sleep of the coked. At least it was light; the sun would quickly banish the gloom in his head. Maybe later he would take the Suzuki Hayabusa out for a blast. He looked at his phone. It opened onto the screenshot of Helen's breasts. He shook his head to dispel the mental image of her body defiled by gunshot wounds. But that could so easily have been the outcome that day. They had been hugging it out only five minutes earlier, then she'd left for the parking structure, before – so out of character – rushing back for one last hug. And to risk her life to save his.

Ten p.m. in the UK. Sophie would probably be asleep. He called anyway. He had to hear from the one family member who didn't hold a grudge against him.

"Hi, Dad." The video showed she was in bed, but propped up, awake.

He grinned at her beautiful little face. "Hi, sweetie. How come you're up?"

"Just playing on my phone."

He smiled. "How are you doing?"

"Okay. I miss you."

Spiller tried not to blub. "Miss you, too."

"Sorry, Dad."

"What for?"

"The puppy. Not telling you."

"Don't worry, I understand. Are you happy with it?"

"Yeah, I love it. I'll send you some pictures."

"Please. So... didn't tell me about David, either, huh?"

She offered a sullen expression. "Mum told me not to."

"No worries. Do you like David?"

"He's nice. He's a cockerpoo."

"David's a cocky poo? I'm going to tell him you said that."

"*The dog!* That's its breed." She tittered.

"So, how's Sammy doing?"

"She's okay. She's still annoyed with you, but no one wants to tell me why."

"Sorry about that, sweetie. It's adult stuff."

"Okay. Dad, I know what I want to do when I grow up. I want to look after dogs."

"What? Like a vet?"

"No, I don't want to see them when they're not well. I want to open a shop and make them look pretty."

"Oh, a dog groomer."

"Yeah. And I know what I want to call it. Doggy Style."

"Oh, dear. I'm guessing Sammy's helped you with that, has she?"

"Isn't that a good name?"

"It's, uh... inappropriate, sweetie. Like... not acceptable. I think Sammy was making a joke."

Sophie tutted. "Is it about sex?"

"Uh... oh, God... it's just... do you have any other names?"

"Dogging Delight."

"Doggy Delight. That's good."

"*Dogging* Delight."

"Jeez... Sammy again, right?"

"Is that rude as well?"

"Just tell your big sister to stop being so naughty."

"I will but she won't listen."

At that moment, a furry white face appeared in the corner of his screen. "Soph, have you got the dog in bed with you?"

She shushed him. "Mum doesn't know."

"Sweetie, you realize pups pee all the time."

"I know; he had a pee on David earlier."

Spiller laughed. "Great judgement, that dog; I like it already. What's its name?"

"Stuart."

Spiller's laughter turned hysterical, to the point that tears were streaming. He suspected it wasn't just the dog's name that had summoned them.

"Daddy, don't laugh, you'll hurt his feelings. Don't listen to him, Stuart."

"Sorry. Sorry." He calmed himself. "You actually named your dog after a one-eyed minion." He burst out laughing again. "That's brilliant."

"I like his breath," Sophie said, putting her nose next to Stuart's mouth.

"Okay, that's just weird. So, any plans for tomorrow? David taking you down the Ferrari showroom to buy you a new car?"

She tutted again. "Dad, you *know* I can't drive."

"Has Mum bought anything new? Still got the old Peugeot?"

"Yeah, it's horrible. Can you buy her a new one?"

"Well, I do send her quite a bit of money."

"I know: Mum puts it in the bank for us. I have *so* much now."

"Good. You're welcome, by the way."

"Oh. Yeah. Thanks, Dad." She gave him a silly, stretched-mouth grin, then had a thought. "If Sammy doesn't start to behave, can you give me her money as well?"

"You, madam, are going to be a very successful, if rather ruthless, businesswoman. And the answer is no. But… I will send some more to your mum, so she can buy a better car."

*"Aaaaaahhhh, Stuaaaaaart!"*

"Oops. I'll leave you to change the bedsheets, sweetie."

*"Muuuuuuuuuuuuum!"* The screen went dark.

It had been the very best way to start the day. Spiller beamed, forgetting that meant it could only go downhill from there. Which it did. Very quickly.

AFTER FINISHING HIS late breakfast, Spiller had been mooching around the house for fifteen minutes when the doorbell rang.

He enjoyed mooching. Since leaving England, his strange, paralyzing fugues had ceased. These odd episodes, where he would grind to a halt, mentally and physically, and sit or stand immobile, sometimes for hours, like a vehicle with a flooded engine, had been debilitating. He'd always assumed they were a symptom of his depression; that his brain, overloaded with angst, like spark plugs drenched in fuel, had to take a breather. The sunshine of LA, the money, the fame, the success, had made a difference, although he suspected he could have deleted the latter three factors from his life, and he would still have felt ninety percent better. He just needed light in his life. Literally that. So, the fugues had faded, to be replaced by mooching. It had a similar cathartic effect, but it was far less disabling. He would mooch from room to room, staring out of the windows for a while, then mooch to the kitchen and savor a coffee for ten minutes, then mooch around the pool, surveying all that he had so swiftly and improbably acquired, then mooch back inside to vacuum a room or two, or to check his Twitter feed. Sitting still, standing still – the inactivity didn't suit him anymore. It felt like it could be a slippery slope, like an innocent shot of liquor to coat an alcoholic's palate.

The feedback on last night's show was extraordinary. #mattspiller, #looneylimey, #bonkersbrit, #crazybastard, #madonamurdercycle, #moamc, #wtaf. There were others, but the crux was that Matt Spiller was trending, thus his new movie was getting insane amounts of publicity.

It was at this moment, while he was scooting through the online comments, that his attention was drawn to the front door.

The genial, Ray-Banned and Botoxed face with the bald head was strangely familiar. Spiller squinted as though trying to identify a pixelated image. Given enough time, he knew he'd put a name to the face, but the mellifluous tones that issued from that face a moment later, and the phrase they shaped, instantly removed any unnecessary guesswork.

"My dear boy! How wonderful to finally be here!"

"Billy? *Billy?*"

"May I be permitted to enter, love? Feeling a tad hot under the collar."

Spiller took a couple of steps back inside his house so he could take in the whole picture. Speaking of collars, his ex-agent didn't have one, and that was a first. The man whose wardrobe had always consisted of velvet jackets, wide collars, cravats, slacks, and mirror brogues, was in full SoCal mode. Tie-dye vest in red and pink, orange Bermudas, and white deck shoes with palm trees on them. On either side of his feet were two large suitcases.

"Well, dear heart?" Billy said. "Or should I say *dude*, given my locale?"

"Sure." Spiller stepped to one side.

Billy pushed his Ray-Bans up onto his shaved head, then entered the house, dragging his cases over the doorstep, until Spiller remembered his agent was in his seventies and offered to carry them, although it was mostly to avoid scratching the wood floor.

"So kind," Billy said.

Spiller grabbed the handles, then let go of them. "What are you doing here, Billy? I mean, is your hotel room not available yet? Probably just best I leave them here, isn't it?"

"No, you can take them up to my room, love."

"Pardon?"

"I'm staying with you – *obviously*. Goodness, what are you like?" Billy guffawed.

"Uh… I didn't even know you were flying over. Did I miss the memo?"

"No." He opened his arms out as though he was about to launch into a song. *"Surpriiiiiise!"*

Dumbfounded, Spiller nodded. "Yep."

"Now… you won't know this about me, but I prefer a yielding mattress and a plump pillow."

Spiller looked his ex-agent up and down again. "Billy, what the hell happened to your hair?"

"Oh, gosh. Love, I looked like I'd been dunked in a black candy-floss machine. I'm not certain I was fooling anyone."

"You weren't. And as for the bed and pillow, you get what you're given, and it's not a given you're getting anything at all yet."

"Oh, I think I am. Lounge this way?"

Spiller watched helplessly as Billy started down the hall, then disappeared into the living room. Something was afoot with the old bugger, that much was clear. Spiller trailed Billy into the room and found he was already settled in the houseowner's favorite chair. Spiller stayed by the door.

"Billy, what gives?"

"I *was* on my way to the hotel when my cab driver shared a little story with me. Actually, quite a coincidence my being here today, dear boy. That's to say, I was flying here anyway – booked it a while ago. But had I not made that booking, I would have certainly been booking a flight sometime in the next few days, so my being here today is… maybe it's fate. Or perhaps I'm clairvoyant."

"Billy, you're rambling and not making sense."

"I have dual citizenship, Matthew. Did I ever tell you? No? Anyway, I came to England when I was five. Never really looked back. Then, you know what happened a few weeks ago? I had a revelation. Why not – I'm not getting any younger – so why not spend the twilight of my life in a sunny clime? I have the money – all that lovely commission from that ghastly movie you just made. And as I'm not ready to cease work just yet, I thought... set up in LA. Why not? I've had an affiliate agent helping me over here for quite some time. That's how Brett found me, and then you. I'm not completely unknown. So... voilà! And you, you lucky chap, will continue having the pleasure of my insightful representation."

Spiller's brain was starting to boil in his skull. "What if I've signed with an agent already?"

"Ah." Billy winked. "I have my contacts. You, sweet cherub, are still up for grabs."

"I did talk to someone. Suzy Cooper."

"Highly influential. But a peculiar woman, from what I've heard."

"Yeah, always in a cream outfit, dark glasses all the time. Not sure I'm that keen."

"Well, problem solved. Here I am."

"It's going to take you weeks, maybe months, to set yourself up, Billy. I can't wait that long to get a functioning agent."

"All done from England. Talent Agency license, business cards, website, the lot. I even leased a little office on Wilshire. Seems to be a popular place for us agents."

There was so much to unpack, and Spiller felt the need to rewind a little. "So... you didn't go to your hotel *why*? And what do you mean about the coincidence, that you'd have been booking in a few days had you not already booked?"

"Any chance I could have a cup of tea, love?"

"No. Why are you here? I mean, at my house, with your suitcases?"

"Is your lovely family out? I was so hoping to meet them."

"If you thought my family was here, you wouldn't be thinking you could move in."

"Oh, I... yes, come to think of it, you did tell me they stayed behind."

"Billy..."

Billy smiled. "*The Mel Banaghan Show*. Have you seen it? I haven't, but I've heard an awful lot about it. Well, not an awful lot, but my cab driver did tell me about last night's episode. Then I found the offending clip on YouTube. I must say, dear boy, you're looking rather *buff* at the moment. I believe that's the popular vernacular."

Spiller needed some time to think. And he needed to put a shirt on. "Tea, right?"

"Milk, no sugar. And mash it *hard*."

In the kitchen, Spiller set the kettle to boil, then went upstairs to cover himself. Billy certainly looked a lot less gay than previously, having transformed himself – apparently overnight – from Quentin Crisp to Patrick Stewart, but Spiller was still keen to be of no assistance in Billy's mental undressing of him.

It wasn't just Billy's appearance, though. The re-invention seemed to go deeper. The genuinely lovely luvvy he'd known since leaving drama school had gained an edge, a spiky bravado that Spiller didn't much care for. Probably it had always been present, simply suffused by the endearing persona Billy had created for himself. He'd always reminded Spiller that nice people like to work with other nice people. It was very odd, after all these years, to think that Billy might not belong to that group. But Spiller had to tread carefully. Billy had seen him do some bad shit; things his agent didn't want to believe were true but had clearly nagged at him ever since.

And he'd seen that bad shit standing right next to Brett Stutz.

## SIX

SADIE WATCHED DISPASSIONATELY as the elderly black actor crawled along the sidewalk with blood oozing from his flank. Despite the telescopic sight, the first round had only winged him, and now he was dragging himself over the hot concrete, leaving a red trail behind him like an alien slug. As the shot had rung out, the area had cleared, shoppers pelting toward store entrances, crouching behind parked cars, seeking refuge from an unseen malevolence whose targeting may have been deliberate and limited, or the beginnings of a massacre. Sadie noted the expression on the actor's grizzled face, frantic eyes searching for the shooter's nest, and generally just appalled that he'd met such an inglorious end so prematurely. Then the second round struck home, and that was the end of it. Theodore Montgomery, legendary Hollywood tough guy, was out of the picture. Sadie climbed back behind the wheel of the Suburban and lowered her window to listen to the aftermath. There was silence for several seconds.

"Aaaaaaaaaaand *cut!* Check the gate!"

Brett Stutz hurried over to the bloodied actor as he began to move.

"I don't need your help!" Theo smacked away the hand that Stutz was offering. "I'm not so old that I can't get to my own goddamned feet!"

"Gate's good!"

"You were phenomenal!" Stutz said, glossing over the rebuff. "Such a poignant demise."

"Poignant?" Theo wiped his hands together, removing the grit from the lot floor. "Two weeks of filming, eight scenes, then I'm shot dead! I'd say that's *tragic!* Who's gonna even know I was in this movie? I used to *rule* this genre! But that was when we had storylines, not all this gory garbage that passes for a plot. I had *gravitas*. You people don't know the meaning of the word anymore."

Sadie watched with a wry grin as Stutz continued to offer consolatory nods.

"Bang, you're dead, bang, you're dead. Bang-bang-bang-bang-bang-bang-bang-bang, you're all dead. The end. That's not a movie!"

"I get you, Theo. I do. It's the public. It's what they want."

"You have no goddamned integrity! Someone get me a cigarette!"

The window went back up. The scene outside now dulled and muffled, Sadie looked through her privacy glass at a couple of assistants as they rushed over to proffer a cigarette and sycophantic smiles. Sadie felt bad for the guy; the ex-leading man being led back to his trailer, like a misbehaving kid to the naughty step. He was attempting the swagger of his glory days, but it was diminished by old bones and nostalgia, the latter as draining as any age-related ailment. These days, his paunch would be first across the threshold rather than his pecs, although Sadie reckoned he could probably still kick the asses of most of the muscular upstarts who'd replaced him.

"Take ten, everyone!" Stutz called.

Sadie reclined her chair, closed her eyes, and waited for the order to take the disgruntled elder statesman Theo Montgomery home.

IF THE REACTION of the mainstream and social media was anything to go by, *Man on a Murder Cycle* was going to be a blockbuster. Stutz had been holed up in his trailer for five of the ten minutes he'd allowed, catching up once more with the tsunami of reaction to last night's shenanigans. The problem was, he would never be able to catch up – not unless he took ten days. There was a good deal of skepticism on social media, with many unwilling to take what they'd seen at face value and accept it was just a pre-arranged publicity stunt. Unfortunately for Stutz, he had taken on several cameo roles in his own movies, and the world knew he couldn't act his way out of a sodden paper bag. Therefore, his Oscar-worthy performance on *The Mel Banaghan Show* was either an unprecedented tour-de-force, or it was a lie, and he genuinely had been on the verge of soiling the seventy-five percent that was left of his leather pants. Despite the barrage of disbelief, he knew he would have to resolutely maintain the official version of events if he and the studio wanted to secure a cinematic release. He hadn't enjoyed being threatened on live TV by a parvenu, but outing him would serve no useful purpose, and would be detrimental to his own career, given the fact that he'd employed the guy despite having witnessed two "auditions" he knew were tantamount to snuff theatre.

The lightest of taps at his door was still audible, and that irritated him. People knew never to interrupt his take-ten time. Today was worse. He had been thoroughly humiliated last night in front of millions on live TV. No amount of spin could alter that fact. Even just having his pants leg desecrated. Only a pussy would have allowed that to happen. Unless it was a performance – which few believed.

He bellowed: *"What is it?"*

Louder this time; a proper knock. And a timid voice: "You got a visitor!"

"You'd better not enjoy your job, whoever that is!"

Stutz got up and opened the trailer door to a suited man with silver hair and a detective's shield on his belt. He looked beyond at the departing production runner, who was literally running away to avoid being recognized.

"Brett Stutz?"

"I don't recall employing you, which means you're a background artist, and a background artist who knocks on my door when I'm relaxing is what I like to call *instantly unemployed*. And who the hell on this set needs to ask who I am?"

"Well, I'm not from this set, Mr Stutz. I'm from the LAPD, West Bureau Homicide. Lieutenant Bartoli."

Stutz peered at the ID held up to his face. It wasn't the same as the ones the props people handed out to the fake cops on set. But he was still wary. After Matt Spiller, he didn't trust that anything was on the level. He had to be ready for an onslaught of impromptu auditions, and maybe this was the first.

"Mr Stutz, I also have a gun, and I can put a couple of live rounds through your ceiling if you're still doubtful." He pulled his jacket open to reveal a big semi-automatic.

"Okay," Stutz finally conceded. "What's up?"

"Really? You didn't think you'd get a visit from the cops after last night?"

"Last night was showbiz."

"Can I come in, or are you coming out?"

Stutz looked past the detective at the faces staring at him, but thought he'd only make it appear worse if he shouted at them to mind their own business. He stepped back inside the trailer.

Bartoli surveyed the luxurious surroundings as he entered. "This is nicer than my apartment."

"How can I help you, Lieutenant?" Stutz sat in his swivel armchair.

"I will do you the courtesy of cutting to the chase. Tell me everything you know about Matthew Spiller. I mean everything. Every single thing that happened back in England between you and him."

"Okay... he auditioned for me, and I gave him the part."

"Bull."

"Beg your pardon?"

"Try again. Only this time bear in mind that I know Mr Spiller of old, so I know what happened last night on Mel Banaghan was a country mile away from being a publicity stunt."

Stutz squinted, smirked. "Sure. See, I happen to know that Matt Spiller has never been in LA before this. He told me."

"But I was in England. I was a DCI – a Detective Chief Inspector. He lived on my patch. Whatever went down between you and him, I can tell you it's the tip of the iceberg."

"So, if you know so much, why would you need my help?"

"Because he is the slipperiest little bastard on the planet."

Stutz shrugged.

"I'm guessing you're acquainted with his English agent. Shots fired in the vicinity of his house?"

"I wouldn't know about that."

"So, if I checked with your PA, asked her to check her diary, she wouldn't place you in England in January, or at his agent's house on the day in question?"

Stutz glanced at his Breitling. "Listen, I need to get back out there. Time is money. And in this industry, it's a lot of money." He stood up, but the detective took a step to block his exit.

"Mr Stutz, I don't think you quite understand my backstory. Isn't that what you movie people call it? If it's the last thing I do on this earth, I am taking Matthew Spiller down. And if you wanna make yourself an accessory, all well and good. If you're protecting him in any way, there's an orange jumpsuit with your name on it, too."

"Sorry, can't help."

## SEVEN

THERE WAS AN imperative conversation to be had, but Billy had put that and himself to bed for a while. Spiller kept staring at the ceiling, hoping to summon some superhero powers that would send a killer laser from his eyes up through Billy's bed and the old bugger himself, slicing him in two. He felt like going for a run, but it was just too hot. He settled in the living room and found a movie to watch. It was strange to think he would be the one the world would be watching very soon. How flawed was his character, yet everyone would look at him, jealous of his perfect life, and how lucky he'd been to get where he was. Even before the opening titles had finished scrolling, he was perusing his phone, checking the social media furor. But it wasn't just Twitter and its ilk; the mainstream media was all over it. He thought back a year, to before all the events that had threatened his life, then changed it for ever. Bored out of his mind, driving from job to job, quietly earning his paltry living, occasionally seeing his kids – neither of which was estranged from him – battling the painful hope that he might one day reunite with his wife and family. Those had been good times, even if they had felt like the worst.

His doorbell again. Why couldn't people just leave him alone? He ignored it, but the caller was persistent. Was it Brett Stutz, following up on his promised visit? Not likely, given Stutz was now rolling on another movie. The ding-dong was replaced by a thud-thud. He let it continue for twenty seconds before accepting it wasn't going to stop.

If Billy's appearance on his doorstep an hour earlier had been startling, this was heart-stopping. Spiller stared at the apparition like the man was the ghost of Christmas past. In a way, he was. He belonged to the dark times of six months ago, a man who'd possessed the power to destroy Spiller's life. But thankfully, a man who'd never been able to amass sufficient evidence to do so. He offered Spiller a cheesy grin.

"Hey, can I get an autograph?"

"Jesus Christ."

"You flatter me."

"DCI Bartoli, what the hell are you doing in LA?"

"Can I come in? We need to have a talk. And it's *Lieutenant* Bartoli."

Spiller stepped outside and closed the door behind him. He couldn't let Bartoli meet his houseguest. He knew Billy had spoken on the phone to Bartoli once, and no one ever forgot having a conversation with his luvvy agent and his superlative endearments. "This way." He used the electronic keypad on the side gate to let them into the pool area.

"You've done well for yourself, Matthew."

"You were heading back to New York. You said: your marriage was over, and you were going home."

Bartoli shook his head. "I said I was heading back to the States. I never said New York. You made an assumption. Do you have a cold soda?"

Spiller dipped into the cooler box behind the bar and handed him a 7-Up.

"*Grazie*. So?" He cracked the can and guzzled some, then burped.

"I thought we had an agreement," Spiller said, aware of his pleading tone.

"Nope. Never said that. Another thing you assumed."

"I saved your reputation, you ungrateful twat."

Bartoli finished his drink. "You wanted me off your case, so you threw me a bone." He burped again.

"Mate, I threw you the whole skeleton."

Bartoli laughed. "Ain't that the truth? Several skeletons, if I remember correctly. And all your handiwork."

"No proof of that."

"Interesting show last night. I nearly choked on my pizza."

"Shame."

"What? That I choked or it didn't kill me?"

Spiller smiled. "Oh, it's so good to have my old sparring partner back. How have you been?"

"I was okay until last night. Then I was assigned to the Harry Sullivan case, which is gonna be a bummer if I don't solve it, right? Then I saw you were here, and my mood dove even more. But then Mel Banaghan told the world you knew Harry Sullivan. So, honestly, right now, I'm verging on delirious." He perched on a bar stool and crushed his can.

Spiller made a face. "Come on… you like me for Harry Sullivan?"

"I like you for him and, uh… what date did you get here?"

"End of Jan."

Bartoli nodded. "Then I like you for Harry Sullivan and every other heinous crime that's gone down in this city since then. Where were you yesterday, early evening?"

"I went for a run."

"Anyone corroborate that?"

"How? How could anyone corroborate that? It wasn't the bloody LA marathon; I run on my own."

"What do you know about Aiden Powers and John Frears?"

"They're dead. They died. What? Is that me as well?"

"Is it?"

"No. Jesus, is that your working theory? I show up in LA and start bumping off the competition?"

Bartoli turned his gaze to the house. "You live alone?"

"Yep."

"Family stayed behind, huh?"

Spiller dipped in to grab a can of beer.

"Starting early," Bartoli said.

"I'm *resting*. Until my next movie, I'm the idle rich." He cracked the can and took a slurp. "Anyway, what are you? My dad?"

As if on cue, like he was waiting in the wings, Billy slid open the bi-fold door.

"Live alone, huh?" Bartoli said.

"Dad!" Spiller shouted, hurrying over. "I thought you were sleeping!" He embraced a befuddled Billy and whispered in his ear. "Change your voice, you spoke to him." He spun around to make the introductions, leading Billy forward. "Dad, this is Lieutenant Bartoli.

He was our technical expert on the movie I just made. Just popped round to say hi."

Billy offered his hand, launching into his best Richard Burton. "Walter. That's very kind of you – looking after my boy."

Bartoli smiled at the old guy. "Angelo. Pleased to meet you, Walter. You doing okay?"

"Exhausted, but very happy to be here."

"Dad just got in this morning. Just flew in. Surprise visit."

Bartoli pointed at Billy's shirt. "Getting in the groove, huh? The old tie-dye?"

"When in Rome," Billy answered, and Spiller prayed he wasn't about to launch into Burton's Marc Anthony.

"Well, you're rocking it, Walter. You must be very proud of your son."

"Well, who wouldn't be?"

Bartoli grinned. "*You* wouldn't be."

Spiller did a double take. "What?"

"Both your folks are dead, Matthew. You think I don't check into a suspect's background? So, who's this guy really?"

"Billy Banbury, darling," Billy said, reverting to his regular voice. "Agent *extraordinaire*."

Bartoli shook his head and appeared suddenly worn out. "I can feel the Matthew Spiller shitshow starting all over again. I wish I *had* gone back to New York." It dawned, and he jabbed a finger toward Billy. "I spoke to you in England."

Billy made a thinking face, like he was trawling his memory.

"Forget it," Bartoli said. "Big question, Matthew, is why you didn't want me to know who this guy is. And you, Mr Banbury... why the hell you went along with it? Ach! You know what?" Bartoli pulled his Kimber .45. "I'm just gonna shoot the both of you."

Billy squealed, quickly glanced left and right for the nearest cover, and decided to jump in the pool. Spiller knew Bartoli and recognized the bluff.

Bartoli looked at Spiller as he re-holstered his weapon. "He knows I can see through water, right?"

"I didn't kill Harry Sullivan, Angelo."

Billy surfaced for a frantic gulp of air and quickly submerged himself again.

"Matthew, in the spirit of openness, I came here direct from talking to Brett Stutz."

"Oh? He say anything?"

Bartoli shook his head. "Not yet."

Billy surfaced for another breath and disappeared again.

"Matthew, you wanna get him out of there? Looks like he's being drownproofed to get in the Navy SEALs."

Spiller headed to the poolside, then turned. "Suppose I'll be seeing you around."

"You can take that to the bank." He put a contact card on the bar. "In case you think of anything. Or you wanna confess. Thanks for the soda."

BILLY WAS DRY within five minutes. Spiller settled him on a lounger and watched from the shade of the bar area as he baked in the sun, and the water evaporated from his clothes. It took ten minutes for his breathing to regain its natural rhythm. What remained was an expression of grim annoyance, and Spiller suspected it was partly manufactured by the old thespian for his benefit, perhaps to inflict a sense of shame to soften him up. Spiller assumed the appropriate look of chagrin, but his heart was impervious.

Eventually, Billy fixed his rheumy eyes on Spiller. "I could have *died*."

"Okay… A, I didn't ask you to come here, and B, you're the silly sod who jumped in the pool."

His ex-agent fumed at the truth of it.

"Billy, shall we have the conversation?"

"All right. I came here because I will not be cut off from the best earner I've ever produced. You don't get to flee the UK and set up here with another agent who then steals my percentage. I put someone in charge of my UK business specifically so I could come here and take what's mine. I don't care if you're my only client in this town; but you *will* remain my client."

"That's odd," Spiller said. "All your luvvy endearments have vanished. Finally given up the charade, have you? The kindly old codger who's only interested in helping other people?"

"Perhaps. Perhaps this is *my* time. *Dear boy.*"

Spiller shrugged. "Hey, you get me work, I've got no issue with you taking your cut."

Billy's grin was as wicked and worrying as any Spiller had seen. It wasn't the grin of a man who'd just got his way. It was the grin of a man whose devilish path had just become crystal clear.

"Billy…"

"I'll take fifty percent, if that's all right with you."

Spiller maintained a calm exterior, although his inner Hyde was bulging at the seams.

"Should I interpret your silence as a tacit acceptance?"

"So… you were heading here to demand your usual twenty percent, then you found out about the show last night, and now you want fifty."

Billy nodded. "Spot on."

"Why? You've always had your suspicions about that day. Why now?"

Billy got up and approached. "You told me it was special effects, all fake blood and squids, and—"

"Squibs, Billy. Squibs. With a B."

"No matter. Anyway, because Brett Stutz didn't bat an eyelid, I believed it."

Spiller laughed. "You never believed it, Billy. You were just too scared of losing your commission to dob me in."

"Think what you like. What is clear to me now, after seeing how you reacted to Stutz threatening to spill the beans last night, is that I definitely did witness you gun down two men on my front lawn." Billy grinned like an attorney after a killer closing argument. "*And* I suspect that detective wasn't here to catch up with an old chum. What did he want with you?"

"Apparently, I'm a suspect in the Harry Sullivan murder."

Billy appeared taken aback by Spiller's candor. It took a moment to regain his equilibrium.

Spiller finished his beer. "So, you have a dilemma, don't you? If I don't agree to cough up half my earnings in perpetuity, do you throw me under the bus and squash the golden goose, or do you back off with your threats?"

Billy nodded.

"Actually, Billy, that's not your dilemma. Your dilemma is this: knowing what I'm capable of, should you threaten me, or should you get on the first plane back to Blighty?"

Billy's quizzical eyes suggested he'd not thought it through properly. "Uuummm…"

"Speaking of planes, remember that incident at the airport, end of Jan? The guy who got shot by the police?"

Billy still wasn't with it. "Uuuhhh…"

"That was the day I left to come here. That man was at the airport to kill *me*."

"What? Why?"

"Because I killed his brother."

"On my front lawn?"

"Oh…" Spiller smiled. "No. Although I can see why you'd assume that. No, this was someone else, completely unrelated to what happened outside your house."

A horrified and baffled Billy made his wobbly way back to his lounger.

"In my defense," Spiller said, "everything I did was in *self*-defense. So, you know, I'm not just some psycho. Having said that, you should probably bear in mind I did drown him in a swimming pool."

Billy glanced uncertainly at the water five feet away. "But… you're not a psycho, so you wouldn't do that to anyone who… hadn't… put your life in danger. Would you? And especially not to a frail old gent who you've known for twenty years."

Spiller grabbed another beer. "Well, infirmity doesn't really come into it. The guy I drowned? He went down in his wheelchair."

Billy's mouth fell open. "But... but... how was a man in a wheelchair any threat to you? Did he have a gun?"

"Not at that moment. He had previously tried to shoot me in the head, though, which was how I put him in a wheelchair – by running him over in my car. So... yeah, you're right: not really self-defense at all. Not after the fact. More just... revenge."

It was a few seconds before Billy's brain apparently managed to catch up. "Oh, fuck."

Spiller hooted. "First time in twenty years I've heard you use that word!"

"Dear boy, to clarify... are you going to drown me in your swimming pool?"

Spiller took a glug of beer. "No. Just as you're never going to blackmail me again. You can have thirty percent, Billy, just because I never knew you had such a set of balls on you. And twenty-five for any TV." He approached and held out his hand. "Deal?"

"If I take your hand, you're not going to throw me in the pool, are you?"

"Billy, if I wanted you dead at the bottom of my pool, I'd have left you to your own devices. You were doing a bloody good job of drowning yourself a few minutes ago."

Billy grasped the proffered hand, and Spiller gave it a brief, sharp tug, which made his agent squeak.

"Matthew, you... you *card*, you. Do I have to move out of your spare bedroom?"

Spiller considered. "Nah. You can stay for a bit. Until you find a rental."

Billy smiled tentatively. "And you're definitely not going to drown me?"

THE RIDE BACK to Riviera was silent, but if simmering fury could be heard, then Sadie had Motörhead in the back. She'd driven Theo Montgomery several times before, so knew not to be offended. He'd opened up to her on their first journey, then not since. Despite his indignation earlier, she sensed he was a gentle soul. His aura was spiky red at times, but it was generally a mix of indigo and the rarest white. The heart of him was sensitive, protective of his truest emotions, but relentlessly open to possibilities. When faced with a perceived injustice, though, such people were often the angriest, unable to fathom how others could live their lives so neglectfully.

She had learned from childhood to hide her gift. Few believed what she claimed to see, even when they professed the deepest faith in things no one at all could see. She guessed it was a form of jealousy. And it hadn't always been helpful. She had seen people with the most amazing auras commit appalling acts, and not just in the heat of battle. She wasn't surprised by it these days. No one was wholly good or wholly bad. Auras fluctuated and misled. It was really only the very young and relatively old whose light was reliable; those who were too innocent to mask their outlook, or sufficiently experienced to have accepted who they were, and the world as it was, not how they'd have preferred it to be.

Theo Montgomery was on the cusp of acceptance. Sadie suspected it was only his continual immersion in the acting world that was blocking it. He was railing against a profession he no longer recognized: the overnight fame that had trumped the apprenticeships of old; the plotless drivel that had superseded the craft of scriptwriting; the bulging biceps and buckets of blood that sought to distract from that creative vacuum. Five years ago, he was done with it. He had withdrawn to spend time with his wife. Then her cancer had returned for one final curtain call. Now only one aspect of his life still made any sense. The acting kept him busy, gave him a focus, but it wasn't the same. Having belonged to a handful of black Hollywood trailblazers in the seventies, the following three decades had proven fruitful. Then the very goal he had striven for had bitten him in the ass. The trail had become too populous. He was yesteryear's stale popcorn.

All this, Sadie had learned the very first time she'd picked him up to take him to the set, just two weeks ago. Eight scenes over two weeks. A glorified background artist. She looked at his mournful expression in the rearview as she waited for his gates to swing fully open. The driveway did a small curve back out to the road through another gate. It was an impressive property, in the Spanish colonial style, one of the oldest on the road dating back to the 1930s, overshadowed by long-established trees. Purchased when he'd been paid the big bucks, it would have been way beyond his earnings these days. Now too echoic for one person, even while it was simultaneously crammed full of bittersweet memories.

Sadie got out and released Theo's door. He climbed out and stood there for a moment, looking thoroughly lost. She went to the trunk, grabbed his bag, and walked him up the path to his grand front door.

"Will you be all right?" she asked.

He offered a shrug.

"Can I make a suggestion, Mr Montgomery?"

"Sure."

"I don't wanna overstep the mark, but…"

"You can speak freely."

"Why don't you stop acting? Or at least stop taking roles that are beneath you. It's really hurting you."

Slowly, he nodded. "It is. It really is. I'm not a hypocrite, Sadie. I was in some violent movies back in the day. But they were of a time. Okay, Sam Peckinpah threw some blood around in the seventies, but today wasn't about that. It wasn't really about the movie."

"Then what was it about?"

Theo sighed and sat on an old wicker chair by the door. "I don't like Stutz. The director."

"What's he done?"

"Maybe nothing. But I don't like him. Something about him." He groaned himself to standing. "I'm just so tired of the whole charade."

"Then get out."

He shook his head. "It passes the time. And it's that damnable fear that keeps every actor in the game: quitting a day too soon and missing out on the big one."

She smiled gently.

"I want my swan song, Sadie."

"I understand."

"Do I owe you anything?"

She smiled; he always asked her that. "No, Mr Montgomery, sir, thank you anyway."

"Do they pay you well?"

"Uh… I do okay."

"Would you let me help you, Sadie?"

"How, Mr Montgomery?"

"You said you don't own this car."

"No, it belongs to the company."

"Could I buy you one?"

Her smile turned crooked. "A car?"

"I can loan you the money if you prefer. I doubt I'll live to see it paid back, but I don't need it. I have more than I'll ever need."

Sadie studied his outline and saw only a shimmering white. His intentions were pure. He just wanted to help. But… was this ethical? Some might view this as elder abuse. A vulnerable old man bilked out of his nest-egg.

"Well, Sadie, you know where I am. Have a think about it and tell me what you need. One car, two, three. You decide. I can't take it with me."

## EIGHT

THE GATE TO the parking lot of the West LA Police Station on Butler Avenue slowly rolled open. The unmarked blue Ford Explorer entered, nudge-bar leading the way. Bartoli watched as it parked in a bay, and Officer Gabriela Contreras emerged, adjusting her utility belt. She looked even better in the hot light of day. He was gratified to see a smile appear on her face as she spotted him waiting by the entrance.

She drew to a halt in front of him. "What's homicide doing at our community police station? You lost, LT?"

"How you doing, Contreras?"

"Same ol'. What can I do for you?"

He was tempted to make a lewd comment, but decided he didn't know enough about her to risk it, so he kept it professional. "I got a favor to ask."

"Shoot."

"Could you look into someone for me? On the down-low?"

She frowned. "I thought you were the detective."

"Your theory... the serial killer? I may have just gone over that with a biro. I found out there's someone in town who might be a good fit for this."

"Okay. Uh... I don't mean to pry, but what's stopping you taking the lead? You know, you *are* lead detective on the Harry Sullivan homicide."

Bartoli waited for an officer to pass by. "So, this person... we have history. I don't wanna put him back on my radar – not officially. Last time, I couldn't pin anything on him. Honestly, it was just embarrassing. If I move on this guy again, it needs to be airtight. And I already screwed up on that score. I paid him a visit earlier. I shouldn't have done that; he'll be on his guard now. But I just needed him to see my face again."

"Was it worth it?"

Bartoli considered, then grinned. "Oh, yeah. He nearly dropped a deuce right there on his doorstep."

Contreras smiled, thought about it. "Okay. I get some kudos, though, if I help, right? You don't take all the glory. I mean it, Detective. I do the footwork on this, you don't cut me out. I take some credit."

Bartoli shrugged. "Whatever. Contreras, I just want him locked up. I don't care how that happens."

"Okay. Guy got a name?"

"Matthew Spiller."

Contreras yelped in amusement. "*El coño loco* from last night on Mel Banaghan? *Him?*"

"Yeah, and he's a bona fide lunatic; that wasn't an act."

"So, you want him locked up, or you want me to whack him? Take him out? You know?"

Bartoli studied her deadpan expression, but there wasn't a glimmer.

"Joke!" she said and laughed. "Jeez, your face. Thought you might appreciate the reference, you being from *Noo Yok* and all. And you kinda looking like a Mafioso."

He'd heard that before and always took it as a compliment. He smiled.

"What exactly am I looking for?"

"Everything," Bartoli said. "Whatever you can glean from the moment he set foot in LA."

*"No problemo."*

He nodded at her vehicle. "Why the unmarked, Contreras? You like being a bit sneaky, huh?"

"I grab one when I can. I don't want a black-and-white to put a scumbag off doing what they wanna do. Just kicks the can down the road. In that, I can be there when it happens."

"When what happens? You get a lot of drive-bys in Bel-Air?"

"It's a pleasant neighborhood, no question. But scumbags are everywhere. Money don't make no difference. Makes them feel entitled, but the law applies to everyone."

"It does. Got a pet hate?"

"Bad drivers. DUI, that kinda thing."

He raised an eyebrow. "Not murder or rape?"

"I can forgive intent more than recklessness. Intent has a sick logic to it, but there's no sense to the death of a person caused by recklessness."

"Yeah." He nodded. "Never thought of it that way before."

"I guess I dislike stupid people more than bad people."

He laughed. "Oh, you got your work cut out in this town, Contreras."

"Don't I just. Give me a couple of days; I'll get back to you about Matthew Spiller."

DESPITE HIS REPEATED denials, Spiller really did want to drown his agent. He observed through the blinds of his bedroom window as Billy sunned his pale skin, occasionally wiping his brow and disgustingly flicking the sweat out of his bellybutton with an overlong fingernail. Although, to give the old bugger some credit, he did still at least maintain a concave abdomen when lying down that allowed the sweat to run to that lowest point.

Thirty percent was better than fifty, but considering his last Hollywood payday, the difference between twenty and thirty was a lot of lost dough. And he would no doubt command even more for his next movie, which was proportionally an even bigger cut for the blackmailing old bastard. Spiller felt cheated, resentful. He'd left a land where people had held sway over him – his future, his finances, his family. This had been a fresh start, a divestment of all that had hampered him in England. Yet, despite his best efforts, here was Billy, trailing after him like a stained piece of toilet paper stuck to his shoe.

It was incredible what money did to people. Billy had always appeared rather content with his lot in life. A notable acting career, although substandard when compared to the McKellen Class of Ten Years Earlier – which had possibly prompted his shift into agenting in the 1990s. But perhaps Spiller didn't have a monopoly on resentment, and Billy had just been simmering gently, awaiting his time to claim the spoils, even if that were just the latter half of the elusive gift of Fame and Fortune. In a way, Spiller understood Billy's need to pounce while his limbs were still robust enough to do so, but... he'd gone about it with such crassness. Blackmail, threats, lording it like he had the upper hand, seemingly oblivious to the fact that the lightest of backhands would so effortlessly send him to a watery grave.

Watching Billy enjoy the hospitality of the house, Spiller seethed. Wherever the next movie came from, even if Billy hadn't sourced the opportunity, he would get involved. Perhaps he would earn his keep by negotiating a higher fee, as he had for *Man on a Murder Cycle*, but any agent in Hollywood could do the same, and they would know the town sufficiently to gauge exactly how far they could push it, and they would only take twenty percent. Billy didn't know the town. He was a fledgling on US soil, liable to be hoodwinked into a lower fee, of which he would take thirty percent. Billy would be stealing what he hadn't earned. He would be enriching himself at the expense of Spiller's retirement fund and his daughters' eventual inheritance. Maybe the passage of time would soften his fury, but it felt pretty well entrenched at that moment.

He had to let off some steam. He changed, wriggling into his armored bike leathers, and went downstairs for his crash helmet in the hall closet. Before heading through to the garage, he went out to the pool.

"Billy, I'm going for a ride. Help yourself to food or whatever. I'll be a couple of hours."

Billy sat forward on his lounger, spilling his bellybutton sweat onto his underpants so he looked like he'd dribbled down below. "Could I come?"

"What? I don't have any spare gear."

"Ha! Piffle-paffle. In my day, our heads were bare and if we wore leathers, they were fashionable not functional."

"You rode a motorbike?"

"A one-seven-five BSA Bantam D-Ten."

"Okay. Cool. Well, in my garage is a specially-commissioned turbocharged thirteen-forty cc Suzuki Hayabusa that'll theoretically hit over two-hundred-and-sixty miles per hour and will – I know – reach a hundred in under five seconds."

Billy's eyes lit up. "Good grief." He moved to get off the lounger. "Let me just put on a pair of slacks and—"

"No, Billy. Not today. I need some alone time. If you've really got the stomach, I'll take you out some other day."

Billy rested back. "Excellent. I shall look forward to that very much."

Back in the air-conditioned house, Spiller stood in the hallway for several minutes to let his skin dry under the bike gear. It wasn't the best time of year to be clad in toughened cow hide, but he figured a sweaty back was preferable to a broken one.

The garage fluorescents showcased two magnificent forms. A Maserati GranTurismo Convertible Sport in *Grigio Alfieri*, with leather upholstery in *Rosso Corallo*, and the Hayabusa in Glass Sparkle Black, with Candy Burnt Gold accents. He genuinely enjoyed staring at these machines in the garage more than taking them out on the open road. In truth, the bike terrified him. While the coke he'd snorted the night before would remain a one-off, the Hayabusa was a drug he couldn't resist, even though it held the power to end his life like a catastrophic overdose.

The plan was to head up North Beverly Glen Boulevard, take Mulholland to the I-405, head north, branch left onto Route 101 all the way to State Highway 27, then head south, winding down through the hills to Topanga Beach, then Route 1 east to Santa Monica, hit the I-10 for a while before getting back on the 405 northbound. It was a circuit he'd done several times before.

Spiller didn't even make it up to Mulholland. The *whoop-whoop* invaded his helmet, and his wing mirror confirmed he had a cop on his tail. He slowed, hoping it would pass, but it stayed put, and hit him with another *whoop-whoop*. He rode a little further, then took a right onto Briarwood, where he pulled over. The blue Ford Explorer followed and stopped behind him, a strobe box flashing blue and red in the windshield. Spiller lent the bike on its stand and dismounted, removing his helmet. The Latina officer climbed out and approached, the heel of her palm on the butt of her sidearm.

"Sir," she said, peering at him through dark glasses. "Do you own this motorcycle?"

"I do." He smiled and hoped she'd recognize him. If she did, she didn't let on.

"Do you have your documents?"

"Under the seat, officer."

"Take them out for me – real slow, please."

"What's this about?" he asked, as he retrieved the paperwork. "I don't think I was speeding."

"You weren't. Just routine." She received the documents. "Key."

"What?"

"Key. Please, sir. Can't have you riding off into the sunset before I've done my checks."

The Hayabusa's ignition was keyless. He unzipped his hip pocket and handed her the RFID fob.

"Thank you." She pointed. "Stand over there, please, sir, face the wall."

"What? Like a naughty kid at a kindergarten?"

The officer was unruffled. "Sir, this'll go quicker if you comply."

He sighed audibly and turned toward a whitewashed wall and a dense hedge. He went to unzip his leathers slightly to cool down.

"Sir! Hands where I can see them!"

He held his arms out very deliberately, then lowered them to his sides. Next thing he heard was a door slamming and an engine starting. He glanced over his shoulder, then swiveled to track the Explorer as it passed his bike and carried on up Briarwood until it was lost from sight around the bend. He glanced at the open seat.

His documents were there, but not the RFID fob.

"What the fuck?" He shifted the documents and searched around the seat compartment. "Bitch!" He hadn't even noted the license plate of the Explorer or the name on her chest badge.

This, after Bartoli's visit? Too much of a coincidence. He froze as a thought occurred to him. He knew the main roads. If she wasn't coming back down Briarwood, she'd be on Angelo Drive now, and that led only one way, straight back to North Beverly Glen. It all depended which way she'd turn at the stop sign.

He popped his helmet on, carefully maneuvered the dead weight of the bike so it was facing the main drag, straddled it, and walked it down to just shy of the road. He lent it again, hopped off, and waited, peeking around a bush at the straight stretch of incline. Five minutes passed, and several cars, then there it was, a solitary vehicle heading his way. He got back on the bike and poised himself, gauging its approach.

The slight slope at the foot of Briarwood was enough to gain some momentum. He let off the brake, and the Hayabusa began to roll.

The Explorer snaked as it braked, screeching its tires, coming to rest at an angle across the yellow center lines, five feet from the bike. The driver's window dropped.

*"Are you insane?"* the officer yelled.

"You took my fob!"

"I don't have your fob!"

"No?" He pressed the start button and the huge engine roared into life. "Well, some arsehole nearby does! Tell Bartoli to get fucked! And you can do the same!" He knocked his visor closed and shot off as fast as he could – without wheelieing the machine back over his head.

Spiller bellowed inside his helmet for thirty seconds until his throat was hoarse, and realized, despite all those months filming, that he'd never felt more in tune with the character of Milton the mental biker.

COMPLETING THE PLANNED route would give him time to calm down, and to think. As he wound his way down through Topanga State Park, Spiller decided he'd return the compliment: pay Bartoli an unexpected visit. He pulled over when he reached the coast, and googled the address of the police station that covered his home. At Santa Monica, he took the Boulevard rather than the I-10, which led straight to Butler Avenue.

Outside the red-tiled public entrance, Spiller realized he couldn't go inside to the front desk. If he switched off the ignition, the bike wouldn't start again. He lifted his visor and waited for an officer to leave the building. An older mustachioed cop was the first out.

"Officer!"

For the second time in an hour, Spiller was approached by a cop with his hand poised above his weapon, clearly wary of a man sitting on a motorbike with the engine running.

"What?"

Spiller pushed the helmet up, so it sat above his brow, like a bulbous appendage. "I need to speak to one of your detectives!" he shouted above the din.

"Turn it off!"

"I can't!"

The cop came closer. "Just turn it off."

"If I could turn it off, I'd have come inside. I can't turn it off."

"You probably need a mechanic more than a detective."

"Jesus… I *can* turn it *off*, but then I wouldn't be able to start it again."

"Why not?"

"It's keyless and I don't have the fob."

The cop frowned. "Did you steal it?"

"What? No, course I didn't steal it. Why would a bike thief come to a police station?"

"Hey, there's some strange people out there."

"Yeah, I don't doubt it. Listen, I need to talk to Lieutenant Bartoli. Can you check if he's around?"

"What's this about?"

"Just tell him Matt Spiller's outside."

The cop suddenly laughed. "I knew I knew you! You're that crazy bastard off the TV!"

Spiller nodded. "Yep. And synonyms thereof."

"Well, we don't have a Detective Bartoli in this building. Bartoli, right?"

"Yeah. Are you sure?"

"Been here fifteen years. Pretty damn sure. What's he do, this detective?"

"I think he's homicide."

"Okay, then you are miles from where you need to be, my friend. You need West Bureau Homicide. Olympic Community Police Station, eleven-thirty South Vermont. Get on the Ten, head east for approximately nine miles. Take off-ramp twelve, left turn onto Vermont. Cross Washington, Venice, West Pico, then start looking on your right."

Spiller absorbed the information, committing it to memory. "So, homicide for this part of the city is ten miles away."

"It's a big division. And it's homicide. You know? Their customers – they don't get impatient."

"No, suppose not. Thanks."

"You're welcome. Take it easy on that thing."

Spiller didn't take it easy, and made it to the visitor parking at the end of the gray-paneled and green-glassed building illegally quickly. Five minutes later, after another awkward conversation with a cop about why he couldn't turn his engine off, Bartoli was sent out to see him. Until that moment, Spiller hadn't even considered that Bartoli might be out on an investigation. He pushed his helmet up on top of his head.

"Switch it off!" Bartoli shouted.

"I can't switch the bloody thing off because you set your little Rottweiler on me."

Bartoli made a face. "Huh?"

"The girl cop in the blue unmarked. Pulled me over, drove off with my sodding key fob."

Bartoli's face gave the game away.

Spiller pointed a gloved finger at him. "It *was* you!"

"No. It wasn't. But I know who you mean."

"You're saying you didn't put her up to it? Pull the other one."

"Matthew, leave it with me." He shook his head.

Spiller grinned, gloated. "Oh, has someone gone a bit rogue?" He erased his smile. "Sort her out, Angelo. I mean it. I've got pots of money now; I can afford the best attorneys. I'll sue you, her, and this whole department."

"Go home, Matthew."

Spiller pulled the helmet down over his face, revved the engine for effect. "Sort it out!"

FOR THE MOMENT, Bartoli decided he would do precisely nothing about the errant Officer Contreras. It was gratifying to see Matthew Spiller's feathers being ruffled. He guessed he'd already tipped his hand with his visit earlier that day, so it didn't much matter if Contreras joined him in pushing a few of the actor's buttons. He decided not to quiz her on the day's events. He didn't want any contact with her just yet, have her confess what she'd done, in case she felt regretful and reneged on her promise to make some checks. She was keen – that much was clear. Perhaps she'd do some digging in places he'd consider out of bounds. It wasn't his problem if she jeopardized her chances of further promotion.

## NINE

THE STRESS JUST kept piling on. His laptop was gone. It was a backup, but it was a monster, housing all his sensitive documents on its four terabytes of twin hard drives. He'd been so busy since the split that he'd not taken an inventory. And he'd not seen any point. She'd left all the expensive designer gear and jewelry he'd bought her over the three years of their marriage, so why would he fear she'd take a laptop, however expensive? Especially as he'd kept it in his personal safe, away from their shared valuables. In full panic-mode, Brett Stutz performed another search of his Crestwood Hills home before concluding it was definitely missing. He felt nauseous. So much on that damned thing that could harm him. Was it accessible? He didn't think so. But just knowing it was out there was enough. This, on top of the excruciating embarrassment of last night's car-crash TV show. And the visit from that detective. Last thing he needed was the cops looking in his direction.

His cell rang. He stared at the caller ID. Cathy Zengler. Did he want to talk to her? What did she have to say? More of the same questions he'd refused to answer as he'd driven her home last night? He wouldn't know unless he picked up.

"Hey, Cathy."

"Brett, hi. You good?"

"Sure, why wouldn't I be?"

"Listen, I know you're pissed off, but Spiller was right. We could not have *paid* for better publicity. I've never seen anything like it. This movie is gonna be off-the-scale colossal. Forget your pride. Whatever happened last night, that obnoxious Limey has done us the biggest favor. The studio heads are ecstatic."

Stutz was scanning his living room as though he might suddenly spot the missing laptop hiding in plain sight. He looked at the view through his panoramic windows, the sparkling lights of Santa Monica and beyond, and the ocean lost against the night sky.

"Brett?"

"That's awesome. Cathy… you think it would hurt the movie if some… *news* was to come out?"

"What *news*?"

"Something bad. Would it hurt the movie? Would the studio pull it?"

"Uh, now you're starting to worry me. Honestly, depends what you're talking about. You know this town these days. Woke as hell. Everyone whining and apologizing for things no one would have blinked an eye at ten years ago. *I'm sorry I'm white, I'm sorry I'm not black enough, sorry I played gay when I'm hetero, sorry I played a paraplegic when my legs fucking work.* People apologizing for acting, for Christ's sake – doing their job."

Stutz gave a laugh. "Yeah, I'm with you. Although… I'm wondering if it works the opposite way. Getting a role because you're *exactly* like the character."

Cathy groaned. "If this concerns a certain Englishman, I really don't wanna know. Not when he's just finished portraying a psychotic, homicidal nut-job. Jesus, I wish I hadn't called you now."

"Okay, just forget about it."

"Easier said than done, but… I don't wanna hear about this again. Okay? And if you need to do something to make sure whatever this is stays buried… do it."

Stutz chucked his cell on the sofa and stepped up to the glass. His ciliary muscles contracted, and the city blurred. He stared at his reflection, distorted slightly by the double glazing. His eyes relaxed again, and he focused on the furthest lights to the right, where they were blocked by the hills. Up the coast, behind those hills, was a big problem; a far bigger problem than Matthew Spiller and his ignoble past. But perhaps one that the ignoble Matthew Spiller could help to cancel out.

NO DOUBT THE Latina cop had thrown his key fob out the window, but Spiller decided he should get the ignition recoded anyway. Between now and then, he had a spare, although he didn't relish even worse treatment now he'd snitched on her to Bartoli, so he decided to leave the bike garaged for a while. Billy was disappointed by the news. He'd genuinely been excited about his upcoming pillion ride.

Strangely, it was quite pleasant having Billy knocking around the place, especially after the sun went down, and Spiller's mood sank with it. It was nice to have that human connection to interrupt the bleak flatlining of his nocturnal thoughts and give them a little blip. Despite Billy's duplicitous intentions, there was something paternal about him, and Spiller still missed his long-dead dad. It was a pale substitute, but better than nothing.

The evening wore on quite comfortably. Spiller had ceded control of the TV to Billy, whose preferred viewing was a re-run of Gerry Anderson's one-off series *UFO*, mainly because he'd starred in a couple of the later episodes. More than fifty years later, he still appeared vexed that his character's potential for greater things had been thwarted by the show being canceled.

Four episodes in, Spiller's enjoyment of his big screen was interrupted by a smaller screen. The caller ID on his phone showed a surprising name. He picked up, hurriedly leaving the living room as he did so.

"Sammy?" he said, as he climbed the stairs.

"Hey, Dad. How are you?"

He closed the bedroom door for privacy. "I'm okay. Better for hearing your voice. How are you, darling?"

"Not bad. Sorry, Dad."

He expected her to burst out crying, then realized how much she'd toughened up last Christmas. "It's okay."

"Mum hadn't told me everything."

"I know. I hope you didn't give her a hard time. We were all messed up back then. I would have stayed, but she said go, and it seemed the right thing to do. Not just for me."

"I just couldn't deal with it. I think it all hit me after you left. I just wanted my Dad. And you'd gone."

"Sorry. On the plus side, you are now set for life financially."

Sammy was not to be deflected. "And then Mum said you'd left her on the floor after a gunfight at the airport, not knowing if she'd even been hit, and you were the cause of it all. Jesus, there is still so much I don't know about last Christmas. Isn't there?"

He wanted to lie. "Yep."

Sammy gave a little laugh to break the tension. "Dad, are we okay to come over?"

Spiller was so taken aback, he paused for thought.

"It's okay if you're too busy," she said.

"No, it's not that, I'm just… surprised. Of course you can come. Hold on, who exactly is *we*?"

"David as well. Is that all right?"

Spiller considered.

She read his thoughts. "We don't expect to stay with you. Well, Mum and David don't. We'd like to – me and Soph. At least for some of the time."

"You can stay as long as you want, darling. I do have a houseguest at the moment, though."

The mocking lechery in her tone was clear. "Oh, *do* you now?"

"No, Sammy, it's my English agent. He showed up unannounced. I can tell him to go. When are you thinking?"

"Mum says soon as we can book. Can't wait to see you, Dad."

"Ditto." His smile quickly faded. "How are you? Honestly. You went through a lot."

"We all did."

"You more than anyone."

"Yeah."

He waited, but that was it. Perhaps she'd managed to lock it away somewhere, and he was picking at the lock by talking about it. He changed the subject.

"When are your exam results?"

"Middle of August."

"Are you feeling confident?"

"Aced 'em." She laughed. "It's how I got through everything. Just stuck my head in a bunch of books."

"Good for you, darling. Which unis have you picked?"

"I'm taking a year out. I might travel. Or maybe I'll be spotted by a film director when I'm in LA and I'll never leave." She laughed harder.

It wasn't a joke Spiller liked — if it was a joke. "You don't want to be an actress, do you?"

"*Actor*, Dad. Gender neutral. Come on, get with the program, lol."

"Sammy?"

"I have no idea, Dad. I just need this year to think."

"You could always go into business with your sister."

"What?"

*"Dogging Delight?"*

"Ah."

"You... honestly." He tittered as he remembered his chat with Soph the night before.

"I think it's a brilliant name. Anyway, how are you enjoying your fame and fortune? I saw that clip of you on Mel Banaghan."

"I think the whole world did."

"Dad, that was insane. And that was not an act. I know you. That was you being *really* angry. What's going on?"

"Uh... it's sorted, don't worry."

"It had better be, Dad. Sorry, but we want to come over and have a lovely time. We don't want to get dumped in the middle of another total nightmare."

Spiller wanted to dismiss her fears, but she deserved better. He took a moment to think, and she allowed him the time. Sit-rep: Billy was paid off and onside; Bartoli was clutching at straws; and for all his bluster, Stutz wasn't about to jeopardize his new movie.

He nodded to himself. "Like the California sun, we are golden."

Feeling more buoyant than at any time since his arrival in LA, Spiller fairly bounced down the stairs. He grabbed a couple of beers from the kitchen and went through to the living room.

"I don't drink beer," Billy said. "Gas."

"I wasn't offering. They're for me. Time and motion." He was just removing his phone from his back pocket, so he didn't sit on it, when it rang again. He checked the caller ID and indicated that Billy mute the show.

"Brett."

"Matthew, I'm having a party."

"Okay." Spiller could hear loud music in the background.

"You need to be here. There are people you should meet. Important for the movie. Important for your career."

"It's happening now?"

"Uh-huh. Couple of folk swing by, they call a few people who call a few people. Impromptu. You know how it is."

"Not really. I'd struggle to fill a phone box on my birthday."

"I'm gonna text you my address."

Spiller looked at Billy, who raised his eyebrows questioningly.

"Any dress code?" Spiller asked Stutz. "You know... are leather shorts okay?"

"You're fucking hilarious. Just get your ass over here. *Stat.*" The call ended.

Spiller waited for the text, aware of Billy's continuing scrutiny. It beeped onto his screen.

"Going out?" Billy enquired.

"Yeah, that was Brett Stutz. He's having a shindig."

"Oh, a little Hollywood *soirée*. Could I be your plus-one, dear boy? I need to start networking if I'm going to make a go of my City of Angels adventure."

Spiller wanted to say no but couldn't really think of why not. "Fine. But no tie-dye. And no velvet, either. Something in between. You're my agent and I'd rather you look the part."

Billy got to his feet. "Won't be a jiffy."

Both men went upstairs to change, then met again on the landing. Spiller was impressed by the subtlety of his agent's outfit. Black jeans and a dark gray paisley dress shirt, tucked in. Spiller wore a white shirt out over blue jeans.

"Very dapper, Billy."

Billy admired himself in the landing mirror. "Do you think so?"

"Absolutely."

"I should have done this sooner, shouldn't I?"

"Decades ago."

Billy turned and gave an endearing smile. "By the way, I am most willing to offer my services as designated driver this evening, should you wish to partake of alcoholized refreshment."

Spiller looked askance. "Someone's been peeking in my garage."

Billy shrugged.

"What car do you own in England, Billy?"

He cleared his throat. "You know what car I own. A Morris Marina. Pristine, I might add."

"Irrelevant. There is no way you are getting your arse behind the wheel of my Maserati."

"I'm an excellent driver."

"Now you just sound like Rain Man. Not happening."

BILLY WHOOPED A lot on the drive over. He whooped in wonderment at every surge of speed. It was a childish reaction that reminded Spiller of the way Billy would often spin his office desk chair once before getting down to business. It seemed to Spiller that Billy had spent much of his adult life pent-up, a self-imposed stifling, outwardly defined by his vintage clothes, his Victorian house, his antiquated language, all intended to anchor him to an era of hope, before he began falling behind his peers, like a thoroughbred gone suddenly lame for no apparent reason. Perhaps that was so much pseudo-analysis, but it certainly appeared to Spiller that his agent had a new lease on life.

"You know you can afford to buy one of these?" Spiller said, as he followed his satnav, turning off Sunset and heading up toward Crestwood Hills.

"Pardon, dear boy?" Billy said, interrupting his humming along to Nickelback's *Rockstar*.

"This car. Or something similar. You made a mint from my movie. You can buy any car you like."

Billy frowned like he'd never even considered the possibility. "Good grief."

Ten minutes later, Spiller was parking up behind Stutz's Ford Bronco. The house was one of the largest on the road, with a view from the rear out over the city. He could hear the thud of music from indoors, but was puzzled by the relative lack of vehicles, which looked like a regular amount for a residential street. Stutz must have been at the window because he opened the door before Spiller could even knock.

"Matty Boy, how are you?"

"I'm all right. Don't like *Matty Boy*, though."

"And who's this? Did you bring your dad?"

Billy scowled. "I am not his bloody father. Brett, it's me."

Stutz leaned forward, creasing his face as though that would help. "Who? Do I know you?"

"It's me, love. Billy. Billy Banbury."

"Wow! What the fuck happened to you?"

"Slight makeover. Not sure that's cause for profanity."

"Come in, come in, straight through to the back room."

Spiller led the way toward the music, followed by Billy, as Stutz shut the door. It wasn't a tune Spiller recognized. Some generic rock band. Possibly a freebie CD of The Dingo Dudes from last night.

The back room was lifeless. Not a soul. Stutz followed in behind and closed the door, then picked up a remote and silenced the din.

Spiller smiled crookedly. "Well, this is rubbish. Although, you're about as popular as I expected you'd be. Even I can get a couple of people round for a party, and I am the original Billy No-Mates. No offense, Billy."

Billy just shook his head. "Brett? I was looking forward to some merrymaking."

Stutz scratched his head. "What can I say? I lied. But it's really excellent that you're here."

"Why?" Spiller asked.

"Okay. I am gonna have a conversation with you, Matty Boy, without Billy. Then a conversation with Billy, without you."

"Or how about I say fuck you and we both jump back in my car and go home?"

"It's a free world. There's the door."

The gleeful grin on Stutz's face was disconcerting. Spiller sensed danger and a distinct lack of choice, despite the offer of a swift departure. He looked at his agent.

"Hollywood intrigue," Billy said. "Do you have champagne, Brett?"

"Refrigerator full of it. Help yourself."

"Rightio." Billy left the room.

Spiller perused a sideboard of awards. "You're very proud of yourself, aren't you?"

"Missing an Oscar, that's all."

"That's a space you are never going to fill. What am I doing here?"

Stutz poured himself a bourbon. "I need you to do me a favor."

"Go on."

"I need you to visit my wife and retrieve something from her."

"Which is?"

Stutz took a gulp. "And then I'm gonna need you to do what you do."

Spiller walked over and grabbed the bottle of liquor. He took a swig, then stepped up so they were practically nose to nose. "And what exactly do I do?"

"This. You do this. You intimidate. And then you… *kill*."

Spiller backed away with a curt laugh. "You know nothing about me. You saw the tag-end of a situation that would have pushed anyone to react with lethal force. You saw the weapons they had; they'd have chopped me into little pieces."

Stutz acquiesced with a nod. "Maybe so. But, Jeez Louise, did you put them down with clinical precision. Double taps to the heart, then headshots to seal the deal. And there's a huge elephant in the room, because this did not happen in open-carry Texas. This was in a country where law-abiding citizens are never armed. Yet you had a gun."

Spiller took a swig of bourbon. "If this is you trying to gain the moral high ground, remember you just asked me to kill your wife. And it's not like I'm a trained assassin. I know how to shoot because I was in that war movie. You know that. Seriously, why don't you just leave me alone?"

Stutz sighed, offered a conciliatory smile. "Matthew, I wouldn't ask if I had any other option."

"Ask someone else. That's your other option. There are plenty of people out there who would do this if you bunged them a couple of grand."

Stutz laughed. "Sure, but how do I find these people? And everyone knows me. I need you to do this. I'm begging you."

Spiller sat down with his bottle on an uncomfortable curvy wooden chair that probably cost more than his Maserati. "But you're not, are you, Brett? You're not begging; you're blackmailing. What the hell am I sitting on?"

"It's a Gaspard Descoteaux. Only four of them in the world."

"I'm not surprised, it's crap. Brett, listen… let's just agree to go our separate ways. Forget this conversation, forget everything. Just ask your ex for whatever it is she took; I'm sure she'll give it back. You don't need to kill her. My neighbor borrowed a ladder from me once, kept it for ages, and he's still alive." Spiller caught himself. "Wish he wasn't now – he's shagging my wife – but that's another story. Anyway, yes? Agreed?"

Stutz shook his head.

Spiller looked at the darkness outside. It was in his head as well. Every night, his mind went dark just the same way. The only consolation was the promise of dawn, and the wondrous light it would bring to lift his soul.

Tonight was different. Stutz had made it different. At that moment, dawn felt a long way off. He spoke quietly, like he didn't need anyone else to hear.

"I've been here before."

"Huh? My house?"

"No, you dummy. This situation. Being pressured to do something I don't want to do. I tell you… it's making me feel really low."

"Boo hoo."

Spiller smiled, then cackled, which broke his reflective reverie. He stood up. "Oh, you have no idea. Do you remember *The Incredible Hulk?* The old TV series with Lou Ferrigno? There was something his mild-mannered alter-ego said to a reporter who kept hounding him: *Don't make me angry; you wouldn't like me when I'm angry.* Well, I have a twist on that: Don't make me depressed; I do really bad shit when I'm depressed."

"I'm counting on it."

"You know, back in the UK, I was *very* depressed. And my depression was like a nuclear sub tearing across the surface of the ocean. It was there for all to see. Here in the sun, I've been better. A lot better. But don't kid yourself. Because I don't. That sub might have disappeared from view, but it's still down there, just under the surface. And its periscope's up, always scouting for some reason to open the tubes and go *absolutely fucking ballistic.*"

Stutz gulped.

"Question for you, Brett, is whether you want to be the one who triggers DEFCON One."

The twisted expression on the director's face suggested he was having a quick conflab with himself. "Okay…" He gave a nervous laugh. "Let's take a step back, shall we?"

"Why do you want to kill your wife, Brett? And what's she got of yours that's so important?" He offered Stutz the bourbon.

Stutz took the bottle and put it back on the sideboard. "She has my laptop. You don't need to touch her. I just want my laptop."

"Why?"

"Because I don't wanna end up like a certain black actor."

"Are you talking *MeToo?*"

"*No!* Christ, no. I mean…" He struggled to say the words.

Spiller thought about black actors who'd been in trouble. "The taxman? You've been lying to the IRS?"

Stutz exhaled heavily, as though a weight had lifted.

"And your wife? What's she done that's so bad you want her dead?"

"Nothing. She left me, but... not that. I don't have a prenup, okay? She could take me for... Jesus, this is the problem. She comes after me with attorneys and forensic accountants, I am done. With or without that laptop. But *with it*..." He shook his head, grabbed the liquor, and took a glug. "Just forget it. The whole thing. I'll deal with it."

"Yeah, why don't you do that, Brett? Go and have a civil conversation with your wife. Ask for your laptop. Offer something in return. Be nice to her. Buy her out of the marriage. How long did it last?"

"Three years."

"So, make her an offer. Surprise her. Be generous."

"You think I haven't thought of that? I can't even talk to her!"

"Just be nice to her."

"No, I mean I am *literally* unable to talk to her."

"You don't know where she is?"

"I know exactly where she is, and I can't talk to her. She joined a fucking *cult!*"

Spiller groaned, dumped himself on the sofa. "God, how the hell did this become my problem, Brett?"

A slightly sozzled Billy popped his head in the room. "Did I hear the C-word? You two aren't having a falling out, are you?"

"Cult, Billy. *Cult.*"

"Oh, I am relieved. I don't like unpleasantness. Eh? What do you mean, cult?"

Spiller stood up. "Doesn't matter, Billy. Go and drink some more of Brett's champagne."

"Right you are, love."

Spiller watched his director as he shuffled on his feet, sipping repeatedly from the bottle in the manner of a chain-smoker with an endless supply of cigarettes. Despite everything, he felt sorry for the man. And despite the stupidity of Stutz's baiting him on Mel Banaghan the previous night, Spiller had to acknowledge his being in LA with an acting career was one hundred percent down to Brett Stutz. Not just that. Stutz's willingness to set aside the truth of that day on Billy's front lawn had saved Spiller from a life of incarceration at Her Majesty's pleasure.

"Brett, do you still want to talk to Billy in private? I'm guessing that was to gang up on me, so I did your bidding."

"No," Stutz said adamantly.

"Do you have a problem with me?"

Stutz had to think about it. "No. Not now."

"And last night?"

He laughed. "Matthew, that was you! Jesus, you walk on stage in dark glasses and cut-off pants, high as a kite."

"What?"

"Sure, you think I don't know how drugs affect people? Man, I've been in Hollywood forty years. The glasses were the obvious sign, but your behavior… It's just a good job people here like to think you Brits are eccentric."

"You wouldn't have thrown me under the bus?"

Stutz shrieked. "No! Why would I do that to my own movie?"

"I thought… you were always a little off with me the whole time we were filming. I thought maybe you were just waiting for the right time to blow the whistle."

Stutz set his depleted bottle back on the sideboard and sat down. "I was terrified every day that you'd do something really dumb. I was terrified that…" he pointed to the wall, then lowered his voice "…*he* might suddenly say something. So, every day I was kicking myself that I chose you, even though you were just *faultless* in the part."

"Oh."

"*Is* he gonna say something?"

"Billy? No way. He's setting up as an agent here. I'm his golden ticket."

Stutz nodded. "Good. Sorry I wasted your time tonight."

Spiller said, "Forget about it," but he wasn't certain he could do the same. He owed Brett Stutz, and he had a fierce sense of loyalty to anyone who helped him, because so few ever had. "Brett…"

"Yeah?"

"Do you want me to try and talk to your wife? I mean just talk. See if I can get your laptop back? I can't promise anything, but... where is she?"

Stutz came over and sat next to him on the sofa. "Matthew, that would be incredible. She's holed up in a place called The House of Sempiternal Love. It's up the coast near El Matador Beach. Hillside of the PCH."

"House of what?"

"I know, I'd never heard the word, either. I had to Google it. It means something that feels as though it's been around for ever. But not like eternal. Eternal is more to do with God. Sempiternal is more earthbound."

Spiller shrugged. "Doesn't help much. What's the purpose of this place?"

"Don't know; there's nothing online. Could be like the Scientologists, the Branch Davidians... the Moonies, for all I know."

Spiller stood up. "Well, all I can do is knock on the door. Take it from there."

"Will you go tomorrow?"

"Sure. Not like I've got anything better to do. Hey, I may take Billy; see if they want to keep him."

## TEN

THE EVENING ENDED on a high note. More accurately, it ended on a collection of rich baritone notes. Having missed out on a pillion ride on a road rocket, Billy had made known another wish on his Bucket List as they drove past a karaoke bar. To Billy's surprise, Spiller had swung a U-turn and parked outside. Between other willing vocalists, the patrons of the bar were treated to a variety of sixties tunes, and as the night wore on, the gaps between Billy's turns grew shorter as people decided they'd rather listen than sing, until it became The Billy Banbury Show.

Spiller found it all very entertaining, but his brain began to tune out after fifteen minutes, to focus on the impending arrival of his estranged family. The best part would be seeing his daughters again. But that would also be the worst part. He wouldn't be too enamored of David's presence as the new daddy figure in their lives, but at least David was providing a service he'd been unable to. David had taken the pressure off, slightly alleviating Spiller's guilt. He guessed the girls would be happy just being in LA with their famous dad, jumping in his swimming pool from sun-up 'til dark. Maybe he'd take them around the studios, the ones open to the public, and the closed sets he'd been on while filming *Man on a Murder Cycle*. He'd drive them to the various locations in his Maserati, take a bunch of photos. Head down to the boardwalk at Venice, take the PCH north aways. The girls would love it all. But he knew he'd still feel inadequate. Like he wasn't doing enough. Like he'd never done enough. Because that was how life made him feel.

But as he looked around the bar, he realized his fame had created a new reality, at least for the people looking in on him. He was being recognized, and these onlookers were sycophants to a person. He could see it in their eyes, their expressions. They were jealous of him. His impending fame was like a precious gemstone worn on the finger of a tycoon. No one wanted to be impressed, but they all were. And unlike so many in that town, Spiller was, as yet, a sealed tome. His first LA chapter was just beginning, and no one knew his history. The veil had fallen away from so many of the established Hollywood players, skeletons crashing out of their closets, sexual peccadillos shared by the spurned and the used, out of spite or in exchange for their own five minutes of fame. Whatever Spiller felt about himself, in this town he was unsullied, an unknown quantity. Last night had been weird, but far from the revelatory catastrophe he had feared when Stutz had taunted about his audition. Spiller needed to keep it that way. He vowed to himself he would offer nothing more during the rest of his promotional tour than chat about the movie, and perhaps a little about his past as an actor in the UK. No one had the right to glean anything more personal.

For the third time in as many minutes, Spiller caught the direct stare of a young man at a corner table. He had a wild, curly mop of fair hair, and looked to be in his early twenties. He was sitting between two women of a similar age, who were struggling to mouth along to the lyrics of The Walker Brothers' *After the Lights Go Out*, a song that likely predated their debut on planet earth by thirty-five years. Spiller directed his attention back to Billy, whose eyes were shut as he crooned his way through a song he knew by heart. No way was Spiller giving the kid in the corner another glance. As a distraction, he took out his phone and began to video Billy's performance.

After five seconds, his gaze was drawn back to the curly-haired kid, like a compass needle pulled back to true north.

The kid grinned, raised an index finger to his temple, and rotated it several times, before jabbing it toward Spiller.

Spiller felt duty-bound to scowl at the insult, but instead found himself smiling, then laughing openly. Shaking his head, he looked back at Billy, until his peripheral vision caught the kid getting up to come over. Without waiting for permission, the kid claimed a seat, setting his bottle of Michelob on the table.

"Matt Spiller, you sorry son-of-a-bitch," the kid said.

Spiller lost his smile. "I know you?"

"Now, don't pitch a hissy fit, just came to say howdy. I was a background actor in that dumbass movie you just made."

"Why don't you fuck off back to your table and look for your filter?"

"Oo, you got your tail up, mister. You fixin' to poleax me? Come on, I could start a fight in an empty house."

Spiller noted the kid's body language hadn't changed, nor his tone of voice. "Mate, I suspect you're winding me up. Very funny, but don't push it. I've had a difficult twenty-four hours."

The kid's eyes sparkled, then he laughed and extended his hand. "Name's Noah. Friends say I'm missin' a few buttons off my shirt. Just my way of sayin' hello."

Spiller gave him a wary look, ignored his hand. "You need to work on your greetings, Noah."

"You gonna lecture me on what's appropriate? After last night?"

"That was showbiz. You know, Noah, when I was your age, I wouldn't have dreamt of approaching a famous person in a bar, let alone mouthing off to them like a little prick."

"Maybe if you hadda done, you mighta got to LA twenty years sooner."

*"What?"*

"Don't ask, don't get."

"Only thing you've asked for so far is a smack in the gob. Why did you come over?"

"I need help." Noah took a swig of his beer.

"You got that right."

"I mean, in the profession. I really was in your movie. Thought you might know some folk, make a few introductions on my behalf."

Spiller raised an eyebrow. "Why would I do that? I just met you."

"Because you were my side of the fence six months back. One wheel down and the axle draggin'. I heard you last night on Mel's show. You can't want me to suffer the same fate."

"I don't give a toss about your fate. Why should I?"

Noah nodded toward his table where the two girls were chatting to each other. "Want me to give 'em a holler?" He leered. "Which one d'you like? Or how about both?"

Spiller smiled. "Sure."

Noah blew a shrill whistle, and the girls came over, dragging their chairs behind them.

Spiller leaned onto the table to talk to them. "This little turd just tried to pimp you out to me because he wants to further his dead-end acting career. I have a daughter your age. You have fathers my age."

"Jerk," one of the girls said to Noah, then grabbed her friend's hand and led her back to their table.

Noah stared at Spiller, shook his head, smiled. "You are dumber than a watermelon."

"You reckon?"

"You don't know me, I could—"

The end of Billy's song signaled renewed applause, and Noah had to pause. Without the music, Noah lowered his voice. "I could be a psycho stalker, for all you know. I could make your life a livin' hell. Is it worth it? All you gotta do is help me out."

Spiller laughed. "Are you threatening me?"

"Could be I'm beyond threats. You think about that? Harry Sullivan, John Frears, Aiden Powers. Ring any bells? Maybe I'm takin' out the opposition. Maybe you're next. Unless you help me out."

With a smile still lingering, Spiller roared his amusement as Billy returned to claim his chair. He settled in it, looking bemused at the mismatch of Spiller's hooting and the snarl of his new table-guest.

Spiller calmed himself, addressed his agent. "Billy! Perfect timing. D'you want to give this guy a business card? He wants to be an actor."

"I *am* an actor."

"But he's a bit thick because he thinks bumping off actors twice his age will improve his odds of getting a lead role."

Billy appeared not to have heard, keener on adding a second client to his LA roster. He looked Noah up and down. "How tall are you?"

"Three inches taller than Tom Cruise, sir."

Billy didn't know what that was, so looked at Spiller.

"Four foot eight," Spiller said.

Noah obliged: "Five-ten, sir."

"Well, you have an interesting look. Maybe not leading man, but…"

"He'd play a good serial killer, wouldn't he?" Spiller said, and smirked.

"Did you train?" Billy wanted to know.

"Amarillo Actors Studio," Noah replied.

"You must hug your pillow a lot," Spiller said.

Noah was stumped. "*Huh?* Man, you are one bubble off plumb."

Billy dug out a crumpled business card from his back pocket. "Drop me an email, dear boy. CV, bit about yourself. Let's take it from there."

Noah snatched the card. "Yessir, I will do that forthwith. Much obliged."

The DJ called Billy back to the stage. As he got up for another encore, Noah headed back to his table, which was now bereft of females. He collected his denim jacket from his seatback, then stared at Spiller for a moment before raising a finger-gun. He winked, then dropped his thumb, pulling his pointed finger back and up as if in recoil, then headed for the exit.

Spiller watched him until he disappeared. He scanned the bar's remaining patrons and wondered how many more of them were simmering nutters. Then he remembered what he'd done in his own recent life, and guessed he could cut the young Texan a little slack. Perhaps the kid was paying bizarre homage to the audacious interview Stutz had alluded to on Mel Banaghan. Perhaps this wouldn't be the last time he'd be accosted by some desperate aspirant who couldn't figure out where to draw the line.

He was still holding his phone, which he slipped back into his inside pocket. He gazed at his agent, swaying on the small plinth, revitalized and SoCalized, warbling his way through *House of the Rising Sun*, and he realized Billy deserved *his* moment in the sun as much as anyone.

## ELEVEN

DESPITE HER RESERVATIONS, Sadie called Theo Montgomery early the next morning to accept his offer. She had half-expected him to tactfully rescind it, having realized the nostalgic gloom, cast by the moonlit shadow of his empty home, had triggered a philanthropy that had overridden his better judgement, but he had sounded elated to hear her voice. Through much of the night, she had battled to fathom the relative morality of saying yes to him, always being hounded by a quote from a movie: "there's no nobility in poverty." *The Wolf of Wall Street*. It had seemed churlish basing her decision on the utterance of a morally bankrupt Jordan Belfort, but you couldn't argue with Leo DiCaprio, right?

Having established the Cadillac Escalade as her favored vehicle, Theo had called ahead to prepare the ground. A half hour later, outside his house, she had given her elderly benefactor a faltering hug, before opening the rear door for him. Cadillac of Beverly Hills on Wilshire Boulevard. They were waiting.

"Did you sleep well, Mr Montgomery?" Sadie asked, as they set off.

"You can call me Theo. And we don't need to small-talk, Sadie. I know you must feel awkward, but there's really no need. I want to do this."

She smiled at him via the rearview mirror, the gratitude alive in her eyes.

As she turned onto Sunset Boulevard, heading toward the city, she heard the growl of a powerful sports car heading her way. She peered questioningly at the driver as the hood-down Maserati approached, and nearly honked her horn at him, but he was too quickly past.

SPILLER FOLLOWED THE twists of Sunset all the way down to the PCH at Inceville, then pointed the Maserati's nose westward. He was aware as he cruised the twenty miles to El Matador Beach that this was the epitome – perhaps the cliché – of his success: an Englishman on a Californian coast road in an Italian sports car, its exhaust notes crying out for a fleeting recognition of its owner, newly baptized by Mel Banaghan into the coterie of Hollywood hard men. He was the person he'd so long aspired to become, and yet it was the outward manifestation of his success that marked his renascence more than anything internal.

But it would suffice. And maybe this was all there was for any of them. Little boys and girls, playing kings and queens.

He arrived at The House of Sempiternal Love. Ten yards off the PCH, tall railing gates blocked access, with no signage. Brett Stutz had sent him a screenshot of the entrance, otherwise he'd never have known where to stop. The drive was wide enough for a three-point turn for those who would be sent back to the road. A high railing fence stretched out from either side of the gates, circling wide before heading up the contours of the scrub rise. The driveway bent to the right past the barrier, then disappeared left after twenty yards. Spiller could see part of a red-tiled roof emerging from a hollow beyond, and the low hills behind that, ascending into Charmlee Wilderness Park.

He edged the Maserati close to an intercom on a short pole. He stared into a camera lens embedded in the box, then pressed the button.

"Welcome, what can we do for you?" A male voice, and not that welcoming.

"I'm here to see Katerina Stutz."

"You mean Katerina Petrova. I have nothing booked in for today."

Using her maiden name. "I know – I'm here on behalf of her husband. My name's Matt Spiller."

A pause, then, "One moment, please."

Spiller waited for a full minute. Vehicles whizzed past on the PCH behind him, a constant rushing soundtrack.

"Hello?" A female voice this time. "I understand you're here to see Kat."

"That's right."

"You're Matt Spiller, the actor."

Spiller smiled into the tiny convex lens. "Guilty as charged."

"What exactly is your business with Kat?"

"Brett asked me to talk to her."

"Kat wants nothing to do with him. Please turn around and go home." The intercom clicked off.

Spiller pressed again.

"What?"

"Sorry to pester, but she really should hear what I have to say. And if you're looking to protect her, so should you."

The woman's sigh was audible. "Okay. But please bear in mind, we have guns up here."

The gates began to open, and Spiller headed up toward the house.

He took a spot in the small parking lot and was met by an armed guard in a tan uniform, standing under the shaded entrance to a modern, white-painted building. Spiller reckoned its size meant there were nine or ten bedrooms inside. Behind him on the lawn, several sun-loungers surrounded an oval pool. All were unoccupied. Too hot for lying out, except for mad dogs and Billy Banburys.

The guard approached without a smile. "Lift your shirt, please."

Spiller stopped walking, pulled his t-shirt high up his midriff, and circled around without being asked. The guard indicated he lift his jeans at the ankles. Spiller obliged. As he dropped the denim back onto his trainers, a woman appeared from the main entrance.

She possessed a shock of red hair, loosely pulled back into a braid, and was dressed in a long, floaty dress, in colors that reminded him of Billy's tie-die vest. She wasn't tall, and appeared to be in her early fifties, but Spiller got the sense that she was a force to be reckoned with. Despite the hippy vibe, she exuded a strength that Spiller knew could only come from bitter experience.

He offered his hand, but she walked past toward the pool, hooking a finger at him. He turned and followed her into the shade of a bamboo-covered shelter over a table and chairs. He took a moment to take in the view before sitting down.

"Nice spot you've got here," he said, staring out over the Pacific swell.

"We like it," she said, settling. "Sit down, please, Matt."

He obeyed, and smiled, but received only scrutiny in return.

"Is Katerina allowed to join us?" he asked.

She made a face. *"Allowed?"*

"I mean…"

"What did Brett tell you about us?"

Spiller had to be honest with this woman; he felt that more than anything. "He said this place is a cult."

She took it calmly, like she'd heard it before. She nodded. "Uh-huh."

"House of Sempiternal Love?" he queried.

"House, yes. Not church. And unless you know who I am and what we do here, who are you to judge?"

He shrugged, tried another smile. "Enlighten me."

"Okay. This is a place of respite for the lost souls of Hollywood."

Spiller turned to the building, looked it up and down. "You're gonna need a bigger house."

For the first time, she smiled back. "Tell me about it."

"So… not a cult."

"*So* not a cult."

"Well, that's good to know. And is Katerina joining us?"

"Shortly. But I suspect that's only because she wants to meet the man who cut the leg off her husband's favorite pants, then put a pair of scissors to his throat."

"Showbiz," Spiller said with a grin.

She shook her head. "Not buying it. You may have been acting; he wasn't."

"And you know this how?"

"Because I was married to Brett for five long years."

Spiller leaned back in his chair. "Oh."

"Katerina is the fourth Mrs Stutz. I was the third." Belatedly, she offered her hand. "Hayley Olsen."

Spiller leaned forward and grasped it.

"My question, Matt, is whether you were also playing a part that night. See, I don't know you to make that judgement. Him, I know. I know Brett very well. You? I need to know if you're here as his errand boy, or you have something to say that Kat might really want to hear. If you and Brett are buddies, I'd guess the first is true, in which case you may as well leave right now."

Spiller considered before replying. "I have come here to fetch something of his. I suppose you'd call that an errand. But Stutz and I are never going to be grabbing a beer together, which is why I also have my own message for Katerina." He turned hopefully to look at the front entrance as though she would appear bang on cue.

Hayley tapped his knee. "Kat will arrive as soon as I give her a call. Not before. Talk."

"Okay. She has a laptop of his; he wants it back."

"Why?"

"Just… I don't know. Financial stuff, I think."

She laughed. "Still screwing over the IRS, huh?"

Spiller shrugged like he didn't know.

"And your message for Kat?"

He shifted awkwardly. "She, uh… needs to watch her back."

Hayley raised her eyebrows. "Did he threaten her?"

"Uh… yeah."

Hayley leaned forward. "In what way?"

Spiller had to be careful. He had a lot to lose by falling out with his director. He couldn't afford to have Hayley panic and call the cops. And yet, he'd known men who bullied women, and they were the pits. Protecting them was the same as endorsing them. He was searching for the optimal way to convey the gist when Hayley spoke.

"Don't worry that I'm gonna drop you in it just as you're starting out on your career. I'm not squeamish, Matt. I'll deal with it, whatever it is. Takes a lot to shock me. My first husband nearly killed me. Beat me to a pulp. Then stuck a gun in my mouth before someone blew his brains all over me. What did Brett say?"

"Jesus… Okay, he wanted me to kill her."

Hayley fell silent, stared out over the ocean.

Spiller realized she was shocked, despite her bravado. He guessed it was all relative. No one was that surprised when a King Cobra struck; it was the worm turning that drew the gasps.

Hayley looked at him. "Kill her to get the laptop back or... just kill her?"

"It's not just the laptop," Spiller said. "The laptop would make it worse, but he's bothered she'll clean him out financially because there's no prenup."

Hayley frowned. "There is a prenup. I've seen it. She takes what she's earned, what's hers from before the marriage; he takes what's his. He learned that the hard way. I had my own acting career for a while, but I took him for millions. Not in a bad way — just what my attorney thought I deserved, but... there was definitely a prenup with Kat. But he told you there wasn't?"

Spiller nodded.

"Right," Hayley said, then something dawned on her. "Why ask you? Why would he think you'd be willing to do it?"

Spiller shook his head. "It doesn't matter. He got the wrong end of the stick a while back, that's all. Listen, just please get the laptop for me, and I'm sure that'll be the end of it."

A willowy figure entered his periphery. He turned to see a slender young woman in a white jogging suit. Barefoot, without makeup, she had the look of a Russian model whose unpainted features were so bland they were beautiful. He didn't recognize her from any movies, but he'd seen a lot of movie folk in the past six months whose street appearance belied their glowing countenance on the red carpet. She crossed her arms as she came closer, a barrier to his intrusion into her sheltered new world. He stood up to offer his chair, but she smiled faintly and declined.

Hayley spoke first to guide the conversation. "Kat, did you take a laptop belonging to Brett?"

"Is that problem?"

"Where was it?" Hayley asked.

"In his safe. I see him take it out once. I see him put code in bathroom mirror. I am writing my poetry and my laptop go wrong. I think he is not using it, so I move my work on flash drive to his laptop and I use it. I put it in my laptop case, and I, uh... intend buy new one, put his back, but I never..."

Spiller listened to her accent and was captivated by the vulnerability in her tone.

"You never got around to it?" Hayley suggested.

"Yes. Am I in trouble?"

She had addressed Spiller with the question, but he was so entranced by her dialect and lilting voice that he had to mentally backtrack before replying.

"No, not at all, Kat. No. Brett just has something on it. Could I take it with me?"

"I must copy my work, make sure I have it all. Should I do it now?"

She looked at Hayley, but Spiller saw more than a hint of reticence in Hayley's eyes.

"Hang on a minute," Hayley said. "Hang on… you keep the laptop for the time being, Kat. Can I continue talking to Matt in private?"

"Of course. Nice meeting you, Matt. Thank you so much for terrify my husband on Mel Banaghan. I enjoy it very much."

He grinned. "My pleasure."

"Yes, I think so, too."

Spiller watched her shuffle back into the house, hoping she might glance back at him, but she disappeared inside the shadows of the open door.

"She's gorgeous, isn't she?" Hayley said, breaking his reverie.

She was smirking when he met her gaze. "Definitely. Why can't I take the laptop?"

"Something's going on," she said. "Brett was abusive, emotionally, verbally, but he was never violent. Not to me, not to Kat. There was a distinct *lack* of physical contact, if anything. So, asking you to kill her? Lying about the prenup? There is something going on, and I intend to rattle the little bastard's cage. Tell him I said no."

"Fair enough." Spiller stood up. "I appreciate you seeing me."

She got up, smiled, then her eyes narrowed. "You knew Harry Sullivan."

"I did. Way back. Why?"

"I knew him, too. Recently. Such a terrible loss."

"Absolutely. Beyond words."

The sound of a car engine drew his attention, and he swiveled to watch an old-model, red Audi TT convertible round the bend into the parking lot and pull up next to his Maserati. He was about to bid Hayley farewell, but she was already hotfooting it toward the Audi, from which emerged a radiantly attractive, light-skinned black woman. In the passenger seat was a boy aged about eight, whose skin was lighter still. Hayley approached with her arms wide open from ten paces away, and the women embraced. They parted, and Hayley opened her arms again to the boy.

"Come give your Aunt Hayley a big squeeze."

The boy reluctantly left his seat and came around the car to be enveloped in a hippy hug, his head half-buried between her breasts.

"You okay, Dodge?" she asked, after releasing him.

He shrugged his reply.

"And how's your mom doing? You keeping her strong?"

"He is," his mum replied.

"Can I go for a swim?" Dodge asked.

"Sure," Hayley said. "You know where the towels are."

He nodded and ran off into the house.

Feeling sidelined, Spiller headed to his car. When he reached the driver's door, the visitor glanced his way, then did a double take. She stared at him intently for a few seconds.

"You're Matt Spiller," she said.

Spiller was getting used to people telling him who he was, as though he'd forgotten. He smiled. "Thank you, Hayley."

Hayley moved her head in his direction, but not enough to meet his eyes. "Sure."

He climbed into the Maserati and hit the ignition, aware that the woman was still watching him. He reversed and headed back down to the gate, buzzing to be let out.

Instead, Hayley's voice came over the intercom. "Could you come back up here, please, Matt?"

Life was so weird of late that he didn't even ask why. This side of the gate, it was too narrow for a three-pointer, so he reversed all the way back. The two women were standing, arms linked, observing his return. He stopped next to them, looked up at them.

"What?"

"Could you hop out?" Hayley said.

He killed the engine and did so. Hayley turned to her friend, who peered at him as though she was sizing him up for a suit. Her eyes went from his face slowly down to his trainers, then back up again, lingering on his biceps, then his pecs. Meeting his eyes once again, she nodded.

"Thank you," she said. "Hayley, could you get his number?"

"Cell," Hayley demanded, palm open.

Still dumbfounded, he unlocked his phone and handed it over. He wondered if she was a casting director, or maybe a director or producer. Hayley input some digits and returned it to him.

"That's my number. Give me a buzz so I have yours."

He pressed to call, and Hayley's right breast began to chirp. She patted the cellphone tucked into her bra. "Okay, cut the call before I get excited."

Her friend laughed, and Spiller touched the red button.

"Get home safe, Matt," Hayley said.

He opened his mouth to ask some belated questions, but they turned and were walking into the house before he could decide which of the many took precedence.

DRIVING BACK, SPILLER realized he was guardedly happy. His world was expanding, capturing as it went some interesting people within its boundary. He'd had no friends in England. There had been one guy, a fellow taxi driver, Gibbo. Younger than Spiller, they'd been mates more than friends. Bitching about life and obtuse passengers for ten minutes in a pub car park before one of them got a job on the datahead and had to scoot. Nothing in common, but they'd clicked, nonetheless. Then some bad guys had mistaken Gibbo for Spiller and had blown the back of his head off, dumping him in the trunk of his own car, but a car that Spiller had purloined to ferry Brett Stutz to a hotel so he could check out some English talent for his new movie, *Man on a Murder Cycle*. The rest, as the saying went...

Here in LA, he'd met Sadie, and now Hayley and her friend, both of whom he was somehow certain would figure large in his life. Then there was Kat, who he could easily imagine hooking up with because she was beautiful and vulnerable, but also to rile her husband. There was Officer Ethan King, who wanted to have a beer with him. And even crazy Texan Noah from the karaoke bar. A strange beginning to a relationship, but the kid had balls, and Spiller had always admired anyone who grabbed at life with both hands. Of course, none of them were friends right now, but he could work on that. If just one of them emerged as a valued person in his life, it would suffice. One true friend was enough. Oddly, despite the multitude of people he'd met while filming, some of whom had spent countless hours in his company, on set, in his trailer, at production parties, not one had survived the transition back to normal life. Maybe that was him. Perhaps no one wanted to extend their acquaintance beyond what was necessary. Perhaps whack-job friends like Texan Noah were all he could expect. Or perhaps he enjoyed acting, but he'd spent too many years being a regular guy to suddenly delight in the company of this strange LA species.

Leaving the PCH and heading inland once again, Spiller's mood crashed. Of course he'd been happy just then. Who couldn't derive pleasure from cruising with the top down along one of the most iconic roads in the world? And now here he was, snaking along Sunset, turning heads in his Maserati, like a pot-bellied old wanker trying to make up for a small dick. What would they make of him fourteen miles east of his current spot? All those heads popping out of their Skid Row tents, spitting vitriol as they viewed the insensitivity of a passing car that they could sell to feed themselves for years.

Fifteen minutes later, rounding the final bend before his home at the end of the lane, he slowed as he clocked the rear of an old black pickup truck with a lone-star flag on the rear bumper. It was parked tight to the hedgerow, ten yards shy of his property. He contemplated stopping, but decided to carry on like he hadn't seen it. The garage shutter lifted, and he drove in and parked next to the Hayabusa. He ran upstairs and peeked out of the front window. It looked like Texan Noah, just sitting there, smoking a cigarette.

"Billy!" he shouted.

Billy ambled in, buttoning a cuff. "Yes, love?"

"Remember that guy from the bar? Frigging nutter's outside. He must have followed us back here last night. Jesus Christ. Just what I need, a stalker."

Billy chuckled. "Oh, Matthew, so melodramatic. I invited him." He headed back out of the room.

Spiller followed him into the spare bedroom. "Billy, what the fuck? Why?"

"He came back to me post-haste."

"What?"

"About representation, love. Quite a nice little CV. I'm going to sign him."

"Billy, you don't work from here. This is my *home*. I don't want anyone knowing where I live, least of all some corn-chewing psycho who probably has a bunch of AR-15s in the lockbox behind his cab. Good God, he's already made threats."

Billy dismissed him with another chuckle. "He's giving me a lift to my new office on Wilshire. I haven't seen it in person yet. Saves me a cab fare."

"Billy... no. You can't do this. This is my sanctuary."

"I'd remind you, dear boy, that you brought two hitmen onto my front lawn and shot them dead before my very eyes. I'd gauge that as rather more of an imposition."

"I didn't ask them to come; you asked this guy. That's the difference. You know what? Fine."

Billy began to remonstrate as Spiller about-faced and headed down the stairs, collecting a baseball bat from the hall closet as he went.

Out on the road, Noah saw him coming, grinned, rolled down his window and flicked his cigarette out. "Hey, Matt, nice to see you again. You off to play some softball?"

"Noah, take Billy to his office, and don't come back."

"Free world, Matt. I go wherever the hell I please. Always have, always will."

Spiller hefted the bat, so its fat end pointed back over his shoulder, poised for a swing. "You can have the whole world; just not this lane."

Noah bit another cigarette from his pack and lit up. "I'll take that under advisement."

Billy hurried down the road toward them, a briefcase in one hand. "Boys! Now, boys!"

"Hey, Mr Banbury," Noah said. "We good to go?"

"I don't want to see your face again, Noah," Spiller said. "Billy, watch this guy – he's not right."

Billy paused at the hood of the pickup. He looked at Spiller. "My love, he can't be any less right than you."

Spiller shook his head. "Thirty percent, Billy. Is it worth it?"

Billy looked aghast.

"You can take twenty percent of what this loser may earn – which won't be much – or thirty percent of the millions I'm going to earn. One or the other."

"Well, if you put it in those terms... sorry, young man, nothing personal." He headed back to the house.

Noah's eyes flared, and he was out of the truck in a second, fists balled, head jutting at Spiller, who gripped the bat resting on his shoulder with both hands.

In an instant, Noah had closed the gap and they were nose to nose.

"See," Noah said, smiling insanely, "y'always gotta keep a little swingin' room if you're gonna bring out the bat, *Matt*. Now, what you gonna do, huh? I guess you could give me a poke with the thin end, but I could always be ahead of you on that and do *this*."

Noah's brow flew into Spiller's nose, which gave an audible crack. Spiller's head exploded in exquisite agony. He crumpled to his knees and let go of his weapon as he felt blood start to gush from his nostrils. Behind him, the departing Billy wheeled round but stayed at a distance. Spiller's vision was a kaleidoscope of black and sparkling stars and all manner of colors. He moaned and cupped his palms under his nose as though he didn't want to stain the concrete, but the blood spilled through his fingers anyway.

Noah stooped and picked up the bat. "Fine piece of hickory. To the winner the spoils." He climbed back in his truck with the bat and slammed the door. "I don't care who you are. You don't fuck with my career." He started the V8, which grumbled menacingly. He gunned the engine loudly, then lurched forward a few yards, performing a raggedy three-point turn that took advantage of Spiller's driveway. Then he was blasting past within a few inches of Spiller, who was kneeling as though in prayer in a pool of his own blood.

Billy approached and stood over his fallen star. "Oh, Matthew, how did you not see that coming? I saw that coming, and I've always made John Lennon look like a rabid warmonger."

"I didn't think he'd do anything."

"I think you may be a tad blinded by your own publicity." He offered his hand.

Spiller wiped his slick palm down his shirt-front and grabbed Billy's spindly forearm, surprised by the strength it offered as he hoiked himself to his feet.

"Are you all right?" Billy asked.

"Do I *look* all right?"

"Not really, dear boy. I meant, are you okay to make it back to your house or do you need a moment?"

Spiller answered by making a few tentative steps. His head was spinning, and the pain was like a machete buried in his skull. He tipped his head back and tried to staunch the flow with two fingers on the bridge of his nose, but realized he didn't have a bridge to his nose any longer, and any pressure on what was left of it just piled on the agony. They made it back to the house, leaving a trail of red to mark their slow progress. At the gate to the pool, Spiller squinted through his watery vision as he input the entry code on the keypad, failing twice before getting it right. He pushed open the gate for Billy.

"Grab a towel from the pool hut, please, Billy. And a bottle of vodka from the cooler." He sank onto the step as Billy nipped inside. He held his shirt to his nose until Billy returned with the booze and a fluffy white towel that soon wasn't fluffy or white. Billy sat next to him and placed a fatherly arm around his shoulders, which brought silent tears, which Spiller allowed himself, assuming they could sneak out under the cover of his already watering eyes.

"Dear boy, it'll all be all right."

Spiller unscrewed the vodka and took several gulps, then laid his head on Billy's shoulder.

"Are you going to call the police?" Billy asked.

"Are you going to give evidence?"

Billy didn't answer.

"Thought not."

"Sorry, Matthew, I'd rather not be falling out with some whacko actor within five minutes of getting here. I mean, I did that already, didn't I? With you. I mean, I don't want to repeat the mistake. If he'd do this to you, what wouldn't he do to little old me? Sorry."

"It's fine." Spiller wondered whether a call to Officer Ethan King might be prudent, but suspected he might have used up his bent-cop quota with Sergeant Alfie Enright back in England.

"What if he comes for you again?" Billy asked.

"He won't. If he's got any sense, he'll just take the win and forget about me. But if he does, I'll handle it. No one gets to do this twice." He buried his face in the darkening cotton and muttered a concealed curse, then pulled the towel away again. "Is it bad, Billy? Honestly?" He lifted his head and turned it to show his agent.

Billy peered. "I'm glad I'm longsighted and I don't have my contacts in."

"Great."

"I think you may need surgery, dear boy. Do you know the nearest hospital?"

"Cedars, I think. Cedars Sinai."

"Okay. Where are your car keys? I'll drive."

Spiller hesitated, then smiled. "Sure, Billy. Pot by the stairs. Thanks."

## TWELVE

WHILE SPILLER WAS at Cedars, getting his nose inspected by people who clearly didn't believe his fable about tripping while running, Sadie was returning Theo Montgomery to his home, her cheeks aching with the grin she couldn't shake from her face. He had given her the option of choosing whatever model she desired, in whatever specifications, and she had spent considerable time with the saleswoman, customizing her ultimate creation via a digital brochure. Theo had chosen to remain in the Suburban outside. He'd wanted her to have the freedom to decide for herself, without appearing to have a sugar-daddy by her side who she felt the need to thank every five minutes. She'd been like the proverbial kid in a candy shop, going back and forth between options, ruling out certain colors, exterior and interior, only to reintroduce them as contenders and find herself back at square one. In the army, she'd had to make split-second decisions. There, in that showroom, that skill had evaded her. As the time passed, a low-grade panic had set in. She'd imagined herself returning to the Suburban, her decision finally made, only to find Theo Montgomery slumped in his seat, every bit as dead as her chance of getting him to posthumously pay for her new car. So, she'd looked around the showroom and spotted something she liked. And the more she stared at it, the more she realized she really did like it, as though fate had dumped the ideal vehicle right in front of her. An Escalade Sport Platinum in Sandstone Metallic. She'd asked to be shown around it. An ex-demonstrator, five hundred or so miles on the odometer, and priced accordingly. Jet black leather interior with natural ash wood trim. More extras than she even knew existed. Sold to the lady with the dopey grin.

She'd felt a bit underhand acting so swiftly to secure the promise he'd made, but she knew that life was precarious and full of surprises, and sometimes life was shorter than anyone had planned for. Perhaps Theo would live another twenty years, but it could have been another twenty minutes.

Now the car was hers. Paid for, insured, certificate of title in her name. No one could take it from her. It was crazy. She owned a hundred-thousand-dollar vehicle, and she lived in a humble apartment in Canoga Park. At least it had a gated parking lot. She laughed out loud at the thought.

"What's funny, Sadie?" Theo asked.

"Just happy, Theo. Thank you."

"If you thank me one more time, young lady, I am taking that car back off you."

She laughed. "Well, that ain't happening! That is *my* car now."

He chortled quietly behind her. "That it is, Sadie. You enjoy it."

"Tha—" She cut herself short and laughed again.

"When I have a few minutes, Sadie, I'll put together a list of folk who I know would enjoy being taken places in that vehicle of yours. I know you're overwhelmed by how much it cost, but with the right clients, it'll pay for itself in a few short months, then you won't feel so bad about owning it. Speculate to accumulate. Gotta have money to make money, Sadie. Or have something that rich folk don't mind paying for. You won't believe what you can charge people to sit in the back of that car. I'm not talking about studio-hopping for a few hundred bucks a ride. I mean folk who won't fly places. You're a smart woman; you must have worked all this out."

She had, and she nodded at him via the rearview.

"Tell you what, Sadie: come around one night soon – if you're comfortable with that. We can talk through a few ideas."

She brought his aura to the fore and saw only kindness. "Sounds good. Give me a call when you're free."

*OH, LAWDY MISS fucking Clawdy. You IDIOT! You realize we have a PUBLICITY CIRCUIT just beginning, right? RIGHT? Fucksake. And "fell over", my ASS. I have never seen ANYONE nosedive their career so early on. You LITERALLY NOSEDIVED your career. What the FUCK is wrong with you?*

Spiller tittered as he re-read Cathy's response to him posting a selfie of his face to her and Stutz. Billy returned with a coffee for himself. Spiller was nil-by-mouth, waiting in his bed for the time when he'd be wheeled away for his emergency rhinoplasty. The X-ray showed one or two splinters that would need removing, but otherwise the break was clean. The procedure to bring the skin back together down the center of his nose, however, would leave a scar. He imagined that Cathy wasn't as peeved as she made out. It would all add to his allure, to the enigma that was Matt Spiller. No doubt, people would think he'd been in a fight with someone, maybe even with Stutz.

"What's tickling you, Matthew?" Billy asked.

Spiller turned the phone. Billy put his glasses on and read the message, wincing at the expletives. "Oh, dear. And so much upper case. Is she always like that?"

"No idea. Billy, will you be my dad?"

"Don't be absurd, Matthew."

"You could adopt me."

"For one thing, you were going to drown me in your swimming pool yesterday. I know it's a technical point, but I'd prefer homicide over patricide."

"Billy, we discussed the possibility of you drowning in my pool; I didn't say I was going to do it. And you're obviously not considering the upside of all this, which is that all your commission would end up coming back to me when you do die."

Billy rolled his eyes. "Rest assured, love, that I would disinherit you."

"Can I at least *call* you Dad?"

"Good God, how much morphine have they got you on?"

Spiller's phone began to ring. It was a WhatsApp call from Brett Stutz. "Brett, *que pasa?*"

"Did you get the laptop?"

"It did hurt, yes. Hopefully, they'll be able to sort it out in surgery shortly, thanks for asking."

"Oh. Sure. How are you? Looks nasty. Who hit you? I imagine there's quite a queue. My laptop?"

"I saw both Hayley and Kat. And no way, José."

"Why not?"

"And why did you tell me Kat was being held by a cult?"

"Did I say cult? I meant cunt."

"Oh, come on, Brett. Hayley might be a bit prickly, but she seems a perfectly reasonable person."

Stutz huffed. "And you were married to her for how long?"

"Fair point. I don't know her; you do. But four failed marriages? Anyone seeing a pattern?"

"The woman's a psycho. I thought it was cute when I first met her. All her talk of spirituality and eternal love and reincarnation."

"What?"

"Oh, yeah. She even wrote a book about it. Supposedly based on *real-life events*."

"Really? What's it called? I might buy it." Spiller beckoned to Billy for a sip of coffee, but Billy shook his head and pointed to the sign on his headboard.

"It's not published. Like that woman could write anything fit for publication. Gotta say, Matty, I'm disappointed. Thought you had more clout. I *know* you have more clout."

Spiller let the insinuation hang for a moment, like a nasty smell that needed time to dissipate. "Listen, she didn't say no, she said not yet. Kat wanted to make sure she had some stuff backed up. I think Hayley just wanted to give her that time. Whilst pissing you off. Which she did very nicely, apparently."

"Keep at it, okay? Please. And, uh, hope the op goes well."

*"Gracias."* Spiller set the phone on his bedside table and closed his eyes. His daughters. How soon would they be with him? Soon enough to see the mess he was in. Their visit was marred already, and they hadn't even left home yet. Guilt swept through him, briefly replacing the embarrassment of the sucker-butt Noah had delivered. He was so much better on his own. No one to let down. He thought to tell Billy not to drive his Maserati anywhere while he was under the knife, then thought he might make a thespian joke about being back in theater, but he was too far gone to get the words out.

"Matthew!"

Spiller abruptly came to, wondering if he was now the other side of the op, and everything had taken place in what had seemed like a split second. But Billy was still sipping his coffee.

"What?"

"I know you took a photograph, but you should probably take a proper video of your face. Just in case you do ever need documented proof of your injuries."

Spiller reached for his phone. "Good idea. What's his full name? You got his details, right? On his CV?"

"Noah Dalton."

Spiller activated the video and switched to the front camera, moving it around his fractured nose and black eyes to catch the different angles, then named the assailant. Beyond his focus, Billy gesticulated, tapping his watch, so Spiller added the time and the date of the recording. As he was about to hit the red button, his phone beeped at him, and the recording stopped of its own accord. He pulled down the notification, which told him his storage was full. He'd have to delete some content before the girls arrived. He wanted plenty of space to document their time with him.

"I'm going to toddle off," Billy said to him, carefully standing, trying not to jangle the car keys in his pocket.

"You got some dollars for a cab?"

Billy wilted a little. "Oh."

Spiller smiled. "It's okay, take the Maserati." He gave Billy the house keys. "Stay by the phone, though, I'll need you to pick me up. And be careful in my car."

"Love, have you seen my Morris Marina? Pristine. Not a scratch in fifty years of ownership. Oh, by the by, could I use your baseball cap?"

"What?"

"I saw one on your back seat. I've never worn a baseball cap. Would that be okay?"

"Absolutely not."

"Oh. All right."

"Billy… I'm lending you my Maserati. Why would I care if you put my hat on?"

Billy chuckled. "Lovely that you haven't lost your sense of humor. Anyway, hope it all goes well, dear boy. Tatty bye."

OFFICER GABRIELA CONTRERAS disliked the LAPD's Basic Car Plan. It made sense in terms of the deployment of resources, but it was too limiting for an officer with aspirations. The same patch, day in, day out. There were seven Basic Car areas for the West LA Community Police Station, which was part of the larger West Division. She was generally assigned to Basic Car 8A29. It was the most easterly of the three larger geographical areas to the north, bordered by Mulholland, but they only covered more square miles because there were fewer roads to patrol in the hills of Bel-Air and the wilderness region further west. The four areas to the south of 8A29 were much smaller, covering as they did the more populous streets of West LA north-east to the border of West Hollywood. Ideally, she'd have liked free reign, to go wherever she pleased in the city, following suspect vehicles, heading for high-crime areas, proactively seeking out crime as it happened, rather than responding to the aftermath.

However, she was perfectly placed to keep an eye on Matthew Spiller, with Beverly Glen at the heart of her patch. His antics yesterday had galled. Perfectly natural for him to feel aggrieved, given she'd stolen his key fob, but most people would have made a complaint, not rolled a motorcycle into the path of a patrol car, then taken off like a bat out of hell, breaking the speed limit with one twist of the throttle. Bartoli wasn't wrong about the hombre being *loco*. And with Bartoli having hinted that Spiller might be in the frame for Harry Sullivan and the others, she was keen to keep up the pressure. What a coup if she caused him to crack and make a mistake.

She reversed the blue Explorer into a side-road off North Beverly Glen Boulevard, just down from Spiller's lane, and waited. She'd done the checks Bartoli requested, so she knew the vehicles Spiller owned. But she knew far more besides. She had proved her investigative skills, following leads that others, she felt certain, would not have spotted, or would have ignored. Incredibly, Matthew Spiller was linked to all three of the dead actors. He had admitted to knowing Harry Sullivan on Mel Banaghan, but there was also a tenuous link to Aiden Powers and John Frears. Perhaps gossamer more than tenuous, but it was there.

Although she wasn't particularly religious, the appearance of a gray Maserati with the top down five minutes later seemed ordained. She smiled, started the engine, and edged forward, pulling out two cars behind. Oddly, Spiller seemed a lot safer today in a car than yesterday on a motorcycle. Pretty soon, he indicated and turned down his lane, heading home. She followed, quickly drawing closer. At a spot where there was a gap in the houses, she gave a single whoop of the siren and lit the police lights at the top of her windshield. The Maserati slowed and pulled over.

Standing by the driver's door, the face staring up at her from beneath the peak of a maroon Dodgers cap wasn't the right one. She scrutinized him for a moment too long, aware of her bewildered expression, but unable to shake it.

He gave her an endearing smile. "Can I help you, officer?"

She had to go through the motions. "Is this your vehicle, sir?"

"It belongs to Matthew Spiller. The actor. I'm his agent. He's at the hospital. He had an accident. Broke his nose, poor love. I do have his permission to drive his car. Is that all right?"

A sinister stratagem settled in her head. "I need proof, sir. Otherwise, I'll need to impound the vehicle. Did he write anything down? Or could you call him?"

"No. No, he didn't. And I don't have my mobile phone with me. My cellphone. Uh… his house is just down there. I have his spare house keys—"

The old guy's hand went to his pocket, and Contreras pulled her nine-mil FN. There was no threat here – she could tell that instantly – but hassling Spiller's agent was a nice touch, and she really just wanted this guy hoofing it down the lane, too scared to remonstrate, while she waited for a tow-truck to haul away the actor's pride and joy.

But the old guy's face contorted once, twice, and then a third time with more animation, like he'd figured out why the first two had happened. He drew in a raspy breath and placed a hand on his chest, clawing his fingers into his incongruously upbeat t-shirt. Then his head lolled forward on an outbreath, and he was still.

*"No me jodas,"* she said, quickly holstering her weapon. She stared at the stricken form, then darted glances up and down the lane. There was no one about. No houses with overlooking windows. She could get the hell out of there like it had never happened. Only, it had. And what if someone had seen her tailing him? Or she passed a vehicle as she fled the scene, and the driver of that vehicle had a dashcam and found a dead man in a Maserati a moment later? Or what if Spiller simply suspected her hand in this, and requested the LAPD pull her in-car video? She dithered, paralyzed by the dilemma. Had she done anything wrong? Something she could be hauled over the coals for? A random traffic stop. What of it? That was allowed. That was her job. If she stayed, called it in, she could bluff it out. If she bolted, only to be discovered later, that would be career-ending. Leaving a heart-attack victim without medical attention? What decent cop would do that?

BILLY COULDN'T HOLD his breath any longer and there was a wasp on his nose, about to crawl up his left nostril. He shook his head to dislodge it and gulped in some air.

"Sir?"

He looked up at her from beneath the peak of his cap with a startled expression. "Good Lord, what happened?"

"I don't know. Are you okay? Do you have a heart condition?"

"Slightly, I take something. Sudden shocks can make me pass out, though. I don't like guns."

"What's wrong with you?"

"I'm English; we don't really have guns in England."

"No, I mean, your condition. What's it called?"

"Oh. Right." Billy blew a sigh, shook his head. "I always forget. Something cardi, cardi something. I can never remember. I'm a tib lesdyxic." He laughed at his joke.

"Huh? Should you be driving?"

Billy peered at her name-badge. "Officer Contreras, I have full permission to drive my client's car. I have his house keys and I know his alarm code. I hope that's sufficient to prevent you towing his vehicle and giving me another funny turn."

Contreras nodded. "Sure. Sure. You'll be okay?"

"Just need to get back and have a nice cup of tea and a little zizz."

She was backing away even before he'd finished his sentence. Billy saw there was a definite air of panic in her retreat, as though she'd bitten off more than she could chew. She climbed in the Explorer and reversed all the way out of sight around the bend, almost as though she didn't want to give him the opportunity to properly clock her license plate while she pulled a three-point turn. Which was silly as he already knew her name. Con— Con—

Bugger. Old gray cells fading on him. Probably the shock. He'd never had someone point a gun at him before. He wondered if he should tell Spiller what had transpired, but that deliberation lasted a mere second. Of course he had to. There was something distinctly devious about that woman pulling him over, and Billy imagined that Spiller would know what was behind it.

He restarted the Maserati and drove the remaining yards to the house, remotely lifting the garage door so he could drive straight in. He sat for a few moments in the relative cool of the starkly lit space with only the burbling exhausts for company. As the shutter settled on the concrete, he stopped the engine and noticed the sudden absence of noise was like a sound of its own. And he realized how much he didn't miss peace and quiet. His house in England had been like a tomb. His only company had been the ticking of his numerous wall clocks. Just sufficient to reassure him he was still in the land of the living, if only a few inches from the threshold of Happy Valley. He'd always envisioned the end of his life would happen there.

Yet, here he was, a man remade, reborn into the antithesis of his prior staid existence. Every aspect an opposite. Here in the City of Angels, ironically, he was beginning to kick against the inevitability of being whisked away to the other side. A gun in his face? He giggled. God, the adrenaline. Who knew his aging body still had a fight or flight response? It was amazing. Provided it was new, from the spectacular to the sordid, he was going to drink it all in; everything this barmy city had to offer. He restarted the Maserati, raised the garage door, and reversed out.

FIVE HOURS LATER, having devalued the Maserati by 250 miles, Billy returned. He'd taken the 405 north through the valley, then branched off onto the Antelope Valley Freeway, skirting the northern reaches of the Angeles National Forest. After completing a big box around Edwards Air Force Base in the desert, he'd headed back the way he'd come. He was hoping his client hadn't called to be collected from Cedars, but truth be told, he didn't really care either way. He'd had a blast, his speed limited only by the prevailing traffic, not any pesky road signs. Perhaps he'd been clocked, and a few tickets were in the works already, but he planned to be out of Spiller's house by the time they dropped onto his door mat. And he'd have to be, with Spiller's family soon to visit.

Looking at the car in the garage, he surmised it needed a wash. Its paintwork had been dulled by the dust of his travels. Nothing that couldn't easily be rectified by a sponge and a hose, but he couldn't be bothered to even search for such items.

Spiller's answering machine showed no messages. Billy put the car keys back in the pot and headed upstairs. He was in the mood for a nosey. In a cobwebby recess of his mind, Spiller's connection to the late Harry Sullivan niggled. Knowing what he knew about Spiller's past, Billy wondered if there might be a gun in the house. Maybe *the* gun. It was a fanciful notion, and he felt excited and a little like Ellery Queen as he began to pull open some drawers and peek in a couple of wardrobes.

Until he opened a narrow floor-to-ceiling closet next to his host's ensuite, and a body fell out on top of him, its dead weight knocking him backward, its lifeless arms encircling him in a mortal embrace, its forehead butting his as Noah's had butted Spiller's. As he hit the floor like a felled tree, Billy let out a falsetto scream like a schoolgirl watching *The Exorcist*.

## THIRTEEN

HAYLEY OLSEN WALKED down the drive to meet her ex-husband. The last of the sun's color was fading from the sky. She noted he was still driving his Kermit-green Bronco, still calling out for attention even when supposedly incognito behind tinted glass. Brett Stutz exited the car to greet her, trying out a smile that didn't sit comfortably on his face.

She stopped and looked through a gap at him.

He extended his smile into a grin, but quickly gave up on the whole amiable-ex approach in the glare of Hayley's stony expression. "Really? You locking me out?"

She stared at him.

"Hayley?"

She continued her mute observation.

"You're not gonna talk to me?" he asked.

"I was just giving you a moment to get used to the view."

"Huh?"

"Looking through bars."

"Yeah, whatever. Can you just get my laptop? Please."

"There must be something serious on that thing; you asking your messenger to kill Kat to get it back."

Stutz looked suddenly bilious. "He said what? That's... that guy can't take a joke. He played a killer in my movie, so I made a joke."

"Sure."

"Listen... I can pay Kat – for the laptop. And give her a lump sum, despite the prenup. Okay? I'm a decent guy."

She shook her head. "You're not, Brett. You knew I wanted to have kids. I was in my last years for that to happen."

"We've been through this. It's ancient history."

"For you, clearly. For me, it's current. I'm not a mom. Every day I'm not a mom. Because you didn't bother telling me you'd had a vasectomy. Christ knows why, as you barely used it the whole time we were married. And you were gonna do the same to Kat, right? Until I talked to her. What is it, Brett? You need a woman on your arm to show people you're not gay?"

"I'm not gay. I'm just busy, and sex has never been high on my agenda. I'm not like all the other guys in this town."

"Then stop marrying women! I know it's old fashioned, but some of us like getting dick and having babies!"

He laughed at her. "Jeez, and you call this place what? *The House of Sempiternal Love?* Yeah, you've really risen above it all, Hayley. So at peace. Such a guru. You know what? I picked you up when you were at your lowest. Your face all beat to hell; busted arm. But I saw you had something, and I gave you a career. And I did love you. Sure, you looked good by my side, but that wasn't the point. And you'll notice I'm using the past tense there. *Looked.* Not sure I'd wanna be seen out with you now. Bit frumpy. You've kinda gone to seed, Hayley."

"How ironic you mentioning seed."

Stutz turned back to his car with an audible sneer and a dismissive wave, then swiveled back because he wasn't finished. He came up to the gate, so his nose was poking through.

"You did very well from me, Hayley. You got a career, great pay checks. Then the divorce. That little settlement? Basically, this is my property. I paid for this. And that other cunt up at the house? Yet another wannabe I made famous. What's her problem? She's still young. She'll find some virile stud to impregnate her if that's what she really wants. All she needs to do is get her skinny ass back out into the world, stop moping. In fact, you should rename this place. *The Sisterhood of Moping Cunts.*"

Hayley found herself smiling at his antagonism. All she had left from the relationship was the pleasure of seeing him riled.

"Just go get my laptop, Hayley. And tell that dreary bitch to look out for an email from my attorney. We need to wrap up this whole mess, soon as."

Hayley contemplated his request. It had always been her intention to hand back the laptop, but at a time of her choosing, when Kat had finished with her back-ups, and her ex had been left to simmer for a few extra days, just for the fun of it. There was nothing to be gained from prolonging their communication beyond that. She knew from bitter experience that situations could spiral out of control very quickly, and you never knew what anyone was truly capable of until it was too late and you were finding out to your cost in real-time.

But before she could respond, she saw Kat heading down the incline, clutching the laptop to her belly. Her hair hung damply from her evening swim.

"Okay, you can go now," Stutz told Hayley. "She doesn't need a chaperone."

Hayley retreated a little way up the slope and waited. She watched Kat stand at the gate for a few moments, and Stutz extend one hand through the railings. Then Kat stood back and launched the laptop high over the gate. Stutz swore, scrambled back, bumping into the hood of his Bronco, and made a catch that would have made Mike Piazza proud.

"Fuck the both of you!" he shouted.

"Oh, *now* you want to fuck us," Kat said, and Hayley laughed.

Their arms linked, Kat and Hayley walked back up to the house, the profanity of their mutual ex dimming with each step, until they rounded the bend, and the landscape muffled the worst of it.

"Did you back up everything you wanted?" Hayley asked, still giggling at Kat's reckless fling of the laptop.

"I did."

Suddenly, the sound of an engine came to them, revving at full pitch. They both looked back toward the PCH, and a pall of white smoke drifted up into view from the area of the front gate. Haley could hear a slight clank, then a creaking of metal.

"Have it your way, asshole," she said, and headed inside.

Her security guard got up from his desk. "I'll see what's going on."

She spoke as she hurried past him toward her office. "Thanks, Nate, this one's mine."

In her office, she unlocked a metal cabinet and grabbed a Mossberg 500 12-gauge. She quickly loaded three shells of buckshot and racked the first one, then marched back outside with it.

"Don't worry if you hear some big bangs," she told them, as she went.

The front gates were bowing inward under the pressure from the Bronco and its bull bar. The air was now thick with smoke and the stench of burned rubber. It drifted up the slope and enveloped her. She watched as the gates broke off their lower hinges and the Bronco's hood burst through the gap. Stutz stopped spinning his tires then, and quickly found reverse before the gates could fall on his vehicle. He backed up a little and stopped, and Hayley figured he was admiring his handiwork. He gave a long victory blast of his horn before he spotted her and curtailed his excitement. She strode into the space where the gates had once come together, and watched his eyes go wide at the sight of a small woman with a large shotgun. Then Hayley sent two quick blasts through the Bronco's re-chromed grille and into the engine, whose grumble became a death-splutter, before conking out. Now there was only the noise of the traffic passing on the PCH, and Hayley could vaguely discern the creaking of the gate's top hinges. She retreated swiftly as one of them detached with a loud crack and collapsed where she'd been standing.

An apoplectic Stutz emerged from his ruined car and surveyed his damaged front end. "My beautiful car!"

Hayley laughed. "You're the one who used it as a battering ram. What did you expect?"

He made a move toward her, but she racked the last shell into the chamber, and he halted, holding his hands in a low surrender. "Now, Hayley..."

She rested the shotgun back on her shoulder. "I want you to call Triple-A, get this piece of crap towed off my driveway, and organize the repairs to my property. Unless you'd like to call the cops." She pointed a finger behind her at a camera pole. "But I got it all on video. And I got Matt Spiller who's gonna verify that you asked him to kill Kat."

"He wouldn't do that."

"No?"

"Not in a million years would he flip on me. Too much to lose."

Hayley wasn't *au fait* with his meaning, so just shrugged. "Fine. The video should do it. You come here, harassing us, you break my gates. What's a poor defenseless woman to do?"

She watched him visibly take stock, his expression one of deep self-contemplation, like a drowning man reviewing his whole existence in three seconds. Only, she assumed he was weighing up his future, not his past.

"Can we keep this between us?" he asked. "Sorry. I'll pay for everything. I can't have bad press right now. The *MeToo* crew would crucify me for this."

"Just stay away, Brett. That's all I've ever wanted. That's all Kat wants." She turned and headed back up to the house.

WHILE BRETT STUTZ was waiting for a tow, ruminating on his questionable career longevity, Officer Gabriela Contreras was experiencing a similar mental crisis, also parked up going nowhere. At least the view was pleasant. She had the Explorer's nose up against the log guardrail at Johnson Overlook on Mulholland. The twinkling valley spread out below her to the north, hemmed in by the mountains fifteen miles away, low and dark against the last light of the day. It was a location for musing about life and the universe, for pinpointing a person's infinitesimal place in the scheme of things, the absurdity of every petty inconvenience that kept a person from seeing the bigger picture and just letting go.

She couldn't let go. The events of her life dug deep into her psyche, her soul, like vicious talons in helpless prey. If anything was going to release their grip, it was time, in its own interminable manner. But only if she stopped struggling, making everything worse.

Every set of headlights in the darkening solitude drew her attention. Then a car slowed and pulled in next to her. A black Chevy Impala. She looked across her empty seat at Lieutenant Bartoli, who gave her a smile and climbed out to stand by her open passenger window.

"All very clandestine, Contreras. What's going on?"

"I know. Thanks for meeting me, LT. Do you wanna…?"

He pulled open the door and took a seat, turning to face her. "So? Got some intel for me?"

"I do. But I can't help you further with this. I'm... Jeez, I'm crossing lines."

"I know. Matt Spiller told me. He dropped by the station to tell me you stole his bike transmitter thing. Pulled him over and stole it."

"Am I in trouble?"

"Not with me. I guess he could always make a complaint, but I doubt he will. He called you a Rottweiler. No one wants a Rottweiler chasing them down. Stay out of his rearview, you'll be okay."

"Yeah, about that..."

Bartoli sighed and looked out over the valley. "Oh, boy. What else?"

"I pulled him over in his car today. Only, it wasn't him driving. It was some old English dude. Said he's Spiller's agent."

"Yeah, I met the guy yesterday."

"Oh. Okay. So... *cabrón* has a heart attack."

Bartoli stared at her. "You scared him to death?"

"No, he didn't die. I don't think he was even ill. I think he was faking. I checked into him. He was an actor himself back in the day. I think he was just playing possum, hoping I'd go away."

"Please tell me you did."

Contreras nodded.

"And your purpose in these traffic stops was...?"

She sighed deeply. "I wanted to disable his bike and tow his car."

He chuckled. "Why?"

"I don't know. Freak him out. Make him make a mistake. Piss him off, at the very least."

"Why?"

"Because he pissed you off, and I like you."

"I like you, too, Contreras. There's a lot to like."

"As a police officer?" she asked.

"Not just."

They sat next to each other and did nothing, despite the signs.

"I gotta let it go, stick to my job," Contreras said. "Something gets in my head, I get fixated. I end up wanting to do everything to the nth degree. Solve everything. Arrest everyone. I need to limit the things I fixate on. It's too much. I go *un poco loca* in my head." She laughed at herself. "Sorry."

"It's okay. It's not a crime to be keen. This job… it's just a job. It can't be who you are."

She felt herself welling up, so he laid a hand over hers.

"Gabriela, what's going on? Really."

Her tears dried of their own accord, like a sluice gate had slammed down. She could only talk about it by cutting off her finer emotions, as though dispassionately reading a witness statement.

"My kid died. Two years ago."

"Christ. I'm sorry. How old?"

"He was nearly five. I had him young. He got hit by a car. Staying at a friend's house. Playing on the front lawn. Car mounted the sidewalk, hit another vehicle, which hit him, and… that was it."

"I'm so sorry." He shook his head, squeezed her hand. "Did they catch who did it?"

"Eventually. He took a corner too fast, didn't even know what he'd done. Knew he'd clipped another vehicle, but not that he'd killed someone. Not until the Captain told him."

Bartoli did a double take. "What?"

"Off-duty cop in his own vehicle. Old-timer, never really off the clock. You know the type. Monitoring the police band. Thinks he can help by heading off the perp. Takes a shortcut down a residential street. Private car. No siren, no lights. But pedal to the metal. My kid never knew what hit him – literally."

"Gabriela, I don't know what to say."

"That's why I don't like reckless. Why I prefer intent."

"What happened to the cop?" Bartoli asked.

"Early retirement, full pension. No blame attached."

"Sorry, that ain't right. Where was this?"

She slowly lifted her hand and pointed an accusing finger to the right side of the windshield. "Mission Area, Valley Bureau. That's why I like to be up here. I feel connected. But then I can drive back down the hill and it's almost like it happened to someone else. Someone I read about in a newspaper. I sometimes... I can't even comprehend I was a mother. That any of it took place. That he even existed. It's like I dreamed the whole thing."

"Did you seek help?"

"Didn't need to seek it; it was thrown at me. Analysis, pills. So many pills."

"You still medicate?"

She shook her head. "They helped, but you feel suffocated. Everything damped down. The pain, but also you can't feel joy. And you need those moments of joy. I need to smile when I think of him. Laugh at the things he did and said. Even if I break down crying a minute later. It's part of grieving, I think. It's necessary. You can't bury it with meds. It's gonna come out sooner or later. Best deal with it."

"What was his name?"

"Benito."

"Blessed."

She smiled, nodded. "Yes."

After a minute's silence, Bartoli spoke. "Leave Matthew Spiller to me. I shouldn't have asked you to get involved. It's not your job." He gently pulled his hand away from hers and made to get out, but she grabbed his arm.

"Don't you wanna know what I found out?" she asked, although she really wanted him to stay so she could read the longing in her eyes and lean in for a kiss. Except that would be so inappropriate after hearing such a sad tale. And she really hoped he wasn't that kinda man; not like her ex-boyfriend, who'd not had the balls to stick around after Benito's death.

"Sure," Bartoli said. "Whatcha got?"

She twisted to face him, bringing her foot up under her opposite thigh. "So, you know about Harry Sullivan. Spiller admitted on Mel Banaghan to knowing him twenty years back. I couldn't find anything connecting them since. Sullivan came to LA, made it. Spiller stayed in England, didn't. Still, a connection."

"And the others? John Frears? Aiden Powers?"

"Frears. Another English actor, but not until he got to LA in twenty-thirteen. Previously a private security consultant, and before that a sergeant in the French Foreign Legion."

"Seriously?"

"And get this: Frears was tight with an actress called Hayley Olsen, who spent five years married to the director Brett Stutz."

"Who just directed Matt Spiller, and had a nationally televised bust-up with him."

"The very same. Tenuous, but…"

"No, that's good work, Gabriela. And Aiden Powers?"

"This is where I had to do some digging. I checked with the studio – who Spiller's spent time with outside of the cast and crew. And latterly, just the one time, he gets picked up by a driver called Sadie Woods. Ex-military. She took him to *The Mel Banaghan Show*. And I thought… I know that name. I don't think I would ever have worked it out, except for the fact I was looking into Aiden Powers. I was on Basic Car A1 that week. I attended the scene. Power's PA showed up to talk to the detectives. And she said a name: Sadie Woods. Woods was the last person to see Aiden Powers alive. She was his driver on his last movie. She took him back to his house the day he died."

He mulled over the information. "Six degrees of separation."

"I know the theory. But if that's the case, it's all bull."

"No, this is a lot tighter than six degrees. And all in the same town? Really good work, Gabriela. You'd be a real asset in homicide, you ever wanna make the move."

"So… you putting a black Sharpie over this now?"

"And a yellow highlighter. What are your thoughts, Gabriela?"

"Jeez, I don't know. Assuming you got a hard-on for Matthew Spiller—"

He barked a laugh.

She raised her eyebrows, smirked at him. "Should I not be talking about hard-ons right now?"

"Uh… continue."

"Well, if you're *looking at* Matthew Spiller, maybe he's killing off the competition. Harry Sullivan's an obvious choice. Maybe some jealousy in there, given how their careers diverged. John Frears, not an actor prior to twenty-thirteen. Handed a career on a silver platter. Jealousy again?"

"What? Spiller rams Frears off the road?"

"Maybe. Frears lived locally. His car was well-known. Easy to spot. Yellow Ferrari two-nine-six GTS convertible."

"Is that rare?"

"You got a spare four hundred large sitting around?"

Bartoli winced. "And Aiden Powers?"

"Maybe Spiller's connection to Sadie Woods predates a couple of nights ago. Maybe she gives him the lie of the land that day. Maybe she even does the job on his behalf. I don't doubt she has the skills. I don't know. Bottom line, we're clutching at straws here. I mean, would you even be thinking of Spiller if I hadn't shot you my crazy serial-killer theory that night in Sullivan's back yard?"

Bartoli considered. "Honestly? Probably not. Spiller's a lot of things, but I never got the impression he's malicious. That time back in the UK, I always felt he was just *reacting* to situations, not engineering them. Like he was caught in the middle and was just trying to find his way out. I can't see why he'd finally get a Hollywood career in his mid-forties and risk losing it. He's high profile now. He doesn't need to be thinning out the herd to get work."

"Unless he enjoys it. Maybe he's just a headcase."

Bartoli shrugged. "Well…"

Contreras read the room and figured the conversation had run its course. "You wanna get a drink some time, LT?"

"Call me Angelo. And yes, I'd like that very much."

She reached and grabbed his tie and pulled him closer, giving him a quick kiss on the lips.

He got out of the car, then leaned in through the window. "Give me a call, Gabriela. And we don't talk shop, okay?"

"Or dead kids?"

"Jesus… listen, you can talk to me about anything, okay? Okay?"

"Sure. Hey, I should have asked: are you married?"

"I was. To an English woman. It ended. One of the reasons I came back."

She smiled. "I'll call. Thanks for listening."

He winked. "You're welcome. Be safe out there."

HIS THIRD WIFE had soiled the Bronco by her attack. It wasn't beyond repair. Nothing was if you had enough money. Swap out the block, new grille, respray the front end. No one would ever know. He would, though. The memory of what she'd done, a final *coup de grace*, delivered years beyond the gut-punch of her divorce settlement, to a vehicle previously unsullied by her touch, bought by him after the split. Stutz had surveyed the wounded Bronco on the back of the low-loader in his mechanic's compound, and had then accepted a low-ball offer from one of the garage grease-monkeys to never see it again. On the plus side, his three-car garage now had a space that needed filling, and what man didn't enjoy spending money on a new car?

Stutz sat cross-legged in the space where the Bronco usually sat, his ass nicely chilled on the tiled floor. He looked at the black Lamborghini Urus SUV to one side of him, and the white Bugatti Chiron Super Sport to the other. He wasn't keen on either of them. Like having a pretty wife on his arm, owning them had seemed the right thing to do for a man in his position; a sign of his status. But he'd always preferred the Bronco. Bright but understated. These two vehicles were monstrous. Not just monstrous – *monstrosities* in his eyes. Too much power, too much noise. Too much of a statement for someone who, more and more, disliked the exhibitionism of Hollywood, and craved a return to the quiet anonymity of his early years.

Matt Spiller had blown that hope out of the water. So far out of the water, his hope was now frozen to death somewhere up Mount Everest. People didn't quickly forget the type of antics that happened on Mel Banaghan. It became the stuff of TV folklore. Stutz had pretty quickly stopped checking social media. The clip was everywhere. No doubt, Hollywood being Hollywood, another crass event would supersede it fairly soon, but his name would always be tied to it. Some day, when they wrote his obituary, it would be there, fouling up his CV the same way Hayley's buckshot had wrecked his Windsor V8.

He just had to make certain his life didn't get any worse. He tipped the contents of his gym bag onto the floor. All the bits and pieces he'd kept in the Bronco. The glove compartment, the door pockets, the seat backs. Pens, pills, tools, glasses, assorted detritus. And next to it all was his old laptop, rescued from his poisoned exes. It was damning. It would steal what was left of his future and blight his past in ways that would make the Mel Banaghan farce seem yawningly trite. He glanced over to his workstation in the corner of the garage, his array of tools. The hammer in its rightful spot on the perforated orange board, outlined in pen, like the tape around a murder victim. The laptop had to be smashed. Not hidden. You couldn't hide something from the police; they were good at finding contraband. Anyplace he could think of, so would they. Perhaps it would never happen, but this had been a wake-up call.

Yet, there were others in the scheme. Big names. Names he could drop into the mix if his own name ever attracted federal interest. Did he want to destroy a potential bargaining chip? Did they have the same on him? Was it all a matter of who caved first, like a *consigliere* timing his exit before the whole criminal enterprise crumbled around them? First man out got to turn state's evidence, claim immunity. The rest were screwed.

Even as he thought this, he was on his feet, clutching the laptop and heading for the hammer. He set the machine on his work bench and unhooked the tool. No way was he going to be the first to break ranks. That would be like throwing himself off a boat as it approached an iceberg, then watching it swerve clear and carry on safely. Right now, he was okay. There wasn't an iceberg in sight.

The laptop flew to pieces under a barrage of blows. The case disintegrated, revealing the hard drive, which he pummeled out of shape, and its information into oblivion.

## FOURTEEN

RATHER THAN RISK Billy getting behind the wheel of his Maserati again, Spiller called a cab to get home in the morning. He couldn't believe he'd let his agent drive anywhere in it, but he supposed he'd felt maudlin the first time, prior to the hospital, being cuddled by Billy, and was later too tired and doped up to care about much at all. As the cab covered the final few yards, Spiller noted the blood pool and the trail of splatters on the concrete leading back to his house. It had darkened in the heat and might have resembled old brake fluid to anyone who didn't know.

He let himself in and stared at his face in the hall mirror. It wasn't so bad. It wouldn't be the first time a denizen of this neighborhood had been seen all bandaged up post-rhinoplasty. His eyes were encircled like he'd been prepped for Halloween by his youngest daughter, using a two-dollar set of makeup. The doc had warned him to be very careful over the next ten days to make sure the bone set straight, and everything stayed in place. Spiller felt totally amenable to the advice. He just wanted to chill. He had food in the house, and no reason to leave. Cathy had set up a couple of publicity gigs for that week, but they would have to be canceled. He wasn't going in front of any cameras wrapped up like that. Cuts and bruises were one thing; they were badass. Bandages told a different story.

He quickly checked in the pot to make sure his car keys were there. They were, which meant the car was in the garage, and that was all he needed to know at that moment.

"Billy!" he called, which only made his sinuses pound.

A moment later, he heard the bi-fold door open and close, and Billy shortly appeared in the hallway in only a pair of Union Jack Speedos.

"Billy, that is *not* a sight for my sore eyes."

Billy scowled and placed his hands on his hips, which only made the visage worse, like he was auditioning for a geriatric Chippendales.

"What's up, Billy?"

"I have a rather large bone to pick with you, my dear."

"Let's not talk about bones when you're wearing skimpy shit like that."

"Come with me," Billy said, moving to the foot of the stairs.

"Billy, I have a broken nose, not amnesia. I remember very clearly I was straight yesterday. Nothing's changed."

"Don't flatter yourself, love. Get up those stairs, go to your bedroom."

Spiller wanted to frown, but he couldn't. "Did you agree to be my dad? Bloody sounds like it."

Billy started up the stairs. "Follow me."

Spiller watched as the patriotic, sunburned wrinkly climbed the stairs. What the hell, he wanted to lie down. He was heading that way anyway.

*"This!"* Billy yelled from ahead of him.

Spiller was cackling as he entered the bedroom, where Billy was standing by the closet, pointing at a familiar figure on the floor.

"What in God's name is this?" Billy asked.

Spiller walked in and bent down, scooping the body off the floor with his forearms under its armpits. He plonked it in an easy chair by the window and whispered to it: "Did that nasty old man disturb you? You sit there for a minute."

"Matthew, I swear, just as I think you've plumbed the depths of absurdity, you come back swinging. What is that thing?"

Spiller looked at the form, dressed in blue jeans and a leather jacket, now relaxing with its head lolled to one side. "That is Manny. Manny the mannequin from *Man on a Murder Cycle*."

"It's hideous."

"So would you be if you'd been sent through a plate glass window at over two hundred miles an hour."

Billy's face scrunched up in puzzlement. He looked at Manny like he could explain himself. "What's he doing in your bloody wardrobe?"

"It's my house, mate."

"It's your *housemate?* What?"

"No, I'm saying this is my house – *mate*. If I want to keep a mannequin in the closet, I'll do that. And more to the point, what were *you* doing in my closet? I thought you'd been out for years."

"Very droll, I'm sure. Looking for a towel."

"You have towels in your room."

"Matthew… he scared me half to death. What's it for?"

"They used him in the movie. Strapped him to a motorbike and sent him through a window. I think he's in pretty good shape, considering. I bought him off the props department. I stick a beer in his hand and sit him in the lounge if I'm away overnight. Keeps the burglars out. He's very realistic. All the joints move in the right direction, he's full weight."

"I bloody know he is! He fell on top of me!"

"Oo, you saucy sod, Manny."

Billy stormed out of the room. "This is a complete *madhouse!*"

"Hey, I never invited you! You're free to leave any time you please!"

Billy swiveled on the landing. "I might well do that. Do you know what happened to me yesterday? Driving back from the hospital – all very sedately, I might add – I was pulled over by a police officer."

Deflated, Spiller sat on his bed. "A Woman? Blue unmarked SUV?"

"I was doing nothing wrong, yet she still stuck her gun in my face!"

"Sorry about that, Billy. What did you do?"

"I faked a heart attack. What else would I do?"

Spiller smiled. "What else? No. No, you're right, it was the obvious choice. Then what happened?"

"I expected to hear her get on the radio and call for medical help, but… nothing. I had my eyes closed, but I think she was just standing there, watching me. The… the… *bitch*. Then I couldn't hold my breath, so I pretended to come to. And she still did nothing. Just scarpered."

"Well, I'm going to have a word with someone about that, don't worry. What's your plan today, Billy?"

Billy breathed deeply to calm himself. "After yesterday's aborted visit, I thought I might pop along to my new office. Set things up."

Spiller nodded. "Right."

Billy narrowed his eyes. "What? I sense disapproval. Be honest. I know you don't really want me here. Speak your mind."

"I just think... you're a Brit, you're getting on a bit, you have no contacts, you don't know this town. I just don't know what you expect to happen, Billy."

"You think I'm going to fail."

"Honestly? I think nutjob Noah has more chance of being cast as the next James Bond."

"Well, thank you for the vote of confidence, love. Which, by the way, does not reflect well on your prospects. I will only fail if you fail."

"Depends what you want, Billy. I'm definitely going to make more money. Do you want to just cream off the top of that, or do you want a proper career as an LA agent?"

Billy dropped a shutter on the topic. "I'm going to my new office."

"Do you want to borrow a duvet?"

"What? Why?"

"Thought you were moving out. Your office has a sofa, right?"

Billy squirmed at the thought. "Could I stay here a tad longer, love?"

Spiller lay back on the bed. "Sure. You're making all the tea, though."

"Rightio. Deal. And I will take your lovely car for a wash, have no fear."

Spiller found himself sitting bolt upright again. "Pardon?"

Billy shuffled on his bare feet. "Oh. You've not been in the garage."

"No. What am I going to find?"

"Uh... slight coating of dust."

"From?"

Billy scratched his bellybutton.

"Billy?"

"You were a taxi driver. I'm sure you occasionally went the long way round."

Spiller stood up and joined Billy on the landing. "Round where?"

"Edwards Airforce Base," he said defiantly.

Spiller fought off a momentary desire to knock him backward down the stairs. Dead easy. Spray the old bastard in pool water, throw some around on the steps and the landing, and there you have it. Unfortunate accident. Wet feet on a polished Maplewood floor. Bartoli might not buy it, but it would be fun watching him flounder yet again. He marched past Billy and downstairs to retrieve his car keys from the pot. He shoved them in his pocket and returned to the landing.

"Billy, you need to sort out your new persona, because right now it's all over the place. This old skin you're shedding? Make sure what's underneath can stand the heat."

TRUTH BE TOLD, Billy felt somewhat fraudulent setting himself up in LA. His small office, in a tall, glass-faced block near the intersection of Wilshire and San Vicente, offered his new venture prestige he wasn't sure he had the pedigree to back up. His relationship with his affiliate agent had been highly spasmodic. It was a link he'd always highlighted on his UK website to maintain the illusion of a transatlantic influence, but prior to Stutz's surprise visit and Spiller's fluke achievement, it had brought nothing of note. Now he was in LA, he was all alone. He was competition, and competition was always to be shunned. Even as the champagne flutes clinked to your success, and the bloated and paralyzed faces tried to smile at you, the daggers were lining up at the grindstone.

Maybe his one and only client had been right. It took more than a shaved scalp and a change of clothes to reinvent a person. The head had to change. The thought processes that had brought a person to a certain point in their life had to be overhauled. If not, there would just be more of the same. And crucially, the heart had to change. It had to become subservient to the new regime in the head, and depending on the desired outcome, it had to soften or harden. Billy suspected his heart would need to become a stone. He needed to be ruthless. He *wanted* to be ruthless. Being the nice guy had never got him anywhere.

He for damn sure needed more clients. Despite Spiller's assurances, Billy didn't trust that he'd capitalize on his current momentum. He was too flaky, too susceptible to acts of idiocy and self-destruction. His career was already hanging in the balance, even before it had properly begun. To Billy's certain knowledge, Spiller was a killer twice over. Three times over if he accepted the veracity of the sinking wheelchair story, and maybe there were even more back in England. And here… had he already started again? By Spiller's own admission, the silver-haired detective seemed to think so. Harry Sullivan had been a contemporary; a Brit of the same age, and in terms of casting, in the same violent mold. That meant competition. And no one liked competition.

Matthew Spiller was a scandal waiting to happen. And Billy was acutely aware that he had made himself an accessory after the fact.

There wasn't much to do in his new office. It was furnished with the essentials: desk, chairs, bookshelves, filing cabinet, sofa – although not long enough to sleep on. But he did need some knick-knacks. The shelves needed filling with books; his desk required a few ornaments. He didn't want a look of transience that would put off prospective clients. His age alone suggested impermanence; it didn't need compounding.

He shivered slightly at the too-cold air-conditioning, then looked out of his sixth-floor window onto a busy Wilshire. He was invisible behind the mirrored glass, and he mused whether that might be a portent. He had arrived, but how was he going to let the world know? Again, it crossed his mind to team up with Brett and turn the tables on his client. Throw Spiller under the bus. At that moment, there was nothing tying them. No contract, nothing on the new website yet. He and Stutz could claim a sudden, simultaneous realization that they'd witnessed two murders and had to clear their consciences. It would certainly raise his own profile if he wanted his name known around town.

Just then, a pickup truck motored past on the street, and Billy thought of Noah, and surprisingly found himself smirking. He knew himself well enough at his age to identify a sign of his true feelings. He liked Noah. He'd liked him before he'd collapsed Spiller onto the concrete, broken and bleeding. And although he normally abhorred violence, Billy apparently liked Noah a lot more now. How peculiar. Then again, how long did it take for a person's heart to harden, if that was their true desire?

Billy took out his phone and found the relevant number in his call history. This would only work if Spiller didn't find out. As he contemplated, his finger hovering above the green circle, a call came in from that very number. He answered as though he didn't recognize it.

"The Billy Banbury Talent Agency, how can I help?"

"Mr Banbury, sir, it's Noah. I just wanted to apologize for my behavior. I was hopin' we could meet up, talk about representation. I understand if you're all het up about yesterday and the answer's no, and I get you're probably busy as a hound in flea season right now, settin' up your new business, but I won't give you no more trouble, you can bet the farm on it."

Billy wondered if Noah was laying on the dialect as a marketing ploy, but he enjoyed the twang and the language. He grinned to himself, but quickly flattened his mouth so his satisfied expression didn't travel in his voice.

"Well, I was rather shocked, I have to say. Although, between you and me, Matthew Spiller can be a little cantankerous at times. I'm surprised you're the first to lash out."

"I'm gratified to hear that, Mr Banbury. Thank you kindly."

"But *you* must understand that this is not my first rodeo – to use your vernacular. I'm quite long in the tooth and I don't have the patience to suffer fools with self-destructive impulses. I tolerate enough of that nonsense from Matthew."

"No, sir, I do understand. It's not in my nature to react so poorly, but I was afeared for my safety – him with that bat and all – and I just reacted. I need you to know, despite my behavior—"

"Noah," Billy cut him off. "It's all right."

"I apologize. I'm just nervous as a fly in a glue pot, talkin' to a big agent like yourself."

Billy felt the need to be a little humble. "Noah, I'm not much different to you. I am a stranger in this city, just trying to find my feet.

Perhaps we can support each other, eh? I'm in my office now, if you'd like to pop in."

"Much obliged. I will be with you like white on rice." Noah ended the call.

Billy unpacked the few items from his cardboard box. Having put everything away in the desk drawers, the office looked no different to the moment he'd walked in. He'd have to raid a few thrift shops in due course. He fancied a stroll along the boardwalk at Venice Beach anyway to check out the oiled-up beach bods, and he imagined he'd find a few eclectic boutiques along the way, although he couldn't see how his taste in curios would gel with such a modern environment. Perhaps quite a minimalist look to avoid offending any potential clients. A couple of posters of Spiller's new film, just for the kudos. Print out and frame a couple of his old black-and-white thespian photographs from back in the day. Pot plant, coffee machine, compact sound system. It wouldn't take much to conjure the right ambience.

SPILLER'S FACE ACHED too much to allow sleep, and he didn't want to be too doped up on painkillers. There were matters afoot that demanded his full, non-medicated attention. He put Manny back in the closet, mooched around the house for a while, made himself a coffee, then summoned the courage to visit his Maserati.

"Old wanker," Spiller said, surveying the car, which had turned from its official metallic *Grigio Alfieri* to its current matt *Grigio Polvere*. He swiped a finger along the driver's door to reveal the contrast, then flicked the dust into the air. Damn, it was inside the car as well. He'd have to call a mobile detailer. He wasn't in the mood to do it himself, as much as he enjoyed buffing the metal in his garage.

A ring on his front door made him swear. He went back to the hall and gingerly put one black eye to the peep hole. Bollocks. Bartoli. Spiller stepped back and regarded his face in the mirror, as he had earlier, like it might have somehow improved. It would no doubt elicit a smile from Bartoli, but this would save him making a phone call.

Bartoli's mouth opened, then his face froze like someone had hit the pause button. Slowly, it began to animate, morphing into an amused grin. He let out a laconic laugh.

"Jesus H. I don't know what happened; I only know you deserved it."

"Thanks. Actually, I'm glad you're here. We need to have a chat about your overzealous minion. She's been at it again."

Bartoli lost his smile. "I know. She told me. She's backed off. Of her own accord. She won't bother you again."

"Not good enough. I warned you."

"Matthew, she's had a lot of heartache, okay? She doesn't need any more. I told her about you, she was trying to impress me. She won't do it again. In fact, you could blaze past her at a hundred miles an hour and she wouldn't do a thing."

"She stuck a gun in Billy's face."

The silence from Bartoli spoke volumes.

Spiller nodded. "Right. That's news to you."

"It is." Bartoli heaved a sigh. "Did he do anything threatening?"

Spiller laughed. "*Billy Banbury?* Have you ever met a less threatening person in your entire career?"

"Fair point."

"Thing is, Billy was wearing a hat – she obviously thought he was me until she pulled him over. So, why didn't she just let it go at that point?"

"I don't know."

"It's not on, Angelo. What if she'd shot him? Mistakes happen. It's a red interior, but I don't think it would hide all that blood. You know how much a new interior on a GranTurismo costs?"

Bartoli harrumphed. "For the sake of argument, I'm gonna assume you're having a little joke."

"Assume away. *Then* the silly bugger faked a heart attack he was that scared, and she just stood there and watched him. No attempt to call it in."

A weary Bartoli shook his head. "I can't excuse what she did. But, Matthew, for old time's sake, give her a pass on this."

Spiller weighed up his position. "Okay. But if you do find evidence I killed Harry Sullivan, you bury it, right? Quid pro quo."

Bartoli grinned, wagging a finger at him. "You are a deeply disturbed individual."

"Oh – and get my key fob back for me. You can drop it through my front door when you're next passing. Don't knock."

"Sure. So, what happened to your face?"

Spiller closed the door on him. He waited to hear a car start up and drive away, then he dipped into the hall-table drawer. Next to Bartoli's card was another LAPD contact card. He took it through to the living room, sat down in his favorite chair, and tapped the number into his phone.

"Who's this?"

"Matt Spiller. Is that Ethan?"

"Hey!" Ethan said, clearly elated. "How you doing, buddy? Didn't expect to hear from you. You okay? You sound funny."

"No, not really. I've got a broken nose."

"Man, that's tough. How'd that happen?"

"Oh, some young actor didn't get my attention. Bit of a stalker. Came to my house and headbutted me."

"You call the cops?" Ethan asked.

"No, not worth it. Not great publicity. Could make me look a bit lame."

"Yeah, guess so. You want me to do something about it? Have a quiet word with the guy? That why you called?"

Spiller shook his head as though Ethan could see. "No, absolutely not. Just checking if you wanted to get a beer sometime."

"Yeah, that'd be great. You doing anything tonight?"

"Oh – tonight won't work." He stared at his dark reflection on the TV screen. "I'm a real mess. I don't want to be seen out like this. Probably at least a week."

"Okay. Well, I've got your number now, so let me call you in a week or so. Really good to hear from you, Matt. You get well soon."

"Cheers, Ethan. You take care."

As the line went dead, Spiller wondered why he'd bothered. Although he liked the idea of having a social life and friends, he'd never enjoyed the reality. Maybe he was projecting, but other people were usually a let-down. Unreliable, flaky, fair-weather. He wouldn't give Ethan another call; this would be a test for the cop to see if he kept his word. It would be a sad indictment if Ethan didn't keep in touch, though. Who didn't want a movie star as a drinking buddy?

Spiller was bored again. He seemed to have spent his entire adult life almost perpetually bored. There had been high points in the UK, but mostly related to his employment as an actor. Strangely, he'd even enjoyed the hours he'd spent sitting in a caravan, his handwritten name taped to the door, waiting to be called to set. It was all part of an environment that gave him an identity he seemed to lack as a regular citizen. There was a buzz to being an active cog in the professional machine, however temporary. The lengthy spells of unemployment that always followed had been like crashing from a narcotic high. There was even a spell of cold turkey that marked his transition from barely tolerable post-job despair back to run-of-the-mill everyday depression. He'd always believed that real success would be the cure, but he was now finding out that wasn't the case. A famous actor in an expensive house seemed a far cry from an impoverished taxi driver in a rented bedsit, but he was learning that they were the same person if both had nothing to do. Bored was bored, and rich and famous and bored was a whole lot worse than poor and obscure and bored, because the former had no dreams left to fulfil, no fantasy scenario where life would miraculously improve and banish all their mental anguish. Sadie had been right: fame and fortune were no panacea. Quite the opposite.

And what else did he have backward? Was he bored because he was depressed, and depression stole his mojo, or was he depressed because he was plain old bored? Sitting there, with everything any rational person could strive for, he could exclude circumstantial depression. And if he was genuinely happy when he was acting, that probably ruled out any chemical imbalance, because wouldn't that persist no matter what was happening?

Spiller decided he needed something to look forward to. He needed more work. Even having something scheduled would lift his spirits. And he really needed that to happen before Helen and the girls arrived. He had burned vital bridges behind him, and he didn't want any of them to realize that the place he'd arrived at hadn't been worth the arson.

To counteract the onset of a bleak vortex, he closed his eyes and quickly nodded off.

BILLY CLOSED HIS eyes, felt his zip being tugged down as he leaned back against his new desk. He looked out through his mirrored windows and felt vulnerable, exposed, even though he knew he couldn't be seen.

"You don't need to do this," he muttered.

Noah peered up at him from under his brow, his eyes partially hidden by the unkempt flicks of his hair. "I can always stop, Billy."

"No, I just… I want to sign you, no matter what. This isn't necessary." He inhaled as a hand stroked skin that hadn't felt the touch of another human in years. "Oh, my God…"

Noah stopped and peered up again. "One thing you're gonna find out about me: I am at no man's beck and call. I choose my path in life at every turn."

Billy felt he'd remonstrated enough to assuage any doubt. He didn't want to stop what was happening. Everything this barmy city had to offer – he'd promised himself. Although he'd never expected this. Thought about it. Never expected it. Not for free.

Now he couldn't keep his eyes closed. They were wide with ecstasy. Besides, he needed to see what was taking place or he'd never believe it later. He glanced down to confirm what his groin and Noah's mouth were telling him, that all was in vintage working order.

In that moment, Matthew Spiller lost his hold over Billy Banbury. Thirty percent, fifty percent, it didn't matter. He would forfeit any amount of money to keep Noah's attention. It was unseemly, no doubt, especially given the age difference, but it was consensual and legal and—

Billy moaned and wanted to cry.

THE MORE BARTOLI thought about it, the more concerned he was. Although only a small percentage of cops fired their guns in anger over their whole career, it wasn't unusual for a cop to pull their piece. There were countless scenarios where the outcome was unknown, and a weapon might be needed. No point having it on your hip or under your arm when a situation went south. But while it wasn't sensible to prejudge any encounter with the public, he couldn't envisage any circumstance in which the Englishman Billy Banbury might appear in the least bit threatening. He certainly had never heard of anyone feigning death during a traffic stop. That smacked of abject terror. He wanted to give Contreras the benefit of the doubt. He tried to picture the scene from her point of view, tried to imagine how she might have been spooked into drawing her weapon. He just couldn't see it. She wasn't a rookie; she knew as well as anyone how to read a situation, which suggested her objective had been to freak the old guy out. She could have let him get on his way once she realized she'd mistaken who was driving, but she had instead chosen to continue her harassment of Matthew Spiller, albeit vicariously.

It was disappointing. They had chemistry. Their rendezvous last night had been laden with sexual tension. Without the heavy topic of conversation, he felt certain the sparks flying would have started a fire.

Sad to say, but Officer Gabriela Contreras was a loose cannon. He'd seen the type plenty of times over his long career. Being a uniformed cop was stressful enough. Pile on some external heartache and it didn't take long for professionalism to start leaching from the job. Objectivity gave way to prejudice. Everything became personal, when pretty much nothing a cop experienced over their day was truly vindictive. People acted out, and a cop's job was to be there to take the brunt of their anger and defuse them. Of course, it certainly *felt* personal when someone was in your face, mouthing off, or you were staring into the muzzle of a gun pointed your way, but the real target was the uniform or the shield on your belt, not the person wearing them. Ultimately, the target was authority. Cops who forgot the truth of that were liable to escalate encounters rather than seek to resolve them.

Perhaps he'd led her on, tacitly given her a task beyond his request that she investigate Matthew Spiller. He recalled his exact words to her: *I just want him locked up. I don't care how that happens.* He had to admit that could have been misconstrued. It had been uttered as a vain hope, but the wrong person could have easily taken that as an instruction.

Bartoli sat in his Chevy Impala outside the station on Butler Avenue. He needed to end what hadn't yet begun. He was divorced, free to pursue whoever he desired, and no doubt he was on the cusp of the late middle-aged fantasy of hooking up with a woman twenty-five years younger than him, but there were pitfalls aplenty down that particular road. He already had four kids from two different women; he didn't want any more. Contreras had been a mother, and she'd likely want to be one again. He imagined it was a natural yearning after losing a child, and probably infinitely more pronounced than in a woman who'd yet to conceive.

Bartoli smiled to himself. Was he hurtling ahead of the facts? Was he being presumptuous even thinking this could be more than a few drinks and a fumbled grope down an alley? Of course. But… if she did want more, he wasn't the guy to provide it. And the bottom line? She was damaged goods. A cruel term for a bereaved mother, and he was fickle for thinking it, but he didn't want to embroil himself in all that such a sad loss entailed.

Had she shown up while he was contemplating, he might have explained all this to her. But she didn't, so he set off down the road and resolved he was just going to duck her calls.

## FIFTEEN

EIGHT DAYS PASSED. Constrained by his injury, and Cathy Zengler's directive that he'd better not destroy her rescheduled publicity a second time, Spiller had stayed home. The Maserati had been washed and buffed by a mobile company, and its keys hidden away from Billy, who had hired himself a convertible Chevy Camaro for a hundred bucks a day. He'd not seen much of the old geezer. Billy had been at his office every day, had stayed out overnight on two occasions, and was now on the lookout for a rental property, having been given notice of his imminent eviction in four days, when Spiller's family, and replacement man-of-the-house, David, were due to arrive.

Spiller had spent the time trying to enjoy the spoils of his success; really trying to infuse his brain with the genuine enormity and improbability of his stratospheric rise. He was like a dud firework, abandoned for years after an aborted launch, then unexpectedly fizzing back into life, and lighting up the night sky for the whole world to see. His broken nose had provided a useful pause, during which he'd realized his life wasn't half bad. He'd smiled more in the past week than in the past ten years, and at nothing in particular. He'd realized that sometimes you needed to step outside your life and look in on it from a stranger's point of view to truly see and appreciate your blessings.

Sadie had pretty much said all this to him the night of *The Mel Banaghan Show*, and he felt inclined now to let her know how shrewd she was – an ulterior motive because he just wanted to see her again. He'd had a laugh with her that night, like she was an old buddy he'd known for years. He imagined most drivers would have stayed in their vehicle, and certainly wouldn't have directed him toward a stash of coke or encouraged his infantile behavior with his trousers. And this, despite her admission that she hated the world he moved in. But that was also the thing that stopped him making contact. Because, given her feelings, a famous actor would be the last person she'd want to hook up with.

The bandage was off his face now, and his nose looked better than it had before the headbutt. Its slight kink, there since a bad rugby tackle at school, had been straightened out. The scar was fading and would be invisible under makeup.

Spiller was still aggrieved at Noah, though. The front of the guy, thinking he could attack a Hollywood actor with impunity. And being right about it. Grudges weren't healthy, but Spiller couldn't shake it off. Some things were personal. His face was his fortune now. It had been hidden under prosthetics and latex for *Man on a Murder Cycle*, but he hoped that type of casting would not persist. Noah had done no less than threaten his future, his earning potential.

Lying out by his pool, thinking about his career, Spiller found himself starting to worry again, and those lazy few days of happily resting on his laurels quickly fragmented into hours of anxious contemplation. He began checking his phone more and more often, as he had done for so many years in England. Only, this was worse. Billy had been an established agent back home. He was a nobody in this town.

Wondering where Billy was up to with setting up his business, Spiller decided to locate his new website. He went indoors, opened his laptop, and was instantly even more concerned about his job prospects.

According to the clients' tab, Billy had signed five actors in the past week. He didn't recognize any of them, so it seemed that no one with any pedigree was jumping ship to be with The Billy Banbury Talent Agency, if they even knew it existed. Not that he wanted competition, but it would have been reassuring to see a face that was at least vaguely familiar, even if it was only from a hemorrhoid commercial.

But the big problem wasn't the faces he could see. It was the one that was missing.

His face wasn't there. Spiller tried to reason it out, but there was no rationale that made sense. He was still being talked about, more publicity was imminent, and the release of his movie would only accelerate his momentum. So, why the hell was Billy not capitalizing on all that?

Spiller was too impatient to wait for Billy to get back – if he even returned that night. And it would be interesting to see his new office, check out if he had the required business paraphernalia. Worse case scenario, Billy was just going through the motions, appearing to be serious, but secretly happy to rely on his thirty percent from Spiller. At his age, Billy wouldn't need any more than that to live out his remaining years in luxury.

Spiller grimaced. That wasn't the worst case. More worrying would be his needing to employ a second agent to secure the work. Twenty percent to them and thirty percent to Billy. Millions lost.

Within five minutes, Spiller was dressed and seated in his Maserati, waiting for the garage door to lift.

WHEN THE ELEVATOR door slid open, Spiller was confronted by a man looking down at his waist as he secured the bull-head buckle on his blue jeans. Spiller frowned as Noah looked up and grinned. Noah's face was flushed, and there was a twinkle in his eyes. He stepped aside and waved Spiller out of the elevator. Spiller stared at him, puzzled, but feeling the cogs meshing in his brain as they reluctantly identified the cause of the young man's demeanor. The door began to close, and Noah placed a hand on its edge, sending it back into the wall. Slowly, Spiller stepped out and Noah stepped in, both turning to face each other again. As the door started to move, Noah made a finger gun, as he had at the karaoke bar, and mimed shooting Spiller twice in the chest and once in the head.

"Well, ain't you a no-account fellow," Noah said laughingly, just before the door sealed them apart.

A wave of nausea weakened Spiller's legs. As he listened to the elevator hum down the shaft, his heart pounded as his head confirmed his suspicion and acknowledged the meaning of Noah's actions.

Spiller turned and spotted the printed plastic plaque on his agent's door. He quickly nipped into the stairwell in case Billy emerged from his office. His instinct told him there was nothing to be gained by talking to the old man. There would be denials and lies, and Billy would be suddenly on his guard, which wasn't how you wanted an enemy to be. Then he experienced the desire to propel himself down the stairs to catch Noah as the elevator door opened on the ground floor. Push him back inside, pummel the life out of him.

The moment passed, and Spiller returned to his car, parked in a residential street off Wilshire. He settled into the hot leather and metaphorically donned his thinking cap.

There was only one explanation for Noah's mime and comment: he knew what had taken place in England at Christmas. It seemed Billy had engaged in a little pillow talk. Not such a problem if he wanted to keep his thirty percent coming in. On his own, Noah could bleat about it, but he'd need Billy to back him up. Without that corroboration, who was going to listen to a vindictive stranger with a grudge? Yet... Noah didn't appear to be holding a grudge. Spiller had been dealt his payback with a broken nose, and it was obvious that his attempt to stamp on the first rung of Noah's career ladder by denying him access to Billy's representation had failed, unless Noah enjoyed blowing old-timers for kicks.

Billy had clearly taken Noah on, and keeping him off the clients' page could be interpreted as Billy keeping his star-turn sweet, protecting the thirty percent Spiller had threatened to withdraw.

But there was still a huge problem, because Noah's profile wasn't the only one missing. Again, Spiller returned to the implications of his own face being absent from the website. Surely, if Billy wanted to draw in a few high-profile actors, having Matt Spiller top of the bill was his best bet. In fact, it was his only play. Lacking a big name, Billy was just a washed-up ex-pat, attempting a risible last act in his twilight years.

Unless... unless Billy didn't consider his future was tied to Spiller's. Maybe he was more concerned with past events. Because what did Billy really want from life now? Money? He had more than enough, more than he could ever spend. If Billy craved anything at all these days, it was the thing he'd never really enjoyed: notoriety. Spiller had always suspected Billy's greatest regret in life was his obscurity, being left behind in his forties after a promising start. Having to abandon hope after acting had abandoned him. Being forced to shift to agenting, creating careers for people he probably considered unworthy to even polish his brogues.

Was Billy about to expose Spiller's past misdeeds? Just for the brief, but intense, notoriety of bringing down a household name?

If that was Billy's plan, it wouldn't work without Brett Stutz to confirm the crimes.

Spiller pulled out his phone and called Stutz, but it went to voicemail. He ended the call, and scrolled to locate Stutz's PA.

A female voice answered. "Hey there, Matt."

"Hi, Bex. How are you?"

"Still picking up calls for the man, so go figure."

"Yeah. Listen, where's Brett today? I mean, right now?"

"You know I can't divulge that information, Matt. He's on location all day. I'll WhatsApp you his itinerary."

Spiller laughed. "You're a really bad PA."

"Ain't that the truth. Anything else?"

"No, that was it. Sorry, I'd chat, but I'm in a rush."

"No problem. WhatsApp incoming. See you around, Matt."

"Yeah, cheers, Bex."

A few seconds later, Spiller had access to Stutz's itinerary for the entire week. For the next couple of hours, the director was at an address in Reseda. Spiller put it in his satnav and set off.

## SIXTEEN

THE SECURITY GUARD at the entrance to the parking lot knew Spiller from *Man on a Murder Cycle*, so waved him through. It was a typical location shoot. Trailers and Winnebagos; camera, lighting, and other tech trucks; vehicles for makeup, costume, catering. Nothing was happening outside the main building, and Spiller repeatedly revved the Maserati's engine as he tootled across the lot, hoping to ruin the scene that was going on inside. He parked his car away from the hubbub, on the edge of the lot. Surveying the location, he felt a pang of jealousy; the idea that a movie was happening, and he wasn't involved.

The building was a single-story gun range. The name above the entrance read *DODGE CITY* – green neon in military font. Every so often, he could hear muffled shots from inside. It was fifteen minutes before Stutz exited the building and sat in his director's chair outside his trailer, calling on an assistant to fetch him something. Spiller got out and sauntered over.

"Brett, how's life?"

The assistant delivered a coffee and received no thanks.

"Matty, what are you doing here?"

"Just passing, saw your Bronco, thought I'd pop in for a catch-up. I have some publicity tomorrow. Wanted to see if you needed me to say anything. You know – about the Mel Banaghan thing."

Stutz offered a cynical look. "You saw my Bronco?"

Spiller nodded. He knew Stutz went everywhere in it.

"Please point to my Bronco." Stutz took a sip.

Spiller looked around. "Uh..."

"Never mind. What do you *really* want?"

Spiller pointed at the trailer. "Little privacy?"

Stutz set his coffee down and led the way.

With the door closed, Stutz peered at Spiller's face. "You're healing well – considering the mess you were in. Now cut to the chase."

"Billy Banbury. Level with me."

Stutz groaned and dumped himself in his easy chair. "This is where you see if I tell you something you already know, upon pain of death?"

"Yep."

"He came to my house, couple of nights back. To sound me out. Would I be on board with throwing you to the wolves once the box office looks healthy and the studio won't take much of a hit."

"Thought so. Did he say why?"

"I didn't give him the chance. I told him to get lost. I can't be associated with something like that; I might never work again. If your threats are genuine, I might never *breathe* again. Matt, what is going on with the guy?"

"He's had his head turned. Actually, he's had his head polished."

"I don't understand."

"Doesn't matter. Thanks for being honest. Were you going to tell me? If I hadn't asked?"

"I was debating. I thought we had time on our side." He peered at Spiller with a hint of desperation. "We do have time on our side, right? You realize, if he talks to the Press before the movie's out, it's gonna bomb. That's if the studio even releases it. No way are they just gonna issue a press release defending you. Best case, they stay neutral, delay the movie, pending investigations. And even if I deny his story, mud sticks."

Spiller gave him an icy look. *"Even if?"*

"Come on... turn of phrase. Matt, I'm on your side. My fortunes are tied to yours."

After a moment, Spiller nodded. "Yeah, they really are."

"What are you gonna do? No, don't tell me." He got up and headed for the door.

"Brett..."

Stutz paused with his palm on the handle. "What?"

"If Billy goes public before I can talk him out of this... you'll have to lie for me. You okay with that?"

"With lying?" Stutz chortled. "Remember why I asked you to get my laptop from Kat?"

Spiller nodded.

"Yeah, I'm okay with lying. I can't act to save my life, but I can lie. Believe me, I am not about to offer myself up as state witness. I don't need the scrutiny. I got it back, by the way."

"Your laptop?"

"Uh-huh. Only cost me my Bronco," Stutz said bleakly.

"You made a swap?"

"Kinda." He pressed the handle and stepped down onto the concrete, holding the door open for Spiller to follow.

Spiller was about to say thank you, but Stutz grabbed his coffee and headed back into the range. Then Spiller committed the unpardonable sin of sitting in the director's chair – on a movie set he wasn't even a part of. A couple of people looked at him and scowled. He offered a palms-up shrug, so they looked the other way like they hadn't seen.

Spiller didn't need to dwell on it to know he believed Stutz. He didn't need to threaten the man's life to keep him in line – although that was a useful fear to instill in a person. Stutz was a criminal himself. A tax cheat. One word to the IRS, and their forensic accountants would be on the case, looking for the slightest discrepancy.

Spiller got up and helped himself to a coffee from a large steel urn on a table, surveying a selection of pastries and cookies under cellophane, to keep the flies off. As he sipped his drink, he caught a figure emerging from the range. He frowned at her as she simultaneously offered him a perplexed look. She came over to him, her expression even more full of profound bewilderment. Initially unsure who she was, he identified her the second before she spoke his name.

"Matthew?"

"We met at Hayley's, right?"

She nodded. "How the hell did you get here so fast? And I said after five."

"Hey?"

"I sent you a text… what, ten minutes ago?"

Her expression was contagious. "Sorry, what? What text? And why are you here? Are you working on set?"

"No. I was a costume designer, but that's not what I'm doing here. This is my business. I own it."

He looked up at the name of the range, and it clicked. "Oh, okay. I heard you call your son Dodge at Hayley's place."

"Dodge was my dad. He owned the range. My son's named after my dad."

"Right. Uh… so, what's this about a text?"

"Check your cell."

Spiller pulled out his phone and found a message instructing him to let her know if he was available to meet her and Hayley at that address later. He looked at her. "Okay… and… who are you? I mean, you took my number without any explanation, and a week later you ask to meet me. Who are you?"

She shook herself, managed a smile, offered her hand. "Virginia. Sorry, this is a little strange. You weren't just passing, right? Just as you got my message?"

He absently took her hand. "Nope. First I've seen of it. I came to talk to Brett."

Bemused, she shook her head slightly. "Wow."

Spiller felt he was being scrutinized like he was the Second Coming. He checked the time on his phone. Just after two.

"Do you have anything on for the next few hours? Virginia asked.

Spiller really wanted to get away and confront Billy. He couldn't afford the luxury of deliberation, now he knew Billy had made such a bold play to get Stutz to turn. Spiller had no clue what *his* next play would be, although he had the uncomfortable sense that it wouldn't be pretty. He shuffled on his feet and wondered if a few hours' inaction might actually be a boon. Perhaps he needed that time for it all to percolate through.

"Well?" she prompted.

He shrugged. "All yours."

"Okay. I'm gonna call Hayley, see if she can get here sooner, but… come to my office."

He followed her. "How come you let Brett Stutz use this place for filming? Hayley hates him."

"Money talks. You know how much I'm getting paid for the day? And I deal with the studio, not Brett. I've worked for the studio before. What happened to your face?"

"I have a stalker. He jumped me."

"You're kidding?"

Spiller could already feel himself planting seeds, preparing the ground for the reaping ahead. "No, but I'm sure the cops are handling it."

Virginia's office was through a door at the rear of one of the sales counters, which was manned by a stocky sales assistant wearing a handlebar moustache and a holstered semi-auto. Spiller scanned the display cabinets and wanted to shoot everything in them. His passion for guns, so long stifled by the laws of his homeland, was burgeoning in this place.

The interior of the office was functional. Business necessities and little else. None of the gun miscellanea he'd expected to find. She offered him her desk chair. Next to a slumbering computer screen was a framed photo of a black man in tiger-stripe camo, holding a Car-15. Once color, it was now almost sepia.

"This your dad?" Spiller asked.

"Uh-huh," she muttered, as she pulled out a drawer in a filing cabinet.

"Vietnam?"

"Yes. The only picture I have of him from that time. I found it tucked in an old book after he died." She pulled out a stack of papers, which she set in front of him. "There you go. Read that."

THE BLUE FORD Explorer that loomed in his rearview mirror made his heart sink. The vehicle was so close to his bumper that Bartoli could see the person behind the wheel. The Explorer's headlights winked on and off a couple of times, and he decided he'd best pull over before she gave him a blast on the siren. His comeuppance was past due.

He'd been in Bel-Air, following up on a couple of duff leads in the Harry Sullivan case, and was driving down leafy Roscomare, heading back to the city. He indicated and stopped outside a palatial house in yellow stucco. As she exited her car, he got out to meet her halfway.

"Sorry," he said, as an opening gambit. "Been so damn busy. How are you, Gabriela?"

She offered a perfunctory smile. "Still a single ex-mother."

He grimaced. "That's…"

"Isn't it? No matter. I just wanted you to know you're off the hook. I shared; you couldn't take it. I don't need a person like you in my life any more than you need someone like me."

Caught red-handed, he sighed. "I'm sorry, Gabriela. I just got too much going on to have to deal with anything else right now. I don't think I could give you what you need."

She laughed briefly without humor. "You see me on my knee offering you a ring, Detective? Maybe I was just looking to get laid. Jesus, you think I could do this job if I couldn't compartmentalize? The moment seemed right, so I told you about my son. Then I moved on. Clearly, you couldn't." She put her hands on her utility belt, the heel of her right palm resting on the butt of her FN.

Something in her demeanor more than her words made him uneasy. "Hey, take your hand off your sidearm."

She made a face. "Seriously?"

"You wanna stand like that with a perp in front of you, be my guest. I don't like it."

"You scared, Detective?"

"Should I be? I mean, Matthew Spiller told me you pulled your piece on his agent. What for? Why do that?"

"Ach," she said dismissively, removing her hands from her belt and folding her arms defiantly across her chest. "You're kind of a douche, you know that? And you suck as a detective. All that intel I gave you? Bet you're still just scratching around, talking to the neighbors, kicking the tires, hoping someone throws you a bone. Am I right?"

He smiled, but she'd targeted a sensitive spot, and his expression felt awkward. Stupidly, he'd let on about his failures in the UK investigation, and now she was taunting him with it.

"Gabriela, stick to your car theft and DUIs. I apologize for involving you." He turned and headed back to his vehicle, feeling he'd not managed to acquit himself that well.

"Hey!" she said, interrupting his departure.

Bartoli turned back to her. "What?"

"Don't even think of trying to deep-six my career. Right now I'm a little upset. You don't ever wanna see me spiteful."

He wanted to remonstrate, to use his rank to slap down her impertinent challenge. Instead, he yielded with a nod, then got back in his car.

The Explorer passed him and carried on down Roscomare, taking a bend out of sight. Bartoli waited a few minutes for his hackles to flatten, but they stayed stubbornly erect. Something about that woman wasn't right. Of course, her recent history was ample justification for bitterness. But it was something else. His police antenna, attuned over thirty years in the job, was pinging like crazy. Her warning not to hobble her career concerned him; the fact that she'd threatened a malevolent response. Back in the UK, it had been known in the force as "doing someone's legs", but it was reserved for serious malfeasance, and he'd not considered her actions went that far. Now he was wondering.

He didn't want to start quizzing her superiors at Butler Avenue, even surreptitiously. Word got back to people, even if the message was non-verbal or veiled. Heightened scrutiny, suspicious looks, apparently motiveless checks on wellbeing. Besides, it might rebound on him. She could easily counter with the narrative that he'd urged her into harassing Matthew Spiller with the tacit promise of career enhancement – which wouldn't be entirely false.

Thankfully, there was another avenue to go down.

## SEVENTEEN

THE ELDERLY COUPLE had left at the end of April to explore Europe with a military-grade itinerary. Everything had been pre-planned down to the hour: where to go, how to get there, where to stay, which sights to see. JoBeth had marveled at the way her husband could construct such a precise campaign, but hers was a wonderment of old that had not been diminished by their fifty-five years together. Jack's mind was sharp as a tack when they'd met. It came with the job, he'd always told her, which was something at the secret heart of government. She had never definitively identified the correct acronym of the department, although she guessed it was defense-related and not one known to the public. There were matters he had never been able to discuss with anyone, including her. Only once, when he was drunk in 1987, had he mentioned working on a nuclear-powered warplane in which the pilot would have to sit in a cockpit filled with a breathable liquid to withstand the speed. She'd thought he was ribbing her with sci-fi, until she'd watched *The Abyss* two years later.

By the time Jack had retired, she'd long since realized it didn't much matter what he did outside their relationship. He'd been a wonderful husband; she'd have been greedy to demand anything more from him. In exchange, she had provided the financial acumen over the years to always bolster their savings. She had found an alternative use for all the tech wizardry he kept in their panic room, learning how to beat the markets, and crucially predict when they were about to tank. She'd been ahead of the game in 1987, had sold off at the peak of the dot-com bubble in 2001, and had been simply awestruck by the so-called experts who had failed to cash-out in time in 2008. Lately, she had become wary again. She didn't like the state of play. Trillion-dollar companies with junk-rated debt, fiat currencies devalued by a mass minting that would make the Weimar Republic blush, millions being splashed on digital objects of no worth in the metaverse – whatever the hell that was – and billions in value tied up in crypto; so-called currencies conjured out of thin air, that were too volatile to ever be used as a form of payment. The world had gone crazy, and she was just waiting for the house of cards to come crashing down, taking the entire system with it this time. Fortunately, her contingency plan was already in place.

Up on Mulholland Drive, the solid steel gate rolled back. The taxi entered and headed down the block-paved drive to their sprawling bungalow home, nestled in a natural hollow. It had been a memorable vacation, except JoBeth was beginning to think that might not be a hundred percent true for Jack. Something in him had begun to dim in the past few weeks. Nothing out of the ordinary for a seventy-six-year-old perhaps, but Jack had never been ordinary. She'd noticed moments when he'd had to check the itinerary in the morning, having checked it the night before, when he would have been able to reel off the entire timetable verbatim with his eyes shut prior to leaving.

Their home was as they'd left it. Her CCTV app had notified her of the gardener's arrival each week, so the lawns and pool area were still immaculate. Apart from that, their perimeter had remained unviolated. They never had to worry about the bungalow itself. For years following his retirement, Jack had been paranoid that his ex-employers would feel the need to silence him, so he'd installed every security gadget available, and some, she suspected, that weren't so readily available.

They unpacked their cases, then slept for a couple of hours. They wanted their body-clocks back on Pacific Standard Time as soon as possible, but there was no way either of them would make it through to bedtime without a little snooze. Up again, and somewhat refreshed, JoBeth made some coffee as she waited for Jack to join her.

"You okay, honey?" she asked.

He nodded. "Not sure how many more trips like that I can take, though." He laughed, then kissed her. "We've had a good life together, haven't we?"

"Of course. Jack, stop it."

"What?"

"Being maudlin. We're still here." She gave him a hug.

"Mind if I check the garage?" Jack asked.

She knew what he meant. "Go ahead."

He took his coffee and left the kitchen. Soon, she would hear the grumble of a V-twin. He hadn't ridden in years, but he still loved to tinker with his bikes. Last time she'd looked, he had three vintage Harleys and a couple of Indians in there. Two were always in a state of repair. He found them, fixed them, and sold them at a loss so that someone without their means could indulge their passion.

JoBeth finished her coffee, wandered into the garden. They had indeed enjoyed a good life. So many, and so close, whose lives were blighted. They were truly blessed. She surveyed her verdant realm beyond the pool.

Her smile faded. She cocked her head. Her timeworn legs carried her as fast as they could toward the green chain-link fence that delineated the boundary of their lush oasis. Beyond that, the untended terrain was now marred. JoBeth stared through the wiring at a blackened patch, although nature had already started to reclaim the land. Her eyes turned up to where the unseen road snaked around the higher, untended part of their property. She traced a path from there down to the charred earth, and noticed deep gouges in the slope. She looked back to the bungalow, to the camera that faced her.

THE MORE HE read, the more excited Spiller became. Six episodes, forty-five minutes a piece. No indication of a working title on the front page of each episode. He was deep into the fifth when he heard the filming wrap in the range. He stopped and listened to the hubbub as the techies carried their trunks and equipment through the store, and the place quietened as the actors and crew filtered out. According to a wall clock with a Colt logo, it was four thirty. Virginia had not returned to check on him, or even to offer him a snack, and he was getting hungry. He ventured out of the office to see if there was anything left to plunder from the catering truck or the table of goodies, but he found it was closed and ready to roll. As he scanned the parking lot for abandoned food, he spotted Brett Stutz in a heated discussion with Virginia next to a black Lamborghini Urus, then he jumped as a horn blasted across the lot. He traced its origin to a huge Cadillac SUV in a silvery beige. Its imposing front vaguely reminded him of the Mandalorian's helmet. The driver's door opened, and he found himself grinning at Sadie, who crooked a finger at him.

"Hey, Sadie. Looks like someone was first to the carpool this morning."

She used the hem of her smart shirt to rub at an imaginary blemish on the wheel arch, and Spiller got a flash of some chiseled abs.

"Very nice," he said.

"The Caddy?"

"That, too."

She caught his drift and smiled. "Actually, this little baby is all mine."

Spiller gave her vehicle the once-over. "Your career plan fairly romped ahead. That's going to take a chunk out of your wages every month."

Sadie shook her head. "*All* mine."

"Gosh. What went right?"

She laughed. "I found Cathy Zengler's coke stash and I put the whole lot on eBay."

It was Spiller's turn to laugh. "Seriously... this is yours?"

"Uh-huh. Anyway, what happened to you? Your face. Your nose. You have an accident?"

"Incident more than accident."

"Who hit you?"

"Nice that you think I'm so punchable."

"So, who was it?"

"Guess you could call him a stalker."

"Are you worried? You call the cops?"

"I'm planning my revenge." He winked.

"Yeah, I believe you. So, what are you doing here? You got some work?"

"No, not on this. I... I don't know. I think I may be about to get some, but... I'll let you know. There's some strange stuff happening, that's for sure."

"And this from the King of Strange."

He shrugged at the truth of it. "Hey, how about I tell you later? Over a drink?"

Sadie frowned at the impromptu pass, then nodded. "Why not? And I can tell you about this." She stroked her car. "Sorry, gotta run, my actor's coming."

"How about you come to my place at eight? We can work it out from there."

"Sure." She gave him a card from her shirt pocket. "That's my cell. In case your plans change." She brushed him as she went to open the front passenger door. "Another one who likes to ride up front."

The young actor walked past Spiller, ignoring him, and hopped in the Escalade.

As Sadie returned to the driver's side, Spiller said, "Must be something up front that people like."

Smirking, she raised her eyebrows and climbed in. He stepped aside and waited for her to leave, but her path was brusquely interrupted by the roaring departure of the director's Lambo. Spiller turned back to Sadie and shook his head, then gave her a salute as she drove past him. By this time, Virginia was striding toward him.

"Everything okay?" he said.

"I was just asking about his Bronco," she replied, smiling. "Apparently, it's a sensitive subject."

He followed her back to the range. "Stutz said he traded it for his laptop."

She chuckled. "Is that what he said?"

"Words to that effect."

"Hayley took a twelve-gauge to it. He tried to bust down her gates, so she shot up his car."

Spiller hooted at the mental image it conjured. "Bloody hell."

"How are you getting on with the scripts?"

They entered the office, and he settled behind the desk and picked up episode five. "So... let's see, Roger had trailed Jimmy to Malibu Beach to kill him."

Any lingering amusement vanished from her face. She nodded solemnly. "Okay. What do you think so far?"

"I think it's brilliant. Am I reading for the part of Paul? He's the only English character. I'm guessing that's why you texted me."

"Let's wait for Hayley, okay? Are you hungry?"

Spiller nodded. "I could do with a bite to eat. And a coffee, if that's okay."

"I'll grab something from the kitchen. You carry on reading. It would be great if you could finish before Hayley gets here."

"Virginia..."

She stopped at the door.

Spiller tapped the script. "What is this? Did you write this? It features a gun range, a Vietnam vet, and I'm assuming you're the Cassandra character, and Hayley's the actress."

"No. I'm not a writer. Hayley wrote it. Well, she wrote a novel, some years back. Twenty-thirteen, to be precise – when it's set. Mostly for herself. But... things have happened recently. So, now is the time. It needs to get out there. She turned the novel into a screenplay and... there you go."

"You didn't answer my question. Or maybe you did. Is this based on real events?"

"Wait for Hayley."

"How far along is this? Have you cast any oth—"

Virginia had put a finger to her lips. "Matthew, I could talk all day about this project, but Hayley needs to be here. We agreed we don't talk unless we're both in the same room. I've already said more than I wanted to. Oh, and we will need to have a conversation about *The Mel Banaghan Show*."

Spiller nodded. "Right."

Virginia gave him a look like he was a misbehaving kid who'd have to wait for his dad to get home to learn his fate. Then she left the office.

THE INTRUSION DETECTION alert was set close to the building, but JoBeth knew whatever had occurred would at least have logged an event on the hard drive. Despite having been away nearly three months, she doubted there would be that many to check. Perhaps the odd coyote skirting close to the fence. She accessed the security system in the panic room, rather than check on her cell, as the larger screen didn't strain her eyes. Assessing that the damage to the terrain was at least a few weeks old, she began on the day they left for their travels. It didn't take long to find the offending frames, a concentrated series of markers to show there had been a period of intense activity. She backed up to the primary event.

JoBeth gasped as the yellow sports car cartwheeled into view, landing upside down, before bursting into flames. Despite having seen the evidence of the scorched ground, she gasped again as the vehicle quickly became an inferno, committing whoever was behind the wheel to premature cremation. She paused the playback, then quickly switched off the monitor before the image could imprint itself in her mind. But it was too late. Some things you could never erase.

She wanted to tell Jack, to share as she always had done, but he wouldn't appreciate it, given his increasingly fragile state. Hopefully, the undergrowth would creep over the charred blemish before he noticed anything was wrong. And if he did spot it, she would pass it off as a brief brush fire sparked by a discarded piece of glass. By all accounts, the start of the LA summer they'd missed had been fiercely hot and tinder dry.

Based on the date of the incident, she performed a quick search to see if she could find out any more information. She imagined it would produce a few results – some rich kid taking a bend too fast in daddy's car.

"Oh, my…" JoBeth said, as the page showed her both national and international coverage of the death of the actor John Frears. She clicked on an Associated Press piece and read through it. She didn't know much about recent movies, but he seemed like a pretty big deal in the Hollywood pantheon. "How awful." She bookmarked the article, in case she ever wanted to show Jack.

SPILLER WAS READY with a big hug for Virginia when she returned to the office with Hayley. He had just finished the final episode and he now knew that Cassandra's dad, Vietnam veteran Roger, had been killed by rogue cop Jimmy on Malibu Beach. He opened his arms to her, and Virginia offered a faint smile and allowed him a brief embrace. Then he opened his arms to Hayley, because she'd briefly shared the bones of her past during his visit to The House of Sempiternal Love, and now he knew for sure she was the actress in the story, thus Jimmy was her ex, and these six episodes had just put some putrid flesh on those bones. Hayley, too, accepted his embrace, thanking him as they parted.

"Come through to the range," Virginia said, and led the way.

Three chairs were arranged to the rear of one of the firing booths, and on the firing table was a disassembled 9mm Beretta with a full magazine of fifteen rounds. Spiller glanced ten yards downrange at a hanging silhouette. The women took their seats and Virginia spoke again.

"Put it back together, fast as, and show me a tight grouping."

Spiller quickly reassembled the weapon, inserted the magazine, worked the slide, then took aim, sending every round through the target's face, grouped so closely that a large hole appeared that looked more like the result of a single 12-gauge slug. He set the Beretta down and turned to them. They acknowledged his marksmanship with unsmiling nods.

"Take a seat," Virginia said.

Spiller settled opposite them, but their impassive expressions gave him pause. "Did I pass?"

"Flying colors," Virginia said. "It's just… we don't like guns a whole lot."

Spiller laughed, but briefly; the women were deadpan. "Seriously? You own a gun range, and you took a shotgun to your ex-husband's Bronco, and you don't like guns?"

Hayley explained: "Given the world we live in, they're a necessary evil. Would I prefer a world without them? Damn right. But am I gonna shun them on principle and leave myself defenseless? Hell, no."

Virginia nodded. "And this is my dad's legacy. This is where I feel his presence the most. In due time, my son will decide for himself. His name's on the building, but it may not be for him. Do you want the part of Paul?"

"Of course," Spiller said. "It's a gift to an actor. The whole thing is. But…"

"What?" Virginia asked.

"If I'm honest, I don't like the ending. I don't mean how you wrote it. It's obviously a true story, so it is what it is, but… I'm not religious. Or even spiritual. I don't believe the whole thing about reincarnation. I just don't. I know you'd have plenty of actors jump at this because they love that final reveal – just the possibility of it – but that's not me."

Hayley scrutinized him. "You don't believe we come back? We meet the same souls? We have unfinished business?"

"No. This is why your place is called The House of Sempiternal Love, right? It's about reincarnation?"

"No one has to buy into it to stay there," Hayley said, a little defensively. "It's just what I believe. Are you saying you don't think we come back?"

Spiller considered his response. "I have no clue. Nothing makes me think we do. Your experience tells you different. I certainly hope we don't. Once and done; I'm good with that. The idea that I might have to do all this again genuinely horrifies me."

To his surprise, Hayley laughed. "Good."

"What?"

Virginia laid a hand on Hayley's. "We don't need you to believe, Matthew. If you did believe, okay, because you can act like you don't. What I find heartening is that you're not lying to us. You're standing your ground; you're being principled, even at the risk of losing the part. I'm glad you don't believe, because John never did."

Spiller frowned at the mention of a new name. "John?"

"My husband. The Paul character."

"Oh, okay. Do I get to meet him? I'd like to."

Virginia looked away, so Hayley answered. "Virginia's surname is Frears."

It took a moment for the cogs to mesh. "Oh, right. God, Virginia, I'm so sorry."

She looked back at him, her eyes glistening. "Thank you. Now you understand what's at stake with this project. Why we need to get it right. Why *you* need to be right."

He nodded. "I'm honored."

Virginia shook her head. "You're not; you're just right for the part. It's that simple. We never wanted anyone with a known face. Ideally, we'd want every actor in it to be unknown, to give it authenticity. We don't want the audience looking at a character and seeing an actor. This being Hollywood, if we want the movie to get anywhere, there will be famous faces involved. But yours doesn't need to be."

Spiller felt slightly aggrieved. "I am quite well known, you know."

"Not really," Hayley said. "People may know who you are, but your face is unrecognizable in that movie you just did. All that prosthetic makeup. It's perfect."

"Right. So… are you seeing other people for the role, or is it definitely mine?"

Virginia looked at Hayley, and they both agreed with a mutual nod.

"It's yours," Hayley said. "Although it very nearly wasn't. Up until ten days ago, the role was cast."

"What happened?" Spiller asked.

"Someone killed our leading man."

For the second time, Spiller laughed when he shouldn't have.

"You knew him," Hayley said. "Harry Sullivan. The guy was over the moon about it. His chance to shed twenty years of violent roles. Do something real, meaningful. He was in seventh heaven. He couldn't believe we'd broken him out of his pigeonhole."

"But why cast him if you wanted an unknown?"

The women looked at each other, both evidently perplexed.

Hayley shrugged. "He convinced us. He was very persuasive. Very…"

"Svengali?" Spiller said.

Virginia peered at him. "That has negative connotations."

"Yep."

"You worked with him once, right?"

"Straight out of drama school. Very charismatic, sure of himself. *Cocksure* is the word. And no great shakes as an actor. Next thing I know, he's made it to Hollywood. Huge mystery, until my agent told me about his family connections in this town. Nice bit of nepotism, but never a word to the masses. What a farce."

"Sounds like you weren't about to catch up over a beer and reminisce about the old days," Hayley said wryly.

Spiller shook his head. "He was an arsehole. When I knew him, anyway."

Virginia smiled. "Well, in the final analysis, looks like you beat him to the punch."

Hayley scowled. "Virginia, come on, the guy was just shot to death."

"Girl, you're the one who thinks shit happens for a reason."

Hayley had to laugh, and the brief tension between them dissipated. "Guess so."

"And Matthew did show up here without even being asked. That is definitely your department."

Hayley nodded. "Sure is."

"Where are you up to with this?" Spiller asked. "Have you cast anyone else?"

"We have a casting director on board," Hayley said. "She's working on all that. And we have a top director, so he's finalizing things with a big studio. It's already greenlit."

"Who's the director?"

The women exchanged reticent glances.

"I won't tell anyone," Spiller said.

"Put it this way," Hayley said. "He's big on Vietnam, so this kinda fits his remit, although he usually doesn't work in TV."

Spiller frowned, then the penny dropped. "*Oh*. Right. Nice. Are you sure he's going to be okay with you casting me? Directors normally want to sign off."

"I'm the one who'll cast my husband and my father," Virginia said. "I reserved that right. The rest is up to them."

Spiller glanced at Hayley, and thought he saw some discomfiture. "You're *both* okay with me? Hayley?"

"We're both concerned about your appearance on Mel Banaghan, I'll tell you that for free. Like I told you back at the house, I know Brett wasn't faking. Which means *you* weren't faking. Unless you just decided to go off-script to freak him out. Did you?"

Spiller shook his head.

"Then, whatever that was, it had better not be anything that can come back and bite us on the ass. If it does, we will sue *your* ass into oblivion. And this woman here? She'll throw you downrange and use you for target practice."

"Matthew," Virginia said, adopting a softer tone than her business partner, "my husband was a simple man – in the best possible way. He lived by a simple credo: you do right in this world. He was noble and honest. I don't want you to act that. I need you to *be* that."

Spiller stood up and went to stare downrange at the faceless target. The women allowed him time to think. For better or worse, he surmised it was time for a little candor. He turned back to them.

"Virginia, your husband was ex-military, right? French Foreign Legion?"

She nodded.

"And your dad was Special Forces?"

"MAC-Vee SOG. In-country January sixty-nine to March seventy-three."

"Four tours. He was a warrior."

"To his dying breath."

"So, they'll have both done things that perhaps didn't sit well with them. Violent acts, but for the greater good."

Virginia considered the fairness of his assertion. "Okay. What's your point?"

"I've done the same. But in a civilian setting." He watched their expressions intently, waiting for it to sink in.

"Brett knows?" Hayley asked after several seconds. "That's your beef with him?"

"He knows some of it. Listen, you want honesty, there it is."

Hayley laughed genuinely. "Man, you really don't care."

Spiller squatted down and picked up an empty nine mil shell casing. He straightened up and rolled it between his fingers, giving himself some time to order his thoughts. He resumed his seat.

"This is all rubbish. I don't mean your story or the movie. I mean Hollywood. For me, acting is just a fun way to occupy my time. I thought it would be so much more. I pursued this for years, and now I'm here… listen, it's better than being poor and driving a taxi, it's just… so *empty*."

"You need a bed at my place for a few months," Hayley said, still amused. "Although it normally takes folk decades to reach your enlightened viewpoint. Virginia, you still want this guy in our movie?"

She met Spiller's stare, then slowly nodded. "Oh, yeah. More than ever. John felt exactly the same about this town – you know that, Hayley." She looked at Spiller again. "John enjoyed the work, never courted the limelight beyond what the studios demanded contractually. He was happy to stay in the house I inherited from my dad. The only concession he made to being a movie star was that car he bought, and that was the death of him. I think John would have liked you."

Spiller nodded. "Yeah, I think we'd have got on."

"Having said all that… I can't have you destroy my husband's legacy, or Hayley's hard work on the script. So, you tell me Brett's squared away, I'll believe you, and the part's yours. Let me hear you say the words, Matthew."

He told them what he believed was the truth about Brett Stutz: "He's squared away."

Had either of them asked how else he might be compromised, he would have lied. He was lying by omission at that moment. His own agent was a far bigger threat; not to mention a certain Lieutenant with a grudge against him. But he would only have issues with the latter if the former decided to cause ructions, and he wasn't about to let that happen.

"What's it called, this series? Do you have a title?" he asked.

"I called my novel *Veteran Avenue*," Hayley replied. "I think that works."

Spiller nodded. "Definitely." He stood up, held out his hand, and sealed the deal.

"Do we contact your agent?" Hayley asked. "I assume you have one."

"No," Spiller said quickly. "I'm looking around. Can you deal directly with me for the moment?"

"Sure. We'll have something drawn up and we'll be in touch."

Heading back to his Maserati, the section of Spiller's brain devoted to plotting murders and evading police was sparking again. It had lain dormant since departing the UK, when he had engineered an implausible yet flawless conclusion to a series of crimes, leaving then-DCI Bartoli baffled and infuriated. Now, seemingly of its own volition, it was scheming anew, presenting him with a cavalcade of future events designed to remove the main impediment to his continued rise to stardom.

He couldn't let *Veteran Avenue* go to anyone else. A handshake wasn't legally binding. Even if it were, his prior illegality, should it come to light, would null and void it.

One way or another, the risk from Billy Banbury had to be defused. Squared away by a placating argument. Or rectangled away with a shovel.

## EIGHTEEN

UNUSUALLY, BILLY WAS at the house when Spiller returned with the gear he'd bought that would make his plan work. He left it all in the trunk of the Maserati, ready for tomorrow. He'd have to load another item into the trunk at some point, when Billy wasn't around to see.

The two actors, one contemporary and one archaic, chilled out in the air-conditioned living room for a while, chatting about nothing in particular, which was the very last thing they should have been discussing. Crucially, Billy was oblivious to the thespian skills being deployed against him. Spiller knew the nonchalance of his ex-agent was a charade, but had to believe that Billy was blind to the reciprocal mendacity of their conversation. If Noah had shared the nature of their encounter outside the elevator, Billy would have gone into hiding by now, or he'd be on a plane back home.

Although it would have taken a miracle to unmake Spiller's mind, he was so intrigued by Billy's duplicity that he couldn't hold back the most pertinent questions, and he suspected it would have seemed odder had he not asked.

"So, how's the agency coming along?" Spiller opened a cold Michelob and took a slurp.

"Oh, you know, still a few teething problems. I'll get there." Billy beamed at the certainty of his claim.

"I looked at your new website."

Billy didn't miss a beat. "Yes, love, I'm holding back on your profile. I meant to ask if you have an up-to-date publicity shot. I'd really like something that places you in Los Angeles. Perhaps with the ocean in the background, the odd palm tree? The one I have of you on my UK website is a good ten years old. Always useful if I'm looking to squeeze an actor down an age bracket, but I'm not certain if anyone would even recognize you from it."

Spiller nodded. "I'll sort something out. You know what? I was wondering if you wanted to take that pillion ride with me tomorrow. I'm assuming you're not far off moving out, with my family heading here soon. We might not get another opportunity. We could stop along the way; take some shots for your new website. How does that sound?"

"That sounds dandy, dear boy. I'll try and get back here for three o'clock. We could capture that wonderful afternoon light. Really make you *glow*."

Spiller raised his can. "Excellent."

Billy turned his gaze toward the pool area, and his chest visibly swelled with a deep breath, as though he felt he'd really arrived. Spiller watched the old man out of the corner of his eye, wondering what machinations that contented grin encompassed, more than the superficial joy of his late-life relocation. He almost felt sorry for him. To have so thoroughly reinvented himself, to have opened an unexpected final chapter in his life, only to now be willfully and needlessly — albeit unwittingly — tearing out the remaining bulk of those unwritten pages.

"Thanks, Billy."

"What for, pray?"

"Getting me this far."

Billy's sunny countenance flickered. It was barely perceptible, like a glitch in an otherwise seamless deep-fake video, but Spiller caught it, and his sorrow intensified. By his own volition, Billy had tipped into the precipice; there was no pulling him back, and he wouldn't know how much hurt was his until he hit the ground.

"You're most welcome," Billy said. "Any plans tonight?"

"Yes. I was hoping you could make yourself scarce, if that's not a problem."

Billy's eyes sparkled as he laughed. "Oh, I think Matthew has a date. Scarce, as in stay in my room, or…?"

"Scarcer than that," Spiller said. "Is that okay?"

"It's your house, love. I have someone I can go and stay with. Mind if I grab a quick shower first?"

"Help yourself."

Billy got up but dithered at the door. "Are you not going to ask who I'm staying with?"

"None of my business," Spiller replied, wondering if Billy was about to come clean on one thing, at least.

"I met a lovely woman in a coffee shop. Really hit it off. She's a few years younger than me, but we seem to have so much in common. I can't quite believe it."

In denial in more ways than one, Spiller thought. "I'm pleased for you, Billy."

Billy left the room, and Spiller stared at the laptop case Billy had left resting against his chair. When Spiller heard the shower running, he went for it.

It was a new machine, minimally set up, with no password protection and only a few files and folders. No deep dive required. A "CLIENTS" folder on the home screen, several folders within it, and one named "NOAH", with two files inside: the Texan's CV, and his contact details, including his home address. Spiller used his phone to take a picture of the information, triggering a notification that his storage was full. He checked his gallery, and his phone had managed to squeeze it in there, but he made a mental note, for the second time, to delete some recordings before the girls arrived so he could chronicle their visit. He powered off the laptop and returned it to its spot on the floor.

During the fifteen minutes it took for Billy to prepare for another Texas Hoe-Down, Spiller sat in silence, eyes closed, playing out the possible scenarios on the back of his eyelids. There was no perfect plan, and if there were, he supposed he'd used up his quota last Christmas. More worryingly, the ruse suggesting itself went far beyond what he had in mind for his agent the next day, and that wasn't even taking into account any unseen repercussions, which might be numerous. Yet... it was all irresistibly enticing; the excitement it would bring, the unpredictability that had made his last months in England equally terrifying and life-affirming.

"What's tickling you, Matthew?"

Spiller opened his eyes to his agent, standing in the doorway in his SoCal gear. "What?"

"You were smiling, dear boy. Were you daydreaming? Something fanciful, perchance?"

"Definitely. How are you enjoying the Camaro, Billy? Think you might splurge on one?"

Billy grinned at the prospect. "You know, I think I might. Unless you think it's too vulgar for someone my age."

Spiller raised his eyebrows. "You care what I think, Billy?"

"Of course. It *isn't* too vulgar, is it?"

"Everything's vulgar in this town, Billy. Who'd notice?"

"Are you all right, Matthew? You seem a little *off*."

"Do I?" Spiller stood up with his beer. He smiled at his agent. "Can't imagine why. Give my regards to your lady friend. What's her name?"

"Oh... yes... Noreen."

"Good for you." Spiller clapped Billy on the shoulder as he passed him and headed upstairs. In his bedroom, he fired up his laptop and used an encrypted browser to anonymously scout around a map of Los Angeles and its environs. He switched to the terrain layer, immediately scrolling to the north of the city, beyond the forests, and into the desert.

Five minutes later, after much zooming in and out, searching for the ideal location, he spotted it. Along Highway 395, north-east of Edwards Airforce Base. Ten miles beyond Kramer Junction, a left turn onto a cracked concrete road, then a mile-and-a-half deeper into the middle of nowhere. A dead-end building on a hillock. The image was grainy at its closest magnification, its purpose initially unclear. But a couple of related photos identified it as an abandoned USAF radio facility. Many miles from the nearest town, many years beyond its heyday, and no reason for anyone to visit, unless for nefarious purposes.

THE SUN WAS dipping just as Spiller heard the roar of Sadie's huge SUV pulling onto his drive. She was just in time to yank his mood back up from beyond the horizon. He pushed out of his pool lounger and headed for the side gate, catching her just as her finger was reaching for the front doorbell.

"What's this?" she asked. "You bringing me in the chauffeur's entrance?"

Spiller laughed. "VIP, more like." He stared at her ride. "I do like that car. You've got to tell me how you managed it."

"A kindly old benefactor."

He held the gate open, then closed it behind her, taking the opportunity to ogle some fine denim contours. "Wow, look at you," he said, vocalizing his interior thoughts.

Sadie turned and faced him. "Thank you."

He read the message on her t-shirt: I WILL NOT COMPLY. Then he realized he appeared to be staring at her breasts. "Sorry, just… uh… that's not aimed at me, is it?"

"I wouldn't be here if it was," she said, perching on a pool chair. "You got some hard liquor?"

"Vodka, tequila, bourbon."

"Bourbon, ice. Thank you. Make it a large one."

"How are you going to drive home?" he asked.

"Who says I'm going home?"

"Oh, okay." He laughed and went to the pool bar to grab the bottle and some cubes from the fridge. "Tell me about the car," he said, while he fixed her drink.

"You know Theo Montgomery?"

Spiller paused. "Really? He just gave you a car?"

"He wanted to help."

He conjured a disbelieving expression and nodded. *"Riiiiiight."*

She laughed as she received her drink. "You know how I know he's legit?"

"Do tell," he said, as he went to grab a beer from the cooler.

"Doesn't matter," she said, and her glass clinked as she took a sip.

"Go on," Spiller said, sitting down.

"You'll think I'm nuts."

"Yeah, that would be a damning indictment, coming from me, right?"

Sadie took another sip. "What the hell. If we're gonna get to know each other, you should know who I am. I see auras."

Spiller felt his eyes narrow, which wasn't the best reaction. "Auras?"

"Since I can remember. When I was a kid, I thought everyone saw them. Never occurred to me it might be unusual. Until I told my mom, and she told me to keep it to myself, it might freak people out. You freaked out, Matt?"

"No. I might be if I believed in that stuff."

"You know you're saying you think I'm a liar?" She smiled and drained her glass. "It's okay, I'm used to it."

"Sadie, I'm sure you see something, but... *auras?* The colors that tell you what a person's like? Sorry, I just think... if you could, you wouldn't be here now."

She went to help herself to another drink. "I can control them. I see them if I summon them; not unless."

"You haven't seen mine?" he asked.

"Sure I've seen yours. That first night." She smirked at the recollection. "It was like a kaleidoscope. I can't make you out."

Spiller made an evil face. "Bit of a risk you coming here."

"Dude, I could kick your Limey ass in a heartbeat."

"I don't doubt that for one second."

"Tell you what," Sadie said. "You turn away so I can't see your expression, then I want you to conjure some emotions. Let's say anger, love, happiness, and sadness. This may not work, but you're an actor so you should be in touch with your emotions. In no particular order, I want you to conjure a memory, or a thought linked to each emotion. I'm gonna see what colors I see, in which order, then I'll tell you what you were thinking."

Spiller shrugged. "Cool party game." He turned his back and instantly thought of his kids for a few moments. He dispelled their images and switched to the fury he harbored against his agent's duplicitous plans. Then he thought of his ex-wife, and the loss of her to another man. Finally, he tried to think of something happy, but he couldn't, so he pictured Sadie naked instead, and making love to her next to the pool. He shook his head to reset his mind, took a swig of beer, and turned around.

Sadie's expression was full of wisdom. "Okay. First, love, but some sadness, too, I think. Then hatred, anger, but still some sadness. Next, even more sadness, but also something bitter in there. Jealousy? Lastly… let's see how the evening goes, huh?" She winked at him.

Spiller felt his mouth had dropped open, so he shut it.

"How'd I do?" she asked.

"Not too shabby."

"So, what have you got in store for me tonight? Apart from the obvious."

Spiller felt a little flummoxed. "Honestly? I wouldn't mind stealing a car."

Sadie set her drink on the concrete. "Then I probably shouldn't drink any more. Any car, or you have a specific one in mind?"

Spiller pointed to the healing scar down his nose. "The guy who did this to me."

"Okay. Did you deserve it?"

"Wow, what a question. I mean, when have you ever seen me confrontational?"

"Yeah, right. Did you?"

Spiller conveniently managed to photoshop the baseball bat out of his mental tableau of that day. "No."

"Then it's fair payback and I'm down with that. You know how to boost a ride?"

"Not really. Tie some wires together, according to the movies."

"Uh-huh. I do. What's he drive?"

"An old truck. Nothing like yours. No new tech to bypass. Just…"

"A few wires." She stood up. "Make and model?"

"Ford F150, I think."

"You know where he lives?"

"Oakwood, near Venice Beach."

She appeared to mull it over for a few seconds. "Okay. I drive us down to Westwood. We take a cab to Venice Beach, and we walk from there, so we don't leave a trail. What happens to the truck once we got it?"

"Park it somewhere for a few days. I may have some sneaky plans for it. Sadie, you can't want to do this. You could get in a lot of trouble."

She thought about it for a moment. "I could. But you know that story you told me about how bored you were driving a cab? So bored that you'd make up stories about being in the military?"

He stared into the hole in the top of his can.

"Right. So, imagine having genuinely *been* in the military."

"Boredom. It's a killer, right?"

"Nothing worse." She smiled mischievously. "You got baseball hats, gloves?"

## NINETEEN

HOLLYWOOD WAS A cesspool, and Theo Montgomery knew that as well as anyone. He'd been there long enough to have seen behind the veil. He'd seen the good fail and the evil prosper, and he knew that the inner cabal that pulled the strings favored the weak and the worthless, because they were easier to manipulate. In some ways, his draft year in Vietnam in 1970 had primed him for Hollywood. You couldn't always tell who the enemy was, and by the time it became clear, it was often too late to mount a defense. He had steadily fallen out of favor over the past fifteen years, and he wasn't certain why that was. It wasn't his age. Some of his contemporaries were still working consistently. He wondered if the cabal had grown tired of his still-frequent public rants against the industry and had decided to commit him to obsolescence.

He sat in his wicker chair and sipped at his scotch, his eyes wandering randomly around a view he'd known so long he could have painted it with his eyes shut. The ornate tiered fountain with its original Spanish tiles, the palm trees, the pines, the acacias, the pink trumpet tree that would bloom in late winter and would always make him smile. He closed his eyes. The scents and the sounds.

Yet, even with his eyes shut, he sensed a sudden change in his vision. A bright red flash that lit one eyelid, then the other. So bright that he feared to open his eyes. Then nothing. For several seconds, nothing, and he mused whether it might have been the precursor to a brain event, a mortal triggering, like an emergency flare going off in some dying part of his head. Perhaps he'd start to smell something burning next, and then he'd fall out of his chair and never regain his feet.

More red light dancing across his eyelids, and this time Theo sensed it was outside his head, not inside, and he figured he knew what it was. Oddly, he waited for it to stop, then opened his eyes and searched beyond the railings of his front lawn, until a tiny spot of red traced up his right arm and across onto his chest, where it jiggled over his heart for a few seconds.

The desire to throw himself on the floor was impeded by his ageing body. So, he moved as quickly as he safely could, vacating his chair and heading for the front door. The wicker took a hit as a shot rang out, then a brick just behind his fleeing form, then the front door as he pushed it open and escaped inside.

Theo hurried up to his bedroom and armed himself with the old .357 Python he kept in his bedside cabinet. He waited for a few seconds, barrel pointed at the open door, but no one tried to break in downstairs, so he relaxed a little and grabbed his bedside phone.

BARTOLI WAS FIVE minutes out from his meeting with Captain Hoyt of Valley Bureau's Mission Division. He had established it had to be off book, so Hoyt had given him the address of a coffee shop near the station. As much as you could read any stranger over the phone, Bartoli had gleaned a pricking of Hoyt's ears at the mention of the name Gabriela Contreras.

Now he was looping off the 405 north at Ronald Reagan Freeway, and back on heading south toward his side of the hills again, activating his windshield lights and calling Hoyt to apologize for the inconvenience. Although he had clocked off for the day, and there were other detectives who could handle the call, Bartoli wanted to be there. Another attack on a Hollywood actor? Okay, it didn't fit the MO of the others, given Theo Montgomery's age, but he certainly had the reputation as a tough guy back in the day.

He left the 405 at Sepulveda Canyon and took Sunset the two miles to Riviera.

SPILLER WATCHED FROM a hundred yards down the road as Sadie walked nonchalantly up to the truck and made entry and drove off in no more time than if she'd had a legitimate key. She'd earlier taken a wire coat hanger from his closet, but he couldn't see if she'd used it. In the few seconds it took for her to arrive at his spot and pick him up, Spiller kept his eye on the sidewalk next to the space that had just been filled by a Ford F150, expecting the appearance of an angry Texan, but Noah was apparently otherwise engaged.

Sadie took it easy to avoid attracting attention. The plan had been to dump the vehicle as quickly as possible on a residential road to minimize the risk, but Spiller felt she was cruising around on the lookout for something.

"Where are we heading?" he asked.

Sadie lifted one finger off the steering wheel – *shut up* – and he felt like a kid who'd been reprimanded by a teacher. Shortly, she pulled over, kept the engine running, and jumped out with a screwdriver. Spiller watched her run across to a tan-colored Ford F150 and deftly remove its license plates.

Behind the wheel and moving again, she said, "Texas plates – dead giveaway. Need them to be local, and these got the same holes."

"Impressive."

After that, Sadie picked a specific route through the neighborhood, finally choosing a quiet residential road that abutted Marine Park. She stopped the Ford, disconnected her makeshift ignition, and left the wires dangling for future use. As she swapped the truck's plates, Spiller decided to check the glove compartment. Among the detritus was a battered service-book wallet, but as he shifted it aside, he noticed it was weightier than expected.

"Ha! Well, happy birthday to me."

The semi-automatic hiding inside the wallet was a 9mm Smith & Wesson M&P M2.0. It had a slightly extended barrel, with a knurled cap that unscrewed to reveal a thread to take a suppressor. Spiller dropped the mag and found it fully stacked. He thought about the other day, when he'd received a headbutt, and now thought he'd been very lucky. His decision to take the gun was split-second. It was in his inside pocket a heartbeat before Sadie tapped on his window. He knew her moral compass was off, but he didn't know by how much.

He hopped out to find her balling the Texan flag sticker she'd removed from the rear bumper. They left the driver's door unlocked. Then they were walking away, and Sadie chucked the sticker and linked his arm like they were just a couple of sweethearts out for an evening stroll.

They trekked a mile in a straight line to end up at Venice Beach. They moved quickly in silence, the threat of discovery too weighty to allow chit-chat. They were walking in Los Angeles. That alone was nearly a crime, and certainly grounds for suspicion. As for the crime they had committed, Spiller guessed that Sadie saw it as a misdemeanor – which it would be as a first offense – and he felt bad that he'd quietly bumped it up to a felony with his possession of an illegal firearm.

When they joined the safety and anonymity of the crowds on the boardwalk, heading up the coast toward Santa Monica, the relief was palpable, and they simultaneously burst out laughing.

"That was insane," Sadie said when she calmed down.

"You've never done something like that before?"

"No way."

"Are you any less bored?" he asked.

She stopped walking, and her amusement subsided. "You know what? No. How can that be?"

"Because you're so skilled. If you're looking for excitement, you need to cock things up. If you'd left it to me, we'd be in the middle of a car chase by now, because I'd have completely bolloxed the whole thing."

Sadie laughed. "This is why I came to your house tonight. I love that you can't get your shit together and you're so open about it. You're so funny."

"Oh. And there was me thinking I was just too—"

*Sexy to resist* is what Spiller would have said, had Sadie not kissed him like he couldn't recall being kissed before. Then she was dragging him across the sand toward a lifeguard hut near the water, like she was parched and craving a desert oasis. He removed his jacket on the way so she wouldn't feel that particular bulge.

It was all a bit of a fumble, his trousers pulled down to his thighs, one leg of her jeans yanked off her foot to allow a spread. All the while, a passion of lips, like first-time teenagers. The ocean side of the hut, against the ramp, but still vaguely visible to anyone who cared to offer scrutiny. The waves drowned out their sounds, which were unbridled. Spiller thrust into Sadie and timed himself to match the impending zenith of her lust.

As Sadie dried herself with his t-shirt, Spiller wondered if she'd now go cold on him. It made him sad to think she might. He watched as she pulled on her jeans and her discarded trainer, making herself decent.

She held out his t-shirt. "You want this?"

"Definitely. I'll need something to remind me I didn't just dream this."

"What? You think this won't happen again?" She leaned in and kissed him. "Are you nuts? You just wait until I get you back to your house."

"Bloody hell, I'm getting another stiffy already."

Sadie laughed, dropping his shirt on the sand. Spiller picked up his jacket but just held it by his side, feeling the weight of the Smith in the pocket.

Back on the boardwalk, they held hands as they walked. Spiller wanted to tell Sadie he loved her, because that's how he felt. Perhaps it was true. He'd always been prey to his emotions. But the years had made him wise enough to keep his counsel.

"Oh!" Sadie said suddenly. "How did things go at the range today? You said you might be up for a part?"

"Actually, I got it."

"Hey, that's awesome. Would I approve?"

"You mean, is it just a load of blood and death? No. I think you'd love it."

So, Spiller proceeded to recount the storyline of *Veteran Avenue*, finding he was even more enthusiastic about the project than he'd realized, therefore even keener to make sure Billy didn't ruin it. Sadie listened, asking no questions until the end.

"The role of Roger, the Vietnam veteran. Is it cast?"

"I don't think so."

"Do you think you'd have any sway in the casting?" she asked.

"Sway? I doubt it. Could I make a suggestion? Of course. Why?"

"Can we grab a cab now? I need to pick up my car, take you to see someone."

"Who?"

"Theo Montgomery."

Spiller stopped walking. "Gosh, he'd be brilliant. But... tonight? Can't it wait? I was looking forward to getting back and... you know. Plus, I need a top."

Sadie broke hand contact. She approached a street vendor and bought an oversized t-shirt from him.

"Here you go," she said, handing it to Spiller. "Can we go and see Theo now? I can't wait to tell him. He said he wants a swan song. This must be it. Listen, come to Theo's now, and I guarantee you won't sleep a wink tonight. Deal?"

Spiller laid his jacket carefully on the concrete and put on his new shirt. "Sure. Let's go."

THE EMERGENCY SERVICES lightshow was visible from a distance. Sadie slowed the Escalade ten yards short of an outer cordon, which was twenty yards down from an inner one, set around Theo Montgomery's home. It was clear from the plethora of police vehicles that this wasn't just an innocent medical emergency.

"That's not good," Sadie said. She pulled into the curb and got out, and Spiller followed suit. She approached the nearest officer, standing just beyond the tape. "What happened? Is Theo okay?"

The young patrolman gave a perfunctory smile. "I can't divulge any information."

"I know that's his house. I'm just asking if he's okay."

The officer looked away, lost his smile.

"I'm a friend," Sadie said.

"Then you're not family."

Spiller stepped in. "We have pertinent information."

"Really?" said the officer.

"Yep. Officer..." Spiller glanced down at the name tag "...Voylan. Should we get back in our vehicle and drive away? We can do that.

But then we'd have to tell Lieutenant Bartoli that an Officer Voylan shooed us away when we wanted to help."

"Uh…"

But Spiller had spotted a familiar figure in the distance. "Never mind. *Angelo! Detective Angelo Bartoli!*"

Bartoli heard his name and stopped talking to an EMT. He looked around and spotted Spiller, who was now waving his arms in the air like he was directing a taxiing airplane. Bartoli's head bowed, then gave a weary shake, before he began trudging toward them.

"What are you doing here, Matthew?" He lifted the cordon and dipped under it onto the civilian side, then walked away from the officer to get out of earshot. Spiller and Sadie followed, and they formed a huddle next to the Escalade.

Spiller indicated Sadie. "My friend here knows Theo Montgomery. She wanted to swing by to tell him about an acting role I may have for him."

"Is Theo okay?" Sadie asked. "Please tell me."

Bartoli scrutinized her for a moment. "You were in the military, right?"

"How the hell would you know that?"

"Oh, I know all about you, Sadie Woods. You are Sadie Woods?"

Nonplussed, she nodded.

"Yeah," Bartoli said. "The last person to see Aiden Powers alive."

"So what? Just tell me if Theo's okay."

"He's okay. Shaken, but unscathed."

"Thank God. What happened?"

"Someone took a few pot-shots at him. You know your way around a gun, right?"

"Fuckin-A. So, if he's still alive, you can bet your ass I wasn't the one pulled the trigger. I shoot at something, it dies."

Bartoli narrowed his eyes. "Did I say you pulled the trigger?"

"You inferred it. And why mention Aiden Powers? What? You think I killed Aiden Powers?"

Bartoli laughed. "Well… here's my situation. Standing in front of me, I have you, the last person to see Aiden Powers alive, and I have

Matthew Spiller, who's a suspect in the murder of Harry Sullivan. And who just had a very public falling out with Brett Stutz, who used to be married to Hayley Olsen, who was best friends with John Frears, who also recently died. Now here you *both* are, *together*, outside the house of a fourth tough-guy actor who someone just tried to kill. Listen, I've only been a detective for twenty-five years, so please do point out if I'm just clutching at straws here."

It was Sadie's turn to laugh; a contemptuous sound. "Sure, I'm that dumb that I'm gonna return to the scene of the crime the same night."

"People do. It's a known thing with perps. Like an arsonist sticking around to watch a building burn."

"Well, that's not me. And why would I want Theo dead? He just bought me this SUV."

"I know; he told me. Maybe you didn't wanna pay him back."

"It was a gift. And I'm sure he told you that, too. Go look for any paperwork; see if it says anything about a repayment plan. Jesus, he even offered to buy me another."

"You own a gun?" Bartoli asked.

"No. I own *guns*. Plural. I work security, close protection."

"You packing right now?"

Sadie scoffed, looked down at her tight-fitting t-shirt and jeans, then slowly turned around on the spot. "Where? You see me bulging in the wrong place, Detective?"

"What about you, Matthew?" Bartoli asked. "I know from back in England that *you* like guns."

Spiller, who had an illegal semi-auto wrapped inside his jacket in the passenger footwell of the Escalade, not five feet away, tried to deflect with a smile. "Allegedly."

The two men locked eyes. Spiller hoped Bartoli wouldn't want to come up empty once again, as he had done so many times, so wouldn't check inside the car to spare himself any further embarrassment.

Bartoli acquiesced with a nod. "Okay. Where have you been this evening?"

Sadie spoke first. "I've been with him."

"And I've been with her," Spiller said.

Bartoli laughed again. "Well, those are the worst alibis since Bonnie and Clyde. I meant specifically where?"

"We took a walk along Venice Beach," Sadie said.

Bartoli looked doubtful.

"I can prove we were just there," she said.

"How?"

"Because next to one of the lifeguard huts there's a t-shirt soaked in our juices. If you hurry, you might find it's still damp. You have forensics, right?"

Spiller sniggered.

Bartoli stared at him, then her. "You two are sick puppies. You know that fucking on a public beach is a crime?"

Spiller looked at Sadie. "I didn't know that."

"Me, neither."

Bartoli growled. "Christ…"

"Can I talk to Theo?" Sadie asked.

"No. See that circus going on down there? That's what we call an active crime scene."

Sadie went to the car to retrieve her cell, and made a call from the open door. "Theo? It's Sadie. Are you okay?" She made a face at Bartoli as she listened. "I'm so relieved. Theo, we're outside up the street. Do you need any help? Someone to talk to? I'm here with a friend. Only, this detective we're talking to won't let us in."

All the while, Spiller watched Bartoli sending her waves of disgruntlement, and he smiled to himself when he thought she could probably genuinely see them.

"Hold on," Sadie said, "let me put you on speaker." She tapped the screen.

"Detective, this is my house!" Theo barked. "If I want visitors, that's my goddamned business!"

Bartoli stepped closer and put his face to the cell. "Your house is a crime scene, Mr Montgomery."

"My front lawn is a crime scene. No one got in my house. If they had, I'd have popped a cap in their ass. Let Sadie and her friend through or I'll come to them, and I'll be sure to walk right through every yellow marker you got laid out."

"Right."

Sadie ended the call, and Bartoli marched to the cordon, lifting it high for Theo's guests.

As Bartoli walked ahead a few paces, Sadie lowered her voice. "Matt, you're a suspect in the Harry Sullivan case?"

"I knew him years back. That's it, really." Then something dawned. "Or it was until…"

"What?"

He stopped walking.

"Matt, what?"

"The part I just got in *Veteran Avenue?* That was Harry Sullivan's until someone killed him."

"Jesus, Matt. Talk about motive. Was that common knowledge?"

"I'm guessing a few people would have known."

"Did you?"

*"Really?"*

Up ahead, Bartoli reached the house and turned around, beckoning them impatiently.

"Matt, I'm only asking what that guy's gonna ask when he finds out. I'm guessing he's lead on the Sullivan case?"

"He is. But I know him from before. Back in England, when he was a detective over there. It's that stuff I mentioned. All the Brett Stutz business that kicked off on *The Mel Banaghan Show.*"

"So, *did* anyone else know?"

"About?"

"This new series of yours."

"As far as I'm aware, nothing's out there. They've kept the whole project very quiet."

A shrill whistle called for their attention. Outside Theo's front gates, Bartoli stood with his hands on his belt, revealing his sidearm like a lawman in a Western movie. They hurried along to join him.

THE CONVERSATION TOOK place in Theo's expansive bedroom, which retained its original 1930s features. Theo propped himself against a bank of pillows, while Spiller and Sadie perched either side of the bed. Militarily, it seemed the safest spot for a debrief. Second floor, center of the room, away from the windows, shutters closed, lights low. Theo's .357 was on the bedside table within easy reach.

Theo recounted the evening's events – all fifteen seconds of it – and unprompted by Spiller, made his own connection to the recent deaths of three Hollywood tough guys. Except, his time as a tough guy was decades past, and the violent content of those movies couldn't hold a candle to the viciousness that lit every frame of their contemporary equivalents. Yesteryear's X-rated was today's PG-13. Perhaps it was a warning, Theo mused. Don't turn today's NC-17 into tomorrow's PG-13. Whoever was doing the killing, maybe they blamed his generation for starting the rot. He guessed it was a fair accusation, although Sadie tried her best to dissuade him of that notion.

Spiller still found it strange to be rubbing shoulders with people he'd seen in movies when he was a struggling actor with no realistic hope of ever joining them, but this was next-level. Theo Montgomery. *The* Theo Montgomery. Thankfully, the elder statesman was sufficiently self-effacing that Spiller felt at ease very quickly. Then he realized he was the one with the status, being the latest talk of the town, and with the potential clout to resurrect the old guy's career with the gift of a role that only came around once in a lifetime, and so very rarely at Theo's time of life.

After providing a brief description of his time in the States, and his prior struggles in the profession, Spiller got to the point, and began to relate the tale of *Veteran Avenue* – as best he could, having only read it once. But there was enough substance that Theo was practically salivating at the thought of portraying Virginia's father.

"Thank you, Sadie, for bringing this to my door," Theo said, when the story was done.

"Least I can do."

"So, Matthew, could you arrange for me to meet Virginia and Hayley?"

"I can only ask, Theo. I know Virginia's adamant that she's the one to cast her husband and father, so it's all down to her. But I can definitely see you in the role. You're about the right age, you're an amazing actor, and you have great presence."

"Thank you. And I was in Vietnam. Just a year. Just a regular grunt, unlike Virginia's pop, but that's gotta count for something, right?"

Spiller offered an encouraging smile. "I'd say so."

Theo grinned and settled back on his pillows. "This just might be the perfect end to an awful day."

"Are you sure you're okay, Theo?" Sadie asked. "Do you need anything to sleep?"

"I may have a bottle of something somewhere." He winked, then tapped his .357. "And this little baby is going *everywhere* with me from now on."

"You need me to stick around?"

Theo considered, then declined, but Spiller could see a thought process ticking away that made him frown.

"What is it, Theo?" Spiller asked. "You look puzzled."

"I don't know... like I said to the detective, the more I think about it, the more I don't think anyone was even trying to kill me."

"Why would you say that?" Sadie asked.

"I was a sitting duck. I was out there, just chilling, fifteen yards between me and the street. Someone had a bead on me for several seconds that I could count. I'm talking laser sighting. Plenty of time to get a shot on target. In fact, they could have emptied a whole magazine into my ancient ass. But they only began to shoot when I moved. And no rapid fire. Just three shots. All where I'd been, not where I was going. It doesn't make sense. Why would someone *pretend* to want me dead?"

No one knew the answer, but Spiller guessed it wasn't the worst question to be stumped on. "I suppose it's better than not knowing why someone *does* want you dead."

Theo laughed. "You look on the bright side. I like that."

"That's the first time anyone's accused me of being an optimist."

"How did you make it to Hollywood in your forties if you're not an optimist?"

"I just kept going."

"Are you shocked you made it?"

Spiller had to think. "Now I'm here, not really. It almost feels destined, like this was mine, no matter what I did."

"Did you make this happen, or did it fall in your lap?" Theo asked. "Your new movie. *Man on a Murder Cycle*. How'd that happen?"

Spiller shrugged. "I went to see my acting agent. I'd not seen him in over two years. He told me Brett Stutz was flying in, and did I want to pick him up from the airport. I'd been driving a cab for years."

"Then you did make it happen. Something kicked your ass to go see your agent after two years, and here you are, a Hollywood actor."

Spiller wasn't sure how to respond, and didn't want an argument, so just shrugged again.

"How do you two know each other?" Theo asked.

Spiller deferred to Sadie with his silence.

"I took Matt to the show the other night. *The Mel Banaghan Show*."

"Heard you caused a bit of a stir that night," Theo said to Spiller.

"You didn't see?"

"Nah. Hate him. And he was talking to Brett Stutz. Especially hate that guy. You, uh… you two together, then?"

Spiller looked to Sadie for guidance.

"Early days," she said.

"You got no family, Matt?"

Spiller smiled at the clear nod to his possible infidelity. "Wife and kids in England."

Theo gave Sadie a look, like a disapproving father.

"We're separated," Spiller said. "In fact, my next-door-neighbor has now moved in with my family, so I'd say all bets are off. I'm a free agent. I'm not looking to deceive anyone." He glanced at Sadie.

"And your kids?" Theo said. "You keep in touch?"

"Yes."

"Good. You should. Too easy to drift apart, then… you can find it's too late to catch up."

"Theo?" Sadie said.

"I fell out with my son over something and nothing. He dug his heels in. I always assumed we'd make up when the time was right, so I never made much of an effort to patch it up. Then he died. How old are your kids, Matthew?"

"My daughters are seven and eighteen. Sorry about your son."

"Thank you. It was a long time ago. You move on, but the hurt never goes away. Unless you've lost a child, you can't know what it's like. That's why you need to cherish your time with them."

"I do know what it's like – to lose my whole family, actually," Spiller said.

Both his listeners frowned at him.

"A police officer came to my house and told me they'd all died in a fire."

"Jesus, how could they make a mistake like that?" Sadie asked.

Spiller shook his head. "No mistake. He was lying. It's a long story, and not one I'm about to share tonight, but I spent around three hours thinking I'd lost them all."

Sadie was peering at him. "It wasn't..."

*Bartoli*, she meant. Spiller shook his head.

"Sounds like you got some serious history," Theo said to him.

"Like you wouldn't believe."

"Could you make the call now?" Theo asked. "About the role?"

"Now? Uh... sure." He took out his cell, grateful for the change in topic.

"Let me hear," Theo urged, before the call was answered.

Spiller hit the speaker button, and Hayley's voice came through.

"Hey, Matt, don't worry, everything's in hand. We'll hook up tomorrow so you can sign."

He laughed. "Hi, Hayley. Thanks so much. Listen, can I run something by you? Actually, can we loop Virginia in somehow? Like a conference call?"

"Virginia's with me. Go ahead."

"Hi, Matthew!" Virginia shouted.

"Hi, Virginia." Spiller looked at Theo's expectant face and smiled. "Okay. The role of Roger. You're still looking for an actor, right?"

"Go on," Virginia said.

Spiller took a deliberately dramatic pause. "Theo Montgomery," he said, and left it there.

Ten seconds of silence. Spiller imagined the women letting the name fill their heads with images of Theo inhabiting the role, moving in character through various scenes.

Finally, Virginia spoke. "Wow. That's genius. He'd be perfect. But... is he still acting? I've barely seen him in anything for years."

Theo beckoned for the phone, and Spiller handed it over.

"Ladies, good evening, this is Theo Montgomery. I am still acting – when someone throws me a crumb. Matthew told me you have a wonderful script, and from what I've heard, I'd be honored to be considered."

Virginia spoke again, and the pleasure in her voice was apparent. "Hello, Theo. Lovely to talk to you. Listen, let's all meet up tomo—"

The line went quiet, then some background noise could be heard, and Spiller reckoned it sounded like a TV news channel suddenly taken off mute. They waited.

After thirty seconds, the TV in the background fell quiet, and Hayley spoke. "Theo, we're watching the news, and we're looking at the outside of your house and a lot of police activity. Did someone just try to kill you?"

Spiller silently waved his arms at Theo and mouthed *no*.

"No, someone just tried to break in. Couple of shots were fired. I'm okay. It's all good."

Inwardly, Spiller was cringing. They'd already lost Harry Sullivan to deadly gunfire; how keen would they be to employ another actor who might still have a target on his back?

They waited.

"Okay, Theo," Virginia said eventually, "how about we all meet up tomorrow? Say one o'clock? I'll let Matthew know where."

"Thank you," Theo said. "I look forward to meeting the both of you." He tapped to end the call before they could change their minds.

He looked at Spiller. "How did that go? I can't tell. Was that a brush off? Is she genuine?"

Spiller nodded. "She is genuine. But we'd better make damn sure you look like you're well protected tomorrow. Sadie? You want to come along? Bring some hardware?"

"Sure. Happy to."

Spiller watched a smile creep onto Theo's face, and his eyes shift to a framed picture of his wife on his bedside table, next to the .357. He smiled at her image.

"Just this one last time," he said to her. "Then I'm coming."

## TWENTY

TOO MANY THINGS were about to happen in a single day. To cope with it all, Spiller should have had a good night's sleep. Yet, after finally nodding off for an hour at five a.m., Sadie was climbing on top of him again at six to take advantage of some morning wood. There were worse ways to start the day.

Afterwards, he made a pot of coffee and told Sadie he had a busy morning ahead with a couple of interviews for his new movie. In truth, that was tomorrow, but he needed all his morning hours free if he wanted to accomplish all that he had planned, and especially if he wanted to meet Hayley, Virginia, and Theo at one o'clock. Sadie said she would await his call, so she could tag along as the hired gun.

As soon as he was alone, Spiller went up to his closet and manhandled Manny downstairs and into the garage. He opened the trunk of the Maserati and removed one half of the items he'd purchased the day before, setting them on the floor beside the Hayabusa. He crumpled Manny into the boot next to the remaining gear, dug out a couple of luggage straps and some lengthy cable ties, and threw those in as well. It was a tight fit, but Manny wasn't about to complain; he'd been through much worse during filming. Spiller closed the trunk and began to think it through. Ordinarily, he would have worked out the permutations overnight, but he'd been pleasantly distracted and unable to grab a spell of time sufficient to complete his plotting.

First on his to-do list was to remove the Maserati's tracking device. It was an aftermarket box, battery-powered, and therefore easy to take out of the car. He also removed the dashcam, which had similar GPS capabilities. He'd also need to remember to leave his cell at the house, so its location couldn't be traced later.

Back in his bedroom, he brought up his intended destination on the encrypted browser and committed the route to memory. He went downstairs and boosted himself with more coffee, draining the pot, then returned to the garage, fired up the Maserati, and set off for the desert. It was 7 a.m.

UNBEKNOWN TO EITHER men, Lieutenant Bartoli was only a hundred or so vehicles ahead of his nemesis, Matthew Spiller, traveling north on the 405. Having curtailed his meeting with Captain Hoyt the night before, they had rearranged. Hoyt had sent a terse message to meet him at 7.30 a.m. at the Seven-Eleven at the gas station just off the freeway in Mission Hills. Bartoli got the impression Hoyt was a little miffed about last night, considering he'd already been waiting at the coffee shop. As Bartoli veered down the off-ramp, a stone's throw from the Community Police Station, Spiller carried on through the neighborhood, heading for the I-5 and State Highway 14.

Bartoli spotted the police Ford Interceptor Utility parked on the street and pulled in behind. He got out of the Impala and approached, tapping on the passenger window and holding up his ID to verify who he was. Hoyt invited him in.

The engine was idling, powering the air-con. Hoyt was in uniform, pale and scrawny-thin, like there was something wrong with him. Perhaps an overactive thyroid, maybe something far worse.

"Captain, thanks for agreeing to meet me; sorry about last night."

"Someone tried to off Theo Montgomery, right?" Hoyt said. "Saw it on the news."

Bartoli smiled. "I got my hands full right now."

"Gabriela Contreras," Hoyt said, getting to the point.

"Yeah, what can you tell me about her?"

"The fact you're here says you got something to tell *me*, Detective."

"Ah… it's not something I can really talk about. It's delicate."

"You get in her pants yet?"

Bartoli recoiled slightly. "Whoa. No, I did not. I'm concerned for a colleague whose behavior is a little erratic, is all."

"Then report it."

"You could have advised me of that over the phone, Captain Hoyt. I'd like to help her, not wreck her career. If I'm gonna do that, I need to know what I'm dealing with."

"Okay. You know her kid died?"

"Two years ago."

"And the guy who killed him? What do you know about him?"

"Another police officer. Old-timer."

"She tell you that?"

Bartoli nodded. "That true?"

"It is. But if you know that, then she's opened up to you, which means she's more than a colleague."

"We're not involved, okay? Might it have gone that way? Sure. But I saw some things I didn't like, and I called a halt."

"And now she's mad at you and you're scared," Hoyt said, smiling for the first time.

Bartoli didn't answer, and nearly reached for the door release.

"What else she tell you about the cop who killed her kid?" Hoyt asked.

"Zilch."

"She didn't tell you someone shot him dead two months later?"

Bartoli experienced a shiver that made him feel like the air-con had dropped ten degrees. He stared through the windshield.

"Oh, yeah," Hoyt continued. "He was parked up right here in this very spot. On duty. Taking a break. Seven-Eleven coffee in his lap, brains on the passenger window."

"Jesus. They catch who did it?"

"What do you think?"

"Was she a suspect?"

Hoyt shook his head. "Not officially. No evidence. A week later, she puts in for a transfer to West Division."

Bartoli didn't respond, too busy trying to picture Contreras putting a gun to a cop's head and pulling the trigger.

"Not what you were expecting?" Hoyt asked. "Or maybe *just* what you were expecting."

After a moment, Bartoli shook his head. "No. Not this. Not at all."

"Really? Come on, you're a homicide detective. You never locked up a perp you thought was innocent all along? My advice – not that you asked – let it go. Not your job. You got suspicions, pass them to

Internal Affairs. Don't make it personal. Don't make an enemy out of Gabriela Contreras. That woman is out to lunch. Speaking of which, I need to eat."

Bartoli took the hint and let himself out. "Thanks for your time, Captain."

"I'd say anytime, but I doubt I'll see you again."

Bartoli closed the door, and the Ford Interceptor took off down the shimmering street. He replayed Hoyt's last words and didn't much care for either possible interpretation.

He was back on the 405 in two minutes, and that was all the time he needed to decide. Hoyt's advice was sound. Leave well alone. He was too close to retirement to embark on a futile mission. He had enough on his plate with Matthew Spiller. He didn't need to be pursuing a fellow cop for a crime he couldn't prove, especially when it could risk his life.

ON HIS WAY back home, Spiller stopped off at an auto accessory store in the Valley. He was in the market for a new dashcam and micro-SD card. He paid for it in cash. The boot of the Maserati was now empty. Manny was awaiting his next role.

He was home by 11.15 a.m. He quickly hosed down the car. Prior to reaching the desert, he'd put the roof up and closed the windows to protect the interior, but the exterior looked much like it had after Billy had returned from his unauthorized spin around Edwards Airforce Base. He quickly grabbed a bite to eat and was on the road at 11.40. Sadie was taking Theo, and he aimed to beat them to the rendezvous. He was still fearful that the two women might be susceptible to a change of heart, and wondered whether adding Theo into the mix might prompt a larger process of reassessment if they decided he wasn't suitable. For that reason, Spiller needed to sign any paperwork before Theo arrived.

An hour later, he turned off the Pacific Coast Highway and edged up to the gates, which were clearly new. He smirked at the thought of Hayley taking a shotgun to Stutz's Bronco, then buzzed for entry.

Hayley and Virginia were waiting for him at the main entrance to the house.

"Can I sign?" he said. "Now?"

"Matt, we haven't even discussed your fee," Hayley said.

Spiller realized he'd not given a thought to the monetary side. He laughed. "It's fine. We can work that out with the studio later. I'm not that bothered; I just want to play the part."

"Come inside."

Hayley led them into her office, which boasted none of the self-congratulatory posters of her short-lived movie career. She went to her desk and slid an envelope toward him.

"That's an official, legally binding letter of attachment," Virginia said. "Fee to be decided when you sign the actual contract. There is a morals clause, of course, which I hope we never have to call upon."

She was referring to their last conversation, and Spiller shook his head adamantly. He tipped the letter onto the desk, leafed through its three pages, taking in nothing of the detail. On the final page, where Hayley and Virginia had signed, was a dotted line next to his name.

"Pen?" he said.

Hayley gave him a black biro, and he squiggled his signature. Then she took the letter to a small copier, creating two more. He received a copy, stuffed it in the envelope, rolled it, and shoved it in his back pocket.

"How's Theo doing?" Virginia asked.

"Let's sit outside," Hayley said. She grabbed a stack of scripts from her desk and headed for the door.

Spiller hadn't spoken to Theo that morning, but he knew the kind of man Virginia's father had been, so decided to bull up the old actor. "He's great," he said, following the women out into the sunshine. "He's a tough cookie. It'd take more than a couple of bullet holes in his front door to faze an old trooper like that. Did you know he was in Vietnam?"

"I didn't," Virginia said. "Interesting."

They arrived at the bamboo awning on the lawn next to the pool and took their seats. A pitcher of iced orange juice was on the table, and a stack of glasses. Hayley poured out three.

"Tell me," Hayley said, "how would you know someone like Theo Montgomery? The guy's a virtual recluse. And you've been here how long? Six, seven months?"

"How are you, Matthew?"

Spiller turned to the source of the Russian accent and saw Kat padding barefoot across the lawn in a G-string bikini. She was everything Sadie wasn't: vulnerable, soft, lacking any muscle definition, but pert where it mattered, and Spiller found himself staring at those bits as she poised at the pool edge, ready to dive in.

"I'm good, thanks, Kat. How are you?"

She looked over her shoulder. "Yes, very good."

Despite being aware of the women's scrutiny, his eyes involuntarily flicked down to Kat's mostly exposed cheeks again, before she took the plunge and deprived him of the view. How fickle was he? Sadie was on her way. The woman he'd made love to all night long. And here he was, ogling another ass. He imagined a fight between the two of them, and pictured Sadie simply pulling Kat's arms from her sockets and beating her to death with them. He smiled to himself.

"Earth to Matt," Hayley said.

He shrugged, opened his arms in admission. "Seriously, where else am I meant to look?"

"Theo?" Virginia prompted, slightly disgruntled. "How do you know him?"

A joke would have been inappropriate, but it spewed out anyway. "I haven't flunked my morals clause already, have I?"

Virginia looked at Hayley for support.

"John would have looked," Hayley said. "Ass like that."

Virginia smiled. "Yeah. He would. He definitely would. And he'd have held his hands up to it." She laughed, and continued until the tears came.

Hayley reached and patted her hand.

Spiller was about to answer the Theo question when he heard the roar of the Caddy as it powered up the driveway. He pointed to the SUV as it rounded the bend and eased into a parking spot.

"Theo's driver. That's how I know Theo. You might have seen me talking to her yesterday at the range. She took me to see Mel Banaghan."

They watched as Sadie jumped out and released Theo from the rear of the Escalade. She was wearing a shoulder rig over her t-shirt, displaying the HK .45. Spiller grinned at her, before she got back in the car and was lost behind the dark windows.

Theo was wearing a Hawaiian shirt and khaki chinos, possibly a nod to the military. It reminded Spiller of the time he'd worn a desert shemagh to bolster the pretense he was ex-army, and what an epic fail that had been, as he'd wound up with a face like a pizza.

"I'm Virginia. It's an honor to meet you, Mr Montgomery."

He gently took her outstretched hand and kissed it. "The honor is all mine, and please call me Theo."

Hayley proved the credentials of her hippy dress and moved straight in for a hug, which was reciprocated. They all sat down under the bamboo, and Hayley poured out two more drinks.

"How are you?" Virginia asked. "After last night."

"Pah! He was lucky he ran when he did. I've not fired a gun in anger since Quảng Nam Province, but I had a three fifty-seven last night that was hot to trot."

They smiled at his swagger.

Virginia said, "How old are you, Theo, if you don't mind me asking?"

"I'm sixty-nine. Is that a problem?"

"*Veteran Avenue* is set in 2013, when my dad was sixty-three. But... you don't look your age. You could play sixty-three."

"We took the liberty of drawing up a letter of attachment," Hayley said. "I hope that won't turn out to be premature. Matt signed his already."

Theo took a swallow of orange juice. "I'm certain it won't."

Hayley grabbed the wodge of scripts from under her seat and handed them to him. "You got the gist of the story, right, Theo? From Matt?"

"I think so. It sounds tremendous."

"I've included a four-page synopsis, to give you a detailed overview, and I've marked your scenes, if you'd like to take some time to read through them. Or you can take them away with you."

"Now is the time," he said, and began to study the synopsis. He looked up at Hayley once he'd finished and gave her an approving nod. Then he found the first of the yellow highlights in Episode One. They all sat in silence while he quickly skipped through the six episodes, reading his dialog to himself, but he couldn't hide how involved he was; his expression creasing this way and that, in tune with the tenor of each silent line.

The only sounds were the distant crash of the Pacific, the hum of the PCH, and the nearer sploshing of Kat as she swam up and down. Spiller had to make a conscious effort not to glance her way, especially when she finally climbed out and prostrated herself next to the pool, ass to the sky, soaking up some rays.

Twenty minutes later, once Theo had exhausted the yellow bits, he began to randomly dip into the episodes, still nodding appreciatively. Then he set the papers on the table and raised his glass to Hayley.

"Well done, young lady. Really. Bravo. You have an excellent ear for dialog. The story is spectacular."

"Thank you," Hayley said. "And all true."

"So Matt tells me. I'd be very happy to sign that piece of paper now, if you're both equally happy with me playing Roger."

Virginia looked at Hayley, and they gave each other a nod.

Theo clapped his hands once, and gave a brief belly laugh that sounded like the release of too much tension.

"I think maybe I just found my swan song."

## TWENTY-ONE

SADIE LEFT FIRST with Theo, then Virginia made her excuses – which did sound like excuses to Spiller – then he hugged Hayley, thanked her again for her trust in him, and hopped in his Maserati to head home.

A half mile up the PCH, he came across Virginia, who was perched against the trunk of her Audi TT on the shoulder. She flagged him down and he parked behind her.

"Car trouble?" he asked, as he approached.

"No. I'd like you to come somewhere with me."

"Where?"

"Follow me." She pushed herself upright and turned back to the driver's door.

"Sorry about earlier," he blurted. "You know… looking at… and then joking. I imagine you're not in the mood for jokes right now."

"It's okay. Life goes on. Best that people don't pussyfoot around me. Just makes things worse. Follow me."

So, he did follow her, all the way back along the PCH, onto Sunset, onto the 405, and off at Mulholland. He tailed her until she indicated, and bumped up the curb onto a dusty verge, bordered by the metal perimeter fence of an unseen property that lurked down the hill. Virginia got out and walked a little way along the road, to beyond the fence, where the terrain dropped off steeply into scrubland. Spiller had guessed the moment they'd hit Mulholland where she was leading him. He stood beside her, staring out to the south, where the salubrious roads trickled down through the wild valleys, like crystal streams toward the stagnant pool that was LA proper. She bowed her head, her eyeline fixed on a patch of charred land a hundred feet away. He was silent, as he guessed he was meant to be.

"I don't know why I brought you here," Virginia announced. "Do you know why I brought you here?"

"I assume John came off the road here."

"I don't mean that. I mean… you don't need to see this. What's the point? This is irrelevant to the character you're gonna play. John was full of life. What happened back in May has no bearing on who he was in twenty-thirteen. I don't want you thinking of this place."

Her confusion was evident. Spiller put a gentle hand on her arm. "Hey. It's fine. I'm happy to pay my respects. I'm honored you brought me here; that you'd share this with me."

"I can't get my head around it. I still can't. It's unreal. I keep hoping I'll feel more…" She shook her head as the words failed her, but her eyes stayed dry.

"You're still angry with him."

Virginia looked at him. "I am. I don't want to be, but I am. You know, you're the first person who gets it. Everyone thinks I'm just sad. Of course I am. But it's buried so deep under all this… this *fury* I feel. Not at life. At him. This was so unnecessary. It didn't have to happen. He didn't have to make me a widow, my son fatherless. That fucking car of his."

"Hayley doesn't know how you feel?" Spiller asked.

She shrugged. "Doesn't say if she does. She's too wrapped up mourning the loss of her *dad*."

Spiller frowned, then thought of the script, the denouement, and he understood. "She thought John was the reincarnation of her dad."

Virginia huffed disdainfully. "It didn't matter until this happened. It was funny. I humored her. John did, too. But it feels like she equates her loss with mine, and I… a part of me hates her for that."

Spiller didn't want to speak his next words. "Perhaps it's too early for *Veteran Avenue*. Maybe you shouldn't make it."

"I have no say. She wrote the book. It's my story, but it's hers as well. And she thinks it's the best way to honor John's life. And my dad's. I guess I'd rather have some oversight if it's gonna happen. I'd rather say who plays John, who plays my dad. I don't know… maybe it'll all prove cathartic."

"That's why you waited on the PCH for me, rather than ask me in front of Hayley. You don't want her to be here."

Virginia shook her head. "Not when I'm here." She smiled. "Hayley leaves a white rose here every week or two." She scanned around, spotted it, a brittle, brown commemoration. "She used to leave one at her dad's grave in Westwood, but now she just leaves one here."

Spiller nodded.

"Sorry, you know that. It's in the script."

"No need to apologize. I'm truly sorry for your loss, Virginia. And I really think you should pull the plug on *Veteran Avenue*, if that's how you feel."

"I don't know how I feel."

"Exactly. You need to know. You need more time. It's all too raw. There's a grieving process and *Veteran Avenue* isn't helping."

"No. How would you feel if it got called off?"

Spiller spotted an elderly woman in blue dungarees walk into the garden that was fenced off from the ruined land where the Ferrari had exploded. She looked up at them.

"Matt?" Virginia said. "How would you feel?"

"Disappointed – professionally. It's a great script. But on a human level, I'd completely understand."

Virginia laughed. "Almost like you think the acting profession isn't human."

"Well, it certainly lacks some humanity. That's why scripts with heart, with a message, need to be made. That's why *Veteran Avenue* needs to be made, but… maybe not yet."

The woman in the garden below them offered a tentative wave. They both raised a hand to her. The woman stared some more, then indicated that they move back to their cars.

"Huh?" Virginia said. "What's her problem?"

But the woman was now smiling, pointing up at her front gate, gesturing that they move toward it. Then she was heading back across the lawn, past a swimming pool.

"I think she wants to talk," Spiller said. "You okay with that?"

"I guess."

They waited outside the solid steel gate for a while before it began to roll back, revealing a kindly face that was already prepped with a sympathetic smile.

"Hello, I'm JoBeth. Sorry to disturb you. I saw you up on the road and thought it rude not to invite you in. Sorry, I'm assuming you didn't just stop to take in the view."

"No," Virginia said. "And thank you."

"I thought you might like a bit more privacy. To sit close. I won't disturb you." She opened an arm, inviting them onto her property.

"That's very kind," Virginia said, entering.

"How did you know the deceased?" JoBeth asked. "Sorry, I'm assuming you did; you're not just a fan paying homage."

"John was my husband."

JoBeth gasped, stopped, and offered a hug, which Virginia accepted.

"I'm so sorry for your loss, dear. I only read about what happened recently. We've been away in Europe. And you are?" she asked Spiller.

"Matt. Friend of the family."

"Well, you're both most welcome. Please come and have some refreshment."

JoBeth led them to the pool area and saw them settled, then disappeared into the bungalow.

"Hey," Spiller said. "You okay?"

"So nice there are people like that in the world."

"The kindness of strangers."

Virginia stared across the lawn, through the green chain-link, at the place where the Ferrari had come to rest. Spiller left her to her quiet contemplation.

"Hello there!" A man's voice.

They smiled at the old guy ambling toward them with a look of slight puzzlement.

"Hello," Spiller said. "Your wife's just getting some drinks. She saw us up on the road."

He extended his arm to them both. "I'm Jack. Up on the road? Uh…" He took a seat.

Spiller sensed more than the confusion of unexpected guests. He'd seen the same lost look in his father-in-law after his diagnosis.

"I'm Virginia Frears," Virginia said, by way of explanation, but from his expression it appeared not to have cleared up anything. She pointed through the fence, directing Jack's gaze. Jack's head jolted at the sight of the ruined earth. He got up and walked to the fence, and stayed there for several minutes until JoBeth called his name. Spiller got up and went to help her with the tray. Jack remained with his nose to the chain-link.

"Jack! Come and sit down!" JoBeth shouted, then spoke quietly to her guests. "Sorry, I don't think he has any idea what happened."

Jack wandered back and sat down. "What, uh…?"

JoBeth spoke, to spare Virginia. "There was an accident, honey."

"My husband crashed his car," Virginia said.

"Oh, I'm so sorry," Jack said. "When?"

"May ninth."

"We were away."

"I know; JoBeth told us. So, you haven't spoken to the police?"

JoBeth shook her head, poured out the lemonade. "Should we?"

Virginia shrugged. "Someone reported hearing a possible collision before the crash, but no one came forward. I can't see any point if you were away."

Jack stood up. "Excuse me."

Spiller could see that JoBeth was struggling with her husband's behavior. She watched him go back into the house.

"I apologize. Jack's… he's… he's not at his best right now. I think he's still exhausted from the trip. We visited a lot of countries."

Spiller smiled, took a drink. Virginia raised a finger toward the house, specifically a camera under the eaves, pointing their way.

JoBeth was quick to respond. "Recordings are overwritten every month unless they're saved. It would have triggered an event log but not a security alert as it's outside the boundary. You wouldn't have wanted to see it, would you, dear?"

Virginia thought about it, shook her head.

"Would you like some time alone?" JoBeth asked.

"Please. Just a few minutes."

"Do you want me to stay?" Spiller asked.

"No." Virginia got up and walked to the fence.

JoBeth linked his arm as they went back to the house. "You like motorcycles, Matt? Jack has quite a collection."

"I do. I have one. I'm guessing Jack's old school. Vintage Harleys, Indians?"

"You guessed right. They're in the garage. I expect he'll be in there, tinkering, as usual."

But Jack wasn't there. JoBeth returned to the house and hollered. "Jack! Jack, honey!"

There was no answer.

"He may be sleeping," JoBeth said. She took Spiller back to the garage, and they could see through the window that Virginia was still at the fence, her fingers clawed into the chain-link either side of her head, as though she needed to cling on to remain upright.

"Do they know what happened?" JoBeth asked. "The police? Was he driving too fast?"

"I don't know. I didn't know him. But Virginia does hate the fact he had that car. It was a Ferrari."

"Yellow," she said, nodding.

"I'm sorry?"

JoBeth seemed to realize she'd been caught in a lie. "Oh."

"You saw the footage? You still have it?"

She nodded. "Virginia wouldn't have wanted to see it, believe me. So, I didn't give her the option. Was I wrong?"

Before he could answer, Jack appeared in the doorway. His expression was ominous.

"Jack? What's wrong, honey?"

"JoBeth, please say goodbye to our guests, you really need to see something." He turned and headed back into the house without awaiting a response.

"Sorry," she said. "He's…"

"It's fine. We'll see ourselves out."

"Thank you. There's an exit button on the gate pillar. Please say goodbye to Virginia for me."

## TWENTY-TWO

BILLY COOED OVER his leathers like an expectant mother might coo over fluffy pink romper suits. Spiller had draped them over the seat of the Hayabusa. They were zip-together and armored, in black, white, and bright orange – the latter a conscious nod to Billy's Morris Marina back home. The helmet matched the suit, as did the gloves and boots.

"My boy!" Billy exclaimed, delighted. "You didn't buy these for me. Surely not just for one ride. They must have cost a king's ransom. I love them!"

"You can't put a price on good protection," Spiller told him. "Well, obviously you can, and they did, but... I mean, there's no price too high. And you never know, you may end up buying a bike yourself. I wouldn't put anything past you these days. Anyway, get yourself ready, I'm going upstairs to change."

Billy nodded, still mesmerized by his new biker persona, laid out ready for him to inhabit.

Upstairs, Spiller checked the time. 4.15. He made some calculations. It was a four-hour round trip, and there would be mischief in the middle to account for. He figured on being back by nine. If he was earlier, he could always pull up somewhere nearby and wait for his guest.

He called Officer Ethan King, not even knowing if he was working later on, or had other plans, but Ethan was free and only too pleased to be invited to the home of a Hollywood star for a few beers. He gave Ethan the address and the time, said not to worry if he was a few minutes late, then changed into his leathers.

Back down in the garage, Spiller admired Billy's outfit. "Snazzy. Let's take a selfie."

"A what?"

Spiller grabbed his phone from a workbench and moved in, so they were shoulder to shoulder, then fired off a few shots.

"You got yours? For your website pics?" Spiller checked.

Billy patted a lump under his jacket.

"Better not have it there, Billy. It might get sweaty. I'll put it under the seat."

Billy handed over his phone and Spiller unlocked the seat. While Billy was pulling on his helmet, Spiller surreptitiously placed both phones back on the bench under a cloth.

Spiller mounted the Hayabusa, steadying it as Billy climbed onto the pillion seat. The garage shutter began to lift.

"Where do I hold on?" Billy shouted through his open visor. "This rail behind me?"

Spiller turned slightly. "Not unless you want to fall off when I accelerate. You need to grab around my waist. Link your hands or grab hold of my leather. Don't worry, I'll take it easy." He started the engine, and Billy gasped at the discord that suddenly filled the garage.

"A bit louder than my old D-Ten!" Billy said, and laughed. "I won't get tittinus, will I?"

"What?"

"Tittinus! You know, love; when your ears ring! I've suffered in the past!"

Spiller left the malapropism uncorrected. "I wouldn't worry about it! I really can't see you of all people being affected by tittinus!" He edged the bike out into the sunshine and dropped the shutter behind them. "We're going to do some serious miles, Billy! You up for that?"

Billy squeezed him in response.

"Enjoy!" Spiller shouted.

"I certainly will! I may even open my eyes at some point!"

SPILLER TOPPED UP the Hayabusa before they left the Valley to ensure he had enough fuel for the whole journey, out and back. He wouldn't be able to get off the bike on the return leg. Billy didn't appear worried by their eventual desert location, perhaps because he'd followed a similar route when he'd taken the Maserati for a joyride. These roads were built for a blast. Given the Hayabusa's turn of speed, and its ability to weave through traffic, he might have halved the official journey time today, but it was imperative he observe the limit and not attract the attention of law enforcement. Only during the last few miles, beyond Kramer Junction on US-395, when his was the only vehicle around, did he start to wind on the throttle and push past a hundred. Billy's grip tightened, but there was no protest from his pillion. He eased back to seventy and took his hands off the bars, spread his arms out wide, and screamed like a banshee.

Billy shouted, "Matthew! God's sake!"

Spiller grabbed the bars again, knocked his visor up and turned his head slightly to be heard. "Try it! Billy, live a little!" He opened his arms wide again and let out another cry as the bike's speed dropped without his input on the throttle.

Billy kept his arms wrapped around Spiller's waist, so Spiller took control again and accelerated to eighty. Then something unexpected occurred. Spiller felt Billy let go. His wing mirrors showed Billy's arms fly out to the sides, and the old man let out a high-pitched shriek for five seconds before his arms encircled the safety of some black leather again.

Spiller laughed hard inside his helmet and felt even more awful about what was likely going to happen. He slowed at the turn-off, taking a left onto the cracked concrete that led to the derelict USAF radio facility, deep in the lifeless desert.

The building wasn't big. Two spaces, a square and a rectangle, linked. The roof of the rectangle had fallen in. Someone had painted two of its exterior walls terracotta red. The rest was the original gray block. A small outbuilding had collapsed. The location had been visited by unskilled graffiti artists over the years, and a few gun-nuts, as countless bullets had pocked its walls, removing concrete chunks of varying sizes.

Spiller felt its primordial sadness, and prayed he wouldn't need to add to it.

He killed the engine and removed his helmet and gloves, ruffling his flattened hair. Billy dismounted and removed his own, then looked around with a concerned expression. Spiller leaned the bike on its stand and got off.

"Matthew... dear boy... what is this place?"

"Good spot for photos, no?"

"Very moody, no doubt. But a nice headshot on a sunny beach would have sufficed." His face altered, took on the hue of the unpainted blocks, erasing his tan. "Why did you bring me here?"

"Sit down, Billy."

Billy unzipped his jacket and pulled it from his shoulders with difficulty, dropping it in the dust as though he knew he wouldn't need it again. He perched on a step outside the collapsed outhouse. He took in the endless view, the parched land, the dilapidated structure. He cocked his head, like he was trying to locate the nearest vehicle, but he was surrounded by miles of nothingness, with nothing to be heard but insects. He simpered at Spiller.

"Talk to me, Billy. Be honest."

"About?"

"That's a bad start. Tell me what you've been up to. Tell me like it's my business. Where you've been, who you've seen."

Billy seemed to search his thoughts, frowning. "I've seen a few clients, a few prospects. And my new lady friend, of course."

Spiller nodded, unzipped his jacket, wafted it to fan his sweating midriff. "This is so important, Billy. This place should tell you that."

"Love, what do you want me to say?"

"Billy, you can say whatever the hell you like. But at some point, I'm going to know it's not what I need to hear."

"Give me a hint," Billy said, and laughed a little hysterically.

"Come on, Billy, this isn't difficult. This isn't *The Times* crossword."

Billy smiled again and shrugged.

Spiller went to the Hayabusa, lifted its seat, pulled on a thin pair of leather gloves, and took out Noah's Smith & Wesson M&P Compact.

"Matthew?"

"Any idea where I might have got this from?"

Billy shook his head.

"I'll give you a clue. *Yee-haw*."

Billy offered another shrug, wiped a hand across his sweating head.

"It's really hot here, Billy, isn't it? That's why I'm not doing this for hours. I want to go home, take these leathers off, and jump in my pool. You've got about five minutes, then I'm leaving you here."

"To walk back?" Billy asked hopefully.

Spiller took a few steps into the narrow shadow of the building and waited. He watched his agent grow more flustered until Billy blurted out one word.

*"Noah!"*

"What about him?"

"I took him on, all right? I think he has prospects, so I took him on. It's a free country. You may not like him, Matthew, but I do. So! There! Sue me!"

Spiller sighed, ran a finger over the gun's serial number. "I'm going to hurry this along, Billy. I took this from the glove compartment of Noah's truck when I stole it last night, when he was occupied getting his rocks off with you. And I saw him the other day at your office post-coital, and he very strongly indicated that you told him what I did to those guys on your front lawn."

"Who I choose to sleep with is my business, young man."

"*That's* what jumped out at you from what I just said? Billy, I couldn't care less where you stick your knob – I mean, kudos that you're able to stick it anywhere at all at your age, but… you broke a confidence. One I explicitly warned you not to break."

Billy seemed about to remonstrate, but looked down at the ground instead, brushing some dust off his new boots as though it mattered. "Sorry," he said quietly. "Pillow talk."

"Right. Finally."

Billy looked up. "Why did you steal his truck?"

"Did he report it stolen?"

"He said he would. What are you up to, Matthew?"

"Mind games. I need him to know he's not safe from me."

"He won't say anything. He knows you're my golden ticket."

"Yeah, but to what? It's not fortune anymore, is it, Billy? You've got more than enough dosh to last you. It's the other half of the deal. The part people really sell their soul to the devil for."

"I gave up on fame years ago, love. It was never in my stars."

Spiller laughed heartily. "No one gives up on fame, Billy. It never goes away. That craving never lets you go. So… give me another name."

"Pardon?"

Spiller pointed the Smith at Billy's head. "Five, four, three, two—"

*"Brett Stutz!"*

Spiller lowered the gun. "Did he approach you, or did you approach him?"

Billy gave a defiant stare. "I went to him. You know that already. You've obviously spoken to him."

"Was he on board?"

"No. He actually seems to be quite fond of you – despite everything." Billy got up and joined Spiller in the shade. "What are you going to do, Matthew? Are you going to kill me?"

"Last question: if I hadn't found out about this, would you have done it? Sold me out for your five minutes of fame?"

"I don't know. I've surprised myself in so many ways this past week, I genuinely don't know. I'm not sure I know my own mind anymore."

"I told you to be careful shedding that old skin of yours, Billy."

Billy moved and collected his jacket off the ground, patting it to remove the dust. He sat down again on the step, cuddling the armored leather in his lap. "Thank you for my outfit. I did so enjoy wearing it."

Spiller squinted. "You would have taken everything from me, Billy. My career, my money, my liberty. You'd have destroyed my kids in the process. I take you back now, you can still go public, with or without Stutz. Just the accusation would ruin me."

"I expect it would."

"And if Stutz caves and confirms, my life is done. It's game over."

Billy stared at the Hayabusa, its engine still ticking and pinking. "You're so undeserving, Matthew. That motorcycle, your car, your house. I think that's what galls me the most. I never put a foot wrong my whole life, and yet the Gods never saw fit to reward me."

Spiller chuckled. "You can't still think this profession works on a sense of fairness, much less morality. You don't think that, do you,

Billy? I no more deserve to be where I am than a ten-year-old kid deserves to get cancer. If that's your gripe with me, you can let it go right now."

His agent snorted.

"You know, Billy, I should have taken the time to explain everything that happened last Christmas. Maybe this is my bad. I let you see the worst bits of my character, like... the opposite of those movie previews that only show the good bits, then you see the whole thing and realize it's mostly shit."

"You're saying you're mostly good?"

"No. I'm just saying you saw a snapshot and decided that was the truth. Then you got jealous."

Billy drew in a long breath and expelled it audibly as his head fell forward onto the jacket. Spiller thought how easy it would be to put a round in the top of his head now he wasn't looking. Well, simple more than easy. Billy looked up.

"I should have worn more leather."

"What? Like a gimp suit?"

"I'm sure I have no clue what one of those is, dear boy, but I expect you're being facetious. I meant, maybe just... less *bloody velvet*."

Spiller had to laugh, and maybe that was the ploy. Billy remained an existential threat. Was the scheming old bugger just trying to soften him up?

"So, Billy... what would you do in my position?"

Billy took a moment. "I'd try to help me get what I truly want. Remember I did that for you, Matthew? You wouldn't be here if it weren't for me. I introduced you to Brett Stutz. That was me. So, that's what I would do, if I were you. I would try and help me get what I want, so I never again feel the bitterness that brought us to this point."

Spiller pondered, took the gun to the Hayabusa, and put it back under the seat. He turned to Billy. "There's a new TV series. I'm on board. And Theo Montgomery. There might be a part you could play. Not a huge part, but it's pivotal. I can't make any promises, but... can you do an American accent?"

"Sure can," Billy said with a twang, offering an unconvincing glimpse.

Spiller nodded. "Okay. Get your kit on, let's get out of here."

"Could I have a hug?" Billy asked, standing up, opening his arms.

Spiller stared at him for a moment. "No. No more hugs. This relationship has changed – you may have noticed. And you can drop the *dear boy* crap with me now. That's not you anymore."

"But we're good?"

"No. But we'll be okay."

As he headed back down the mile length of arrow-straight concrete toward the 395, Spiller increased his speed to eighty and lifted his arms off the bars, giving an almighty whoop. He put one hand back on the throttle and slapped Billy's knee with the other.

"Come on, Billy!" he bellowed, and whooped again.

Billy let go and threw his arms out wide, and Spiller twisted the throttle, lifting the front tire.

Aside from the thump of Billy's booted toes momentarily kicking up into Spiller's triceps, Spiller wouldn't have known his pillion had gone. He checked his wing mirror and saw Billy flip-flopping along the road, pitching up sprays of dust. He slowed and stopped, looked around. Far away on the highway, a semi-trailer was passing, nothing more than a liquid red outline in the intense heat. He U-turned, stopping at the twisted form that was only held together by the double stitching of the new leathers. He hopped off and retrieved a short towrope from under his seat, tied it to Billy's ankles, then jumped on and dragged him back to the derelict building.

Spiller stood over his ex-agent for several minutes, looking for signs of life. The black visor was down, cracked but still there, and Spiller was glad about that. Perhaps he'd have used the Smith on him if he'd twitched, or wrenched at his ruined helmet, breaking his neck. Or perhaps, in total remorse, he'd have raced to the highway to flag down a car so they could help try to revive him. It hadn't been a cut-and-dried decision. Until the moment when Billy, full of trust, had let go, Spiller hadn't known for certain what he'd do. Had Billy clung on, it was possible he might have ridden all the way home, pushing the problem into another day. Because Billy would have remained a problem; he had been twenty years too old for anything in *Veteran Avenue*.

Or maybe Spiller was kidding himself. Perhaps Billy's fate had been as indelibly etched in stone as the bullet holes in the gray and red blocks. Maybe just the mention of *Veteran Avenue* had steeled him, sealed Billy's fate; the very idea that such an opportunity could be ripped from his grasp. And why the hell should he have kowtowed? Billy had pushed his luck too far, tested Spiller's patience and generosity once too often.

Spiller untied the rope and dragged Billy into a corner of the roofless building. He threw a tarp off some rubble, which also revealed Manny, dressed identically to Billy from top to toe. Spiller stripped Billy of his bike gear, not looking as he pulled the fractured helmet off his shaved head, then hid Billy under the tarp. He went and retrieved the Smith from under the bike's seat, returned and fired five times into the covered corpse. He carried Billy's gear outside and across to a defunct car, a boxy brown thing from the eighties. He pushed it underneath, out of sight, and was just about to throw the gun into the desert – to be sniffed out by the police dogs later on – when he paused, his arm pulled back ready.

He looked at the Smith and recalled a similar situation in early January. Standing on a bridge across a reservoir in the snowy English hills. The dead of night, a murder weapon in his hand, desperate to get rid of it. Out across the water it flew, landing with a plop. Then, days later, a risky and farcical return trip with scuba gear to retrieve the damn thing, knowing it was the one item that could frame his nemesis and free himself to manifest his Hollywood dream. Keeping hold of Noah's gun was risky, especially considering the imminent journey home in a stolen truck, but something told him it hadn't fully served its purpose yet. He stuck it in his back pocket and returned to the building.

He grabbed the luggage straps and cable ties he'd left next to Manny, and dragged the mannequin outside. He wheeled the Hayabusa up to the wall, then manhandled Manny onto the pillion seat, resting him against the wall so he didn't topple off. He lifted his feet onto the pillion pegs and cable-tied them in place. He had already doctored his and Manny's leathers, and he now looped the straps around Manny's back, beneath the jacket, and out through some cuts in the leather under his arms. Spiller climbed on, reached behind and grabbed the straps, and pushed the ends through some cuts he'd made in his own jacket at his flanks. He pulled them tight around his chest, clipped them together, and zipped up. He connected another cable tie loosely, then brought Manny's hands up in front of him, and secured them at his waist. Manny was fairly rigid, but Spiller had added extra duct tape at the pertinent joints, especially the neck, so his head wouldn't loll and make him look like he'd fallen asleep. He imagined a traffic cop might stop a biker with a napping pillion passenger.

## TWENTY-THREE

SPILLER RODE THROUGH the dusk and arrived home in the dark. He felt awful. He wished Billy was sitting behind him, rather than a dummy. But Billy had been the real dummy, and Spiller couldn't envisage how this could have ended much differently. There was a level of duplicity beyond which life-changing events were set in motion. Trust vanished, banished by treachery too gross to pardon. All that was left were implausible promises and hollow pleas for last chances that were undeserved. Despite the warnings, Billy had breached that boundary. No matter how bad Spiller felt, there was comfort in knowing that this had been a binary choice: him or Billy.

He slowed the bike as he rounded the last bend, in case Ethan hadn't arrived yet. It was just after nine. There was a car outside his home, a modern Dodge Challenger in red. Spiller hit the garage shutter remote on the instrument cluster. He flashed his headlight and saw Ethan raise his hand, then he quickly edged past the nose of the Challenger, past Billy's rented Camaro on the driveway, and slipped the Hayabusa into the garage next to the Maserati, making sure to drop the shutter to prevent Ethan following in behind. He parked close to the work bench, removed his helmet and gloves, and grabbed a utility knife, slashing the tie that bound Manny's hands. He unclipped the luggage strap and jumped off, and Manny slowly bent at the waist and headbutted the gas tank, like he was exhausted. Spiller cut the ties at the foot pegs and pulled Manny off the bike, quickly carrying him inside and upstairs to Billy's bedroom. He set the shower running and hurried back down to the front door.

Ethan was already waiting on the step, a six-pack of Miller Lite in his hand. They shook, and Spiller invited him inside.

"Great to see you, Ethan, how's life?"

"Always good, Matt."

"You sold my pants yet?"

Ethan laughed. "I told you: I'm hanging onto those bad boys. So, how are you, buddy? Where've you been?"

Spiller led him into the living room. "Just out and about. My agent's staying here for a few days and wanted a pillion ride. He's a daring old sod. Take a seat."

Ethan tore one off the six-pack and handed Spiller the rest. "You getting changed?"

Spiller looked down at his leathers. "Yeah. You want a glass?"

Ethan shook his head, cracked his can, and Spiller took the beers to the kitchen and put them in the refrigerator, then headed upstairs. He switched the shower off, changed into some black joggers, and shouted "Night, Billy!" on the landing.

"Good night, dear boy!" Spiller shouted into his sleeve in a Billyesque voice.

"First things first," Ethan said, as soon as Spiller entered the living room with his beer. "Your face. The guy who did it. You described him as a stalker. Any more problems?"

Spiller saw another opportunity to plant a few seeds. "I bumped into him at my agent's office. I think he's desperately trying to get on his books. He sort of made a threatening gesture. You know, the old finger-gun to the head thing."

"To you or your agent?"

"To me. Although I get the feeling my agent's a bit worried as well."

"You got some home defense?"

"Not sure I could get a gun on a work visa."

"A baseball bat?" Ethan asked.

"I did have one. He stole it after he broke my nose."

"Oh, man." Ethan sniggered. "Sorry, I don't mean to laugh. You know his name?"

"Noah. Texan kid. That's all I have. My agent should know more. Should I get him?"

"No need. Just find out his surname and let me know if he steps on any more toes. And, uh… if you need anything for home defense, give me a holler. I could point you in the right direction."

"Interesting. I'll keep that in mind. Cheers."

Over the next couple of hours, the two men chatted like old buddies who'd known each other since they were kids. Ethan had three cans, while Spiller returned to the kitchen to refill his glass eight times, becoming progressively less coherent and more outspoken with each beer.

As Spiller opened the front door to let Ethan out, he was yawning uncontrollably and quite unsteady on his feet. They agreed to catch up again soon.

In the living room, Spiller collected up the last of Ethan's cans and the empty chips packets and took them to the kitchen, dropping them in the trash on top of his bottles of alcohol-free Heineken.

Five minutes later, he was exiting his garden onto the reservoir, cap on his head, backpack on his shoulders, tac-light leading the way.

Spiller followed a well-worn path nearly to the south end of Stone Canyon Reservoir, then branched off through the undergrowth to arrive at the end of a lane lower down North Beverly Glen Boulevard. As he started walking down the hill toward Westwood, he kept his eye out for a passing cab, and his brain began to pore over the day's events. Momentous as they had been – securing a coveted movie role and offing his agent to protect that role – it kept settling on the more innocuous memory of Jack curtailing their visit with his request that JoBeth come see something. Theirs was a relationship that had most likely lasted many decades. There could be little that was new under the sun after so many years. That was why old folk with their means took long trips to Europe. Yet something in their familiar home had spooked the old fellah; an imperative that had annulled the social niceties and implanted a look of dread in his rheumy eyes. *You really need to see something.* Perhaps it was nothing more than a colorful spider that was suddenly fascinating to a mind slowly flaking away its layers. But Spiller recalled the moment when Jack had abruptly excused himself by the pool. Virginia had just mentioned a possible collision prior to the crash, and the date it had happened. *You really need to see something.* Then JoBeth had revealed the existence of a video that hadn't been overwritten in more than two months.

The first cab picked him up after a mile, which took him to Westwood. A second carried him from Westwood to Venice Beach. From there, he retraced the route he'd taken the night before with Sadie, a one-mile walk to Marine Park and Noah's F150.

He approached with caution, although he wasn't expecting a welcoming committee; he was the one who imbued the vehicle with evil intent. To anyone else, it was just a hunk of old metal. Had it been spotted, it would have been towed already.

Spiller put his gloves on and let himself in. He connected the dangling wires, firing up the engine. He drove a couple of streets away, stopped, and removed the new dashcam from his backpack. He disconnected the GPS, set the date one day ahead, muted the sound, installed it on the windscreen, and started recording.

For the third time in less than twenty-four hours, he was heading to the desert.

As he had done previously, he kept to the speed limit, arriving at his destination at just after 3 a.m. He'd been alone on the 395 the last few miles, and that had been reason enough for a bored cop to pull him over, but he hadn't seen any. He switched off his headlights just shy of the turn; the moon was enough. He didn't want a passing motorist to spot any illumination so far from the highway.

Spiller parked the truck facing away from any business he'd need to get up to. He left the engine running, powering the dashcam, then fetched Billy's bike gear from under the old car and threw it into the Ford's cargo bed. He stood there, wondering if there was anything left to do. Billy would stay where he was, so the cops could find him when the time was right. Their footprints from earlier? The Hayabusa's tire tracks? He reached into the cargo bed and grabbed one of Billy's long gloves, then crouched and proceeded to slap at the ground where he'd ridden in, and wherever he recalled having walked. Maybe it was overkill, but it would help settle his nerves to know he'd literally covered his tracks when he finally got to bed and lay awake, reviewing his actions.

He waited for ten minutes. He figured that was sufficient to cover a foreshortened timeline of events. Noah arrives, unloads Billy, kills him, strips him, hides him. Would Billy's injuries stand up to scrutiny? Spiller guessed he'd snapped his neck or fractured his skull. There would be other broken bones, no doubt, and internal injuries, and bruises, all denoting a frenzied attack, perhaps a crime of passion. Ultimately, though, it wouldn't matter if a pathologist couldn't explain every bodily insult. Such minor enigmas would be rendered moot beside the signs that did make sense, like five bullet holes.

A potentially lethal exhaustion suffused Spiller's brain as he headed back the 125 miles. He'd been awake for forty-something hours. Sex with Sadie had been amazing, but now he wished he'd slept instead. He dropped the windows and played the radio and sang along, even if it amounted to gobbledygook because he didn't know the words. More than once, he nodded off and jolted awake just in time.

At some point along his route, he veered off deep into the desert again. He doused Billy's motorcycle gear with lighter fluid and set it ablaze, destroying any skin cells in the leathers and stray hairs in the helmet.

Rather than return the truck to Noah's neighborhood, Spiller left it near the UCLA campus, on a residential street lined with fraternity and sorority houses. He needed to be the one who dictated its discovery, which had to happen after Billy's disappearance had been logged with the police, and a few breadcrumbs had been laid out for them.

He removed the dashcam from the windshield and popped the micro-SD data card out from its slot. He pushed it just under the driver's floor mat, packed the dashcam into his backpack, locked the doors, and walked home, latterly taking the same route along the reservoir.

## TWENTY-FOUR

THE NEXT MORNING, Spiller loaded Manny's leathers and gear into black sacks and into the Maserati's trunk, then headed across the city to the Angeles Public Dump. Later, following his interviews for *Man on a Murder Cycle*, he drove up to Mulholland Drive and parked where he'd parked the day before. He walked to the end of the fencing and looked down into Jack's and JoBeth's garden. He stared at the CCTV camera on the bungalow that faced toward the pool area and the place where the Ferrari had come to rest. He shook his head, confirming what had been bugging him since yesterday. There was no way that camera could have caught anything up on the road. At best, even with a fish-eye lens, it might catch a figure standing where he was, at the very edge of the level ground. Was it conceivable that Jack had reviewed the footage and spotted someone standing there, gloating over the burning wreck below? Who would do that? How stupid would you have to be to get out and risk being caught there if you were at all culpable? He looked back at the trees that bordered the property, shielding it from passing eyes. His eyes darted around the branches as he moved slowly toward the entrance gate. He stopped, squinted, searching, finding nothing.

As Spiller reached the gate, it began to roll open. On the other side, Jack was waiting for him; short pants and the Parisian equivalent of a Hawaiian shirt, Eiffel towers for palm trees, Arc de Triomphes for pineapples.

"Matt, right?"

Spiller nodded. "How did you know I was up here?"

"Come in," Jack said.

Spiller entered, and the gate rolled shut behind him. Jack turned and headed down to the house, so Spiller followed. Jack led him into the kitchen where JoBeth was making a sandwich.

"Oh, hello, Matt," she said. "What are you doing back here? *Jack!*"

Spiller turned to see Jack standing with a suppressed Sig-Sauer semi-automatic, which he'd produced from seemingly nowhere.

"Jack, have you taken leave of your senses?" JoBeth asked. "This is Matt; he was here yesterday."

Her husband scowled. "I know *that*. I may be a little slow these days, but I'm not cuckoo just yet. Move." He indicated with the end of the huge suppressor for Spiller to leave the kitchen.

*"Jack!"*

"I knew this day was coming, JoBeth. Walk. End of the hallway, take a left."

Spiller obeyed, heading into their bedroom. He wanted to say something but didn't know Jack's mind sufficiently well to pitch a comment, and especially feared that neither did Jack. He stopped in front of a floor-to-ceiling bookcase, and watched as Jack took his cellphone from his pocket and handed it to his wife.

"Punch us in," Jack told her.

"Jack…"

"JoBeth, just do it."

JoBeth took the cell, touched the screen several times, then the bookcase behind Spiller slid back, and the steel door it was hiding made an audible clunk.

"In," Jack urged Spiller.

Spiller pulled on the heavy door, then stopped as the interior was revealed as fluorescents flickered on automatically. A bank of screens sitting on and above a metal desk showed various images of the driveway and garden.

"In," Jack repeated.

Spiller stepped forward, and Jack and JoBeth followed him into the panic room. Metal cabinets lined the walls, their contents a secret, but not beyond an educated guess.

"Sit," Jack said, pointing to a small cloth couch at the end of the room. He closed the door.

"Jack, what the hell is going on?" JoBeth asked.

Spiller took a seat, and finally figured out a reasonable question. "Who do you think I am?"

"I don't know. But I think you'd have been here sooner had we not been in Europe at the time."

"At the time of what?"

"You're a fixer. Come here to make sure we don't talk."

"A fixer?"

"A cleaner. A mechanic. Thing is, I can't figure out if that crash was a ploy to get you inside, the company taking care of loose ends finally, or it's unconnected, but you know I know what happened."

Spiller gave JoBeth a pleading look, but she looked equally perplexed.

*"What happened?"* she echoed. "Jack, what are you talking about?"

"You know when I called you yesterday? To come see something?"

"Of course, honey. You showed me the video of the crash. You didn't know I'd seen it already."

"There's more. Go to the security app. Open the settings. Tap the Build Number option quickly five times."

JoBeth followed his instructions, then caught a change in her peripheral vision and looked up at the bank of monitors. The views had altered. Two angles on Mulholland Drive, traffic heading both east and west past their property. And the interior of each room in the house.

"My God… Jack? We have hidden cameras in our home?"

"Sorry."

"And where the hell are the cameras up on the road?"

"They're disguised as branches. I didn't want you to know the extent of the CCTV coverage. I thought you might get spooked knowing the steps I was taking. How real the threat is."

"What threat?" Spiller asked.

"Jack worked for a clandestine government department."

"Which one?" Spiller asked.

Jack sat down at the desk. "You know which one."

"When did you put all this extra security in?" JoBeth asked.

"Last year. When you were away visiting your sister."

"Why then?"

"JoBeth, I see tech on the news every day that we were working on in the eighties and nineties. The problem is the projects that are still in the dark, just waiting to be deployed. It's getting close, I can feel it. These last three years are proof of that. It's just the start. And I know things. I know too much."

"Jack, honey, if the company wanted you dead, you'd have been bones for decades already. And so what if you opened your mouth? The world is full of crackpots with aluminum hats. Who'd take a blind bit of notice?"

The logic appeared to quell Jack's disquiet. He slouched a little, rested the pistol on the desk, its bulbous end still aiming Spiller's way. Not for the first time did Spiller feel dissociated from a mortal dilemma, as though the outcome was of no concern. He guessed his comeuppance was long overdue.

JoBeth glowered at her husband. "Direct that weapon someplace else, please. I'm sitting here as well."

Spiller looked at the old man, so thoroughly lost in the fog, no longer able to quantify the risk of harm. Slowly, Jack rotated the gun so it pointed at the wall.

JoBeth softened her manner. "Honey, why don't you let Matt tell you who he is? I'm sure he's not who you think he is."

"I'm not," Spiller said.

Jack sat upright again. "Okay. Talk. But remember you're a long way from the road, sitting in a sound-proof box, and these are subsonic rounds waiting to leave a big suppressor."

"No problem. My name is Matthew Spiller. You can Google me. Believe me, there's plenty to find. I'm an actor, I just completed a movie here, and I just got a part in a TV series. It's about John Frears, the guy who died in the Ferrari. That's why I was with his wife yesterday – Virginia. JoBeth, just Google me."

JoBeth typed the name into Jack's cell. Jack kept his eye on Spiller the whole time.

"He's here," JoBeth said. "It's true. Matt's an actor. He was on Mel Banaghan the other night. Jack, take a look."

Jack woke up a dark screen on the desk and tapped in the search. His eyes flicked between the images and Spiller's face.

"He's all over the internet," JoBeth added.

"So, what did you come back for, Matt?" Jack asked. "I'm still not convinced. Why did you come back here today?"

"You saw something, didn't you?" Spiller said. "On the cameras out front. Yesterday, when you called JoBeth, I knew you'd seen something important. I'm just looking out for Virginia."

"We don't want to get involved," Jack said.

"Speak for yourself," JoBeth said. "*You* don't want to get involved."

"And I don't want *you* to get killed."

"Jack… honey… no one is out to get us."

"Don't patronize me, JoBeth. You don't know what I saw."

"Then why don't you show me?" She got up and stood beside him. "Jack, lose the gun. Matt is not here to hurt us."

Jack took the semi-auto and put it in the drawer. Spiller hadn't been invited but decided to join JoBeth by the desk. He watched as Jack went into the system and found a video file.

"I cut the relevant clips together so you can see it more clearly; exactly what took place."

He clicked to play, and Spiller furtively held his phone to his side and started recording what followed, but his phone instantly beeped about its lack of storage. He quickly shoved it in his pocket.

"What was that?" Jack asked.

"Text message," Spiller said, and carried on watching with mounting confusion and horror.

AT THE END, Spiller stood there dumbfounded. It was clear that Jack's time at the government department had involved next-level tech that would have knocked Elon Musk back in his chair. His fingers belied their liver spots, skating around the keyboard like a young wizard's casting a spell, but it was his brain that was truly remarkable. Whatever synapses that may have been fading in his gray matter were seemingly bypassed by a genius network that was hardwired and still firing on all cylinders. The edit he'd produced of the crash looked like a professional movie; short, but packing the hardest of punches. He'd also put together an album of still shots, pulled from the video, of the relevant moments. Zooming in, clearing up the faintest pixilation that only showed at the closest magnification. Jack's tech acumen, his ability to frame a compelling story, was a prosecutor's wet dream.

JoBeth slowly retreated to the couch and sank into it like her legs had lost their strength. Her skin had the pallor of shock. "Jack?" she said.

He shook his head. "I don't know."

"We call the cops, right?"

"Seriously?"

"Honey, Virginia deserves to know the truth. We need to help her find some peace."

"JoBeth, right now that woman is most likely alive and kicking precisely because she *doesn't* know the truth. And the peace you want her to have? That could be the kind she rests in permanently. You just watched what I watched, right? Matt, am I right?"

Spiller shrugged. There was so much he wanted to say, but so much he couldn't explain. So much information that was barely credible, and so damn close to home.

"Matt," JoBeth said, "we have to call the police. Tell Jack."

"Sorry, but... I can see why Jack might not want to."

"Thank you, Matt. I need some time to think, JoBeth. *If* we make the call, it can't go to the wrong person. We don't know what that was about, but it may go very deep. And that's not me being paranoid."

"All right, honey." JoBeth got up and opened the door. "I'm sure you know best."

Jack followed his wife out of the panic room, growling something about being glib and condescending, and Spiller took those few seconds to commandeer Jack's pistol from the desk drawer. Who didn't love a free gun? He unscrewed the suppressor and slipped both into his waistband under his shirt. No doubt at least one of the steel cabinets in that room was crammed full of weapons. Jack didn't need it, and probably wouldn't miss it. Might not even remember he owned it.

Spiller said his hurried goodbyes to the elderly couple, who were in the kitchen, verbally jabbing half-heartedly at each other. Jack stopped and followed Spiller outside and up to the front gate, then out onto Mulholland. He touched Spiller's arm.

"You can't spot them, can you?"

Spiller understood the reference. His eyes scoured the trees for the cameras. "Nope. I give up."

Jack put a fatherly arm around his shoulder and pointed. "There's one, and..." He led Spiller along the verge to the Maserati. "There's the other. See?"

"Vaguely. Difficult, even with you pointing them out. Listen, Jack, if you do decide to talk to the cops, I know someone you can trust."

"Trust is a big word, Matt."

"I know. Look, I don't like him, and he sure as hell doesn't like me, but that's not the point. This guy's by the book. If he wasn't..." Spiller struggled to elucidate without revealing too much of his own dark past.

"What?" Jack asked.

"I wouldn't be here talking to you now. He'd have stitched me up. I gave him every reason."

Jack smirked. "Well, now you're making me think *you're* the one I can't trust, Matt."

Spiller became acutely aware of the stolen steel pressed tight against his skin under his shirt. "Let me give you my number, in case you want to talk it through." He slipped behind the wheel of the Maserati and took a scrap of paper and a pen from the glove compartment. He jotted down his phone number and handed it to Jack.

"Why don't *you* want to get involved?" Jack asked. "I'd have thought, given the footage you just saw, that you'd be disgusted I'm in two minds about this. You don't think Virginia should see it?"

"Honestly, I've courted some controversy lately. I don't need to get in the middle of any more. And even more selfishly, I don't want

Virginia to pull the plug on the TV show." He looked down at his lap, feeling slightly ashamed. Or feigning it. It was becoming increasingly difficult to tell.

"It's okay, Matt. The job I did for thirty years was never lighter than gray. Mostly dark gray to black. I'm no angel. I understand conflicts of interest all too well."

Spiller thought he saw a glint of pride in Jack's eyes, as though he were surviving on the memory of past deeds, however inglorious.

"I'll maybe call," Jack said. "So long, Matt."

## TWENTY-FIVE

NOAH DALTON PERCHED on a large, white, ornamental rock outside the LAPD's Pacific Station on Culver, under the shade of a sidewalk tree. He looked at the modern brick and concrete façade, then at the incongruous stone obelisks off to the right, standing like misshapen tombstones in an old Texan graveyard. The hell was wrong with this town?

He was in a quandary. Confused as a goat on AstroTurf, as his pa used to say before he got T-boned running a red on his way home from watching the Dallas Cowboys at the bar. After, he didn't say much of anything. Just drooled a lot while he sat in his wheelchair facing the TV every night, while Ma Dalton popped her Oxy in the bedroom and prayed for him to pass in his sleep. To get away from all that, it had been the army or acting, and Noah had decided he'd rather be shot by an Arri Alexa in Hollywood than an AK-47 in Afghanistan.

By rights, he should have marched inside and reported his truck stolen. Should have done that first thing, soon as he'd woken and seen it was gone. But there was the Smith & Wesson to consider. He wanted to assume whoever stole the truck would have rifled the glove compartment and found it, removing the risk of a firearms charge against its rightful owner. Then again, his assumption that he would always bring it inside for home defense each night had proven false; so, so much for assumptions.

Now, though, he had a bigger worry. Billy wasn't answering his cell. To his immense surprise, he'd grown genuinely fond of the old Brit. Billy was just so different. His accent, his words, his sense of humor. And his kindness that seemed unrelated to any carnal favors, because Noah had come to realize that Billy had been honest when he'd told him that first time in the office that there was no need for sex.

He tried working through the scenarios. They ranged from the best case of the cops returning his truck, along with the gun still hidden inside the service wallet, to the very worst case of him being arrested for Billy's murder because Matt Spiller had stolen his truck and used his gun on his agent – a gun that could be traced to him from his fingerprints on the magazine and the bullets, if not the frame. He'd always hated it when his ma told him if his brains were ink, he couldn't dot an i. But she'd been right. Antagonizing a fellah he damn well knew was a homicidal lunatic. Why the hell had he revealed outside the elevator that Billy had told him all about last Christmas in England? Doing so, he'd hung targets on his and Billy's back, and Billy's may well have been perforated already.

Shoot, what was that cop's name? The one Billy had told him about. The one from England who was now working here. He'd understand. Maybe he was the only one who would. Best talk to the man first, get ahead of the game, fess up, even about the gun, rather than risk the worst case coming true and having to defend the indefensible.

Noah headed inside. The desk officer welcomed him with a dutiful smile.

"Officer, I need some help. I need to talk to a detective about a fellah called Matt Spiller – the actor. No doubt you saw him on the television a few nights back. There's a detective who knows him from England. I gotta talk to that detective *tout suite*."

"Okay, slow down. This detective? You got a name?"

"No, sir, I don't. He would be recently arrived from England. You know of such a detective?"

"I don't. You know which area he works?"

Noah remembered Billy saying the detective had paid a visit to Spiller's home. "Uh, possibly Beverly Glen."

"And what's it concerning?"

"I can't be sure. Could be a homicide."

The officer's brow furrowed. "Okay. Well, you'd need West Bureau Homicide. But—"

"Began with a B! Something Italian."

"Pardon?"

"The detective's name. Can you check, please, sir? I really need to talk to him."

The officer looked down at his monitor and tapped something in. "There's a Lieutenant Bartoli at West Bur—"

"*Yes!*" Noah shouted. "Yes, sir! Bartoli. That's his name. Definitely Bartoli. And where would I find this detective?"

"Why don't you come through to the office and we'll see if we can get in touch with him?"

Noah took a moment to assess the offer, and noticed the cop seemed slightly agitated, like he was about to pull his sidearm. He wanted out of there. There was a conversation to be had, for sure, but it had to happen right now and off the record. He couldn't risk sitting in a jail cell, waiting to be interviewed, only to have the unsavory facts of his agent's disappearance pre-empt the utterance of his fears.

"Sure," Noah, said, and dithered. Then he heard the door behind him opening. He turned and ran, barging past an elderly guy who cursed at him. The desk officer called after him to stop. He took a diagonal toward the street, crossed some paving stones, but then an area of gravel tricked his hurried gait and he stumbled. Then he was up, briefly, before his muscles were filled full of lactic acid and he dropped like a dead weight.

OF ALL THE types of maniac Spiller suspected he might be, klepto wasn't one of them. And yet, he'd stolen a truck and now a pistol, and he didn't even know what he wanted the latter item for, although he guessed that was probably a characteristic of any self-respecting klepto. It was another gun he'd need to hide out by the reservoir.

Too much was happening in his life. He'd been overloaded even before his visit to Jack and JoBeth. Now, having watched the video, he didn't know where to turn. Virginia certainly needed to know. And Hayley. And Bartoli. But the women could end up canceling *Veteran Avenue*, and he absolutely didn't want to embroil himself in the matter of John Frears by having the LAPD redesignate his death. If Jack and JoBeth decided to surrender the footage, that was their choice, although Spiller knew Jack was also reluctant to attract attention, given his paranoia.

But, boy, these were exciting times, and not just because he was in Hollywood about to begin his second project. He'd realized over last Christmas that the very events that threatened to upend his life, or literally end it, were also the most life-affirming. It was perverse, no doubt, but he'd become hooked on the taste of fear and adrenaline. In a town full of people addicted to booze or drugs or sex, this was Matt Spiller's chosen fix.

The sight of Billy's Camaro outside his house brought him somewhat to his senses. The cost of his macabre sense of gratification was high. He parked the Maserati on his drive and looked at Billy's rental. It reminded him of his last visit to his parents' house after his mum had so swiftly shuffled off to follow his dad. The emptiness, the finality, knowing a vital essence had gone from his life.

"You stupid, stupid old man," he muttered to himself.

Now it was just a waiting game. At some point very soon, Noah would report his agent missing. Spiller hoped that would be tomorrow, as the micro-SD card he'd left on the floor of the F150 showed a night-time trip, and Ethan had apparently witnessed Billy's return the previous evening. But it didn't matter. If Noah did talk to the cops, they would just assume he was pre-empting a crime he was yet to commit as a gambit to fool them. Either way, tomorrow or the day after, Spiller would make an anonymous call to the cops to alert them to the existence of an abandoned truck.

AFTER REQUESTING THE custody officer uncuff the young Texan, Bartoli had taken the poor kid to an interview room for an unofficial chat. What he'd listened to had been both horribly reminiscent, and no doubt disconcertingly prescient. This schmuck was in a ton of trouble. He watched Noah fight back the tears, and guessed the kid probably hadn't cried in front of a stranger since he was in diapers. Yet, despite his sympathy, Bartoli was pissed at him. If Billy Banbury really was dead, then that was one less person in the world who could definitively put Matt Spiller in the frame for all that had happened back in England. And that pool of people wasn't big to begin with. Now there was only Brett Stutz. By confronting Spiller outside the elevator as he'd described, Noah had sealed Billy Banbury's fate.

"I gotta ask, Noah... why? Why would you reveal to Matt Spiller that you knew what he'd done? That Billy told you? And after you broke his nose, for Christ's sake. Knowing what you knew about him, you didn't think maybe you should keep *schtum?* Let Billy come forward when he was good and ready? Sorry, kid, but if your agent's dead, a lot of that's on you."

Noah sniffed some snot back in. "I know. So? What are you gonna do about it?"

"I'll go talk to Spiller – for all the good that ever does. See what he has to say for himself."

Noah shifted uncomfortably in his chair. "I still feel funny."

"That's because you got your ass tasered. Next time you mention a possible homicide to a cop, don't then turn around and run away."

"Yeah, that was dumb." Noah seemed to consider his next question. "Am I in any trouble?"

"With me?" Bartoli shook his head. "All off the record. Can't tell you it's gonna stay that way, though. Cops find that gun of yours, and it's missing a few rounds, I'm guessing illegal transportation of a firearm's gonna be the least of your worries. And if Spiller's behind all this, they *are* gonna find that gun. Meantime, God knows what else that psycho has in store for you. My advice would be to get the hell out of Dodge."

"Huh?"

"Leave town. Go back home. Where is home?"

"Amarillo."

"Okay. Go there. Get out of LA while you can. If we need to come looking, we'll find you. Point is, Spiller has you in his sights, and that's a place you don't wanna be. Even I wouldn't wanna be in your spot right now, and I have a legal forty-five on my hip and the might of the LAPD behind me."

Noah's expression twisted, like he was finally coming to the realization that no one could help. "Is he really that bad?"

Bartoli smiled queerly at the recollection. "Hate to say, but he ran rings around me a few months back. Most of the time, I don't think even he knew which direction he was running, but he seemed to have this knack of changing course at just the right moment, figuring out his next move on the hoof. I don't know. I haven't decided yet if he's a criminal genius, or just the luckiest dope I ever met. Thing is, it amounts to the same thing: he gets away with behavior that you or I would be locked up for inside of five minutes."

Noah groaned and leaned his head on his arms. Then he jerked bolt upright.

"Noah? What?"

"Could he be killed?"

Bartoli revealed his prior thoughts on the possibility by laughing. "Well, I don't think he's immortal, so…"

"Would anyone really care if he was killed?"

Bartoli adopted a stern attitude. "Noah, don't even think about it. Two reasons: A, I'm gonna know it was you and I'll come for you; and B, it won't stop anything he's already set in motion. Worse, if I can't question him because he's dead, then I can't trip him up, which leaves you hoping he made a mistake that's gonna let you off the hook. And to date, Matthew Spiller has not put a foot wrong."

## TWENTY-SIX

LOUNGING NEXT TO his pool, Spiller could hear a commotion on the road outside his home. A car engine and slamming doors. His first thought was that Bartoli had finally given up on catching him legitimately and had resorted to sending in SWAT to perforate his sun-bronzed torso. They could plant a weapon, make it look like a righteous kill. It wasn't that far-fetched, given he'd executed a similar plan in England that had seen gang leader and barrister Dominic Ward turned into Swiss cheese at the hands of a tactical firearms unit.

Then a voice he recognized made his heart leap. He got up and opened the side gate.

"Daddy!" Sophie yelled, then grinned, showing gaps and teeth in various stages of growth and shedding.

He crouched down and opened his arms so his youngest could pelt into them. He encircled her and stood up with her held tightly, then opened one arm for his eldest to receive a hug. Sammy smiled, and sauntered as an older teenager does who's too cool to run, and who was clearly still smarting from their recent estrangement.

"So good to see you both. I've missed you so much."

Sophie pulled her head away. "Can I go swimming?"

"What's that?" Spiller asked. "You've missed me, too?"

"Can I?"

He lowered her to the concrete and looked at his wife, who offered a faint smile. Sophie grabbed her sister's hand and dragged her into Spiller's back garden, which audibly wowed her.

"Hey, Helen," he said. "Everything okay? I thought you weren't arriving until tomorrow."

"Today, Matt."

"Pretty sure it was tomorrow."

"Two possibilities. You're wrong, or we're wrong but the airline didn't give a toss."

He nodded. "Easy to lose track of the days here." He stared past her at a figure still seated in their rented Tesla. "Should have known he'd go electric. Is he getting out or what?"

Helen retreated a few steps and tapped on the window. David exited and came around with a beaming smile and his hand outstretched.

"Matt, how are you?"

"I'm all right. How are you, David? How are you enjoying my wife?"

David looked at Helen. "Should I go; pick you up later?"

"No, David, you can stay. Matt's just being a prick. Give him a few minutes to get the bile out of his system, he'll be all right."

David smiled at Spiller. "I didn't cause your break-up, Matt. You know that, right?"

Spiller blew a long breath, nodded. "Yep. All on me. Totally my bad." He extended his arm, and the two men shook, although Spiller noted David's grasp was like a limp flannel in his palm. His dad had always told him you could judge a man by his handshake.

David dithered for a moment. "I'll go and check on the girls. May I?"

Spiller stepped aside unnecessarily. *"Mi esposa es su esposa."*

"What? It's *casa*, isn't it?" David asked. "The expression?"

"Oh, yeah. Bit rusty on the Spanish."

David entered the pool area, leaving the exes to their awkwardness. But Spiller quickly realized he was the only one who felt uncomfortable. Helen had dealt with it and moved on, and if she hadn't, he would never know.

"Don't be a twat this holiday, please, Matt."

"Matt the twat."

"I mean it. We all want to have a happy time. *All* of us. David has been brilliant. Good for me, great for the girls."

"I know; he bought them a dog."

"Don't be so cynical. You should be thanking him. He's been a solid, dependable influence on our lives since you left. And I do know what *esposa* means. I still remember my school Spanish."

"Sorry," he said, and meant it. "And… I'm sorry I couldn't measure up."

"It's okay. It's who you are. You're good at a lot of things. Family life isn't one of them."

Behind him, there was a splash, then a bigger one.

Spiller laughed. "They're not wasting any time. What are your plans today, Helen? You can kick around the pool for a bit, if you like. Are you hungry? I have a big freezer full of stuff."

"Thanks. We need to ring around a few hotels first. We went to ours and really didn't like the neighborhood. Just a vibe."

"Why don't you stay here?" Spiller's mouth said, before checking in with his brain. "For a couple of days, at least. I can stay somewhere else if you feel awkward. I mean, you know... cheaper for me to get a single room than for you to get a family room. Right?"

Helen had him figured. She smirked. "Ah, Matthew has a girlfriend."

"Early days. Very early days. I didn't grab someone the moment I landed here. I want you to know that."

"Matt, it's okay." She nodded at the Camaro. "Whose is that? Thought you had a Maserati."

By this point, Spiller had run through a worst-case scenario in his head, and his offer of *gratis* accommodation didn't seem so smart anymore. He imagined a severely aggrieved Noah landing on his doorstep, having slipped the clutches of the cops who were after him for a murder he'd been framed for. Damn, he really needed Noah in custody ASAP.

"Matt?"

"What?"

"The Camaro?"

Perfect excuse. "My agent's. I thought you were getting here tomorrow so he's meant to be moving out in the morning."

"Your *agent* is staying with you?"

Spiller realized he'd not clued her in – for good reason. Now he had to. "Billy. My English agent. I've been putting him up for a few days. How about you get a room tonight, then you can all come and spend a few days here once he's gone."

She stared at him. "Billy Banbury's here?"

"Uh-huh."

Helen lowered her voice, moved closer. "Is this about last Christmas? Does he know what happened?"

"No-no. Just... silly bugger upped sticks and followed me out here."

"Matt, I *know* there's stuff you didn't share about last Christmas, and I was okay with that. Plausible deniability. And because I thought it was all over. So, *do not* tell me you're getting some blasts from the past. Not since we flew all this way."

Spiller searched for a plausible denial of his own, but he was too slow.

"Jesus Christ," Helen said.

"It's fine. Helen, it's fine. Honestly, give me a day." He laughed. "You've given me twenty years; what's another twenty-four hours?"

She didn't echo his mirth. She shook her head and went through to the pool.

Spiller considered. Would it be weird if he reported Billy missing so soon? Could he pre-empt Noah and not appear suspicious? He still needed another night to pass so the dashcam footage made sense.

The sound of a car engine drew his gaze, and rendered his deliberations moot. Exactly the person he wanted to see, at precisely the wrong time. He stepped to the gate and quietly drew it closed, then hurried up the lane to flag Bartoli down before he could make it all the way to his drive. Bartoli passed him and parked behind the Tesla and the Camaro.

"Listen," Spiller said, as Bartoli stepped out. "Not a good time."

"Got a little party going, huh? What? You don't invite your old buddy Angelo?"

"I've got family visiting, okay? My kids. Whatever you're here for, I don't want them involved. I don't want them upset. I mean it. You need to go."

"What I need to do is my job. And right now that's talking to LA's own resident English psychopath."

"Right. What is it? Quick."

Bartoli leaned against his car. "Your agent. When did you last see him?"

"Yesterday. We went out for a ride on my bike. Why?"

Bartoli raised an eyebrow. "You're telling me Billy Banbury went pillion on that motorcycle of yours?"

"Here, look." Spiller took his phone from his pocket, cued up some photos. "That's him in his leathers yesterday afternoon, in my garage, before we headed off. Look at his little face; how happy he was."

"Sure. And you both got home safe?"

"Of course. If you don't believe me, ask one of your officers. Ethan King. You know him?"

Bartoli shook his head. "Lot of cops in this city. Why? He pull you over?"

"No, he was here when we got back. We had a few drinks together. Quite a few."

Bartoli snorted, then laughed. "Well, ain't that convenient."

"Ethan King," Spiller repeated. "Go and talk to him."

"And this morning?"

"I heard Billy get up early."

"Right. One of these his?" Bartoli indicated the cars.

"The Camaro."

"So, he's still here."

"No. He likes to wander around the reservoir in the morning. Or maybe he took a cab somewhere. I don't know. Not really my concern."

Bartoli sighed. "Are we game-playing again, Matthew?"

Spiller shrugged. "I'm not with you."

"Okay, I'll save us some time. Noah Dalton reported Billy Banbury missing today, so now you can go ahead and make an anonymous call to let us know where his truck is, so we can find the evidence you left in it that Noah killed him. Probably that Smith and Wesson from his glove compartment, right?"

"You have such a negative impression of me."

"Just trying to speed things up, Matthew. That kid's a mess because of you. He knows what's heading his way, so, do the guy a favor and put him out of his misery, why don't you?"

The pool gate opened, and Helen stepped out. She eyed Bartoli's car, and Spiller could see she'd pegged it as a cop vehicle – the door spot, the lightbox in the windshield. He swore under his breath as she came over.

"Hi," she greeted Bartoli. "Detective…?"

"Mrs Spiller, right? Helen Spiller?"

She groaned like the title pained her. "For my sins."

Spiller watched the cogs meshing in Bartoli's head, resulting in a cruel smirk. Was he about to rat him out to his wife for being with Sadie the other night?

Instead, Bartoli extended his hand. "We never met – last Christmas."

She loosely grasped it, frowning at the riddle. "Uh…"

"Lieutenant Bartoli. I was DCI Bartoli back then. Your husband did a damn fine job of keeping me away from you." He grinned. "But all good things…"

Helen sent daggers flying Spiller's way. "*Another one* who followed you out here? And you didn't tell me?"

Bartoli answered. "No, Helen. We got here roughly the same time. He got a job in LA, I got a job in LA. What are the odds, huh?"

"And you're here now why?" she asked.

"You may wanna ask your husband. Been up to his old tricks again, the little *sod*." He chortled at his Britishism. "Anyway, enjoy your vacation. And a word of advice? Don't stay with this loser. You wouldn't believe what he's been up to while you've been out of the picture."

Spiller spoke up. "She knows I have a girlfriend, Angelo."

Bartoli laughed. "Like *that's* your greatest peccadillo. Toodle pip."

Spiller made a supreme effort not to notice Helen's scrutiny as he watched Bartoli get in his car and drive away. "What?" he said to her.

"You're asking me? What the hell is going on, Matt? You promised me, and especially Sammy, that you had no problems here. Despite that absolute car crash on *The Mel Banaghan Show*."

Spiller dismissed her concerns with the waft of a hand. "Ah, he's just fishing. He's on the Harry Sullivan case and he's drawing a blank, so he's trying to pin stuff on me because he's still annoyed about last

Christmas." He attempted to walk past her, heading for the pool, but she grabbed his wrist.

"Define *stuff*."

"I don't know... apparently, my agent's gone missing."

"Oh, Matt..."

"Listen, the old codger hooked up with some young Texan stud. The same guy who broke my nose. They'll be getting their rocks off somewhere."

"Thought you swam into the pool wall," Helen said. "That's what you told us."

"Well... it's done. It's over."

She still had a hold of his wrist, and now she squeezed it. "Okay, then there's no problem. That's what you're telling me, right? And I should believe you, right, Matt? Because you wouldn't have let us come out here if you had any problems. *Right, Matt?*"

"Right."

"So, we can all stay here tonight."

"Yeah," he said quickly, to block the avalanche of objections that was about to gush out of his mouth.

"I mean, if Billy's not around, then his room's free. And he was about to move out anyway, right? So, I can just help you pack up all his stuff and put it in the garage for when he does show up. *Yes?*"

Spiller felt like he was being manipulated by a master hypnotist. "Yep. Sounds like a plan."

"Good." Helen turned and headed back to the girls.

The pool gate closed on him, and he heard his wife morph in an instant, the gaiety his daughters craved returning to her voice. Then they were all laughing, David growling playfully as he no doubt stalked Sophie around the pool edge, being the father figure Spiller would have needed months of Method Acting to emulate. He wondered if they'd miss him if he left, whether they'd even notice if he just headed off to Sadie and the allure of her undemanding affection.

Helen was punishing him. Installing her reconfigured family in his home so he could look on like the outsider he'd become. The horrendous sequence of events last Christmas had not been set off by him. That had been down to Sammy hooking up with a drug dealer, and Helen filling said drug dealer's throat and facial cavities with expanding foam. It had then been left to the man of the house to clear up that mess, and everything that had followed. Still, when it *had* all settled, he had waltzed off to Hollywood. Not just for a job, but to start a new life on his own, leaving Helen to deal with the emotional aftermath, especially in Sammy. The house, the pool, the Maserati, his career – these were the things he was being punished for.

But there was usually an upside to any apparently luckless situation, and Spiller didn't have to search that hard to find the advantage in this one. In fact, it could not have worked out better had he planned it. Because tonight was the night that Billy would officially be taken to the desert, and there was no better alibi than having a houseful of guests. Especially when at least one of them wouldn't lie to get him off a parking ticket, let alone a murder rap.

ONCE THE EVIDENCE was in, the cops would know that the perp couldn't have made it from LA out to the desert and back in much less than four hours. Therefore, Spiller had to make his presence in the house known every three hours or so throughout the night. The girls went to bed early, but he had managed to keep Helen and David up until one a.m., chatting about life in Hollywood and the stars he'd met. Latterly, their expressions had suggested they'd rather go to bed, or have multiple root canals, than listen to him regale them. He had noticed Helen start to snuggle into David on the sofa, presenting a distasteful image that she correctly hoped would drive Spiller to bed and end the evening. Fair play, he thought, that she was giving her estranged host at least a little respect by feigning interest in the very thing that had destroyed their marriage.

At four o'clock in the morning, Spiller was still reading in bed, and wondered how he might wake his houseguests without making it seem like he was trying to wake his houseguests. He wasn't sure he'd have slept very well had he even wanted to. Every sound outside made him think Noah was creeping around the property, trying to locate the easiest way in, a weapon in his hand and the blackest of thoughts in his heart.

"Ah," he said to himself, as an answer to both problems came to mind. He stared across the bedroom at the closet door and was out of bed before he knew it. He hadn't dressed Manny since stripping him of his leathers that day, so now he laid his stand-in on the bed and gave him a fresh outfit of a hoodie and jogging pants.

As intended, Manny's heels thumped on each step as he was dragged downstairs. Spiller stopped halfway and listened for any stirrings from the adults' spare bedroom. All that came to him was light snoring, so he let go of Manny, who instantly bolstered his stunt résumé with Stair Fall.

Helen was the first to appear on the landing, a look of genuine terror on her face. "Matt, what the fuck is going on?"

"Sorry."

She glanced beyond him. "Who is *that*?"

David appeared by her side, yawning, and impressively unperturbed by the whole thing.

"He's not real," Spiller said quickly. "He's a dummy. From my last movie."

Helen moved to pull the girls' door closed, but Sammy slipped out to join them on the landing before she could.

"Sorry," Spiller repeated.

Helen lowered her voice to avoid waking Sophie. "And why are you throwing him down the stairs at four o'clock in the morning?"

"Is that what time it is? Is it four o'clock?"

"Yes."

"Four o'clock, really? Bloody hell, sorry."

"Matt, I know it's your house, but what are you doing?"

"I was putting him in the lounge. He normally sits by the window as a burglar deterrent. I put him back in my closet because he freaked Billy out, but since he's not here anymore…"

Helen shook her head. "And you don't think it's going to freak out our youngest daughter?"

"Nah, she'll think it's funny."

"*I* think it's cool," Sammy agreed.

"I'm going back to bed," David said through a yawn. "Night-night."

"Night, David," Spiller said. "Sorry I woke you at four o'clock in the morning."

"Matt…" Helen said.

"What?"

"You're fucking deranged."

*"Mum."*

Helen closed herself inside the guest bedroom.

Matt shrugged at his eldest. "Oops."

"You need a hand with that?" Sammy asked.

FATHER AND DAUGHTER settled with their mugs of tea. Spiller watched Sammy, who was squinting at Manny as though she knew him from somewhere.

"He looks like you," she said.

"Charming," Spiller replied, eyeing the vacant pupils of his inanimate stunt double.

"He's got more hair, though."

"When are you going home?"

"LOL. You've got to admit, Dad, this is all a bit weird."

"Your mum shacked up with David in my spare room? Tell me about it."

Sammy chuckled. "No, I mean *that*. At this time of night."

"Sorry. Just couldn't sleep."

"I thought that was better since you've been here."

"It is. I still have bad nights, though." He smiled at her. "How are you?"

"I get on with stuff. What else can you do? No point dwelling."

"No." He took a slurp of tea. "You like David?"

She nodded. "He's a decent guy. Takes care of mum. And us. Dad, why did you leave?"

He groaned. "We've talked about this."

"Not face to face."

Spiller gave it a moment's thought, then shrugged. "I don't know. Fate. Destiny. Stupidity. Sammy, it's a Hollywood career. It was a big movie by a top director. What was I going to do?"

Sammy was shaking her head. "You don't have to live here to work here, Dad. I know it's more convenient, but there are British actors who fly here to do a movie, then fly home."

He drained his tea, stared out at the night sky, still two hours away from dawn. "That day at the airport… we both knew what it meant. Your mum knew when she waved me away. Forget the police involvement had I stayed. It was bigger than that. She wanted me out of her life. She's happy with David, right?"

"She doesn't swear when she's with him. That was the first time in ages."

"Soph seems to like him."

Sammy tried not to grimace at the truth of it. "Yeah."

"You looking after your little sis?"

"Of course. Always got my eye on her."

"Good. Thanks." Spiller offered a fatherly grin, but he felt neither paternal nor happy.

## TWENTY-SEVEN

JUST AFTER SEVEN o'clock. Spiller's phone was ringing. He sat up in bed and looked at the caller ID, which showed a name attached to a number he'd only recently added.

He pressed the green button. "Good morning, Angelo."

"Matthew. Just wanted to let you know, there's no need for you to call in with the location of that truck you stole, because someone just called it in. I'm heading there now. Should be interesting."

Spiller's mouth opened, but the line went dead before he could say anything. He guessed it was good news. No need to go to a payphone, no fear of any cameras catching who made the call, no chance of any techie cops using voice recognition software on the recording. He lay still for a moment, musing. It was too tempting. Like an arsonist peering with flickering eyes at a fire he'd just set, he had to witness the aftermath. He needed to know that the data card had been found.

His bike and car were too obvious; Bartoli might spot them. But Billy's Camaro was still parked outside. It wasn't far to Westwood. He felt certain he could beat Bartoli to the scene.

AS SPILLER NEARED the foot of North Beverly Glen Boulevard, approaching Sunset, he wondered if he was being wise going anywhere near Noah's truck. In truth, he'd known from the second Bartoli had hung up on him that it was a stupid move, and there was nothing he could do at the scene if the cops didn't find the data card. He was hardly going to walk up to them and suggest they missed something. Anyway, with Bartoli's input, they would know it wasn't just a stolen-recovered vehicle. He would have CSI crawling all over it, and how likely was it that a seasoned CSI would fail to check under the floor mats.

Despite his qualms, he continued onto Sunset, shortly branching off to skirt the north of the UCLA campus, heading for the frat and sorority houses on the west side.

As he stopped at the junction with Gayley, about to cross over onto Strathmore, and the truck's location on Landfair, a more troubling thought occurred: that perhaps he was being played. He checked his mirror and could see a black car three vehicles behind. The route ahead was clear, but he waited, causing the two cars behind to honk at him and quickly overtake. In his mirror, he could see the black car was holding back, and he knew it was Bartoli in his Chevy Impala.

Spiller moved across Gayley onto Strathmore and continued, passing Landfair, and eventually exiting onto Veteran Avenue. The Impala followed. He hopped on the 405, then came off and headed east across the city on Santa Monica Boulevard. He kept his tail until South Beverly Glen, when he saw the Impala take a left and abandon the wild goose chase.

DESPITE SENSING AT the junction with Gayley that he'd been spotted, Bartoli had carried on a while, until he felt certain that Spiller was more than likely going to keep driving until he ran out of gas. What would it matter? It wasn't his car, and Billy Banbury wouldn't be asking where it had been abandoned.

Bartoli cursed as he pulled over to think, but it didn't take more than a few seconds to figure out where the truck might be. Spiller had taken a specific route, heading for Westwood's student community; at which point, when he'd noticed his tail, he'd driven right through it and out the other side.

He got going again, up to Wilshire, then headed back to Westwood, where, within ten minutes, he'd found it. The old Ford pickup was parked on Landfair, incongruous among all the modern, reasonably priced student cars that lined the street. It was parked outside the Delta Sigma Phi frat house – so the green lettering on the white building professed. He stopped adjacent to the truck and switched on his cop lights, a guard against anyone questioning his antics and requesting a black-and-white. He tried the door handles. The truck was locked, so he used a baton to smash the passenger window and open the door. The sound of breaking glass drew attention. Several frat boys in various states of undress began filtering out of their houses. Bartoli peered into the bed of the truck, then climbed in. He broke open the lockbox and rummaged around, before lowering himself back onto the road. Next, he leaned in the passenger side and checked the glove compartment, reached across to unlock the other door, then hunkered down to check under the seat. He went round to the sidewalk and opened the driver's side, squatting again to search.

And there it was. Not the gun he'd hoped for, but perhaps something much more useful.

LUCKILY FOR HIM, Noah hadn't taken Bartoli's advice to leave town. There was nothing left for him in Amarillo, and he didn't have any place else in mind. And whatever was hurtling down the track toward him, he was never going to outpace it.

Standing outside the small, rented bungalow he shared with three other wannabes was the person he'd expected, but sooner than he'd have liked.

"Don't tell me," Noah said to Lieutenant Bartoli. "They found my truck, my gun minus a few rounds, a map showin' X marks the spot, and Billy Banbury dead on the X with my bullets in his head."

"Hold out your hand," Bartoli said.

Noah offered up his wrists to be cuffed.

"No, just one hand. Open it."

Puzzled, Noah withdrew one arm and cupped a palm, as instructed. Bartoli laid his hand over the top, then closed Noah's, although he couldn't feel that anything had been placed there. He opened his fingers just sufficiently to see what it was.

"I don't get," he said.

"You will. Watch it. You'll know what to do. By the way, your truck's on Landfair in Westwood. Sorry, I had to smash your glass to get that. I'd go pick it up before it gets stripped for parts."

Noah was still staring at the micro-SD card in his palm. "But what if I watch this and I still don't know what to do?"

"Then I guess you're going to jail." He turned to leave, but Noah grabbed his arm.

"Detective, please… you made a real effort for me – I see that – and I surely appreciate it, but… it's all gonna be for naught if I can't figure out what to do."

Bartoli looked to his left and right, but there was no one around. He lowered his voice. "I found your truck, but there are still two things outstanding. One without the other, you should be okay. Put the two together, you're in big trouble. Listen, kid, I already broke the law for you. That right there is evidence. I watched it. You mentioned X marks the spot? Well, there you go."

Noah felt his expression twisting in confusion as Bartoli returned to his car. He guessed the detective was just trying to cling onto some vestige of professionalism in not spelling out exactly what the next steps were. Maybe if he didn't hear himself speak the words, he could somehow minimize his moral decline.

*Two things outstanding.* At least that part was easy. His gun and his agent.

Noah went back inside and found his laptop.

SPILLER STILL HAD Noah's Smith & Wesson. He was grateful for that, at least. His phone had beeped with a text message shortly after he'd arrived home. It was from Bartoli. One word: *DELETED*. Vague enough that it wouldn't mean anything in court, but sufficient for its recipient to get the gist. Bartoli had discovered the data card and had disposed of it to protect Noah. Spiller was quietly impressed. Bartoli had never seemed the type to go rogue. Still, Spiller smirked, because Bartoli had only delayed the inevitable. His destruction of the evidence didn't alter the fact of Billy's body lying poorly hidden at a desert location that could be made known to the cops at a time of Spiller's choosing.

Or maybe never. The aim had been to remove a wobbly cog from his carefully constructed Hollywood adventure; to make sure Billy could never threaten him with blackmail again; to reduce by half the number of people in that town whose eyewitness testimony could put him in jail. Now there was only Stutz, and he would only hobble his own career by admitting to knowledge he should have confessed to six months ago. Providing Noah stayed out of the picture, Spiller supposed there really wasn't any need to frame him, and he felt genuinely buoyed by his sense of benevolence. Was Death Row fair payback for a broken nose? Probably not.

With his alibi now set in stone, Spiller no longer needed any of his guests in the house. Helen and David as a couple made him want to retch, even though his ex-next-door-neighbor had clearly been a boon to his family. Even his girls made him uncomfortable right now. Perhaps it was just the strain of a fractured relationship that was his responsibility to mend. Who was he to them? A Method actor who'd been offered a mystifying role. Still, he was in Los Angeles, and there was plenty to do that wouldn't involve conversation. Places to visit, and some that would only be open to famous people like him. He'd take his kids out today, wherever they wanted to go, buy them a ton of souvenirs, and he'd record it all, so, in years to come, he could watch a highly selective outtake of smiles and laughter, and ignore the larger blooper reel that surrounded it.

Time, finally, to cut some of the media that was bloating his phone's storage. First, the bulky files.

Five minutes later, Matt Spiller was laughing his ass off at the funniest video.

AT KRAMER JUNCTION, Noah stopped referring to the notes he'd made from the journey on the data card. The signs had been clearly marked, illuminated against the night sky, above the highways that had taken Matt Spiller to that point, two nights earlier. He pulled in and refueled the Ford at a gas station just shy of the crossroads. He watched the comings and goings on the highway. Lots of semi-trailers taking advantage of the services. A glorified truck-stop in the middle of the desert. An ugly electric substation to his left; no reason to linger here, except to gas up, grab a bite to eat, or a little shut-eye. He paid for his fuel and climbed back in. The dusty desert air had coated the cab through its windowless door.

He perched his laptop on the dashboard and set the video going, forwarding to the precise moment the light turned green and Spiller cruised through the deserted junction. He paused it at that point. He'd already timed this last leg of the journey at around eleven minutes, and he figured if he kept an eye on the clock and matched his speed to the one indicated on the recording, he would know the exact moment he arrived at the correct turn-off.

Noah moved back onto the blacktop and joined the queue at the lights. When the light turned green, he set the recording to play, and began to feel nauseous at the thought of what he might find a few miles down the road.

Really, he just wanted to locate the gun. If he could do that and dispose of it where no one would ever find it, that would suffice. Bartoli had told him without spelling it out. The gun without the body; the body without the gun. Both would work to smash the frame. But of the two scenarios, he preferred the former.

Spiller had stuck to 55mph, and Noah did likewise. He passed a vast solar farm on his left and headed into the desert again. It reminded him of Texas, and he felt a pang that took him by surprise. He felt homesick. Not for the old family house, or the ruined folk who still dwelled there, but for his life before all this. When Hollywood had been a mere idea; letters on a hillside that spelled a mythical future, unsullied by the experience of actually meeting its weird inhabitants.

Ten miles and eleven minutes later, the speed on the recording slowed, and Noah eased off the gas. There were no vehicles heading his way, and none behind close enough to see where he turned, so he followed the route, taking a left off the highway onto a cracked concrete road. His eyes flicked between the glaring view through his windshield, and the smaller one on his dash, showing a set of headlights reaching into the darkness of two nights past. Ahead, maybe a mile away, on a small rise, he suspected he could see his destination. The vague shape of a low building, the only manmade thing on a barren landscape.

Two minutes later, at the dilapidated structures, Noah switched off the engine and wiped some dusty sweat from his top lip. Hot as Hades out here. He glanced at the laptop's screen, at the yellow tunnels of light, stationary now, and hazy with the disturbed dust of an abrupt halt. He reached for the machine and lowered its lid.

Noah surveyed the scene, and knew he was never going to find the gun. If it was here, Spiller would have left it somewhere a team of CSIs might find it, sifting yard by yard with the special dogs that could sniff out anything, but nowhere obvious that it would look like the perp wanted it to be found.

Billy's body was a different matter.

Inside the roofless building, Noah made a point of revealing only as much as he needed, to know for sure it was Billy. He could see the bullet holes in the tarp. Although the walls of the building were riddled with gunshots, this was a tight grouping. He gingerly pulled the tarp back and saw a bare foot, a sock hanging off the big toe, like it had been dragged down with the removal of his footwear. It was a distinctive sock; one he'd seen Billy wearing. Black, with colorful smiley faces.

Weeping for a man he'd barely known, but who'd been more compassionate to him than almost anyone in his entire life, Noah dragged Billy's tarp-wrapped body outside, and hefted it up onto the pickup's bed. The lightness of it made him cry louder. So empty. Hollowed out. The essence within, gone. He wiped his nose with his sleeve and closed the tailgate, and vowed in that moment to stay in LA. He would drive further inland toward the mountains, branch off onto some dirt road that led to nowhere, and dig a deep hole. Then he would return to the city, where he would remain, at least until Matt Spiller was in jail, his career in tatters. Or until he, too, was six feet under.

## TWENTY-EIGHT

"OKAY, WOMAN, YOU tell me: what should I do with this information?"

JoBeth raised a disapproving eyebrow. "Don't you *woman* me, Jack. What should you do with it? What would any sane person do with this kind of information?"

"They'd go to the cops. But as you've pointed out many times over the years, I might not be that sane."

"You're—"

Jack submerged himself to cut out her voice, then swam underwater to the opposite pool wall.

"Come back here," JoBeth ordered from her recliner, as he surfaced. "I'm not raising my voice."

Jack obediently returned to her side of the pool and rested his forearms on the warm coping stones. "Sorry."

"You're not insane, Jack, you're just paranoid. You had a crazy job, and you can't unknow the things you know. I get that. But that was years ago. This has nothing at all to do with that. We need to tell someone."

Jack wiped his eyes, ran a hand over his thinning hair, clawing it back. "Matt did say he knew a cop we could trust, if we wanted to talk to someone." He moved to the pool steps, shuffled back into the corner, and opened his elbows out on the side, leaning back and tilting his face to the sun.

"Call him and get the number."

He sighed as he relaxed. "Okay."

"Now, Jack."

"Can't a man chill in his own back yard?" But he didn't need to be told twice, and was out of the pool and walking toward the house before JoBeth had a chance to call out.

"Towel! Don't you go dripping on my clean floors!"

He stopped, shook his head, made an annoyed noise in his throat, and came back to collect his towel.

BARTOLI NUDGED THE nose of his Impala out from its space in the parking lot of the Olympic Community Police Station on South Vermont, but he was cut off by a vehicle stopping in front of him. He peered at the driver, cringed, but received a friendly wave.

Gabriela Contreras got out of the blue Ford Explorer and came up to his window.

"Hey, LT," she said. "How you doing?"

"Good, thanks. Sorry, Gabriela, I need to be somewhere."

"Sure. I just wanted to apologize for the other day. I was way outta line."

He smiled crookedly. "You don't work here. You came all this way to say sorry?"

"I did. And I was hoping we could try again. You know? Maybe grab a beer. Nothing heavy. Just a bit of good, clean fun. Well... maybe I'll throw in a little dirty fun if you play your cards right." She flashed her teeth in a big grin.

Bartoli's eyes flicked down to her breasts, held down by her Kevlar undershirt, but straining for release. His manhood stirred. "I don't know..."

"Sure you do. You getting it someplace else?"

"That would be my business."

"Thought not." She laughed. "Come on, life's too short to hold a grudge."

Bartoli was instantly reminded of his recent chat with Captain Hoyt over at Mission Division. He frowned at the memory. But her lips pouted, and Hoyt was erased from his thoughts.

"Come on, Angelo, you wouldn't believe what I can do with this mouth. I'm very lingual. Spanish, English, and there's that other thing."

"Jesus, Gabriela." He gulped. "Listen, I'll call. I will." And his groin meant it. "I just gotta run."

"How's the Sullivan case going?" she asked. "Any leads?"

"No. But I just got a call from a guy who wanted to talk to me about John Frears. And he mentioned Matthew Spiller. You know, I think you were right about him. There is a link. Everywhere I go in this town, he pops up. He was even there the night someone shot at Theo Montgomery."

"Well, that can't be a coincidence."

"No, it can't. Listen, I've got your number. I will call this time."

*"Prométeme."*

He smiled at the sound of it. *"Te lo prometto."*

She reached a hand in and squeezed his arm. "Oh, your native tongue," she said huskily, and chuckled. "Good luck today. Catch you later."

BARTOLI COULDN'T RECALL much of the journey up to Mulholland. He drove on autopilot, guided by the part of his brain that wasn't engaged in projecting onto his windshield a new porn movie, titled *Cops Get Down and Dirty*. What had just happened? Propositioned in a parking lot by one of the sexiest officers in the whole of the LAPD? Did it really matter that she might be nuts? With those lips? Those tits? Those hips? And how many years did he have left when he might grab someone like her and not have to pay for it?

The gate rolled back, and he eased the Impala onto the property, heading down the incline toward the expansive bungalow.

"You gotta be shitting me…"

Emerging from the front door were two elderly folk, and Matthew Spiller, who strode ahead to be the first one to greet him. Bartoli got out and reluctantly grasped the hand offered to him, just for show.

"Angelo," Spiller said.

Bartoli beamed at the homeowners waiting fifteen feet away. "Hey, guys, how you doing today?" He squeezed Spiller's knuckles, eliciting a pained intake of breath, and moved to introduce himself. "Lieutenant Bartoli. Angelo."

"JoBeth."

"And I'm Jack."

"So, you say you got some video evidence relating to what happened to John Frears?"

"Correct," Jack said. "Follow me." He turned, speaking as he led them all inside to the kitchen, where a laptop was set up on the counter. "We were away traveling in Europe, so we only just saw this."

Bartoli turned to Spiller. "You've seen this, have you, Matthew?"

"Of course."

Bartoli shook his head, miffed at yet another example of his nemesis possessing more facts than him. "Okay, Jack, show me what you got."

Jack woke the laptop and set the compilation video to play.

Bartoli felt his eyes go wide as he watched.

"You know that vehicle, right, Angelo?" Spiller said.

Bartoli put on a pair of glasses, leaned in closer. "Again, please, Jack."

After the second viewing, he said, "Shit," then looked at JoBeth. "Sorry. Jack, can you zoom in on the license plate?"

"Already did." Jack produced a still image of the front of the offending vehicle.

"Fu...God's sake," Bartoli said, redirecting his profanity into something less offensive.

JoBeth laid a hand on his shoulder. "It's okay, Lieutenant. If now's not a good time to curse, I don't know when would be."

"CA Exempt," Bartoli muttered, reading the words above the numbers on the license plate.

"And you see what's behind the wheel?" Spiller asked, rather too chirpily.

"Of course I see what's behind the goddamn wheel, Matthew."

Bartoli squinted at the image. The visor was down, obscuring the face, but the silver shield on the dark uniform was clear to see. He perched on a kitchen stool, feeling the strength ebb from his legs, and the chance of a world-class blowjob recede with it.

"You know that vehicle, right, Angelo?" Spiller said again. "*I know that vehicle. It stopped me when I was on my bike the other day.*"

"Play it again, please," Bartoli said, and he watched as John Frears came into view in his yellow Ferrari two-nine-six GTS convertible, and the unmarked Ford Explorer accelerated alongside and barged the Ferrari off the road and down the ravine.

"Do you know who that is?" Jack asked, suddenly understanding there was more to it.

Bartoli nodded. "And look at that good citizen. What a scumbag."

The video had run on, showing another vehicle appear, pull over to survey the crash scene, then speed away.

"Not much they could have done," JoBeth said. "We have another angle, from cameras on the house. His car blows up the moment it comes to rest. Poor soul."

Bartoli turned to Jack. "You have this backed up? You have all the originals?"

"Affirmative."

Bartoli frowned. "I didn't see any cameras up on the road."

"They're well hidden."

"Why? Why not a visible deterrent?"

Jack looked at his wife, who shrugged. "I worked for some people. Back in the day. Government people. I always figured they might come for me. I figured it's best if they don't know that I know when that happens."

"Government? What? CIA?"

Jack laughed. "We were ghosts. Even the CIA were clueless about us. Lieutenant, the things we did – you wouldn't believe me if I told you."

"We're getting off the point," Spiller said. "Angelo, you were about to tell Jack who's behind the wheel."

"I can't see who's behind the wheel. But… yeah, I could take an educated guess. Jack, could you put all this on a flash drive for me, please?"

"Sure." Jack left the room, and shortly there was a loud metallic clunk from down the hall.

"It's okay," JoBeth said, responding to Bartoli's puzzlement. "We have a panic room."

Bartoli smiled. "You know, of all the people I've met, I think your husband may be the last person on earth to panic about anything."

MIDWAY ACROSS THE lawn, beside the pool, Bartoli halted and turned to Spiller. "Are you stalking me, Matthew? Did I ask you to follow me? Your job here is done. Thank you for passing my number to Jack. Now you can go."

"I think you need to thank me for something else, no? Solving John Frears' murder? Which you didn't even know *was* a murder."

"You didn't solve it, Matthew; Jack's surveillance system did."

"But you're here because I gave them your number. Otherwise, this could have been put through to any detective. You're in need of a win, Angelo. Say, *thank you, Matthew.*"

"Fuck you, Matthew."

"You're welcome."

Bartoli carried on toward the perimeter chain-link fence, and Spiller followed.

"You still here?" Bartoli said.

"You may also want to apologize to me."

"Why would I wanna do a thing like that?"

"Because you had me pegged for this, didn't you? This, Harry Sullivan, Aiden Powers, maybe even Theo Montgomery."

"Well, you're the only person I know who's linked to all of them. And you do have a track record."

"Allegedly." Spiller smiled. "Anyway, if I didn't do this, you think it's possible you're wrong about the others? And have you thought that she might have killed them *all?*"

"Why would she?"

"Who knows. *Puta loca.* Do you need a reason if you're crazy?"

Bartoli shook his head. "I can't see it." He looked from the crash site up the slope to the road. "Poor schmuck didn't stand a chance."

"You're not asking why she did it?"

"Gabriela?"

"Oh, first-name terms."

"No, Matthew, we weren't *shagging*." He paused. "But she did share. She lost her kid to a dangerous driver. Ever since, she told me she's been on a mission to take them off the road. I didn't know she meant that literally."

"What do you think happened?"

"I'll find out for sure when I pull the footage from her shopcam that day, but I'm guessing Frears was speeding. Maybe he didn't notice the unmarked, made a dangerous maneuver, overtook her on a bend. Who knows? Whatever happened, she obviously saw red."

"And what about that twat who stopped a few seconds later and did nothing? Are you going to look for them?"

"Definitely. They may have seen what happened beforehand to cause it. Maybe they got a dashcam. You know? Like Noah did in his truck? You weren't gonna ask me how that went?"

"No."

Bartoli grinned. "I performed a completely by-the-book search of his vehicle – on my own with a baton – and I found a data card that must have fallen out of a dashcam onto the floor. You got my text, right? *Deleted?*"

"Oh, I was wondering what that was about."

"Sure. So, I said *deleted*. What I really meant was, seeing as how I'm a nice guy as well as an upstanding cop, I knew it must be Noah's property, so I returned it to him. Along with his truck."

Even summoning all his acting skills, Spiller only just managed to feign disinterest. "Okay, that's good."

"Isn't it? Because that saves you another phone call. Now you also don't need to call in a dead body off of Route Three Ninety-Five, ten miles past Kramer Junction."

Spiller hoped his tan might hide the sudden grayness he felt crawling under his skin.

"See, Matthew, if that kid's got any sense – which, I admit, is up for debate – he'll have gone out there already and moved your dead agent. Taken it some place it'll never be found. No dead body means no ballistics. His gun, whatever you did with it, is now useless. The kid's off the hook."

"No idea what you're on about."

"And I'm warning you, Matthew: don't even think about trying to put him back on it."

Spiller shrugged cluelessly.

"Back to the here and now... I assume your connection to Jack and JoBeth is via Brett Stutz's ex, Hayley Olsen, who's best friends with Virginia Frears? How well do you know Virginia?"

Spiller stared at the burned patch of ground. "I just signed a contract to appear as her dead husband in a TV series."

Bartoli slapped a hand on Spiller's chest. "Don't fuck with me."

"I'm not. Although I suspect this might delay their plans. Maybe even cancel them."

Bartoli sneered at him. "How sad for you. Anyway, if you wanna talk to Hayley, tell her what's happened, let her break the news to Virginia before we do, so she hears it from a friendly face... go ahead. Just make sure they keep it quiet until we make the arrest."

Spiller nodded. "Thanks."

"Oh, that bitch!"

"What?"

Bartoli's private revelation made him look skyward, and he laughed briefly. "Clever bitch."

"What?"

"The night Harry Sullivan died... that's when I first met Contreras. She had this theory; really made a point of planting it in my head. She said, what if it's a serial killer, targeting Hollywood tough guys. At first, I didn't buy into it. Frears crashed, Powers slipped, and Sullivan looked like a botched street robbery. The possibility of a serial killer seemed far-fetched. Then she joined all the dots on you, linked you to everyone, and I started to think."

Spiller chuckled. "That I'm a serial killer? Please..."

"You know, I bet it was her who shot at Theo Montgomery. Reinforce the whole scenario for me. He told me he didn't think anyone was genuinely trying to kill him. Damn, she led me a merry dance. Well, not anymore." Bartoli suddenly made a face. "Why the *hell* am I telling *you* all this?"

"I think you're secretly quite fond of me, Angelo. We're like some dysfunctional crime-fighting team."

"Whatever. Just go talk to Hayley and Virginia."

HIS MIX OF emotions was too disabling. Bartoli edged out of the driveway, and the gate rolled shut behind him, but he pulled up onto the verge rather than head back down to the city. It felt like he had a dozen lines of Christmas lights in his head, all tangled together. The brightest, flashing like crazy among the anger and sadness and shock, was disappointment. Not in Gabriela; in himself. He'd been fooled. He tried to work out if a better man might have seen through her, but the truth was that he *had* seen through her. He'd known to visit her old Captain, and his suspicions had been confirmed. But he'd still not been able to resist the lure of sex, and just as in England, another headline case was about to be solved because Matthew Spiller had taken pity on him and placed the evidence, neatly bowed, at his feet.

He stared through the windshield at the trees that fronted the property. Jack had hidden the cameras well. Inquisitive, he got out and walked the length of the fence, looking up at the branches, searching. They had to be up there somewhere, but damned if he could spot them. He went back to his car.

As he was cruising down Mulholland, his cell rang, providing a welcome interruption to his continuing self-flagellation. He answered without checking the caller ID. "Lieutenant Bartoli."

"It's Matt, listen—"

Bartoli ended the call, but it rang again immediately. He was approaching Johnson Overlook and decided to pull in rather than risk the conversation fusing all his tangled lights at once and making him crash. He moved off the road and nosed the Impala up to the token log barrier. He remembered the last time he'd parked there; his first rendezvous with Gabriela that had promised so much.

"What is it, Matthew?"

"Don't hang up. Listen, I'm still at the house. Jack's been running some license plate recognition software for a couple of hours already, to see how often the blue Explorer's been past lately. Fairly regular hits, but probably nothing unusual for a beat cop. But the last hit was thirty minutes ago. She arrived just after you, parked along the road, just in range of the camera."

"Bitch followed me."

"Watch your back, Angelo. Literally. She set off right after you."

Bartoli turned just in time to see the Ford Explorer bearing down on him, veering off the road onto the dusty shoulder. It flashed through his mind that his current location, parked next to a sudden drop, probably wasn't ideal, considering her MO. Then, weirdly, she hit the brakes, and the Explorer slid toward him, throwing up a brown cloud that enveloped his car. He braced for impact, but there was just the smallest *dink* as her nudge bar lightly touched his passenger side. His car rocked once and was still.

Belatedly, his hand went to his side, but his .45 was under his jacket, which was held down by his seatbelt. Then he looked at her, and quickly raised his hands where she could see them.

Held directly in front of her face, pointing his way through her windshield, was her 9mm FN. Slowly, her gun trained on him the whole time, she exited her vehicle and came to his front passenger door. She lowered the weapon to her side, so it wouldn't be visible to a passing motorist, and he dropped the window.

"Hey, Gabriela." He nodded at the drop in front of him. "I guess I should be grateful I'm not down there already, huh?"

"Give me what they gave you."

"What did they give me?"

"Don't lie to me, LT. I saw you peering at the trees."

"What can I say? I'm a keen ornithologist."

"They got surveillance. Has to be. Only reason you'd be up here after all this time. I'm guessing they've been away until recently. Anyway, if I'm wrong, I reckon you'd be real confused right now – me pointing a gun at you."

"See, you would have made a great detective. What happened, Gabriela? That day."

"Like you care. Like anyone cared when my kid died."

"Yeah, but you got even, didn't you. Shot the cop who did it. Outside a Seven-Eleven."

Contreras looked surprised. "You talked to Hoyt." She nodded. "Yeah, I blew his brains out." She laughed. "Yet you'd still have humped *my* brains out."

"You got even," Bartoli repeated. "You didn't have to run some innocent off the road."

"*Innocent?* No one buys a yellow Ferrari who doesn't want people to look at them driving it fast."

"Is that what happened? By all accounts, John Frears was a good family man. Not reckless, not a risk-taker. Pretty humble life for a movie star."

"He was driving like a bat out of hell."

"Well, I guess we'll see when we review your shopcam footage for that day."

Contreras laughed. "That's a big leap of faith, LT, thinking you might go from this spot right now to the safety of the station."

"Maybe so. But assuming I do live through today, do me a solid, will you? So I can tick it off my list? Theo Montgomery. That was you, right?"

She showed a sickly smile. "Amazing how a little red dot can roll back the years. You should have seen the old goat run."

Bartoli nodded to himself, bowed his head, and noticed his cell resting between his thighs, the screen bright against one leg, still connected to Matthew Spiller.

"Gabriela, I can give you the flash drive they gave to me, but it's all saved up at their house. And if they've got any sense, they'll have called the cops by now, and they'll have locked themselves in their panic room."

Her face creased. "Fuck are you talking about?"

Bartoli pointed between his legs. "You still there, Matthew?"

Spiller's voice whined up from his crotch, so he slowly retrieved the cell from his thighs and put it on speaker.

"Matthew, you're someone who can wriggle out of pretty much anything, right? So, please tell Officer Contreras if you can see any way this goes in her favor."

"Uh, no, she's proper screwed," Spiller said. "Cops are on their way."

Bartoli saw the pinch in her eyes that prefaced her finger moving on the trigger. The engine was still idling, so he dropped his cell and shifted into reverse. As the gearbox clunked into place and the car jumped backward, her first bullet caught the top of a knuckle and blew it off, but better a knuckle than the chest shot it would have been, had the car been stationary. The utility truck heading up Mulholland caught the rear of the Impala and spun it heading downhill in an involuntary PIT maneuver, and as a second and third bullet smashed harmlessly into his car, Bartoli thought he'd best go with the flow and follow his nose, rather than try and head back up the hill toward Jack and JoBeth.

Spiller's voice came from the footwell. "Angelo! What's happening?"

Bartoli shouted back, "What's it fucking sound like?"

"Are you hit?"

Bartoli inspected his missing knuckle sitting at two o'clock on the steering wheel, and reckoned it wasn't much different to the broken knuckles he'd suffered in the street fights of his New York youth.

"Angelo!"

"I'm good!"

He rounded a bend and pulled a handbrake turn, squealing the tires, and set the lights and siren going as he blasted back up the road toward Contreras. But as he approached Johnson Overlook, he could see the Explorer had disappeared. He shot through the pall of dirt hanging in the air and put his foot down.

"Matthew! She's coming! She's heading your way! Get them safe! I'm two minutes behind her!"

"YOU HEARD THE man," Spiller said to Jack and JoBeth, who were gathered around his phone, completely enthralled, like people used to huddle around the wireless. "Let's get you into the panic room."

"You're coming?" JoBeth asked.

"Damn right. This isn't my business. Bartoli's on his way, and likely every cop within ten miles. If she's heading here, they're going to kill her. If I was all you had, sure I'd step up, but I'm not about to get shot by a psycho cop when I have a Hollywood career ahead of me." Spiller suddenly thought to add his poor, grieving kids into this worst-case equation, but realized it was too late not to sound extremely lame.

He ushered the homeowners out of their kitchen, but Jack barged past and let himself into the panic room ahead of them. Even in those three gained seconds, his intentions were clear. As they followed in behind him, he was standing at an open metal cabinet, eyeing his hardware.

"Jack!" JoBeth shrieked. "No!"

He grabbed an AR-15 from the wall, checked the magazine, and worked the bolt.

JoBeth stood in his way, blocking the exit. "You want to hold that, Jack, fine, but you do it on this side of the locked door. You are not going outside with that thing."

"I'm not going outside, no, JoBeth. She wants to stay on the driveway, wait for her colleagues to show up, I'm good with that. But she steps one foot inside our home, and she's getting a full magazine." He stepped up to his wife, who stood her ground.

"Jack…"

"Honey, I don't want to move you aside, but I will. I am not a well man. We both know what's happening to me. My mind… it's all wrong. It's fuzzy and…"

"You're still my husband."

"But I won't be. Few months, will I even know who you are? You'll tell me, and maybe I'll understand, then two minutes later you'll have to explain it all again. We've seen it with our friends. I'm not going out that way, JoBeth. Whatever happens today, I am not going out that way."

JoBeth was horrified. "What are you saying? You'd kill yourself?"

"JoBeth, step aside. Please."

The enormity of the conversation made her wilt, and she shuffled out of his way, and closed and locked the door behind him.

"JoBeth?" Spiller said.

"I can't choose for him. Not if I love him." She moved to the desk and woke up the bank of monitors, then sat heavily to watch.

THE FORD EXPLORER busted through the front gate. Spiller and JoBeth watched as the impact caused it to snake its way down the incline into the first obstacle in its path.

"My car!" Spiller yelled, as his Maserati was shunted into the brick wall of the garage.

JoBeth gave him a sharp look that read: *get your priorities in order, mister.*

"Sorry, it's just..." Spiller said, then trailed off.

The female cop got out of her vehicle and pulled her sidearm. On another monitor, Jack was hunkering down behind the sofa, AR-15 resting on the chair back, with a clear line to the door. The cop approached the house and loosed off a bullet at the front entrance.

"She's not staying outside," Spiller said needlessly.

JoBeth was silent, seemingly holding her breath. She switched her attention to the hallway camera, and the image of an open door, with the cop standing stock still just inside their home, apparently listening. Then the cop was creeping along, as though she hadn't already made enough noise to wake the dead. At the door to the living room, the cop halted, then walked in.

"Now, Jack," JoBeth whispered at the monitor. "*Now.* What are you waiting for?"

"Stand up!" the cop screeched at Jack, aiming straight at him. "Drop the weapon and stand up!"

"Jack, kill the bitch," JoBeth pleaded desperately. "What are you doing?"

Jack let go of the gun, which tipped forward onto the cushions. He stood up and held his hands at chest level.

"Let me have the footage and I'll leave you alone," the cop said. "I'm only here for that. I'm not looking to kill anyone."

Jack started chortling.

"God's sake, Jack... don't laugh at her."

"You think this is funny, old man? What about me looks funny?"

Spiller tapped JoBeth and pointed to the driveway monitor. Bartoli had arrived. But JoBeth quickly looked back at the living room.

"Ma'am," Jack said, with a calm civility. "Even if I were to hand over all the equipment in my panic room. Even if Lieutenant Bartoli were to surrender the flash drive I gave him. Even if I were to erase my laptop... it's all in the cloud. You can't get it back from the cloud, not in the time you have." He cocked his head. "You heard that siren? It's over, sweetheart."

"Don't you *sweetheart* me. It was an old bastard like you killed my kid. You think you got some special dispensation because you're old? That just means you got less years to lose when I shoot you."

"Okay, you're no sweetheart, I can see that. What's your name?"

"I'm Officer Gabriela Contreras."

"Well, I can't see you holding onto that title for much longer."

JoBeth gasped. "Matt, why is he taunting her?"

*Suicide by cop*, was Spiller's instant thought, but he just shrugged.

"I'm Jack, by the way."

The sudden movement of Contreras's head showed she'd heard a sound. She quickly moved to grab Jack and stand behind him, gun at his head.

Bartoli's voice in the hallway: "Gabriela, I'm coming in. Okay? I just wanna talk. I'm not holding a gun." He extended his arms so his hands appeared past the jamb. Spiller could see one was injured. "Don't shoot anyone." Slowly, Bartoli appeared in the doorway. "Why are you doing this, Gabriela? This is beyond salvation. You're going to jail for John Frears. But you might at least get out with some good years left if you give up now. You could maybe even cop an insanity plea if you tell people about Benito."

"*Don't*... don't you dare mention his name."

"Okay, listen..."

"Lieutenant," Jack said.

"What?"

"She's gonna take me down, and you, if you stand there much longer. In case you didn't know, Gabriela here has a death wish. You need to leave my house right now. I mean, really leave my house, go back up to the gate and stay there, and keep your colleagues back when they arrive. Go. I'll be okay."

JoBeth laid a hand on Spiller's. "Matt, I don't like this."

"You should do as he says," Contreras said. "Five, four, three—"

"Okay!" Bartoli backed out of the room and retreated to the front door.

"All the way!" Jack shouted. "Get away from the house!"

Bartoli left the bungalow and was seen heading back up to the gate, as instructed, halting the first police cruiser that had just arrived.

"Gabriela, can I talk to my wife?"

Contreras stepped away, keeping the nine-mil aimed at his heart. "Sure." She perched on the arm of a chair.

Jack pulled out his cell but didn't use it. "Honey?"

Spiller watched the tears appear from nowhere and roll down JoBeth's cheeks. She tapped a button on the desk. "I'm here."

Contreras jumped at the extra voice in the room. She darted glances around the walls and ceiling. "You got cameras in here? An intercom? She's been listening to everything?"

"JoBeth, whatever happens in the next two minutes, stay in that room."

"No," Contreras said. "No. You come out of that room, JoBeth, or I put a bullet in your husband's brain."

"Stay there, honey."

But JoBeth was already on her feet. At the end of the room, she barged aside the sofa and pushed down on one of the floor tiles, which popped up slightly, then she opened it like a small trap door. She took a chain of keys from around her neck and inserted one in the floor, opening a safe. She reached in and pulled out a small velvet pouch. Then she closed everything and shoved the sofa back in place.

JoBeth came to the desk and put her lips close to the mic. "Gabriela, you can have money, whatever you want. It's all in here. Millions. Let my husband go and you can leave with it all. Take me hostage, get away from here, set up a new life for yourself."

"JoBeth, stay in that room. *JoBeth!*"

Behind her, Spiller was eyeing a new development on one of the monitors. Jack now had his cellphone in his hand and was tapping at the screen as though he was sending an urgent message.

Contreras was unperturbed. "Who you calling, *estúpido?* Cops are here already." She cackled as though the madness had finally found a vent.

*"Stay in that room, JoBeth!"* Jack yelled.

JoBeth stopped at the door and handed over the chain of keys. "Matt, if Jack and I die today, we have no kids, no relatives of any note, so please do some good with what's in that safe. And that's not all. So, *look*." She unlocked the door and walked outside, closing it behind her.

Spiller peered at Jack's face, a kind of delirium oozing from every pore as he tapped the screen one final time.

Until he saw his wife in the doorway.

"Oh, JoBeth, no. No, honey, I told you..."

As JoBeth made to tip the contents of the pouch into her palm, her face pleading with Contreras, Jack closed his eyes, and the room went dark.

## TWENTY-NINE

STANDING AT THE ruined gate to their property, Bartoli was still holding back his colleagues, arguing with a SWAT Lieutenant about who had the authority. Even as he remonstrated, he wasn't quite sure why he wouldn't just allow them to do the job they excelled at. Except that Jack had told them all to stay away, and Jack had worked for the government on some shady projects, and something in his tone would not be dismissed so glibly.

He swiveled on his heels mid-sentence as multiple shutters dropped noisily all around the property. Every window, every door. Five seconds later, the whole house hummed as though a monstrous machine had come alive in the very fabric of the building. There was a loud *whoosh*, like the structure had taken a huge gulp, then the several air-con units around the exterior walls simultaneously belched out a blueish vapor that vanished against the California sky in two seconds, before it all fell silent, and the shutters lifted.

"What the hell was that?" Bartoli said to his SWAT counterpart.

"Damned if I know. Forty-David, move your team in."

Bartoli watched as ten heavily equipped and gas-masked officers swept down the incline and made entry at various points, which had, just a few seconds earlier, been barred. A minute later, the team filtered back outside in a more relaxed manner. The sergeant approached his commanding officer, unstrapping his helmet and removing his mask.

"Three dead, two elderly and one of our own. A female. Name tag says Contreras. One alive in the panic room. Says he's the actor Matt Spiller. Won't release the door to anyone but a Detective Bartoli. That you?"

Bartoli nodded.

"Cause of death?" The SWAT LT asked the sergeant.

"Beats me. No one got shot in there. No one got stabbed. They just died."

"How long have they been dead, you figure?"

Bartoli answered: "Seconds. When I walked out, they were all still breathing."

"What the fuck was that effluence?"

The sergeant shrugged again. "No readings. Air in there's as clean as a mountain breeze."

"You know anything about what went down in there, Detective?"

Bartoli considered for a moment. "A secret government acronym is what went down in there."

He headed to the bungalow, smiling as he properly noticed Spiller's Maserati caught between the Explorer and the garage. In the hall, he peered into the living room and saw the three bodies.

"Angelo!" came a voice from the ceiling. "Am I okay to come out? Is the air safe?"

"You see me standing here, don't you?"

"Yeah, I don't think I'm going to come out just yet. I'm going to give it fifteen minutes. If you're still standing then, I'll come out."

"Suit yourself."

Bartoli spent the time jotting down notes and taking pictures on his cell, being careful not to touch anything, especially the bodies. Latterly, CSI joined him in full hazmat suits, and tried to usher him out.

"If I was gonna die, I'd be dead already," he told them. "You won't find anything. At least, not related to what killed them."

As Bartoli waited for Spiller, the three bodies were zipped up and taken away, and no one returned. Finally, Bartoli heard a releasing clunk from the bedroom. Then Spiller appeared in the doorway, sniffing the air.

"You had eyes on this, Matthew? I'm guessing there are cameras in here as well as a speaker."

"Yep. The room went dark, the cameras switched to infrared. Then, looked like some sort of mist came out of the air vents. Few seconds later, it all gets sucked out of the room, the shutters lift, and they're on the floor."

"Jack wasn't kidding about his old job, huh? My guess is they autopsy these three and find nothing. Maybe heart attacks. Murder by natural causes. CIA were talking about it back in the seventies. Science fiction back then. Or maybe it wasn't."

"What happened to your hand?" Spiller said, as he squatted down where JoBeth had collapsed.

"Gabriela shot me. You feeling okay? Are you having trouble standing?"

"I'll be fine. Delayed shock, probably."

Bartoli peeked outside the door, down the hallway. "Show me the panic room."

"I'd rather get out of here in case that mist thing goes off again."

"Don't be such a pussy."

"I'd take being a pussy right now. At least I'd have eight more lives."

"Stand up, get moving," Bartoli said.

Spiller obeyed, leading Bartoli down the hall.

"Why are you walking funny?" Bartoli asked, as he followed.

"Tired. And the adrenaline; it's made me feel really heavy and slow."

"You're not kidding. You don't seem too great. You should get yourself checked out, in case you inhaled any of that mist."

"I'm touched you care."

"I don't. I only want you alive so I can put you in jail for Harry Sullivan and Aiden Powers."

"Not Theo Montgomery?"

"Gabriela confessed to that one. Oh, and not forgetting your erstwhile agent, of course."

They entered the panic room, and Bartoli began opening the wall cabinets. "Jeez, straight out of a John Wick movie." He went and sat on the sofa and perused the area. "You take a weapon, Matthew?"

"Yeah, I shoved an AR-15 up my arse."

Bartoli shook his head. "Listen, I'll need to get a statement from you at some point, so don't go on vacation. Right now I need some medical attention."

"After you," Spiller said, stepping aside to let Bartoli pass.

"Uh, no. I don't like you behind me."

"That's what she said."

"Just move."

Spiller stopped at the front door, staring forlornly at his Maserati. He went and sat on the hood. "You have kids, Angelo?"

"I have four. Why?"

"Aw, a litter of *Bartolitos*. Well, imagine if some bad people threatened them. Threatened to kill them. *Tried* to kill them. Now, let's say all your cop powers are no good to you. The law can't touch them. Would you do something about it? As a man?"

"You're talking about last Christmas?"

"I'm talking about you being in a hypothetical situation. Would you do anything and everything to protect your family?"

"Of course. Matthew, this isn't the time. I have work to do. This is an active cri—"

"When is the time, Angelo? When do I get to convince you to just *leave me the fuck alone?*"

A couple of nearby cops started paying attention, but Bartoli waved them off.

"It's not just last Christmas, though, is it, Matthew? You're up to your neck in this town as well. Okay, my turn to hypothesize. So, I've protected my family. They're safe. Then some old guy shows up who knows what I did, but not why. And he wants to expose me. Not because it's the right thing to do, but – I'm guessing here – maybe because he just wants his face on the news. I reason with him, pay him off, beg him, and he still doesn't care; he's gonna expose me anyway. What then? Should I kill the guy? Is that where we're going with this? You want me to give you a pass on killing your agent?"

Spiller started laughing, but quickly stopped. "You're so blinded."

"Meaning?"

"This vendetta you have against me. It's even got you tampering with evidence."

Bartoli moved closer. "To save an innocent kid. You know, I can't listen to you anymore." He turned, but Spiller grabbed his sleeve.

"Listen to this, then, you prick." Spiller brought out his cellphone and went to his videos. He set something to play and held it up to Bartoli's ear.

The first thing Bartoli heard was someone crooning along quite passably to The Walker Brothers' *After the Lights Go Out*.

Then Noah's voice: *"You are dumber than a watermelon."*

*"How so?"* Spiller's voice.

*"You don't know me, I could—"*

A round of applause.

Noah again, quieter now: *"I could be a psycho stalker, for all you know. I could make your life a livin' hell. Is it worth it? All you gotta do is help me out."*

Spiller's laugh, then: *"Are you threatening me?"*

*"Could be I'm beyond threats. You think about that? Harry Sullivan, John Frears, Aiden Powers. Ring any bells? Maybe I'm takin' out the opposition. Maybe you're next. Unless you help me out."*

Spiller pulled his cell away and shoved it deep in his jeans pocket.

Bartoli stared at him. "What did I just hear?"

"You know what you heard. And that's not just a voice recording; that's a video."

"How did you get that?"

"I was filming Billy singing when Noah came over. I didn't even know I had it until yesterday. I'd forgotten it was still recording. But Noah's face is on there, speaking the words, admitting to three murders."

Bartoli took a moment. "Noah said *maybe*. *Maybe*. Sounded a lot like bluster to me. And we now know who did kill John Frears, and it wasn't Noah Dalton."

"True. Perhaps he wanted to bolster his CV a little. Fact remains, you still don't know who killed the other two, and there you have Noah practically confessing. But, hey, who knows what a jury might think."

"I need to seize your cell." Bartoli held out his hand.

"Fuck off. I know what you do with important evidence. You really want to make a fuss about this here? In front of all these cops? Go ahead. You think Noah's got the steel to front it out in an interview room? Or you think maybe he cracks and tells them you gave him that data card, just to lighten his sentence. Me? I'm going with box number two. You want to bet your pension, your *liberty*, on box number one... be my guest."

Bartoli seethed.

"In case the fact had escaped you, Noah Dalton is an *actor*. Just like me, it's his job to fool people. You just bought into the whole little-boy-lost-in-LA act. From what you told me, you handed him a data card that tracked his truck to where he killed Billy. So, now he's moved the body, you have no proof of *anything*. Bravo."

"Matthew, *you* led me to his truck this morning. If it wasn't you driving that night, how come you knew where it was parked?"

"What? I led you to his truck? I went out to a studio this morning for an interview. Hold on... were you following me?"

Bartoli was shaking his head. "Nuh-uh. No way. No way are you dragging me down this fantasy rabbit hole with you." But in his head, the demented bunnies were already hopping. "Why would Noah kill Billy? Tell me that."

"Because they were giving it each other up the ass, and I'm guessing Noah had second thoughts about that. Maybe he didn't want his start in Hollywood to come that way. Or the *good ol' boys* back home to hear about it."

With his brain nudging critical mass after the events of the past hour, Bartoli could only grunt. He looked at his knuckle and felt very sorry for himself. Then a thought occurred.

"Why did you call me to warn me about Gabriela? Did Jack make you?"

"No. Jack came out to tell me, then went back inside."

"I don't understand. Why were you looking out for me?"

"Because, Angelo, I've never wanted anyone to get hurt who doesn't deserve it."

"Oh. Then... thanks."

"Welcome." Spiller pointed to the Ford Explorer. "Can you get someone to shift this, please? I want my car. I'm going home."

## THIRTY

SPILLER DIDN'T GO home. He called Sadie to check where she was, and invited himself to her Canoga Park apartment when she said she was in. She came outside the complex and buzzed him into the gated parking lot, then directed him into a visitor spot, smiling crookedly at the Maserati's recontoured bodywork.

"Hey, stranger," she said. "What happened to you?"

He got out. "Sorry I haven't called. So busy."

"I didn't mean that; I meant your car."

"Not sure you'd believe me if I told you."

She sat on the hood. "Sorry, am I okay here? Don't wanna scratch it."

"Funny."

"What happened?"

"In a nutshell? A psycho cop rammed my car."

"What? Where was this?"

"Mulholland. It's fine – I wasn't in it. I was in a panic room waiting for another cop to arrive so he could arrest her for murdering John Frears."

"No way."

"It gets worse. I was left in the panic room while the owner of the house killed himself, his wife, and said psycho cop, using some toxic agent that will never be identified, because the guy apparently used to work for an agency that would make the CIA look like the girl scouts."

"Never a dull moment with you, huh?"

Spiller laughed at the understatement. "Oh, and my wife and kids arrived yesterday. With the new man in their life. A day early. Well, on time, but a day earlier than I'd thought, because, as you rightly pointed out the night we stole that truck, I can't really get my shit together. Speaking of which, the police recovered the truck, but they now think it might be linked to the disappearance of my acting agent. Do you still want to be with me?"

"Hell, yeah." She pushed herself to standing. "Can I get a hug?"

"No, a hug would freak you out right now. Can we go into your apartment? I'd really like to get naked."

SADIE LED HIM into her bedroom but frowned at him. "You sure you wanna get naked? I don't think you're well. You were walking weird. You sure you didn't inhale any of that toxin?"

Spiller shook his head. "I'm okay. Just need to lose my clothes."

"Okay, big boy." Sadie began to pull up her t-shirt.

"Not you; just me."

She stopped. "You want me to watch? I'm not into that. I usually like to be involved."

Spiller said nothing. He removed his denim jacket, then his t-shirt, then his shoes and jeans.

Sadie regarded him with a bemused smirk. "*Okaaaaaaay*. You kinda look like that dude from *Midnight Express* – when he gets caught at the airport. What you got under there?"

Spiller stared at his reflection in her full-length mirror, then looked down and found an end to one of the wraps of duct tape near his wrist, and pulled it back, grimacing as it removed his arm hairs. He laid it on the bed, sticky side up.

Sadie stared at the twelve one-ounce gold coins. "Are they real?"

"Yep." He stared in the mirror again, at the duct tape that covered nearly every inch of his skin above and below his briefs. He peeled the highest band from around his chest. He stifled a moan but couldn't stop his eyes watering. He laid it on the bed, revealing around thirty ten-ounce gold bars.

"This is why you didn't wanna give me a hug outside," she said. "You know how much they're worth?"

"About twenty grand each."

She looked at the four remaining wraps around his torso, and the ones on his legs and arms. "And you got them taped *everywhere*?"

"Coins or bars – yep. One-ounce coins, and five- and ten-ounce bars."

"That one wrap is worth more than a half mil." She giggled.

Spiller stared at her. "Don't you want to know where I got it all?"

"Sure – if you feel like telling me."

"But you don't need to know?"

"How would that change anything? You'd still be here; the gold would still be here. Why would I care?"

"Maybe I killed someone for them."

"But you didn't. You wouldn't. Not for money."

He'd almost forgotten. "Oh. The auras."

"That, and I can read people. Your auras are messed up, no question, but there's something at the heart of you that means well. A kernel of…"

"Of?"

She took a moment. "Necessity. Yeah. You do what has to be done. Sometimes, life takes you a bad route that makes you do things you wouldn't normally do. When I was in the army, I made decisions over there that I'd never make here. Did things I'd never do here. Circumstances. It's about self-preservation. Most natural human instinct. That goes, there's no point. Once you're okay with people walking all over you, it's time to check out."

Spiller was confused. "But that first night we met, you said you hated the movie business – or at least the violence it portrays. I don't understand why that would anger you so much when you seem able to dismiss genuine wrongdoing."

"I said: it's about necessity. Who *needs* to go watch your new movie, Matt? The whole thing's premeditated. Someone *planned* the book. Someone *planned* the movie. Why? It's not necessary. It's sick. It infects people. *Inures* people. Pretty soon, you got a world full of people who just don't care."

Spiller felt her argument was ambiguous, possibly even specious, but he wasn't in the mood to butt heads.

As they unwrapped his body, depilating it in the process, Spiller offered an explanation of events that she hadn't requested. They peeled off the gold and set it aside, balling the tape into one sticky mess. At the end, they surveyed the duvet, weighed down by millions in bullion. He stuck a hand down his briefs and produced a velvet pouch, which he tipped onto the bed.

Sadie's mouth dropped open. "A girl's best friend."

He bent and plucked another from inside his sock; the one he'd furtively grabbed when he'd squatted down next to the chair where JoBeth had collapsed. He emptied it out.

"Nice," she said.

"And I have a few more in my jacket pockets."

"Diamonds?"

"Pouches."

Sadie stood for a moment, then backed up to a wall and slid down it onto her ass.

"Sorry," Spiller said, sitting on the bed. "All a bit much, eh?"

Sadie got on her cell, tapped something in. "What size are those diamonds? A carat? Two?"

"I'd say a mix. Probably some a lot bigger."

She read the results. "A top quality two-carat can be worth up to seventy thou. This is crazy. This is tens of millions. Millions in rocks, millions in metal. How d'you think they got it all?"

Spiller shrugged. "Maybe they were both as paranoid about the financial system as Jack was about home security."

"She must have trusted you'd do the right thing with it."

"That's what she wanted. She said to do some good with it. I'm guessing they have a will, but they probably weren't expecting to croak on the same day. Possibly they didn't name a beneficiary if that happened. Anyway, she overrode that by telling me to take it. You got any bright ideas?"

"I know of some veterans' charities that need help."

Spiller nodded. "Sounds good."

"Where d'you get the tape?" she asked. "The duct tape."

"Desk drawer. Next to some big cable ties. I'm guessing the old guy envisaged having to restrain someone at some point."

She nodded. "Okay. And… did you clear them out? Is that everything?"

"Some gold left. And a big stack of cash."

Sadie shuffled on her knees to the bed and surveyed the fortune on her duvet. She looked up at Spiller with an awkward expression.

"What?" he asked.

"Am I wrong to want keep some of it?"

"No. I'd be amazed if you didn't. Sadie, take what you want. You said it: self-preservation. We all need money. I know money isn't everything—"

"Unless you don't have it. Then it's all you think about." She picked up a ten-ounce bar, still tacky from the tape's residue, and rubbed it between her fingers.

"Seriously," he said. "JoBeth said to do some good with it. I'd say improving your life is a good thing. Theo Montgomery thought some of his money was well spent on you, didn't he? It's not like you'd keep it *all*."

She peered up at him with a cartoon-evil look, then smiled. "No. I wouldn't." Then she placed a hand on his hairless leg. "So, you had diamonds in your shorts a few minutes ago. Can I look at those crown jewels of yours again?" Her hand shifted higher.

LYING THERE POSTCOITAL, Spiller wondered if life could get any better than that room at that moment in time. An amazing kick-ass woman beside him, a balmy Californian afternoon, surrounded by gold and diamonds. Gold and diamonds that he didn't even need because he was already rich. And famous.

But the Spiller of yesteryear was still around, like a little devil on his shoulder, and it made itself heard above all the fluffy mood-music in his head.

He still had work to do. Unpleasant work, like breaking the bad news about John Frears to Hayley, so she could talk to Virginia, with all that might mean for *Veteran Avenue*. And going back to his home, where his place had been successfully usurped by a man he really wanted to dislike but couldn't find reason to. And taking his kids out. Pretending to be a father but second-guessing every action he took and every word out of his mouth. And waiting for Bartoli to stumble upon a clue that would destroy the doubt he'd tried to sow in the detective's head about who really killed Billy. And waiting to see if Noah would just take the win and fade away, or if he'd bust back through the saloon doors like The Man With No Name, looking for payback.

And there was another thing. About the Frears crash. But a good thing this time. Something that could help to fully close a door that Billy's demise had left ajar.

Sadie got up and headed to the bathroom, and Spiller watched her. A stirring told him he was up for more, but Virginia deserved to hear the news from Hayley, not from CNBC, and the day was getting old. He hopped off the bed and got dressed. Sadie padded back in and made a face at his clothed appearance.

"Sorry," he said. "I have some stuff I really need to do. He gave her a kiss, emptied the remaining diamond pouches from his pockets onto the bed, and headed out of the room.

"Matt…"

He stopped at the apartment door. "Yeah?"

She was incredulous. "Are you leaving all that with me? You know I have nothing keeping me in this town. I could pack my bags and disappear and never look back."

"Nothing?" he asked.

"Of course, there's you. I meant… most people would happily trade a few days' relationship for tens of millions in gold and diamonds. You're not worried about that?"

He smiled. "You're not most people, Sadie. You'll do the right thing. Keep a little, keep it all. If you do stick around, I'm not going to ask what you did with it."

"You'll know if I buy a house next to yours."

Spiller laughed. "You want to live on my road, you don't need to buy a house."

Sadie offered a puzzled smile. "What are you saying?"

He winked. "Sorry, gotta run."

## THIRTY-ONE

BARTOLI HAD BEEN sent home with his bandaged hand. But, like Matthew Spiller, he'd headed someplace else. Noah's truck was outside the small bungalow, and the Ford's window had already been replaced. The truck had also been detailed, presumably to remove any trace of dirt, dust, fauna, or flora that might link to Billy's final resting place, should it ever be discovered.

Noah was in shorts and a grubby white singlet. From the state of his hair and his bleary eyes, he'd been sleeping. He yawned in Bartoli's face, and the smell suggested his teeth also required detailing.

"Detective," he said on his odorous outbreath.

"Noah. Can we go inside?"

"You got a warrant?"

"I just need to talk to you."

Noah stepped outside and pulled the door shut behind him. "My roomies are home." He walked to the wire fence, drawing Bartoli with him. "Shoot."

"Okay, I need to know what you found."

"Where?"

"Noah, I'm on your side."

"Ain't no one on my side, Detective." He instantly teared up. "Not anymore."

"Guessing you found Billy, then. X marks the spot?"

Noah wiped his eyes, gave the minutest of nods.

"You moved him?"

"Well, I wasn't gonna leave him there. You told me not to."

"You find the gun?"

Noah shook his head. "Why are you here? I appreciate what you done for me, but…"

"Spiller is still trying to put you in the frame."

"How's he gonna do that? Shoot someone else with my gun?"

"Honestly? It wouldn't surprise me. But he may have a much easier way."

"Huh?"

"He has you on video bragging you might be responsible for the deaths of Harry Sullivan, Aiden Powers, and John Frears."

Noah was aghast.

"You were in a bar. Sounded like karaoke."

The recollection made Noah reel on his feet. "That was just... I was puttin' on a show. I was tighter than bark on a log that night. I just wanted to impress the guy, give him a little of what he gave Mel Banaghan. I got it all wrong, the booze talkin', but I thought he'd be impressed. You got his cell, right? You took it off him? You can erase it, right?"

"I didn't get the chance."

"Ah, shit."

"For what it's worth, Noah, I still believe you. But that video... that's not great for you. For a while, Spiller even had me doubting I made the right decision, giving you that data card. He comes forward with that video, shows it to cops who don't know him like I do... he's gonna be believed."

Noah smiled, in spite of himself. "That fellah's got horns holdin' up his halo."

"You need to leave town, kid. He still has your gun, and Christ knows what he might do with it next. Make distance your alibi. Go to New York. Try off-Broadway. Come back here to movie-land when I got all this settled."

Noah appeared to think about it, but Bartoli guessed he'd done all the thinking he was going to do.

The Texan sneered in defiance. "I ain't runnin'."

"A man's gotta do, right?"

"You all finished?"

"No. Tell me about the body."

Noah stiffened. "You're burnin' daylight, Detective. I got nothin' to say on that. Anyhow, you ain't never gonna find it."

"I need to know. Could be important later on."

Noah moved onto the lawn and lowered himself into a striped deck chair. He closed his eyes. "Only clothes he had on was his shorts and socks. I tried to keep him wrapped in that tarp; I didn't wanna see him. But he slipped out as I was unloadin' him." He squeezed his eyes tight, but the moisture seeped past. "Five holes in the torso. Very little blood. Meanin' he was already buzzard bait before he got shot. He had some bruises, scuffs. Especially his head. As though he'd been in an accident."

"What kind of accident?"

Noah opened his eyes. "The fatal kind."

Bartoli gave him a withering look.

"I guess... as though he'd taken a bad tumble."

"From a height?" Bartoli asked.

"Nope. Nothing tall out there."

Bartoli felt a click in his head. "At speed? Like maybe he'd fallen off a motorcycle?"

Noah considered, then nodded. "I guess so. *Damn*, Matt Spiller owns that motorcycle from the movie. He told everyone on *The Mel Banaghan Show*."

Bartoli nodded slowly. "He did indeed."

THE DAY OF sightseeing and activities he'd envisaged with his daughters was fast approaching its vanishing point. If he hurried home, he could maybe eek out a late afternoon jaunt that might give the vague impression of a day out, but that was assuming Helen and David had decided to stay by the pool. More than likely, they had all ventured out together in the morning, as functional families do when on vacation.

But he'd just arranged to meet Hayley and Virginia at Dodge City. It was a couple of miles straight down Sherman Way to Reseda. He'd be there in a few minutes, which would be way too early. Hayley had said she couldn't get over to the valley for at least an hour. He didn't want to be in Virginia's presence, sitting on news he'd want to spew, so figured he'd just wait in the parking lot outside the range until she showed. Then there'd be another hour explaining the macabre business on Mulholland. So, maybe take his kids out for an evening meal instead; make amends tomorrow.

His cell chirped, and it was obvious he wasn't the only one struggling with his daily planner.

"Hey, Helen," he answered.

"Where are you?" she asked.

"Sorry, had a lot of stuff to deal with. Crazy stuff. Are the kids at home? I was heading back in a bit."

"Soph's with us. Sammy's at home, waiting for you by the pool. For some weird reason, she thinks you're not going to let her down today. She's convinced you're going to turn up and show her the best time ever. Bless her."

"I'll give her a buzz, let her know I'm on my way."

"Now?"

Spiller thought of his rendezvous. Could he get over to his home and back to Reseda to coincide with Hayley's arrival? Would an afternoon at a gun range count as *the best time ever?*

"Matt?"

"Yes, now. Heading there now." He ended the call, took a right, and aimed his Maserati toward the 101.

THE BEEPING SOUND of the pool-gate keypad being pressed made Sammy sit up on her sun lounger. She was still wet from a swim, and nearly got up to dry herself, anticipating her dad's return to take her out somewhere. But she stayed still, frowning at the multiple attempts to gain entry. She almost called out, wondering if her dad had forgotten the code, but her instincts told her there was something amiss. Quietly, she slipped off the lounger and darted to the pool bar, where she hid under the counter. The sound of someone climbing over the gate, and the thud of shoes on concrete. Then silence, and she pictured the intruder surveying the scene, waiting to see if anyone appeared to challenge him. Footsteps, away from her position toward the house. The bi-fold doors were closed to keep the air-con cool. She heard them being pulled apart.

Sammy wondered if she should run. Run for the pool gate, or maybe for the gate to the reservoir. Bad idea, the reservoir. Too deserted. Even the pool gate was fraught with danger. She couldn't see where the intruder was, without peering over the bar, and she didn't dare make her presence known, in case she did so at precisely the wrong moment. Best stay hidden. Minutes passed, and she realized she could easily have got away, but the more time she delayed, the more likely he would leave the house and bump into her. Her chance had passed, so she stayed put.

Finally, she heard him slide open the door and close it behind him. Then nothing. No footsteps back to the gate. Thirty seconds, and no movement, then she remembered she'd left her cellphone under the lounger. Slow footsteps down to the poolside. She looked at the concrete on her side of the bar and saw the water she'd tracked there was still visible under the shade. And still visible from his point of view. Footsteps moving closer. A voice from the other side of the counter.

"Hey, darlin', you wanna come out?"

Sammy looked to her right and saw an icepick on a shelf, next to a bucket. She grabbed it and held it upside down, flat against her wrist.

"Come on, darlin', I ain't gonna bite. *Yet.*"

Sammy stood up but kept the bar between them.

"Guessin' you're Matt's daughter, huh? Unless he just likes 'em young, but I made him that offer in a bar once, and he flat-out rejected it. His only redeeming feature, far as I can tell. This your cell?" He offered her phone to her. "I could tell you was female from the tassels on the cover. Go on, take it."

Sammy kept her arms by her sides, so he put it on the counter. She suddenly felt very aware of the skimpy two-piece she was wearing.

"How old are you, darlin'? I'd say about eighteen. You sure are pretty."

Sammy saw the lechery in his eyes. She squeezed the icepick.

He grinned. "Maybe your pa would let me take you out sometime."

"I think that's unlikely."

"Sure he would. We're friends, me and your pa. He didn't tell you about me? I'm sure if I asked nice, he'd let me fuck you into next week."

Despite the adrenaline making her shake like a leaf, Sammy snarled at him. "You really need to leave before he comes back. And you *definitely* don't want to meet my mum after talking to me like that. You wouldn't believe how protective *she* is."

Noah laughed. "Don't you worry, I'm leavin'. Say hi to your pa from me. Tell him I want my gun back. The deal is, I get my gun back, or I get to fuck his daughter." He winked. "Heads up, that's you, sugar tits. Make him understand."

BARTOLI EXITED THE 405, taking the off-ramp, heading for Sherman Oaks. He'd managed to catch Officer Ethan King on a day off, and while King had agreed to meet, it was on his terms, in a place of his choosing, which happened to be the gym. Bartoli had never picked up a dumbbell in his life and found the whole notion of pumping iron to be alien. He figured if God had wanted us to work our biceps, he'd have made our hands weigh thirty pounds.

King was paged from reception, and Bartoli was kept waiting fifteen minutes, listening to deafening music that he surmised must be motivational in some way he'd never fathom. When he finally did appear, King was carrying a gym bag, and his hair was wet from his shower. They'd never met before, but King extended his hand, and Bartoli guessed it wasn't difficult to identify a gym-phobic paunch, shield or no shield.

"Lieutenant, what can I do for you?"

"Can we talk outside? I can barely hear myself think."

"Sure." King led the way, and they sat at a picnic bench just outside the entrance.

"Sorry to disturb your downtime, Officer King."

"No problem. It sounded urgent. What's up?"

"Matthew Spiller."

King grinned. "I know the guy. I might even call him a buddy. Is he okay?"

"You mean, is he alive and kicking? Sadly, yes. Is he okay? No. And sorry, but I got a feeling you won't think he's much of a buddy after this conversation."

King lost his amusement. "Go on."

"Two nights ago, you went to his house."

"Yeah. I spoke to him on his way back from The Mel Banaghan Show. He was parked up, talking to his driver. Early hours, like, two a.m."

"His driver," Bartoli said. "Blonde woman?"

"She didn't get out, but, yeah. Anyway, he seemed like a good sport. I gave him my card. Who doesn't want a movie star as a buddy? I didn't think he'd call but he suggested a beer."

"You think that was odd?"

"Not really. I'm pretty personable."

"You think maybe *he* just wanted a *cop* as a buddy?" Bartoli asked.

King shrugged. "He did say he was having an issue with a stalker. Some guy broke his nose. He said his agent had concerns as well. Lieutenant, where is this going? I have some errands I need to run today."

"Okay. Full disclosure: Matthew Spiller has basically given you as an alibi."

"For what?"

Bartoli grimaced, knowing that nothing about his suspicions had been made official, and wouldn't be unless he was certain he had an airtight case.

"Lieutenant?"

"I can't share details of the investigation, and I'd ask that you keep this to yourself. Suffice to say, I need you to corroborate – or not – what he told me about the other night."

King took a pink protein shake from his bag and took a swig. "Which was?"

"He said you saw him return on his motorcycle."

"Uh-huh. I was waiting outside. He came back with a pillion passenger, went into his garage. Came out a few minutes later and let me in."

"Tell me about the pillion."

"Not much to say. Armored leathers. Black, white, orange. Matching helmet, gloves, boots. Dark visor, pulled down. Could have been anybody."

Bartoli smiled. "Good memory."

"It's kinda photographic. Pretty useful in our line of work, huh?"

"I'd say. So… would you say the pillion was built? Like you? Or slight? Just trying to get a vague idea of his frame, at least."

"Difficult to say. Armored leathers are bulky, whoever's inside them. I mean, they didn't look like they were saggy or oversized."

Bartoli tried to conjure in his mind the cellphone picture Spiller had shown him of Billy in his leathers, but he didn't have the mental recall of the officer across the wooden table from him. He pictured the color scheme only because he'd just been given it. Were the leathers loose fitting? He couldn't remember. That image, like the video of Noah in the karaoke bar, would need to be seized.

"Few more questions," Bartoli said. "Did you see the pillion once you went inside?"

"No. He went upstairs and took a shower. Matt said it was his agent. I heard Matt say good night to him, and I heard his agent reply."

"You heard his agent?"

King nodded.

"You actually heard his agent?"

"Well…" King finished his shake. "I heard a response. Obviously, I can't say for sure it was his agent, as I've never met the guy."

"What did he sound like?"

"Like, uh… that wizard guy from the *Lord of the Rings* movies. You know?"

"Never watched them."

"Ah, what's his name? Uh… Ian… Ian McKellen. Posh, English. My kid loves all that fantasy nonsense, so I have to sit through it."

Bartoli could feel his disappointment mount, and could almost see Spiller standing over King, working him like a master puppeteer.

"How long were you there for?" Bartoli asked.

"Couple of hours. Left just after eleven."

"So, Spiller could have gone out after you left."

King laughed. "Not in his state. He sunk a lot of beers."

"Too drunk to drive?"

"Too drunk to walk, almost."

"That bad?"

King nodded and pointedly checked his watch, which was one of those fitness gadgets.

"Tell me about the beer," Bartoli said. "You take any booze along?"

"Six-pack of Miller Lite."

"You drink any of it?"

"Two or three."

"From the can?"

"Yeah, why?"

"What about Spiller?"

"He used a glass. Poured it out in the kitchen. That it, Lieutenant?"

"Could he have been faking? Being drunk?"

King made a face like it was a dumb question. "I guess. If he had reason to. I mean, he's an actor. I guess most actors have drunk acting in their repertoire. But... why would he?"

Bartoli stood up, stepped back out of the picnic table. "You should keep away from Matthew Spiller. He's not a nice guy."

"You think he was faking? Using me?"

"Thanks for your time, Officer King. I may circle back on this."

"Knock yourself out," King said, then headed toward his red Dodge Challenger. Halfway across the lot, he halted and stood there for a moment, then returned to Bartoli, who was pondering what to do next.

"One thing," King said. "I got this image in my head. Like a photograph. It just popped in there. When I went to the bathroom, I passed the kitchen and noticed a bottle on the counter. There was blue on the label. I can picture it. It was Heineken, but there was *blue* on the label."

As a man who was partial to a few beers, Bartoli understood.

## THIRTY-TWO

SPILLER COULDN'T GET into his own house. He tried the key again, but the door had been bolted on the inside. He tried the pool gate, but that, too, was locked. Someone had to be in, so he went back to the front door and started banging. After a moment, he heard Sammy.

"Dad? That you?"

"Yeah, can you let me in, please?"

She opened the door, and Spiller could see instantly that she was distraught. She stepped out and hugged him tightly.

"Sammy, what's up?"

"Some guy came by. Hopped the gate. He went inside the house for ten minutes."

Instantly, Spiller knew who it was. "Where were you?"

"Hiding outside behind the bar. Anyway, he came back out, hadn't taken anything that I could see. I've checked around the house and he's obviously had a good search through drawers and wardrobes."

Spiller was wondering how he could spin it as a random burglary if nothing had been taken, but his cogitation was rendered moot by her next comment.

"Oh, then he spotted me and threatened to fuck me if you don't give him his gun back."

Spiller wanted to go ballistic but didn't want to verify the seriousness of the situation with such a reaction. "Young Texan lad, right? Noah Dalton. He's a stalker. Listen, he's all talk. But now he's said *way* too much. I will sort this out, okay? You're not in danger. I will deal with this today."

"Mum's going to go apeshit."

Spiller cringed. "I know this is a big secret to keep, but please don't tell your mother. After castrating me, she's going to cut short your holiday and you're all going home. And I really want to spend some time with you. Honestly, I will handle that wanker. And if I can't, I'll take you to the airport myself."

Sammy drew in a huge breath, like the air was lacking oxygen. She nodded on her sigh out.

"Thanks," he said. "Now, just let me make sure the house is okay, then I'm going to take you somewhere. I think you'll enjoy it."

IN TRUTH, SPILLER wasn't at all sure Sammy would enjoy it, so he kept their destination a mystery until it was a done deal, in case she balked at the idea of shooting guns and decided to hop out in the middle of the 405.

Hayley was waiting outside Dodge City in a Volvo SUV, and she had a passenger with her.

Sammy squeaked excitedly as Spiller drew up nose to nose. "Oh, my God, is that Katerina Petrova? I love her! And who's the woman with her? I know her face as well. Dad, is that…"

"That's Hayley Olsen."

Sammy turned to her dad and kissed him. "Dad, this is so cool. But… is this a gun range?"

Spiller looked up at the *DODGE CITY* in green neon, listened to the muffled gunshots from inside, and squirmed. "Yeah, sorry. It's owned by John Frears' widow. I have some business with these people. Hayley's written the script for the new TV series I'm going to be in. Sorry."

"Am I going to shoot some guns?" she asked.

"Uh… do you want to shoot some guns?"

*"Hell, yeah!"*

Spiller laughed. "Right, then. Just… you know, don't tell your mother."

The introductions were made, and Spiller was gratified and relieved to see his daughter all starry-eyed as she was hugged by two B-list Hollywood actresses. Then Kat draped her willowy arms around him and gave the obligatory cheek-to-cheek air-kiss, before Hayley gave him a perfunctory hug that spoke of irritation.

"Matt, what's going on?"

"As I said on the phone, I really need to talk to you and Virginia. Or you need to talk to Virginia after I talk to you."

"What's it about?"

"It's about John. There's been an incident up on Mulholland, where he crashed."

"I know, it's all over the news. No details yet, but... what? You know something about it?"

"I know *everything* about it. Can we go inside?"

Hayley led the way. Virginia was at a counter, showing a semi-automatic to a customer. She spotted them, asked another member of staff to take over, and beckoned them through to her office.

Another hug for Spiller, but even more mechanical than Hayley's. "Matt, what's happening? Hayley said you needed to talk to me. Is this about John? I heard something's happened up on Mulholland. Sorry, uh..." She looked belatedly at the unknown face in the room.

"This is my daughter. Sammy."

Virginia shook Sammy's hand, then addressed Hayley. "You bring Kat for some more target practice?"

"Uh-huh. Okay if Sammy joins in? Can you get Bobby to look after them?"

*"Bobby!"* Virginia bellowed, and her stocky sales assistant with the handlebar moustache popped his head in. "Bobby, can you take care of these young ladies for me? Whatever they wanna shoot. On the house. Take good care of them."

"Sure thing, boss," said Bobby, and offered a grin that was mostly concealed by his facial hair. "This way, ladies."

Spiller grabbed his daughter's hand. "You listen to every word he says, okay? Safety first."

"Don't worry," Bobby said. "It's cool. Who wants first go on the bazooka? I'm kidding."

Alone with Hayley and Virginia, Spiller felt like he was under the spotlight of the greatest audition of his life. His heart was hammering. The background noise of random gunshots didn't help matters.

"I don't know if it's best you hear this from Hayley," he said feebly.

"I wasn't there, Matt. What's going on?"

Virginia did a double take. "What? *There?* Where? Matt, were you up on Mulholland?"

He sank into a chair. "Okay, you need to sit down. Both of you."

Spiller relayed everything — if *everything* meant leaving out the part where he was made beneficiary to tens of millions in gold and diamonds. As he spoke, Hayley shifted her chair closer and put her arm around Virginia, who wept through it all. Spiller could see Hayley wanted to cry but was staying strong for her friend.

"This is insane," Virginia whispered finally. "A *cop* killed John? Hold on... why did Jack call you and not me?"

"Not sure," Spiller said. "I think he wanted my advice."

"On what?"

"Whether to tell you."

"Why wouldn't he tell me? This is a homicide!"

"I don't think he was well. Mentally. You know? Paranoia. And maybe dementia. Anyway, I told him you needed to know." Spiller recoiled inside as he spoke the lie, which conveniently glossed over the time that he'd known and said nothing. He desperately wanted to ask what this all meant for *Veteran Avenue*, but that would have been too cold-hearted.

Thankfully, Hayley was more forthright. "Virginia, I'm so sorry. But where does this leave us with the project? It's all in motion. You wanna call it off? I'm okay with that. Really. In the scheme of things, I couldn't care less about a stupid TV series. I'm sure Matt agrees."

"Absolutely," Spiller lied again.

Virginia put her face in her hands. "I can't think right now." Then she looked up, visibly aggrieved. "It's not just a *stupid series*, Hayley. It's my husband's life story. Our *love* story."

Whether by accident or design, Hayley had said exactly the wrong thing, which was exactly the right thing to ensure Spiller's career advancement.

Virginia stood up. "We are making *Veteran Avenue*, Hayley. It's getting made. And you're adding a new epilog. The world is gonna know that my husband was not just another rich actor who drove too fast."

Hayley rose to her feet, and the two friends embraced.

"It's gonna be *awesome*," Hayley whispered in her ear, then turned her head slightly. "Right, Matt?"

"Absolutely."

"I really wanna shoot something," Virginia said. "Let's shoot something."

As they went through to the store to choose their weapons, Spiller felt he couldn't breathe, like the elephant in the room had decided to sit its arse on his chest. Thankfully, unlike most conspicuous but overlooked pachyderms, the women genuinely didn't know it was there. They had no clue that the star of their story was skating on such thin ice, and it suddenly seemed staggering to him that the lumbering Dumbo next to him hadn't already sent him crashing through to the freezing depths. Billy, Noah, Bartoli. And Stutz. Brett Stutz. The one remaining link to his past misdeeds, who he'd thought was all squared away, but who was imminently to be bathed in a glare that would make the hardiest individual crack wide open.

An hour later, the floor of the range booths was covered in brass casings. They cleared their weapons, hung their ear-defenders, and pulled in the last of the perforated targets.

Out in the parking lot, Spiller saw his still-gleeful daughter settled in the car, before he turned to Hayley and hooked a finger, indicating he needed to chat further. Hayley, who'd been about to reverse, got out of the Volvo, and Spiller walked with her away from the cars to the sidewalk. He looked back and saw Kat exit the Volvo and go and sit with Sammy in the Maserati.

"What else, Matt?" Hayley asked. "What are you not saying?"

He had to get out in front of it. The cops had the video evidence, and the women now knew he'd seen the evidence with his own eyes. When the cops went public with what they knew, his silence would be suspicious.

"Tell me about Kat," he said.

"You're interested in Kat?"

Spiller shook his head. "Not like that. I mean, what happened with her and Brett?"

"That's not for me to say. Kat's a friend, and I guess a client while she's staying at the house. Either way, I'm not sharing anything told to me in confidence."

"I get that. Okay, well... what was Brett's connection to John?"

Hayley made a face. "I'm guessing those two questions are linked."

"And what was John's connection to Kat?"

"Hang on, Matt. You're telling me there *was* a connection? Okay, rewind. Brett and John? John worked on a Stutz movie earlier this year. Just before he died. It's in the can, but being held back, out of respect. Why?"

"And Kat and John?"

Hayley turned and watched the traffic pass by, taking a moment to collect her thoughts. "Matt, it's obvious you have a knack of knowing things before other people. Don't pussyfoot around. Are you saying Kat and John had a relationship? Is that why you kept this from Virginia?"

"No. But they would have met, right? Possibly. If Kat came to the set when John was filming?"

"Possibly. Why?"

Spiller was confusing even himself. "I'm trying to join some dots."

"Tell me the dots you can see. Start with that."

"That day, up on Mulholland, Brett was there."

"*What?*"

"The cop bumps John off the road, then another car arrives. A black Lamborghini Urus. It drives to the edge, then drives away. No question the driver saw the explosion, the flames; the smoke was billowing up onto the road. He was following close enough that he might even had seen the Ferrari go over."

Hayley was biting her lip. "And Brett drives the same model."

"Brett drives the same *car*. I saw it when Brett was filming here. Personalized license plate. Same license plate in the video."

"Ah, fuck. Matt, what's it mean?"

"You tell me, you're his ex. You told me you knew him better than anyone. Best case scenario, it's a coincidence, just the same road at the same time, and he knows John's gone, so he doesn't want to be caught at the scene. But why not call it in? Why not report the vehicle that bumped him?"

Hayley nodded. "Unless he was up to no good."

"So, I'm just wondering… these are the dots: John works for Brett, Brett follows John, Brett says nothing about the crash, Kat takes Brett's laptop, Brett goes crazy, to the extent that he wants her dead. Hayley, can you join any of that up?"

Hayley swiveled to look at Kat and Sammy, laughing together in the Maserati. "I don't know. But I think only a moron wouldn't try."

"Could John have known about Brett's dodgy taxes?" Spiller asked.

Hayley laughed briefly. "He wouldn't have cared if he did. John kept his life very private, and afforded others the same courtesy. He knew what a viper's nest this town is."

"Listen, maybe we should both keep quiet. I can always say I never got to see that part of the video, if Virginia asks. Or maybe I didn't recognize the vehicle."

Hayley laughed again. "Sure. Let's forget about it. You can do that? What are you, a sociopath?"

Spiller smiled, and suspected he might be. "No."

"Okay, I'll talk to Kat quietly. See if she's been holding anything back. I'll let you know how it goes."

Spiller remained by the sidewalk for a minute to compose himself, and for the first time since Mel Banaghan, he wished he had a line of coke to snort.

By the time they pulled up outside his home, Spiller had finalized his plan for Noah. It had been floating around his head ever since Sammy had told him about the threat, but it had just clicked into place. The arsehole missed his gun? No problem. They would be well and truly reacquainted. No way would he ever let another guy hurt his daughter, like back in England.

He noted David's rented Tesla was home.

"Sammy, we went to Santa Monica Pier, okay? You want to say we bumped into Kat and Hayley, fine. But we did not spend any time going bang-bang."

Sammy chuckled as she got out. "And I didn't meet any deranged Texans."

"Definitely not that. Love you, kid."

"Love you, too."

Before Helen could come out and catch him, Spiller did a U-turn and sped away.

## THIRTY-THREE

BRETT STUTZ'S PA, Bex, was no less keen to divulge her employer's whereabouts than last time. He was at his shiny, high-rise office in Century City. Spiller made his way up to the top floor, where all socially inadequate people liked to locate themselves. He entered the glass-walled office to find Stutz standing with a scotch, looking out over the darkening city, in a vignette that looked staged, and ripped straight from JR Ewing's status playbook. He kept his back to his visitor for an insulting moment too long.

"King of all you survey, huh?" Spiller said.

Stutz returned to his desk. "I like to think so."

"Well, make the most of it, buddy, because you're about to come crashing down to earth."

"What d'you want, Matty?"

"You've not seen the news? Checked social media?"

Stutz reached for his cell.

"Don't bother," Spiller said. "I'm the one with the inside track here, not Twitter. Interesting times up on Mulholland Drive today, Brett. At the precise location where John Frears died. I know because I was there. I recently got to know the people who own – *owned* – the house next to the crash site. Lovely couple. Now dead. Well, I say *crash site*, but more accurately known as the *scene of the crime*."

"What's this got to do—"

"Shut up, Brett. Just listen. You don't have long before the cops arrive. Hidden cameras in the trees, owners back from vacation. They learn about John Frears and check their CCTV. And what do they see?"

"How would I know?"

"They see an SUV pushing Frears off the road."

"That's awful."

"And then they see a black Lamborghini Urus stopping to take a look."

Stutz deflated in his chair, then cracked. "Matt, the guy was *ash*. Okay? Nothing I could have done. Nothing anyone could have done. I could have been driving a fire truck and he'd still have been ash. Ferrari hit the ground and *whoof!* Game over."

"But you didn't call it in, did you? You didn't report the crime. Why not? Why were you following John Frears? Did he know about your tax business? Would you have run him off the road if the other car hadn't?"

"No! Christ, no. I was just following him. He'd been talking to Kat. More than just chit-chat. On the set of my movie. A job *I gave him!* Deep conversations when they thought no one was looking. I thought they were having an affair. So, I was holding back in the Lambo, but I guess he saw me. He put his foot down and I wasn't about to give chase. Way too much power under my foot. Then this maniac overtakes me, and both of them disappear. Next thing I know, I hear a thump of metal up ahead, I come round the corner, and just catch the rear of the Ferrari going over the edge. Hits the ground. *Whoof!* The other vehicle doesn't even stop. I stop, but what can I do? Someone just killed John Frears. What? I'm gonna stick around and hope the cops don't think it's me?"

Spiller smiled. "And that, your honor, is the case for the defense."

"I didn't do anything, Matt! I swear."

"Yeah, and that's the problem: you did nothing. And your main worry isn't a criminal court; it's the court of public opinion. You'll get crucified for this, Brett. The studios aren't going to fund any more movies no one wants to see because you're an industry pariah all of a sudden."

Stutz looked horrified, then enlightened. He drained his scotch. "Sure. And no one's gonna go watch *Man on a Murder Cycle*, even if the studio releases it. So, this is a big problem for you, too."

Spiller felt relieved that Stutz viewed this as his only concern.

"Except…" Stutz grinned crazily "…if I don't have a career to protect, maybe I don't need to protect you anymore. Right, Matt?"

"Ah, but you said you'd never talk about last Christmas, Brett, and I'm going to take you at your word on that. Because the first rule about last Christmas is? Never mind. Anyway, this is a really tall building and you've just seen on social media that the cops have video evidence that John Frears was murdered right in front of you, and you did fuck all. So, you know… you couldn't live with yourself. *Splat*."

Stutz held his hands up. "Okay. Can we not trade threats? I assume you didn't come here just to gloat. You got a plan to save both our asses?"

"Of course. When have you known me not to have a plan?"

ALONG THE PACIFIC Coast Highway, three miles short of The House of Sempiternal Love, and a half hour before dark, Hayley pulled the Volvo across the carriageway into the nearly deserted parking lot for Zuma Beach. She cut the engine and sat for a moment, listening to the surf crashing against the vast shoreline, still dotted with people enjoying the setting sun. She shifted to face her passenger.

"Kat, we get on, right?"

"Of course, Hayley. I love you. Like I love my mother."

"That's nice. I love you, too, Kat. We have a lot in common. And you trust me?"

"Yes. You take me in, look after me. Of course I trust you."

"Good. And if there was anything you hadn't shared with me already, would you share it now? If I asked?"

"I don't lie to you, Hayley."

Hayley noted Kat's pouting lower lip, like a child's. "I know. But sometimes we lie by omission. We tell the truth when we're asked, but maybe we don't say something important if we're not asked. Yeah?"

Kat nodded. "Keeping secret. It is kind of lie."

"Exactly. Kat, is there anything you need to tell me? About Brett? Maybe about John Frears?"

A tear rolled from one eye, and she wiped it away.

"Kat, this is so important. Brett was on Mulholland Drive when John was killed. He was right behind him."

Kat inhaled sharply. "You think…?"

"No. No. Not that. A cop killed John. Some crazy bitch in a uniform. But Brett was there. Matt thinks maybe he thought you were having an affair."

Kat reached and held Hayley's hand. "You know Brett is not good man."

"He's a dick."

"No. *No*, Hayley. Brett is not good man. You are with him many years before me. You know this."

Hayley clamped her other hand over Kat's. "What do I know, Kat? Tell me. That he cheats on his taxes?"

Kat shook her head, extracted her hand. "There is more. I don't know, but there is more. I sense it. You must believe in sense. You write book about other world."

Hayley fell silent, weighing up her feelings, belatedly trying to tap her intuition.

"You are hypocrite, Hayley. Sorry, I love you, but you say tell truth, but you are not honest. Brett is not good man. John know this. We talk about it. John hear things. He ask me if I feel bad about my husband. If I have trust. I say I trust he does not want other woman, but something is not right. I sense."

"You think he's *gay?*"

Kat gave a shrill laugh. "No. And I don't care. That is not it."

"Girl, you married an older guy, a famous director, to get ahead in the business. You're the fourth Mrs Stutz. Did you really think it would last? That it would be all hearts and flowers? This town stinks. No one made you come here."

Kat fell into a sulk, and Hayley started to count the trash cans spaced evenly along the beach from left to right. She tried a different tack. "Okay, what *things* did John hear?"

"Bad things."

"Jesus, girl, give me something to work with. Rumors are rife in this town. Being badmouthed just means you made it. It's a badge of honor."

Kat looked down at her sweatshirt and started fiddling with the zip. "John think Brett have laptop with information. Bad information."

Hayley understood. "The laptop you took. The one he was so keen to get back."

"Yes. John ask me to look for one in house, but I cannot find. Then John die and I forget. After many months, I see Brett open safe in closet. I see him put code in mirror."

"So, you didn't need it for your poetry and other stuff? You took it because John asked you to?"

Kat nodded. "Our marriage was very bad by then, and I want to take something that make Brett angry."

"In that, you surely succeeded. I never told you, but Brett wanted you dead for taking it."

Kat's mouth fell open, before her lips pursed into a venomous pout. "Fuck that asshole. Wait... why do you keep secret? Secret is kind of lie, yes?"

"Because I didn't wanna worry you. That's my job at the house. I protect my residents. And the problem went away. He got his laptop and backed off. He was never gonna do anything anyway, Kat; he hasn't got the balls. Don't worry."

But Kat was suddenly smiling. "Why do you think he follow John that day? Hmm? Not because he think we have affair. Because John *ask questions*. And answers, I think, are on laptop."

"Well, then, too bad we gave it back. Anyway, tax evasion... who gives a crap these days?"

Kat nodded. "Yes, it is great shame."

Hayley eyed her. "Are you holding anything back, Kat? I need to know."

"That is all."

Hayley didn't believe her. "Then let's go home."

## THIRTY-FOUR

IN THE EXCITING life of a Hollywood actor, especially one new to the city, the LA Sanitation's residential trash collection schedule wasn't even a blip on the radar. You paid your local taxes, left your bins out, and they got emptied. People like Matt Spiller had bigger fish to fry, and he guessed the remains of those fish should go in the green bin, but he'd never been terribly sure and had never really cared. Now he did care about the collection schedule, and he wished his blue bin had been emptied a day earlier.

He stared up his driveway at the recyclable objects that had been lined up neatly in front of his garage door. Three cans of Miller Lite and six bottles of Heineken 0.0, with a small gap between the two groups.

He left the Maserati on the road and approached the small arrangement. In front of the empty Miller Lites, written in black marker on his concrete, was the word *ETHAN*. In front of the bottles of alcohol-free Heineken was the word *MATTHEW*.

"Bartoli. Tosser."

He collected the cans and bottles and threw them back in the wrong bin, just to be obtuse, then let himself into the house. His guests were still in residence.

"Hey, Matt," David said, stepping out of the kitchen. He was wearing a brand-new apron that Spiller had never intended to use, which was now splattered with orange sauce, but not enough to cover the message, which read: *I'll Feed All You Fuckers*. "We're just about to eat. Want to join us? By the way, we found a hotel, so we'll be out of your hair after dinner."

"Sure. Anything left in the pot or is it all on my child-friendly apron?"

David laughed. "Oh, sorry. I couldn't find any others. Plenty to go around."

"Daddy, you swear *all* the time," Sophie told him, as he entered the room and took a seat at the central island. She clambered across the island to kiss him, and Helen ticked her youngest off and gave her ex a little nod, like he was some hobo they'd stupidly asked to dinner. Sammy smiled, and furtively blew at the end of two fingers, like she was clearing smoke from a barrel. Spiller gave her his best Lee-Van-Cleef eyes.

"Let me guess... spag bol," he said.

*"Correctamundo,"* David replied, busying himself at the range cooker.

"Helen makes a mean spag bol. Don't you, dear?"

*"Matt..."*

"Or maybe she's just mean when she makes a spag bol. One or the other."

She flared her eyes at him, warding off further references to the last supper that Sammy's abusive ex-boyfriend had nearly enjoyed at Christmas.

David turned around, puzzled. "You don't skimp, do you, Helly?"

*"Helly?"* Spiller said, trying not to splutter a laugh. "Smelly Helly."

"You are such a child," she said, but she clearly wanted to smile.

"Anyway," Spiller said, "I have to go out again after dinner."

Sophie moaned theatrically.

"Sorry, kid, movie stuff. I might not be back until the morning, but then—"

"We'll be gone," Helen said. "Great timing, Matt. Oh, Sammy said your car's all smashed up."

"It is. Don't look so amused, my love."

"What happened?"

Spiller looked at Sophie as he spoke, addressing her like it was Halloween by the campfire, and he was delivering his best spooky tale. "It got rammed by a crazy, murderous policewoman outside a big house, high up in the hills, then she died when the house poisoned her with its deadly mist, but I hid, and finally I escaped with *millions* in gold and diamonds. So... happy ending, eh?"

Sophie tutted, shook her head. "You're so silly, Daddy."

Spiller looked at Helen, whose slightly horrified expression suggested she was far more gullible than her daughter. She opened her mouth, a question on her lips, then she grabbed her glass of red wine and washed her futile enquiry back inside her head.

"Oh," Spiller said suddenly. "Soph, what do you think of Manny? Manny the mannequin from *Man on a Murder Cycle*. Is he still in my spot by the window?"

Sophie grinned, nodded. "He's funny."

"See," Spiller said to Helen, "told you she'd like him."

"Can I take him home on the plane?" Sophie asked.

"Don't know. Depends if David wants to give up his seat and stay here with me. What say you, David?"

"I'll pass. Thanks, anyway."

"That's a lovely pendant," Spiller said to Sophie. "I meant to say. Who bought you that?"

Sophie put her fingers to her neck and pinched the bulbous gold heart. "Sammy."

"Is that a locket?" he asked.

Sammy answered: "No. It's just so full of the love we all have for Soph. Isn't that right, little sis?"

"Oh, your cop friend popped round earlier," Helen said, with a touch too much nonchalance. "Wanted to know if you were in."

"Bartoli? Yeah, we were—"

"No, this was a younger guy. Said he was a drinking buddy of yours."

Spiller suddenly felt very nauseous, and he flushed with warmth. "Oh. Yeah. Ethan. David, I'm starving, dish it up. I'm just nipping upstairs."

He shut his bedroom door and leaned back against it. Brilliant. Another peeved cop with an axe to grind. Too hot. Roasting hot. He shrugged his jacket onto the floor and heard a light clink. JoBeth's keys. He took his jacket to the bed and dipped into the narrow inside pocket, designed to take a pair of glasses. He pulled the silver chain out and laid it on the bed. Three keys. Maybe one for the front door, one for the panic room, and the safe key, a flat thing with complicated teeth that resembled those used for safe-deposit boxes. Suddenly, he heard JoBeth's last words echo in his head. In the heat of the moment, they'd slipped into his brain, consciously unheard. But the brain was amazing, and now it sent her message out to him:

*And that's not all. So, look.* The last word emphasized.

He did look – at the safe key, which he'd noticed had something faintly inscribed on it. A series of letters, numbers, and special characters. Perhaps so she could order a replacement if hers got lost?

What had she meant? She had to know he'd raid the safe once the door closed behind her. She'd *asked* him to take it all. She'd given him the keys so he could. Therefore, she wasn't just stating the obvious – that the pouch of diamonds she'd taken wasn't the sum of it.

Was there another safe? The thought of it only made him feel queasier. The excitement of a treasure hunt.

"Dad! Food!"

He had to go back downstairs. Spiller shoved the key chain back in the pocket and realized it wouldn't go all the way down. He pulled it back out again and felt inside with his fingers, which touched some velvet. He tipped the overlooked pouch onto the duvet and spread the rocks apart with one finger. Perhaps twenty, and some sizeable, at least three or four carats.

"Dad, foo—king *hell*."

Spiller looked at Sammy, gawking at the diamonds. She pushed the door closed behind her and approached.

"You weren't joking," she said. "About the house in the hills."

He gathered the stones into a pile and pinched them back into the pouch.

"What have you done?" she asked.

"Nothing. Wrong place, right time. Or right place, wrong time. Either way, these were gifted to me."

"And the gold?"

"Pardon?"

"You mentioned gold. And millions. That's not millions."

"So says the Queen of Hatton Garden."

"Dad… what the hell?"

He put the pouch away before anyone else could barge in, then took her hands. "Sammy, now's not the time. I will tell you sometime, but not now. Rest assured, though, these will be in your future. Okay? When you need them. Same for Soph."

"Yeah, she won't want them. Once she's got *Dogging Delight* up and running, she'll be fine."

Spiller laughed. "Nice try, kid. Give me a hug."

ODDLY, SPILLER RATHER enjoyed the evening with his extended family. Even if the extension comprised an interloper who was cucking his wife. To be fair, there was still nothing to dislike about David. The kids seemed fond of him, and Helen appeared to have found an even keel after so many years being thrown around by her husband's stormy presence.

In Sadie, Spiller wasn't entirely sure what he'd found. After eating, he returned to his bedroom and called her to ask if he could stay at her place that night.

"You can stay here until the landlord finds a new tenant," she said. "I'm on my way to Chihuahua, baby!"

His momentary silence caused her to have a giggling fit that lasted a full minute.

"Sadie?"

"I'm home. Come anytime, lover."

"Sadie, are you drunk?"

"Sure am. I just came into a *lot* of money." She cracked up again. "Buzz when you get here. Bring *booooooooooze*."

The fact she wasn't already halfway to Mexico, Spiller found fascinating. It wasn't so much her unwillingness to flee with an untraceable life-changing fortune; it was that she seemed to be sticking around for him. She was an enigma, a moral conundrum. Her intention to donate to some veterans' charities had been noble, but she had somewhat undermined herself by asking if she could keep part of the loot. But if she wanted to keep some, all she had to do was disappear with it. And why ask his permission? Although JoBeth had genuinely wanted him to take it, who else on this earth would have believed that to be true? Yet, she clearly did. And why had she been so amenable to his request for some coke the night of *The Mel Banaghan Show*, and why so entertained by his subsequent antics? And why had she been so willing to go and steal Noah's truck with him? He knew from experience that boredom could make recklessness a naïvely attractive pattern of behavior, but there was a balance to be struck in everything, and most people simply weren't willing to risk exchanging their future liberty for a few hours of memorable idiocy. And none of his extraordinary capers had begged a single question from her.

Down in the living room, the new, improved Spiller family was bunched up together on his three-seater sofa. Manny was still in the only armchair, guarding the bi-fold doors.

"Okay, I'm off," he told them from the hallway.

"Cheers, Matt," David said, and the other three just waved, too engrossed in a *Mission Impossible* movie to speak or break their gazes away from the screen. "We'll pack and get going shortly, if that's okay?"

"No worries," Spiller replied, then creaked down the hallway in his leathers. He fired up the Hayabusa and headed for the valley, by way of Mulholland Drive.

HE SLOWED AS he approached the home of the late Jack and JoBeth, stopping at the spot where John Frears had gone over. Looking down at the property, he could see yellow tape across all the windows and external doors, and warning pictograms of skull and crossbones. But there was no activity and no lights, and no one standing guard, so he assumed that whatever the cops had needed to remove had been removed, which he guessed was all the property's ducting, and probably any receptacle that might conceivably contain a noxious substance. Naturally, every computer would also have been seized, along with every firearm. The big question was whether they had also gone to the trouble of ripping up the floors, but he supposed he would have seen the associated detritus outside in a skip, had that been the case.

He moved a little further along and saw that their front gate had been returned to its spot and temporarily secured in place by wooden battens and canvas straps, although the assault by Contreras's Ford Explorer was clearly visible. More yellow police tape had been attached to the damaged gate in large diagonals, with another skull and crossbones pictogram in the center.

Having confirmed the place was unguarded, Spiller got on the throttle and pointed the Hayabusa toward his extremely sozzled girlfriend. It was good that Sadie was so drunk already. After the champagne he planned to pick up near her apartment, she'd sleep right through. No need to dose her with any pills.

Twenty minutes later, he was unpacking his rucksack in her living room. He changed into a black jogging suit, uncorked one of the two bottles of Moet, and sat beside her. She proposed a toast to their literal good fortune, and to having met each other, which Spiller was profoundly touched by.

"You okay?" she asked, as he wiped the corner of his eye.

"I can't believe you have any interest in me," he said. "And that it's nothing to do with my fame, or the fortune sitting in your bedroom. I am so flawed."

"I know." She gulped her drink and hiccupped.

He laughed. "I'm guessing you don't drink very often."

"Am I gonna feel bad tomorrow?"

"You'd best not wake up tomorrow. Give it a couple of days."

She drank some more.

"Seriously, Sadie, you don't know me. I am a deeply flawed individual."

"Who isn't? Welcome to the human race. You know how flawed I am? I'm gonna keep a bunch of that shiny shit in there. You said I can, right? And why not? I don't wanna look back when I'm married with kids and know I could have filled my kids' college funds in a day, but I was too noble to make the decision. Why should I be the one to plug the shortfall in VA funds? You know how much the SIGAR assessed in twenty-twenty was lost to waste or fraud in Afghanistan? Nineteen billion."

"SIGAR?" Spiller queried.

"The US inspector in charge of reconstruction over there. Nineteen billion. Gone into the pockets of the corrupt politicians of a puppet government, corrupt generals, cops, warlords, the Taliban. And who's back in charge now, after twenty years of fighting? The fucking Taliban. Billions that could have gone to our own people, to help them handle the injuries and pain from that futile clusterfuck." She downed her champagne and poured herself a refill. "So, if you say I got a greenlight to hold some back, that's what I'm gonna do."

Spiller wondered whether to tell her there was probably a load more where that came from, but thought the revelation might sober her up, and he needed her comatose-drunk for his plan to work, and his alibi to stick.

TWO HOURS LATER, Spiller was putting a sodden Sadie to bed. It was past midnight. He'd had just one glass of fizz, but she'd been too hammered to notice him lagging so far behind. He lifted her arm and it fell back heavily onto the mattress. He tickled her nose, which only twitched. Her breathing was deep, and carried a slight snore that he found incredibly cute. He took her cell to the kitchen and put it on silent, so she wasn't disturbed, and left his there as well, similarly muted.

From his rucksack, he retrieved his tac-light, his black knit hat, black gloves, and black trainers, and he tied a black bandana around his neck that would lift up and cover his nose and mouth when the time came. As the bike would be too noisy and conspicuous, he found the keys to Sadie's Caddy, and headed out.

As he made his way back home, he reviewed his plan. He was going to employ the same tactic he'd used when he'd slipped out to take Noah's truck to the desert. Cruise to the end of one of lower cul-de-sacs off North Beverly Glen, then trek up along the reservoir to the gate that gave entrance to his back garden. This wasn't just to avoid the inconvenience of having a camera along his road recording his arrival; he needed one of the guns he had stashed under a rock in the undergrowth near the shoreline.

The weapon he needed to use was Noah's Smith & Wesson. The gun with the Texan's prints on it. Maybe a little smudged on the frame, but clear as day on the magazine and the bullets, and a serial number that might even track back to him or his family – although Texas wasn't big on logging firearms.

With his hat pulled down and his bandana up, Spiller navigated his path with the tac-light on its lowest power. He located the rock and found to his relief that the suppressor from Jack's pistol fitted onto Noah's. Same thread size and twist. He shoved Jack's back into its Ziploc bag, and hid it under the rock again, gathering in some earth and brush to cover the hollow. He worked the slide, lifting a bullet into the chamber.

A hundred yards away from the rock, he reached his gate and pushed it open. He'd left it unlocked, as he'd left his bi-fold doors unlocked and the security system unarmed. Across the pool area, on the other side of those doors, was Manny, still sitting in the armchair – Spiller's non-sentient sentinel.

Spiller crept quietly past the pool, keeping low, even though he knew he wasn't overlooked. Dressed as he was, with a suppressed semi-auto in his hand, it just wouldn't have felt right to stroll. He knew there would be a significant noise, even with the suppressor, but he only intended one shot. One shot would be enough for the plan to work, but hopefully insufficient to cause his neighbors more than a cock of their heads. A single noise could easily be written off.

He reached the doors, brought the gun up level with Manny's head, and placed his finger on the trigger, disconnecting the inbuilt safety. He eased the door open a few inches and—

Manny moved.

Spiller recoiled, but his brain couldn't sever the impulse that was already curling his finger.

The gun fired and there was a howl as the bullet caught the thing that wasn't Manny in the shoulder, pitching it forward onto the floor.

Then Spiller saw the real Manny, also laid out on the floor, but partly behind the three-person sofa that David had obviously decided was too cramped for four people.

Spiller turned and fled, and his plan to make it seem like the assailant had tripped as he bolted the scene in panic, dropping the weapon, became horribly prophetic, as he caught his foot going through the gateway and sprawled into the dirt and lost his grip on the Smith, which skittered into the darkness.

Then he was up and running, with the sense that the pool area behind him was now awash with light, and the home he'd thought would be empty was suddenly filled with shouts and screams.

## THIRTY-FIVE

SADIE WAS ALREADY up, making some breakfast. Spiller could smell the coffee in the pot and the bagels in the toaster. Possibly the aromas had woken him. He sat up and felt his hangover intrude around his temples. He'd returned in the early hours to find Sadie hadn't moved a muscle, and he'd proceeded to belatedly catch up with her inebriated state. He'd sat down in the kitchen, finishing the half bottle of Moet as he'd watched his cellphone silently flash with each missed call from Helen. He'd counted ten before he'd turned it face down, but he'd imagined there'd been fifty more while he'd been driving back to the valley. The rum had followed the champagne, and the vodka had chased down the rum. And now he felt terrible. But there was no way he would have slept sober.

He felt like a coward for ducking his ex all night. He imagined his daughters would have been especially grateful for his presence, considering their surrogate dad had been shot and would have found it difficult to hug them. But the alternative would have been for him to answer Helen's call last night, and then she might have wondered why it had taken him thirty minutes to do so, which Bartoli would answer with great ease: that half hour was his traveling time, returning to Sadie's apartment from the scene of the crime.

A horrible thought came to him, and he nearly threw up over the duvet.

Could David have died? Spiller was pretty certain the shot had hit his shoulder, given the movement he'd made and the spin of the body upon impact, and the fact of his moan, which at least ruled out the headshot he'd intended. Spiller shivered and swallowed some bile. He had been a second away from putting a bullet in the back of David's head. The next-door-neighbor he'd known for years, who he'd always quietly loathed for his flirty ways with Helen, but who'd turned out to be a Godsend for his abandoned daughters. A Godsend he'd nearly sent back to God.

The need to confess, to end the farce of his LA existence, overwhelmed him. Then Sadie walked into the bedroom naked with his coffee and bagel, and Spiller's whimsical thoughts about voluntary jailtime dissipated like the killer mist in the house on Mulholland. You didn't get room service like this in lockup. And as his bagel went down and he began to feel better, Sadie ensured something else came up, and the fact that she could have this effect when his hungover head was so full of turmoil said everything about how captivated he was by her.

After making love, he nonchalantly checked his phone in the kitchen, and felt terrible that he had to feign such panic at the sight of so many missed calls. But the real acting was to come.

"Helen, what's wrong, are the girls okay? I just saw all your calls and messages."

"Where have you been, Matt? *Where?*"

He looked at Sadie and proudly told the only truth he would utter that day. "I'm at my girlfriend's."

Sadie smiled, but her expression remained concerned for him, and he hated his pretense for doing that to her.

"Are the girls okay?" he asked again, as he imagined he would with the real deal.

Helen took a breath. "The girls are fine. But David isn't. He got shot last night."

"Jesus. Where? At your hotel? In the street? What happened? Is he okay?"

"Just a flesh wound, thankfully. And it happened at your house."

"My *house?* When? I thought you left my house."

"We were all really tired, so we decided to stay another night. What a terrible decision that was."

Spiller silently concurred. "Is David in hospital?"

"No, they let him out. He was so lucky. Matt, why the hell would anyone try to kill you? I'm assuming you were the target. What are you mixed up in? The cops are here and they really want to talk to you."

Spiller looked at Sadie, tried a smile. "Helen, I told you I was having an issue with that Texan guy. The one who broke my nose. Has to be him. Is Bartoli there?"

"No. There's a female detective. Just get over here, Matt."

"How *are* the girls?" he asked. "They must be in bits."

"We managed to keep the worst of it away from Soph. We told her the noise was David falling over, but she's not stupid. Cops are everywhere. Anyway, Sammy's been sitting with her in the bedroom, playing games on her phone."

"And how's Sammy?"

"Dealing with it, as she always does. She's pretty amazing, that girl. Tough as nails since last Christmas."

Spiller doubted that was true, and suspected there would be a long-term relationship with a shrink somewhere in her future. A tear crept into view, and Sadie put a hand to his cheek for comfort.

"Give me half an hour," he said to Helen, and hung up.

Sadie looked at him. "Sorry, I'd let you take the Caddy, but I need it for a job later."

"It's okay, I've got the bike."

"I don't like you on that thing. Especially not in your state of mind."

He kissed her, then hugged her, and nearly said he loved her.

BARTOLI DIDN'T KNOW why, but Hector Hernandez had the stench of Matthew Spiller about him. He didn't trust the story he'd just been told, and felt the hand of his adversary weighing heavily in the deceit. Was that paranoia? Could Stutz have been acting independently? Could he have had this guy standing by since May, ready to step into the line of fire if the fan turned brown? Stutz himself had come across plausibly in his interview, if a little too assured. Bartoli had sensed an element of gloating, of the kind he'd often felt emanating from Spiller when he was certain he'd outfoxed Bartoli's best efforts.

Sitting across the interview table from the ageing Mr Hernandez, Bartoli identified a similar nonchalance. How could anyone not feel guilty at such inhuman inaction? Unless the crucial action had never been theirs to take, so the guilt wasn't theirs to own.

Bartoli wanted to shout at Hernandez. Instead, he said calmly, "Tell me again."

"What part?"

"All of it. How long have you been looking after Brett Stutz?"

Hernandez stared at the wall to the left of Bartoli. "Uh… I've looked after his vehicles for twelve years now. Twelve or thirteen. I'd have to check my books. It was the year he made that movie – can't think of its name – about a guy who goes postal in his hometown?"

"That could be every movie he ever made," Bartoli said. "So, let's say twelve years. And you service his cars how often?"

"Twice a year. Like clockwork."

"And you had possession of his Lamborghini Uranus early last May for a week, is that right?"

Hernandez smiled. "No."

"No?"

"No. It's called a *Urus*. Uranus would be a pretty stupid name for a Lamborghini. For any car. But, yes, I had Mr Stutz's *Urus* in my workshop for about a week."

"And the day in question?"

"I was checking it drove right. I never return a car to a client if I don't drive it myself first."

"And you took a cruise along Mulholland."

"It's a good road to test the handling. And it's a nice car. Maybe I test-drove it a bit more than I should. *Sshh,* don't tell anyone." He laughed.

"Hmm. And you're a qualified Lamborghini technician, is that correct?"

Hernandez frowned. "You know I'm not."

"So, you don't have all the diagnostics machines and tech gizmos to make sure a supercar like that runs according to spec."

"I got a diagnostics machine. Does everything it has to. Anyway, Detective, I've been working on cars since I was five years old. I got an ear tells me everything I need to know."

"Sure. And Brett Stutz is happy to have *your* stamp in his service-history book, instead of Lamborghini's. Yeah, makes sense. Depreciation. Who cares, right?"

Hernandez laughed again. "I guess rich people don't."

Bartoli leaned back in his chair, closed his eyes. "Okay…"

"I told you everything, Detective. All I saw was the Ferrari go over. I didn't know he'd been bumped, but you say he had been. I don't know. Anyway, I stopped, but there was nothing I could have done. And I wasn't gonna wait around in case someone tried to say I was involved. And as I *wasn't* involved, I didn't have to say anything. California law states it's not mandatory for a witness to report a car accident."

"It does. You're right. And well done for genning up on that fact already."

"For doing what?"

"Genning up. Finding information. It's a British phrase. I spent—" He stopped himself, shook his head. "You know what? Never mind. Thanks so much for your time, Mr Hernandez, you've been very unhelpful. I guess you're free to go. Don't spend it all at once."

Hernandez stood up. "Huh?"

"However much Stutz paid you to say you were driving. I'm gonna check it all out, you know. Your garage records, your employees – their recollections of that time – your invoices, bank statements, Stutz's service-history book. All of it. You better hope to God your ass is covered on this, Mr Hernandez. Obstruction, wasting police time, *perjury*. That last one? That's five years jailtime." He chuckled. "It's kinda ironic, right? A *genuine* failure to report an accident as a witness, you're okay. A *hypothetical* failure, however…" Bartoli stood up and opened the door for him.

Hernandez looked a bit gray, dithered as though he wanted to sit back down, but decided he just wanted to leave.

As for Bartoli, he just wanted to retire, or at least move to some small town in the middle of nowhere and become its sheriff, spending his last days on the job dealing with missing dogs and the local drunks. He wasn't going to pursue Hernandez, as he'd threatened. Way too much legwork involved, and so what if Stutz had been the one driving? It still wouldn't be a crime if he'd driven away and kept quiet. And Bartoli did understand why he wouldn't want the public to know the truth. The more pertinent issue was why he was following Frears in the first place.

He checked his watch. Not even noon yet. This day was so old already. And now he had to go out to Matthew Spiller's home, because someone had apparently just tried to kill him. And if Bartoli had believed that, he would have been furious at the incompetent perp. But he didn't believe it. This was more Spiller chicanery, and he had no doubt that Noah Dalton would be the net loser when everything shook out. A part of him wanted to go to Noah's home and warn him, but he guessed an arrest team might already be knocking on his door.

USED TO BEING quizzed by a cynical old detective, Spiller found the difference quite sublime. Here was a younger, female detective who knew nothing of his past, so was treating him with respect, like he was a regular human being, even a victim, because although he'd not been the one to get shot, his home had been violated. And in a break he hadn't hoped for, Sammy had just come clean about Noah's menacing visit the day before, so he didn't need to do much more than confirm that the Texan had already threatened him in a bar, then broken his nose, before his agent had mysteriously disappeared. That he hadn't been asked about Noah's missing gun meant Sammy had been somewhat judicious with the facts.

As Noah had been inside the house, surfaces were currently being dusted, so Spiller was talking to Detective Rainey out on the street. Helen, Sammy, Sophie, and a sorry-looking David, were huddled on plastic chairs in one corner of the pool area.

"Okay, Mr Spiller, I've got Sadie's details if we need to confirm your whereabouts last night."

Spiller smiled, and thought Rainey reminded him of Hayley, diminutive but ballsy, only twenty years younger. He imagined she hadn't long been out of uniform.

"Anything else you can think of?" she asked.

Spiller feigned deep thought. He wondered if he should mention that Bartoli knew all about Noah, but he wasn't certain what, if anything, Bartoli had bothered to officially record. He didn't even know if Billy's disappearance had been logged. If not, it would only complicate matters that, on the face of it, were fairly straightforward. Spiller had picked up an unhinged stalker, who had turned out to have homicidal tendencies. What would have made it even simpler was the dropped Smith & Wesson, but he'd not heard anyone mention such a discovery, and wasn't sure how to prod them in the right direction without raising suspicions.

"No, nothing," he said, and immediately suspected his assertion would be countered by the arrival of a black Honda Civic being driven by Angelo Bartoli.

Spiller decided to play it dead-pan and take his lead from Bartoli, whose agitation was evident in his hurried gait.

"I can take it from here, Detective," he said to Rainey.

"And you are?"

"Lieutenant Bartoli. West Bureau Homicide."

Rainey wasn't fazed. "Okay. You see a coroner's van here, Lieutenant?"

"What's that?"

"No one died here. I'm Detective Rainey, and I've been assigned to this case."

"Who are you with?"

"CAPS."

Bartoli sneered. "Crimes Against Persons? Whatever this is, it ain't that."

"No," Rainey said. "Sounds like it could be aggravated stalking, so it may get passed off to DSVD. But right now, Lieutenant, in the absence of a DB, I can't see how this concerns you. Unless you'd like to clue me in on something?"

"Aggravated stalking?" Bartoli said. "You got a name?"

"Noah Dalton. I got officers looking for him now. Mr Spiller's had a few run-ins with the guy. He even has Dalton on video, threatening him, *and* would you believe, making out like he killed Sullivan, Powers, and Frears – although we know the last one can't be his."

"Well, I'm lead on the Harry Sullivan case, Detective Rainey, so, obviously, this may be connected." He looked at Spiller. "Matthew. Lucky escape, huh?"

Rainey frowned. "You two know each other?"

"Previous life," Bartoli said. "So, who's the vic, if it's not Mr Spiller?"

"My wife's new boyfriend," Spiller answered. "David. Poor fellah."

Bartoli stared at Spiller for a moment, then addressed Rainey. "Mind if I talk to David? That okay with you?"

Rainey smiled facetiously. "Sure. We're all on the same team. Mind if I tag along?"

Bartoli grunted, and Rainey and Spiller followed him through to the pool area.

"Mrs Spiller, hello again," Bartoli said. "David, right? How you doing?"

"I'm okay. Shaken, but…"

"I bet. What happened?"

"I told Detective Rainey here. I was asleep, I heard the door open, I started to turn, and I got shot. That's it."

"You see the guy who did it?"

"Barely. All in black. Hat and mask. I wouldn't recognize him if he was standing right here."

Bartoli looked at Spiller. "How tall? As tall as Matthew, who's standing right here?"

David shrugged. "No idea."

"So, you turned, got shot, and then what?"

"I fell forward, looked back, saw him running away."

"You're sure it was a man?" Spiller asked.

David pondered. "Well, no. Why?"

"Just a bit sexist, assuming it was a man."

The four of them stared at him, so he wandered away toward the rear gate, and stood there, kicking at a loose stone in one of the steps.

Behind him, David caught the subliminal hint and said, *"Oh!"*

"What?" Bartoli asked.

Spiller casually sauntered back to listen.

"He fell," David said. "As he was running out through the gate. He went his length."

Bartoli looked at Rainey. "You check out there already?"

"Uniform did a quick sweep. Couldn't find anything."

"Okay, nev—"

But Rainey had already whistled a couple of officers, and now the Field Investigation Unit was leaving the house, so she corraled them as well.

"Anything?" she asked them.

"Plenty of prints. Those places the young lady thought the perp had touched yesterday. Need to rule out the homeowner and guests, then see what's left."

"Excellent," Rainey said. "Can you and these officers take a close look around the gate and beyond? Apparently, the perp fell as he was exiting the property."

"Sure."

Spiller looked at Bartoli, whose squinting eyes said he'd already calculated the result of their search.

It didn't take long.

"Weapon!"

Rainey hurried to the gate and disappeared through it.

Bartoli smiled at David and Helen. "I don't have any more questions, if you wouldn't mind giving me a moment alone with Matthew."

Helen looked suspicious, but they both headed into the house.

Bartoli lost his smile and could barely contain his rage. "You are fucking evil, Matthew."

Spiller shook his head. "Nope. You're behind the curve, Angelo. Noah came here yesterday and threatened to rape my daughter. Ask her. She told Rainey already."

"You put her up to it."

"I didn't, but think what you like."

Bartoli fumed.

"*He* caused this, Angelo. I would have let it go."

"You shot your wife's boyfriend."

"I imagine whoever pulled the trigger expected to shoot a mannequin. I expect whoever pulled the trigger thought those four people in the house had *left* the house."

Bartoli appeared to be struck by a revelation. "Jeez, when did I become your confessor? Seriously. I used to be a cop. I'm more like a fucking priest with you. All I do is listen."

"You could always arrest me."

"Sure. And look like an idiot, like in England."

"I recall you came out of that pretty well. Cleared up some very high-profile cases."

"Cases *you* created," Bartoli said, then sagged and sat down. He raised his bandaged hand in front of his face, like an injured dog offering a hurt paw. "Christ, I can't even catch a decent gunshot wound."

Spiller thought he looked broken.

## THIRTY-SIX

SURPRISINGLY, HELEN DIDN'T want to rearrange their flights and leave early. Spiller supposed it was her feisty side coming to the fore, refusing to kowtow to any threats. Besides, she fully expected the cops to arrest the Texan and remove said threat. Even more amazingly, she had no rebuke for her husband, although Spiller was not overly encouraged by this. He felt he'd probably now sunk beneath contempt, which would be the prelude to him essentially becoming *persona non-grata* to her reformed family. As private penance for David's near-death experience, Spiller had offered to stump up for them to stay at The Beverly Hills Hotel. Rather than stand on principle and refuse to accept, Helen had called the other hotel and canceled with them. If she'd known how many diamonds he had in his pocket, and how many more he expected to collect, his "generosity" would not have elicited even the grudging thanks he'd received.

The house without them in it felt oddly empty. He'd grown used to living on his own, having found a strange peace in knowing his circumstances limited the damage he could do to others. No one had to bear the brunt of any moods, so their shelf-life was limited, as they never rebounded on him. There was no one to validate him, one way or the other, so he felt what he felt for as long as it lasted. Now their absence made his solitude feel like a negative.

He called Sadie, but she was out on a job and wouldn't be back until late at night. He briefly wondered if she'd absconded with the loot, because why would she need to work if she was going to retain a life-changing portion of it? But a person couldn't just sit on their arse, however rich they were. If that's what money did to people, what would be the point of it? Life would be essentially over.

Spiller wondered whether he should venture up to Mulholland and try to requisition the remaining stash, but decided he just wanted to sleep for a while. Not knowing if Noah had been arrested, he went out to the reservoir and retrieved Jack's Sig-Sauer. The risk of being caught with an illegal firearm bothered him, but worse was the possibility that Noah might elude capture, locate one of his own, and seek revenge.

He locked the house, positioned Manny in the window, set the alarm downstairs, and went to sleep.

Thirty minutes later, his slumber was interrupted by someone banging on the front door. He woke and grabbed the Sig. He descended the stairs but stopped on the last step, using the wall for cover, in case it was Noah about to unload on him through the door.

"Who is it?"

"Your old buddy! Ethan!"

"I'm busy, mate!"

"No, you're avoiding me! There's no avoiding me!"

Spiller nipped along the hall and into the kitchen, where he hid the Sig under a dish towel in the sink. Then he went to the door and talked through it. "What's up?"

"Don't take me for a fool a second time, Matt! It won't go well for you! Just open up! You know what this is about!"

Spiller unbolted the door, opened it two inches, and was already back in the kitchen by the time Ethan pushed it wide. "In the kitchen!" Spiller called, standing beside the sink.

Ethan entered and settled on a stool at the central island. He was in civilian clothes, off duty. He shook his head. "Oh, Matt. So disappointing. I guess that's on me. I should have known a big star like you wouldn't have any genuine interest in being my buddy. I'm just a lowly patrol cop, right? You got a beer, Matt? Non-alcoholic, I'm driving."

Spiller smiled. "Sorry, I drank them all."

"Don't I know it. What the fuck was that about? Don't tell me you were practicing for a part. You used me. For an alibi. But for *what?*"

Spiller shrugged. "I can't tell you. You know I'm not going to tell you. If it was serious enough that I needed a cop for an alibi, it's serious enough that I'm not going to *tell* a cop."

"Wow. I guess that night on Mel Banaghan, the world got to see the real deal. You were hiding in plain sight. A genuine psycho."

"For what it's worth, Ethan, I don't think you're a lowly cop. Before my life here, I was driving a cab, no money, struggling every day. I actually admire you."

Ethan fake grinned. "A psycho admires me. I'm so flattered."

Spiller wasn't sure what to say, so he just waited. At some point, Ethan would realize the futility of his visit, and leave.

Ethan nodded. "Pleading the fifth, huh? Okay. Oh, I heard you had some trouble here earlier. Someone tried to shoot you. Your stalker? Or was that just a big mirage as well? All part of the show."

Spiller said nothing.

"Yeah, I thought so. Well, you know how you thought having a cop on your side was a good thing? You ever consider how it might feel if you had a cop forever on your case?"

Spiller chuckled. "Been there, bought the t-shirt."

"Bartoli? What I hear, he's a good guy. He won't do anything unless you clearly step out of line. Even then, maybe he rolls over your toes. Me? You make me your enemy, I'm gonna be standing behind you and I'm gonna *push* you out of line. Then I'm gonna run you the fuck over."

"So, what are you saying? I tell you about the other night, or you're going to... what?"

Ethan suddenly looked confused, like he hadn't finalized his closing argument. His tough façade crumbled. "Damn it, Matt, I'm so pissed at you. I spend my professional life distrusting folk. Are they lying to me? About to pull a gun on me? I like it when I feel I can trust a person. It lifts my spirits. We got on, right? That night? Didn't we have a real laugh?"

Spiller nodded. "We did."

"Then?"

"I'm sorry. There are things going on that I can't explain. Things that date back many months. Did Bartoli tell you he knew me in England? When he was a detective there, before he came here?"

"No."

"Right. Well, it's very complicated, and you got caught up in it. I used you. I did. And I owe you for that. We can still be friends, if that's okay with you. We can always reset."

Ethan made a face like he wanted to say yes but his pride wouldn't let him.

Spiller had a thought. "You took my trousers that first night. Remember?"

"Why? You want them back?"

"No, it's just… you said you might sell them in years to come and put your kids through college with the proceeds."

"I was joking."

"You don't have kids?"

"I got kids; I just think, by the time they get to eighteen, no one will even know who you were. The way you're going, you'll have been dead or in jail for a decade already."

Spiller quietly gulped. "Maybe. But what if you knew, right now, that their college fund was secured?"

Ethan laughed raucously. "I got three kids! If they all choose to go, that's over a hundred thou at today's prices, and that's a two-year in-state college. A private four-year college, I'm looking at seven-fifty large. Are you kidding? On my pay? I'm talking about maybe giving them a few thousand each, so they don't have such a loan-burden for the rest of their lives. What are you gonna do, Matt? Set up a trust fund for me?" He hooted.

"Wait here," Spiller said, and left the kitchen.

NOAH DALTON HADN'T bothered changing the license plates that Matt Spiller had swapped onto his truck, and he was glad of that. He guessed his plates would be the subject of a police BOLO right now, and perhaps the bogus plates might allow him to get out of the city and lie low for a while. Hopefully, Lieutenant Bartoli would figure something out and acquit him in his absence, although it didn't bode well that Bartoli had so far failed to offer the protection he'd promised.

The police cruisers outside his house had stopped him in his tracks. Three of them, lights flashing, blocking the street. He'd slowed and taken in the scene, before reversing away and turning around. He'd kept his eye on the news, but hadn't yet seen anything to verify exactly why the cops would want to talk to him. Best case – which would still be bad – was that Spiller's daughter had reported him, and he felt stupid for being so brazen in confronting her, especially with lewd talk that hadn't been serious. But he'd wanted to freak Spiller out, and it had seemed like a good idea at the time. Worst case, the cops had his gun, and it would link him to a crime that would see him jailed for a very long time.

He had an old school buddy who now lived in San Diego, working at the Naval Air Station on Coronado Island. They'd kept in touch, and since he'd been in LA he'd already had the offer to drive down and stay for a while, sink a few beers, reminisce about the old days. Noah had deferred, but now he was going to turn up unannounced and explain the whole sorry episode – hopefully before his face hit the news, and his buddy had his mind made up for him.

THE DIAMOND SITTING in front of Ethan King was perhaps four carats. Ethan stared at it for a few seconds, seemingly unimpressed. Spiller waited, his eyes twinkling like the stone under the ceiling spots.

"What's this?" Ethan asked.

"What's it look like?"

"It looks like a diamond. But as you're a conman, I'd say it's cubic zirconia."

"Nope."

Ethan pinched it between his fingers and set it in his palm, then nudged it around, making it sparkle. He put it down and took out his cellphone. He googled something and read for a minute. He picked it up again and knocked it around his palm.

"Hmm. No rainbow colors inside."

Spiller wasn't sure what that meant, and started to worry that Jack and JoBeth were frauds, and he'd left a bunch of worthless glass and shiny base metal with his girlfriend.

"So far so good," Ethan said, starting to smile. "Article says real diamonds only show rainbow colors on the outside. Inside, the sparkle should be gray and white. That's its *brilliance*." He breathed on it, and his grin widened. "It's not fogging. That's good. Diamonds don't retain heat. You got a newspaper? A book?"

Spiller opened a drawer and found a local guidebook.

Ethan placed the diamond over a word and tried to read through it. "Can't see anything but white."

"Meaning?" Spiller asked.

"The light's scattering inside, blocking the print."

"That's good as well?"

"It's *awesome*. You got any sandpaper?"

"Might have some in the garage."

"Get me some," Ethan said. "Last test."

Spiller found a small square in his toolbox and returned with it. Ethan rubbed the diamond, then inspected the result. His grin broke open and he began laughing.

"Not a scratch. This is a diamond."

"I know," Spiller said, his faith in his fortune restored.

"Are you giving this to me?" Ethan asked.

"That and a few more."

"How many more?"

"How many d'you want?" Spiller dipped in his pocket and placed five more stones on the counter.

Ethan's laughter faded as the enormity of his predicament fully registered. "Jesus. Should I be worried where these came from?"

"I didn't steal them, if that's what you mean. And no one's ever going to look for them."

Ethan collected the rocks in his palm and pushed them with a finger. "How much is this?"

"I don't know exactly. Hundreds of thousands, probably. Don't quote me."

Ethan looked up. "Can I have some more?"

Spiller laughed. "I suppose. Might be some gold and cash I can give you, too. Thing is…"

"What?"

"I might need a look-out. Sorry if I'm making use of my cop buddy again."

"What would I have to do?"

"Just sit in your car outside a certain house. Anyone shows any interest, gets nosey, flash your shield."

"And what if it's a fellow cop?" Ethan asked.

"You're plain-clothed, special op. They'll believe you. They won't want to get involved."

Ethan frowned. "Why not?"

"You'll understand when you see the house."

Ethan suddenly shook his head, appeared dazed, as though he'd just surfaced from a hypnotic trance midway through playing an invisible piano as Liberace. "Whoa. Matt, how can I explain suddenly coming into this much money?"

"Don't buy yourself a gold-plated Hummer. Who's going to know?"

"What if IA ever checks my bank statements? What if I turn these into cash so I can pay my kids' fees in ten, fifteen years, and my bank asks where it all came from? They're very keen on money-laundering these days."

Spiller thought for a moment. "Start gambling."

"Do what?"

"Start visiting casinos. Let it slip to your colleagues you're having a little flutter. Then take a trip or two to Vegas. Start boasting about some big wins. Fill out the tax forms, tell the IRS you won big. Or, I don't know... go on holiday to a state where lottery winners can remain anonymous. Come home, say you won. Both your parents still alive?"

"Yeah, why?"

"Well, sorry to say this, but maybe one or both croak in the next ten years. They leave you some shiny stuff. Ethan, you've got a lot of years to figure this out. Get creative. You said it: set up trust funds. Sell a diamond now and then, filter the money in slowly. Come on, fellah, if you're not careful, you're going to overthink this and think yourself out of it. It's gold and diamonds. D'you want it or not?"

Ethan nodded. "I do. Who wouldn't?"

"Then you'll make it work."

BARTOLI SPENT THE afternoon at his desk, going through files. He had an awful feeling that at least four crimes were about to be dumped at the door of the vanished Noah Dalton. For sure, this latest episode at Spiller's house. A broken nose, a threatened daughter, and a wounded houseguest. Noah's presence at the house confirmed by the daughter, his prints all over the house. A gun found at the scene, his prints on that, too, and a pending ballistics report that would no doubt match the through-and-through slug found in Spiller's living room to the gun. And that was just one crime of attempted murder. Then there was Noah on video boasting that he might have killed Harry Sullivan and Aiden Powers. And there was the case of the missing agent, Billy Banbury. So, potentially three more murders to add to the tally. Poor kid had come to the city seeking fame, only to find infamy.

Part of him hoped they would never track down Noah; that he might find a new life, a new identity, and somehow fade into Hollywood folklore as a bad guy who got away with it. Bartoli hoped this for Noah's sake, but also for his own, because he'd been complicit in Noah's apparent escape from justice. Had he persuaded Noah to officially report his truck stolen, and to share his fears for his agent, the data card would have been logged into evidence. Billy's body would have been found, and Noah would have been arrested. He would still have been innocent, but so would Bartoli. Now Bartoli was horribly compromised, because Noah would sing like a stoolie if he was caught. Then there would be only one option left: Bartoli would have to lie like Matthew Spiller. Deny, deny, deny. The problem with that was the official record that they'd met. That day at the police station, a report filed by the cop who tasered Noah, and a request that Bartoli come talk to the kid. A conversation that was off the record, which made it even more suspicious.

The only way out for them both was if Bartoli could finally nail Spiller. Expose just one of his lies, and hope it brought the rest of them tumbling down.

Spiller's relationship with Sadie Woods certainly irked. Contreras had been right about that. In a city of nearly four million people, how likely was it that Spiller had known Harry Sullivan, and Woods had known Aiden Powers? Spiller, whose house was a half mile away from Sullivan's across the reservoir. Woods, who was the last person to see Powers alive. Sullivan and Powers, both rivals for acting roles.

Bartoli contemplated. Yesterday, Spiller had mentioned his new TV project, playing John Frears. Virginia Frears was linked to Hayley Olsen, who was linked to Brett Stutz, who'd also been up on the road when Frears crashed, no matter what the mechanic said. A circle so tight it was practically incestuous. But considering Olsen and Stutz had parted on the most acrimonious terms, according to the Hollywood gossip columns, how had Spiller got to meet her? Stutz didn't seem like a likely conduit.

After a little digging, Bartoli found some information on the retired Hayley Olsen, and found the number for The House of Sempiternal Love. He waited as he was put through to her office.

"Hayley Olsen. Detective...?"

"Bartoli. West Bureau homicide."

"Is this about John?" she asked.

"In a way. I'm sure you're busy, Miss Olsen, so I'll get right to it. Matthew Spiller. What can you tell me about him?" He poised a pen hopefully above a clean sheet of paper.

"He approached me by way of my ex-husband."

"Approached?"

"Like a go-between. Brett and I had a personal issue, and Brett used Matt to reach out to me."

"I see." Bartoli drew a big question mark, which was of no help. "And... how was Matthew Spiller cast in the role of John Frears? I know you're friends with Virginia Frears, but what I'm asking is how did that come about?"

"That isn't even meant to be common knowledge. How would you know that?"

"I was the detective on Mulholland yesterday. Spiller and I go back aways."

"So, you're the one we need to thank for cracking the case?" she asked.

"Correct," he lied, and waited for gratitude that didn't come.

"What's the issue here, Detective? Should I be concerned about employing Matt?"

Bartoli's lip curled with relish. "Oh, I can't see it's gonna reach that point."

"I know Matt's not squeaky clean, Detective. He has a past. Everyone in this town does. I didn't ask him to elucidate, but he assured me it will not be coming back to haunt us. If you know different, you need to put up or shut up."

Bartoli didn't like that. "You know you're talking to a police Lieutenant, right?"

"I was married to a cop once. You can look it up. He beat me, nearly killed me, knifed Virginia's dad to death on Malibu beach, shot Virginia, then tried to kill a few of his cop buddies, before a sniper blew his brains out while he had a gun shoved in my mouth."

"Gee, that's dreadful."

"Yeah, it really was. So, you'll forgive me if your job title means jack shit to me."

"Guess I'll have to."

"More important to me is character, Detective."

Bartoli couldn't help but laugh. "You think Matthew Spiller has *character?*"

"More so than you, yes. It wasn't you who broke the case yesterday, it was Matt. He put the homeowners in touch with you after he saw the video. Or is he lying?"

Bartoli yielded. "No. One of his few truths."

"Was there a point to this call, Detective?"

"I'm trying to make some connections, Miss Olsen. Right now, I'm investigating one murder that's likely linked to two others, and to an attempted murder. And they're all linked by one person: Matthew Spiller. Can I run a couple of names by you?"

"Go on."

"Aiden Powers."

"What about him?"

"Any connection? To you? To Virginia Frears?"

"Not to me. I can't be sure about Virginia, but I don't think so. Who else?"

"Harry Sullivan."

Hayley Olsen fell quiet for a moment. "What about Harry?"

"You knew him?"

"We originally signed him to play John."

Bartoli silently punched the air and wrote SULLIVAN!

"Detective?"

"So, Harry Sullivan was meant to play John Frears until someone shot him. Then Matthew Spiller showed up and you gave him the part. That pretty much the nub of it?"

"Basically." She chuckled. "Listen, if you're thinking Matt killed Harry to get this role... no way. No one knew about it. Not the part, not the script, nothing. We kept a very tight lid on it all. Unless Harry himself told Matt, then no way he could have known. And that's highly unlikely because Matt told us he had no love for Harry."

"He said that?"

"Said he was an *arsehole* back in the day. Called him *Svengali*."

Bartoli drew a sad face next to the name he'd written. "Interesting. Thank you, Miss Olsen."

"Don't louse up our project, Detective. I mean it. We have a really big director on board, a big studio, some very big names. There's a lot of money already tied up in this. So, you have definite proof that Matt did something, you go right ahead. But you cast unfounded aspersions and wreck our plans, we will sue you for every cent you have, and we'll get the rest from the LAPD."

"Gotcha," Bartoli said, purposely casually. He hung up and stared at the sheet of paper, adding one more word: *MOTIVE!*

Feeling he was on a roll, Bartoli decided to head out and knock on some doors.

## THIRTY-SEVEN

"*THIS* HOUSE?"

"You should switch off the ignition; this engine is really noisy."

Ethan stared through the windshield at the reconstructed gate with the diagonal yellow tapes and the sign in the middle that warned of instant death. "Are you serious? You were here yesterday when it all went down?"

"I'm sort of the reason it went down," Spiller said. "Engine."

Ethan quelled the Challenger's grumbling V8. "You can't go in there. Look at the sign."

"Ethan, you're not going to hear it on the news, but whatever killed the people in there, it's long gone. No trace. Not anywhere."

"They said it was some sort of chemical leak; that the guy was an amateur chemist who mixed the wrong liquids."

"*They* say a lot of things, Ethan. You need to stop watching the news."

Ethan checked the clock. "It's nine now. How long am I meant to sit here?"

"Hopefully no more than twenty minutes. If there's any more inside, it'll take—"

"*If?* I'm sitting here with my ass hanging out, and now you tell me *if.*"

"Chill," Spiller said. "I told you. I know there *was* more. The question is whether the cops found it." He picked up the large gym bag from the footwell. "Don't leave without me, okay? You've got my number. You have a problem out here, let me know." He put his hat and gloves on and got out before Ethan's second thoughts could develop.

With Mulholland temporarily deserted of passing traffic, Spiller was quickly over the gate and scampering down to the bungalow. A quick kick broke the cheap hasp and padlock from the bullet-holed front door. He illuminated his tac-light and checked the rooms. The ceilings throughout the house had been taken down, the walls opened up, the detritus left where it was. Spiller swore, but noticed all the floors were okay, and he surmised that they'd traced any ducting in the roof and walls and figured none of it led underground.

The door to the panic room was open, as though they'd decided there was nothing left inside of any interest. He went to the sofa, which had been pushed aside slightly, but was essentially in its original spot. He shifted it and looked at the tiled floor. Even up close, he wouldn't have known. The tile he knew to be a trap door just looked to have regular grout around it. He pressed his heel on the front, and it popped up. Spiller kneeled and inspected the grout line, which was actually a thin flexible plastic strip, aged to look worn and discolored to match the rest of the floor.

He used the flat key with the weird teeth to open the safe. The cash and the remaining gold were still there, so he quickly transferred it all into the gym bag. He figured another safe would have to be on the edge of the room, or it would have been forever popping open when Jack or JoBeth stepped on it. He started using his heel, putting pressure on all the tiles closest to the walls. He got to where the desk was, pushed it aside, and tried the tiles underneath, but none of them moved. He completed a circuit of the room, then looked at the cabinets that had housed Jack's personal armory. The doors were open, revealing a bare wall and empty gun hooks. Spiller stuck his sneaker inside and began pressing on the edges of the tiles again.

The last tile he tried, in the corner of the room, released with a click.

NOAH'S TRIP WASN'T a complete waste of time. His buddy had welcomed him into his home, listened to his tale of woe, and decided he could stay until his face got plastered all over the TV and social media, and a simple sleepover became harboring a fugitive. This was especially pertinent, given his buddy was now a Master-at-Arms – a Navy cop. Noah knew his name could be aired at any minute. He'd tuned into the news on his drive down the coast, and his worst fears had been realized. According to the dumbass mainstream media, someone had tried to kill Matthew Spiller, and the pundits were drawing parallels to Harry Sullivan and Aiden Powers, even if recent developments had meant they weren't able to include John Frears in their spurious assessments. A suspect had been identified, but the cops weren't releasing his name. Noah imagined that meant they were waiting for prints and ballistics.

One night's accommodation had not been worth the journey. He could have checked into a motel or slept in his truck. What had been worth the journey was the Navy-issue Sig M17 his buddy had kept at home. *Had* being the operative word.

Noah went out for some beers and never returned.

EVEN AS HE filled his gym bag with more loot, Spiller wondered why he was doing it. He already had Bartoli nipping at his heels. There was also the slight problem of a Texan who probably surmised he had nothing to lose anymore, which was never the best basis for decision-making. Yet, here he was, knocking on trouble's door again, appropriating the last of his unofficial inheritance that only the amazing Sadie would ever believe was his to take.

His career was on the line. His liberty. Perhaps even his life, if some trigger-happy cops decided to pull a U-turn and investigate the Dodge Challenger. In Ethan's shoes, Spiller would simply say he was off duty, was passing, and saw someone clamber over the gate. Then they'd all go in together, and the intruder would most likely be shot on sight; probably with Ethan as the triggerman to prevent Spiller from blabbing the truth.

But... all that money. A triumvirate of treasure. Cash, gold, and rocks. How could anyone resist? How would a person justify such a lack of balls in years to come? It was beyond him. If he'd learned one thing last Christmas, it's that he'd been living in a coma up until that point. The events of that period had taught him to live, to take chances, and how invigorating it felt to do so.

Spiller put his hand into the metal container one last time, reaching deep into its unseen extremities, checking for any leftover goodies. As he started to bring his hand out, he felt something touch his knuckles.

He turned his hand over and felt the underside of the box, and his fingers closed around a small object, stuck out of sight. He unpeeled the tape and pulled it out. A black flash drive. He tucked it down his sock, closed both safes, clicked the two tiles back down, and headed out of the panic room with his weighty haul.

Ethan asked him only one question when he got in the car. "Was it there?"

Spiller grinned and patted the bag.

It wasn't far from Mulholland back to Beverly Glen. Spiller half-expected that Ethan would pull over and pull a gun, then leave him by the road and drive off with the gym bag. As they arrived home, Spiller realized how nice it was to have met someone whose moral compass was only slightly defective.

Ethan switched off the engine. "Can I take a look?"

Spiller lifted the bag, unzipped it, and dumped it on Ethan's lap.

"Ho lee shit." He looked at Spiller. "How much is here?"

"Don't know. *Muchos millones*."

Ethan giggled like a child. "What do I take?"

"Listen, I am going to give a lot of this to some good causes. Take what you feel is appropriate, Ethan. Take enough so you never have to worry about money again. Don't take so much that it's *all* you worry about."

Spiller granted the wayward cop some privacy by staring out of his side window for a minute. He could hear Ethan removing some of the contents and placing them behind his seat.

"Okay," Ethan said.

Spiller offered his hand. "Mate, I'm really sorry I used you the other night."

Ethan maintained his grip. "Are you a bad person?"

The question was too big. "Does it matter? You just got rich."

Ethan released the handshake. "I was onto you."

"You knew nothing. You still don't. I could have just told you to fuck off."

Slowly, Ethan nodded, and dumped the bag back on Spiller's lap. "Are we gonna grab another brewski, Matt? A real one this time?"

Spiller smiled. "Definitely."

UNTIL HE WAS certain he wouldn't need to pack his bag and disappear into the night, Spiller wasn't going to share his news of the extra floor-safe with Sadie. He had no clue if or when Bartoli might finally catch a break and find a compelling bit of evidence he'd actually be happy to take to his superiors, but he figured running away was a lot easier if you had a ton of money standing by. He totted up the contents of the gym bag, and calculated Ethan had taken maybe a cheeky two million, plus the diamonds he'd already received. Even leaving Sadie's stash untapped, Spiller estimated he had at least ten million, depending on the quality of the stones. If he'd believed in an afterlife, he'd have imagined JoBeth looking down on him right now with extreme rancor. Then again, what would have become of it all without his intervention? Unearthed at a later date by the authorities and seized by Uncle Sam? Or left undiscovered beneath the feet of the new homeowners for decades?

Spiller wasn't keen on lugging his bag around with him, and he couldn't think of a terribly cunning place to hide it around the house. He checked on his phone and found a twenty-four-hour self-storage facility near Reseda, and decided to drop by on his way to Sadie's apartment. He added some clothes and Jack's Sig to the loot and felt quite excited that he actually now had a go-bag, like all the best badass movie villains.

As he was about to reverse the Maserati onto the street, his cell rang, and showed the name *HAYLEY*. He let it ring out, then got on his way.

The storage facility fleeced him, but they at least let him pay in cash, didn't request any ID, and the guy in the office didn't seem to recognize him. A full house of anonymity. The only item he retained from his evening exploits on Mulholland was the flash drive, and he wanted to look at that with Sadie, because he would have no clue what to do if it contained a list of Swiss bank accounts.

They made love the moment he walked in the door. In the closest room, which was the kitchen. Jeez, this woman made him feel like he'd just gone through puberty again, walking around school with a perpetual hard-on. Sadie was a new lease on life for him. He'd always thought that would happen when his dreams came true and he made it to Hollywood, but perhaps he'd been wrong. Maybe he'd just needed to meet this woman. There had been someone many years ago who'd made him feel this way. Before Helen. It had ended badly, and he'd thought he'd never feel that way again. He had loved Helen, but it wasn't a match for his earlier relationship. There were levels of love. Some loves burned brightly and suddenly died, starved of something essential. Others smoldered for decades, never threatening to catch light, but generating sufficient warmth to ensure their longevity. And a rare few were spontaneous combustions whose fuel was infinite. His love of long ago was like that. And this felt the same.

They sat together, cuddling, watching TV.

"Oh," he said, after ten minutes. "I forgot to mention. I found a flash drive when I found all that stuff on Mulholland. At the back of the safe. I've not even looked at it."

"A flash drive in a safe? That sounds ominous, knowing what we know about Jack. The job he did. Why don't you grab my laptop?"

Spiller returned with the computer and the flash drive and settled next to her again. He handed them to her. "Here you go. I'm not much of a nerd."

Sadie challenged him with a wry look. "I look like a nerd to you?"

He kissed her. He was lying to her again, and he hated himself for doing so. For not revealing the extra safe. For his side-deal with Ethan. For taking her SUV last night. For everything he hadn't told her about Noah and Billy and Bartoli and last Christmas. It felt like the most perfect relationship, but it was built on lies and omissions.

Sadie powered up the laptop, slotted in the flash drive, and clicked on it. "No go, Matt. Password-protected. I'd guess it's military grade, at least two-fifty-six-bit AES encryption."

"Thought it might be. Can it be cracked?"

"A brute-force attack? Maybe with a supercomputer running for trillions of years."

He smiled.

"I'm not joking. I read an article recently. It'd take over twenty-seven million trillion trillion trillion trillion years. Give or take. How long are you here for?"

"Can it be *hacked?* I mean, people hack into the Pentagon, right? That can't be easy. Any ideas?"

Sadie pulled out the flash drive. "Wrong arm of the military, Matt. You need Army Cyber Command. I can shoot it, if that'd make you feel better."

Spiller had a thought. "Hold on..." He left the living room, returning with JoBeth's keys. He inspected the safe key with the strange inscription, then showed her.

"Hmmm," Sadie purred. "This is way too long and complex to be a key-cutting code." She smiled at him. "No... they couldn't have been dumb enough to put the password on here. Could they?"

"Maybe Jack did it when he knew he was losing his mind."

Sadie stuck the flash drive in the slot again. "Here goes nothing. Let's hope it doesn't leak some of that killer mist if we get it wrong."

"That's not funny."

"That is funny. Jack gets the last laugh. That's funny."

"I'm going to wait in the car park," Spiller said, moving to get up.

She laughed and blocked his exit with her arm. "You can sit the hell down. I'm okay with dying sitting next to you."

Spiller returned the laugh, but she wasn't smiling any more. "You know what? Me, too. Go for it." He pinched his nose, which made them both cackle.

Sadie slowly typed in the mix of letters, numbers, and special characters, then read them out loud three times, seeking verification from Spiller as she spoke. Then she went to press ENTER.

"Hold on, hold on," Spiller said. "If this could kill us, we should probably have one last bonk."

"*Bonk?*"

Spiller slipped his hand under the laptop and offered a preliminary translation.

Sadie squirmed and moaned. "*Ooooh.*" She set the laptop on the floor.

WHAT WOULD SPILLER do? Although it wasn't a credo Bartoli intended to live by, it seemed a useful exercise in working out the precise events of the previous night. The gunman – hereafter known as Spiller – had reportedly fallen as he fled the scene through the rear gate. It seemed logical that the safest approach would be via the reservoir, away from prying eyes and streetlights. So, leave as he'd entered. It also seemed logical that Spiller wouldn't have wanted a lengthy escape on foot, in case a police chopper was in the area. Although, from what Spiller had implied, he hadn't expected anyone to be in the house, so probably hadn't foreseen the need for a quick getaway. Then again, Spiller had been known to plan for every eventuality in the past, so he would still have deemed a swift exit to be preferable. That meant he would have parked on one of the nearby lanes. He would also have wanted to avoid using one of his own vehicles, which were too recognizable, and too noisy. That left a rental car as an option, or perhaps Billy Banbury's Camaro, which Bartoli hadn't seen since he'd tailed it the day he'd discovered Noah's truck in Westwood's student area.

Or, as Spiller had given Sadie Woods as an alibi, maybe he'd used her the same way he'd used Officer King.

And it was this supposition that had finally led Bartoli to his present location, two lanes down from Spiller's home, where for the second day running, a homeowner's CCTV had worked the oracle. A Cadillac Escalade had rolled past the camera on its way to the end of the road, and The Department of Motor Vehicles' database had confirmed the owner to be Sadie Woods.

Bartoli sat in his Honda Civic outside the property, spinning a small flash drive between two fingertips, but still not satisfied. The footage showed the car passing out of sight. No coverage of who got out. But the timeframe was a perfect match, according to Detective Rainey's incident report.

Had Spiller finally made a blunder? Or had he simply taken the window of opportunity presented to him, however imperfect? Had he known that the LAPD lacked the resources to properly pursue

Crimes Against Persons offenses, especially when no one was badly hurt? Again, Spiller had implied that his target had been a movie mannequin, not his wife's boyfriend. Had that been the outcome, even without a probable suspect, very little effort would have been made to solve the crime. But *with* a definite suspect, implicated by prints and ballistics, if not circumstances, why would Spiller have worried the detective in charge would bother exploring other avenues? He likely didn't even think Bartoli would get a look-in, with it not being a homicide.

But there was another, totally different, scenario to consider. That Spiller hadn't done this. That he also hadn't killed Harry Sullivan. And that he hadn't killed Aiden Powers, because Bartoli had to admit that was a long shot. Officially recorded as an accident, and no indication it was anything other than the tragic result of too much disposable income splashed on too many designer narcotics.

Except… Sadie Woods had been the last person to see Powers alive.

Bartoli felt malevolent thinking his thoughts, and he smiled at his reflection in the rearview mirror. He didn't believe Sadie Woods was at all culpable, but there was enough here to give him an angle, because this would be the biggest test of Spiller's character. If he had any genuine feelings for his new girlfriend, would he really stand back and risk her taking the fall?

THE FLASH DRIVE OPENED like Aladdin's cave. Even the most cursory scan of its contents, however, warped that metaphor into Pandora's Box. With Spiller watching, Sadie opened one folder after another, and the complexity of the images and data left Spiller feeling regretful he'd even found it.

"Matt?"

"I know."

"No, this is terrifying. I don't know exactly what I'm looking at, but this is serious. Blueprints, diagrams, formulas, and most of it photographed, like Jack really wasn't meant to have any of it. I'm guessing that lethal mist is in here somewhere. And some of these blueprints look a lot like weapons tech. But nothing like I ever saw in the military. Look at the stamp on every page: *Top Secret: Special Access Program.* That's the highest classification. Look at this one. Dated nineteen eighty-seven. Is that some sort of nuclear propulsion system? For a fighter jet?" She zoomed in on the accompanying text. "Oxygenated perfluorocarbon? That's like a breathable liquid. Do we have airplanes that fly so fast that the pilot needs to sit in liquid? And that was thirty-five years ago. Oh, Matt…" She looked above the lid of the laptop at the TV, and seemed grateful for the banality of a gameshow.

Gently, Spiller took the machine off her, and continued exploring several of the folders. "Menticide… Cybernetics… Soulcatcher… Blue Beam… Directed Energy… Voice of God… Havana Syndrome. Sadie, you ever heard of any of this?"

She nodded. "Variations on a theme. Conspiracy theories – supposedly. What are we gonna do with it?"

Spiller didn't know. It was like an extra headache when he already had a migraine.

"Do we speak out?" Sadie asked.

"What's the point? As you said, it's tinfoil-hat stuff. The drive gets discredited, then we end up dead in mysterious circumstances."

"Hmm." Sadie immersed herself in the gameshow again as a distraction.

Spiller removed the flash drive from the slot. He thought of the storage locker he'd just rented. "I'm going to hide this somewhere tomorrow. It'll be safe. I need time to let all this settle."

She took the laptop, shut it down, set it on the floor, and looked at him. "Your life is nuts."

He grinned. "So, what does that say about you?"

"Guess I must be in love."

## THIRTY-EIGHT

THEY FELL ASLEEP in each other's arms, a comatose audience for TV fare that demanded no higher level of engagement, only to be disturbed an hour later by the buzz of the apartment intercom. Sadie merely uttered a grunt, as though the sound had entered only her subconscious, which had chosen to dismiss it. Spiller eased out from her embrace and headed to the door before the caller could wake her.

"Who is it?" he whispered into the box. "It's late."

"That you, Matthew? Wanna buzz me up?"

"What is it, Angelo?"

"Actually, probably best you come down. Interesting development in the matter of who shot your wife's boyfriend."

"You catch Noah?"

"Oh, he's in the wind. You should come down, Matthew. Before I come up and talk to you about your girlfriend's Cadillac Escalade – in front of her."

Spiller experienced a wave of sickly adrenaline. "Wait a minute." He wondered what to do. Could he take Sadie's gun and kill him? Stupid idea. Maybe it was nothing. Maybe Bartoli was being his usual inept self, mistaking harassment for detective work. But he'd clearly made a link, and Spiller couldn't have him expound his theory in front of Sadie. He quickly put some clothes on, took Sadie's apartment key, and went downstairs.

Bartoli was perched on the hood of his Honda, looking smug. The air was still warm, and he was in shirtsleeves, his .45 visible on his belt.

"What?" Spiller asked. "What about Sadie's Caddy?"

"Okay, you're playing dumb again. Her vehicle passed a camera on Dellwood last night. In and out. I could give you the exact timings, but I'm guessing you already know the upshot."

Spiller searched for an innocent answer, but he was stumped. "So, why aren't you arresting her?"

Bartoli smiled. "Because she didn't do it."

"I know she didn't do it, but the procedure would be to arrest her, listen to her denial, then check the CCTV in this car park, and identify who really did drive her car out of here last night. Why aren't you doing that?"

"Because that just gets you for last night. And I want you for more than last night. I want you for Harry Sullivan, your agent, and everything you pulled last Christmas."

"Not Aiden Powers?"

"I don't care about that. I don't think you did that. But I know you killed Harry Sullivan. I spoke to Hayley Olsen, who told me Sullivan was cast as John Frears until he got himself shot. Then you waltzed in. Real fortuitous."

Spiller stepped forward.

Bartoli placed his hand on his holstered gun. "Shooting you also works."

Spiller stopped. "I had no clue about that part. It was a secret. Hayley must have told you that."

"She did. But would a jury believe anyone in this town can keep a secret?"

"So, what do you want?"

"I told you."

"No. That was an opening gambit. This is a negotiation. Because you know I can wriggle out of anything if I want to."

Bartoli nodded. "But can Sadie Woods? She was the last person to see Powers alive, and then she went to your place last night and tried to shoot you. Maybe she just hates actors."

"But I was here last night, so why would she go to my house to kill me? All you'd have to do is check the CCTV here to confirm that."

"If the system here works. And even if it does, maybe the past week somehow gets deleted. Evidence disappears; you should know that. Then what we got is Sadie Woods, prime suspect."

"And what about Noah? His gun, his prints in my house, his threats to my daughter?"

Bartoli put on a thinking face. "Maybe they were in it together. Honestly, I don't know how all this pans out. In the final analysis, though, whatever happens, you lose the girl. You betrayed her. You took her car, tried to frame her."

"Make your mind up, Angelo. Did I frame Noah or Sadie?"

"Maybe both."

Spiller lost his temper. "I would never hurt that woman!"

Bartoli laughed. "*Awww*, little Matthew's in love. It's okay, I could see it the other night at Theo Montgomery's house. I guess it's nice to know you're not a complete sociopath. You at least feel something that you *think* is love."

Spiller stared coldly at Bartoli, and knew it was a good job he hadn't brought Sadie's gun downstairs with him. "So? What now?"

"Fess up. To last night. And to killing your agent. I'm good with that. Noah gets off, your career ends, you go to jail. Basically, justice is served. Because if you don't… I will switch all my energies to your new squeeze, and her life will go up in flames. Who knows, she may *genuinely* try to shoot you."

For only the second time in his life, Spiller could summon no sense of hope. The first time had been in England, when he'd been told his family had been murdered, because he'd not been able to envisage a life worth living without them. Then he'd learned it was just a wicked lie, and he'd realized a part of him craved a new life without them in it.

"What?" Bartoli said. "Have I managed to dumbfound the famous Matthew Spiller? Well, chalk one up to the good guys."

Spiller stepped closer and held out his hand. "Well done. You win."

"You want me to take my hand off my forty-five?"

"Listen… at least give me twenty-four hours. I need to talk to Sadie, explain stuff. And speak to my family."

"You're not wriggling out of this, Matthew. There's no clever plan to get you off the hook. You can take all the time you want, it's not gonna happen. Not this time."

"I know. Just a day. Pretty please. I did try and save your life, remember?"

Bartoli peered at him. "That's fair. Okay, midnight tomorrow. Be at your house. I'll come for you."

"Thanks."

"Or you could take off. Like Noah. I wouldn't mind hearing that you got shot dead by a US Marshall in some lonely Nebraska barn."

Spiller shook his head. "You got me, Angelo. I'm done."

SPILLER SPENT AN hour watching Sadie sleep. His eyes traced her lithe form, covered only by a t-shirt. What a life he might have had with this woman. He'd been right to feel bereft of hope. There was no scheming in his head. No grand plan would come to mind. And it seemed there was a sad inevitability to his current predicament. Everything he'd ever wanted was his. A promising career, plenty of money, a nice home, a Maserati, a Hayabusa. And a new love. All perfectly concrete, his to have and to hold. But, ultimately, as gossamer as the dreams of fame and fortune that had so plagued his younger years.

"Sadie," he whispered, not really wishing to disturb her. "Sadie." A little louder: "Hey. Sadie."

She stirred, opened her eyes, smiled at him. "What time is it?" She sat up. "Are you okay?"

His eyes welled, but he didn't feel he had the right to any sympathy, so he blinked it away. "I have to tell you something."

"Are you getting back with your wife?"

He laughed. "No. Nothing like that. I love you."

Sadie grinned. "I know. I'm kinda fond of you, too. Was that it?"

"I took your car last night when you were asleep."

"Oh. Where d'you go?"

"I shot my wife's boyfriend."

Sadie burst out laughing, then quickly stopped. "Is this acting? You're having a bit of fun with me?"

"No. It was on the news. They're after that Texan whose truck we stole. It was his gun. But I did it. I gave you as an alibi."

"Why? Are you jealous?"

"No. Actually, I'm very happy for her."

"Then..."

"They weren't meant to be home. They said they'd be leaving. It was meant to be a dummy. A mannequin I own from the movie. I wanted to shoot that."

Sadie leaned forward on her knees. "Why?"

"To get the Texan off my case. Because he broke my nose and threatened my daughter, and..."

"And?"

"He knows I killed my agent."

Sadie put her head in her hands, stared at the floor. "I must be dreaming. I'm still asleep on the couch. I'm gonna open my eyes and—" She looked up at him. "Matt, why?"

"He was trying to blackmail me. I was happy to pay him off, then I found out he didn't care about the money. He just wanted to be famous. Even just for five minutes. The guy who put Matt Spiller in prison."

"For what?"

"The bad stuff back in England. I killed people. And some other people died. I was just protecting my family."

"This is why that detective's got such a boner for you?"

"And now he's got me. He was here earlier. An hour ago. He has footage of your SUV from last night, just down the road from my place. He said he's going after you if I don't admit to at least some of the things I've done."

"But you gave me as an alibi. If I say you were here, then you're *my* alibi, too."

"So, who was driving your car?" Spiller asked.

"Did they arrest the Texan?"

"No. He's on the run."

"Okay. Then he stole it. Matt, it's reasonable doubt. You left his gun at the scene?"

Spiller suddenly felt a spark of optimism. "I did. And his prints are everywhere."

"Then what's the problem?"

He stared at her for a while, utterly bewildered and even more in love. "Why aren't you annoyed? You should be furious. I took your car, gave you as an alibi. I've kept so much from you."

"You think you know about *my* life, Matt? Have I shared? About my time in the military? What went down over there?" She shook her head. "No. You said the first time we met: it's a need-to-know thing. You don't blurt your life story the moment you meet someone. And why would any of this surprise me? I try not to, but I see your auras, dude. I mean, *wow*. Come on, I knew what I was buying into. You snorted coke that first night. You cut the legs off your pants. You put a pair of scissors to someone's throat. On live TV! What? You think I think you're *sane*? You're hysterical. And I love you."

Spiller was laughing quietly, his eyes moist again.

"So," she said. "That detective? He can go fuck himself."

He calmed down. "I can't take the risk, Sadie. He's not going to let up. If he can't get me, he'll get you. He's already got rid of evidence. What if he *plants* some? To frame you. To hurt me."

"Frames me for what?"

"Aiden Powers. Maybe even Harry Sullivan."

Sadie's face went slack, and she looked suddenly ill.

"What? Sadie?"

She got up and went to grab what was left of the rum from the kitchen. She returned and swigged from the bottle. "We're confessing, right?"

He nodded.

"Powers made a move on me. He invited me back to his pool. I knew he was loaded, but I wanted to maybe get some contacts for my business. He read it the wrong way. Stripped down to his shorts, laid a hand on my tit. I just swatted it away. I would have walked, but he grabbed my face, so I threw him a little Tai Chi. Basically stepped out of his way and let his weight work against him. And it did. He fell and cracked his head open on the poolside."

Spiller went and sat beside her and held her hands. "Hey, it was an accident."

"It was. But when I got home, I noticed I was missing a hoop earring. I think he pulled it out."

"So, *if* the cops ever ask, you had a drink with him before you left, and it must have fallen out."

"Problem is, I told the cops I dropped him off at the curb. They didn't pursue it because his death didn't look suspicious. But what if that detective goes after me, and they check and find my earring in the pool area… with my DNA? Or they check nearby cameras and see me get out and follow him? I'm caught in a lie, and why would I have lied if I had nothing to hide?"

"Because you're a veteran, and they'd have said you were suffering from PTSD. I don't blame you for getting the hell out. No one would. Listen, I'll take the rap for Powers. I can't risk you getting in trouble just because you met me."

"Matt, no. No man left behind. We can bluff this out."

Spiller sat for a few minutes, contemplating, then he nodded at his girlfriend.

Boy, Bartoli was going to be so pissed off.

## THIRTY-NINE

THE OTHER SIDE had not offered any help. Oftentimes, when she was in turmoil, Hayley would take a step back and wait for guidance from the Universe. She tended not to confront problems in the moment they presented themselves, because, given a surprisingly short amount of time, they usually faded into a cosmic shrug. This time, though, a night's sleep had brought neither answers, nor a diminishing of the questions.

She wasn't happy with Kat's response yesterday. Mrs Stutz the Fourth had sidestepped the issue of her relationship with John Frears, shifting the focus onto what a bad man their ex-husband was, without providing much detail there, either. It galled Hayley to know Kat thought she had more of an inside track on Brett than her; with the implication that Hayley had been willfully blind or painfully stupid during their marriage.

And if anything, she was even more concerned about Matt Spiller's involvement in *Veteran Avenue*. The detective had raised her hackles, bolding the doubts that Spiller himself had sown regarding the quality of his character. Perhaps the frank admission of his faults had, by design, served to bar her further inquisition. The notion of replacing his letter of attachment with an official contract now gave her real pause. Even with a morals clause, the moment any film ended up in the can, the cost of potentially having to reshoot would begin to mount.

She needed to talk to him in person. She sent him a message: *Matt, please come over to the house, we need to discuss something. I will be here all day.*

It would be a shame if they had to give him the boot. He was perfect. But there was no lack of actors out there. It was easy to become fixated on a certain face in a role and develop a mental block to anyone else. How many times were characters replaced in TV shows to the public's utter dismay, only for the original cast member to be forgotten inside one episode? People were fickle.

Her thoughts returned to Kat, and she realized just how angry she was with the girl. She asked for no payment from the people who stayed at the house. If they wanted to contribute, that was their decision. She ran it as a non-profit. All she did require was honesty. Her residents didn't have to spill their life stories, but in matters pertaining to the safety of her other guests, the truth was important. If someone had a stalker, she needed to know. If a jealous ex was about to show up at the gate with a gun, she needed to know. And if a resident had been screwing her best friend's husband shortly before his violent death, she damn well *wanted* to know, because that was a betrayal on two fronts.

Hayley left her office and went to knock on Kat's door.

"Good morning, Hayley," Kat answered through a yawn, as she knotted a kimono. "Everything okay?"

"Not really. I think maybe there's someone out there more deserving of this room."

Kat pouted. "You want me to go?"

"I don't think this place is helping you. This is a sanctuary, a place of healing. I don't think you need any healing. I think maybe Brett was right to move on from you."

"Hayley, what is wrong?"

"Please pack your things." Hayley walked away before Kat could remonstrate.

Twenty minutes later, a sheepish ex-resident pushed open Hayley's office door, dragging a gold-colored suitcase behind her. She approached Hayley's desk and set a bulky hard drive down.

Hayley tapped it. "What's this?"

"I am sorry, Hayley. I am not totally honest. That is hard drive."

"Yeah, I know what a hard drive looks like. Why are you giving it to me?"

"Remember I say I copy my work from Brett's laptop? Not true. I have no work on his laptop. But I copy. I copy everything onto hard drive."

"And?"

"One folder I cannot open. It has password. I try everything but I cannot open."

Hayley sighed. "It's his taxes, Kat."

Kat became suddenly animated. "No! Not taxes. He want me dead over that? Pah! And too big for taxes."

"What is?"

"Folder. One terabyte. If it is taxes, Brett hide seventy-five million pages from IRS."

Hayley stared at the hard drive, picked it up. "What about videos? How many hours would it hold?"

"I think maybe five hundred."

Hayley found a cable in her drawer. She spoke as she connected the drive to her desktop computer. "Why do you think Brett's a bad person?"

"I don't know. Maybe I am wrong."

"No, you were pretty damn sure last night. You think there's something nasty in this folder? I mean, that he'd go to jail for?"

"You mean children?"

"*Jesus...* seriously?"

"That is nasty, yes? What else? He worship Satan? He have evidence of UFO?"

"Maybe it's just a ton of gay porn. That would certainly account for his disinterest in the bedroom." Hayley made a few mouse clicks, then swore. "How d'you get into something like this? Are there programs? Kat, take a seat."

Kat parked her suitcase and sat down. "You need hacker."

"What passwords have you tried?"

"Names, dates, movies. At least it does not wipe data after try too many times."

Hayley typed in a few guesses, to no avail. And why would Brett have used a password that was easily solved? All he'd have needed was a special character in there somewhere. An ampersand in the middle of a simple word would suffice.

Kat reached and held Hayley's hand. "I do not betray you. I do not betray Virginia. John is kind to me, but nothing more."

Hayley suddenly felt vindictive for asking her to leave. "It's okay. Listen, if you wa—"

"I will go. You are right, Hayley. I do not need to stay. Brett is in past. I am much better. You help me greatly."

"Okay."

"Hayley?"

"What?"

Kat appeared awkward with the question she had in mind. "What happen if you get in folder and it is very bad? And people ask how you did not know. How I did not know. Or they think we know, but we say nothing."

Hayley was poised to press *Submit* on another guess. "You're suggesting it might be so bad that we'd have to go public?"

"Or we can forget," Kat said. "Throw away hard drive. Then there is no knowing."

Hayley pressed *Submit*. "No knowing, just wondering. Kat, we need to get into this folder."

"In my country, we have saying: "*Волков бояться – в лес не ходить*. It mean, if you're scared of wolves, don't go in woods."

Hayley tilted her head back and shut her eyes. "Oh, man…" She could only think it *was* some kind of porn. But why would anyone store that much in a private folder? Porn was everywhere online. You could go incognito, use a VPN if you were totally paranoid, and watch a thousand hours of filth for free. And who'd care if it was gay? Gay was the new straight. The new gay was a hundred different genders whose proclivities were mind-boggling and were now mostly enshrined in laws that made the silent majority feel *they* were the aberrant.

"I think it is not strong security," Kat said. "There is hacker who can break it."

Hayley tried to think of anyone she knew who might know of such nefarious figures, and immediately thought of Matt Spiller. She frowned, disturbed by the association her mind had so easily established.

"You think of Matthew," Kat said, smiling. "I think of him, too."

Hayley picked up her cell.

A PHONE CALL chasing a text message was a bit too keen for Spiller's liking. Not that he was too surprised. Bartoli's chat with Hayley had clearly been designed to queer his pitch. More and more, Spiller was beginning to think his Hollywood adventure was a mere dalliance, and that he and Sadie should just take off together. Take the cash, the diamonds, the gold, and just disappear. Forget the acting. Such inherent emptiness in the abandonment of self, even temporarily. He'd let the profession destroy his happiness for two decades. It had wrecked his mind, stolen his joy, detached him from his family. He had yearned for a private pool in the hills for so long, it had blinded him to the fact he was now swimming in a vast septic tank.

He'd not been awake for long. He slipped out of bed quietly, and stared, as he'd done last night, at Sadie's slumbering form. He focused on her face, so innocent and pure in its release from the world's angst. Her brain, dreaming its dreams, levelling the psyche, immersing her in a world shared by everyone, and understood by no one.

As he got on the road in his battered Maserati, heading up the coast toward The House of Sempiternal Love, Spiller realized he wasn't scared anymore. Hayley could take *Veteran Avenue* from him. Helen could take his kids from him. But no one, *no one*, was going to steal his second chance of real love, from a woman who saw him warts and all, and genuinely wasn't fazed by any of it. And if it seemed Bartoli was about to succeed in that theft, Spiller would end him.

The gates were already opening as he turned off the Pacific Coast Highway. The vehicle waiting to exit was a sleek, black Mercedes, and Kat was behind the wheel. Spiller let her through, and she stopped alongside him.

"Hey, Kat. How's life?"

"I am leaving. It was nice meeting you. Maybe we work together some time."

He opened his mouth to respond, but she'd hit the accelerator and was now twenty feet behind him, waiting to join the passing traffic.

Her tires squealed as she set off in the direction of LA, leaving a cloud of dust in the air.

"Bye, then." He nipped through the gates before they could close and headed up the incline to the house. Hayley was outside, sitting at the pool edge, dangling her feet in the water. He got out, removed his shoes and socks, rolled up his pants legs, and joined her. Neither of them spoke for a couple of minutes, they just leaned back on their arms, and tilted their faces to the morning sun.

Eventually, Spiller said, "You talked to a Detective Bartoli."

"Uh-huh."

"You want me off *Veteran Avenue?* It's fine. I won't lawyer up, if that's your concern."

Hayley lay fully back and closed her eyes. "I pretty much never use this pool. I barely ever walk across the highway and take a swim in the ocean. It's what people think the rich and famous do. Lounge about, enjoying their spoils. I never did."

Spiller flattened himself beside her. He knew the answer, but he asked, "Why not?"

"It's boring. Doing nothing. Owning things you don't need. You maybe don't remember the movie *Wall Street*."

"Michael Douglas."

"Bud asks Gordon Gekko: *How many yachts can you water-ski behind? How much is enough?* It's true. How many cars can a person drive at the same time?"

"Nice to have a choice, though," Spiller said.

"The theory's great, sure. It's what brings every young wannabe into town. It's not the acting. If someone wants to act, they can do some amateur dramatics in their hometown. Or they can adopt a persona, change who they are every day, so the world never sees the real person. It's all acting. The difference here is the money and the notoriety."

"It's something to strive for. What else is life about?"

"But actors strive for the whole world, don't they, Matt? So, the absence of it feels like a catastrophe, and the attainment of it is just an anticlimax that leaves nowhere to go."

Spiller smiled. "I've had this conversation with my girlfriend."

"She's an actress?"

"God, no. No, it's Sadie – Theo's driver."

"Oh, okay. She looked impressive."

"She is."

"Are you gonna wreck it?" Hayley asked.

Spiller sat upright. "Why would I?"

"Because that's what we do in this town. We destroy the good stuff while striving for toys that can never replace it. We lose the people we love, then soon after we lose ourselves. Just as the public finally notice us and believe that we made it, we start taking stock. We have to, because we caught the thing we were chasing, so we have to stop, take a step back and work out if it was worth it. I did it myself. Kat did it. Every person who's been through this house has done it. And believe me, I've had some huge names under my roof."

"Did that answer my question? Maybe it did, but I'm a bit thick. Am I off *Veteran Avenue?*"

Hayley sat up. "I don't know. I can't figure you out. You can clearly see through the bull, which is one reason we liked you for John. It's just…"

"I'll back out if you want."

"You won't fight for the part?"

"I think anything that's meant for me, I won't have to fight for it. It'll just land in my lap."

"That detective thinks you killed Harry Sullivan," Hayley said. "To get the part."

"The part I didn't know about and that I'm happy to walk away from? Yeah, that makes sense."

"Why does he think that?"

"We have history. He was a cop in England before he came here. My oldest daughter got us caught up with some bad people. Underworld people. Things were terrible for a while."

"And how did that end?"

"Badly for them. And that's all I'm going to say. He resents not being able to figure it all out, so now he's hounding me. If that's a problem for you, I get it. *Veteran Avenue* is brilliant. I wouldn't want it screwed up if I'd written it."

"I didn't just write it; I lived it. So did Virginia. In fact, both of us nearly *didn't* live through it."

Spiller got to his feet, rolled his pants legs down and put his shoes and socks on. "Your call, Hayley." He offered his hand, but she stood up without taking it.

She stared at him for a moment, weighing him up, but he spoke first.

"You're not happy, are you, Hayley? And it's got nothing to do with me."

"Pardon?"

"What was all that philosophizing just now? That was about you, not me. Something got you soul-searching. What's going on?"

"Nothing."

"All this sempiternal love stuff, the hippy vibe? It's cool, but it's a front."

"You figure?"

"If it was real, you'd be living on a commune far away from here. But you're not. You're twenty miles up the coast, and you're still immersed in the profession. You're not running a refuge for battered women; you're trying to fix the broken souls of Hollywood. And you know that doesn't happen. I bet everyone who leaves this place takes a left out of the drive. Back to the city. No one turns right, leaves it all behind. You're just a pleasant place to go cold turkey for a while, before they head back to their drug of choice."

Hayley's eyes were starting to blaze, but they softened. "You're right. But why would you point that out? When I'm already on the fence about you, why would you try and tip me off?"

Spiller shrugged. "Resolution. For both of us. You take me on, I'll give you everything I've got. But you also need to be committed. *Veteran Avenue* is your baby. Don't take risks with it."

Hayley sat on a pool chair. "Gee, you're a little crazy."

"So, what's going on with you? Why the soul-searching? Did you have to kick Kat out? Is that it? Did she admit to something?"

"Kinda."

"About John?"

Hayley nodded. "But not that. Not an affair. They were just friends."

"What then?"

"John asked Kat to take Brett's laptop. But she only found it recently."

Spiller sat next to Hayley. "Why would he have wanted it? The tax business? Why would he be bothered about that?"

Hayley was shaking her head. "It's something else. How are you with cracking computer passwords?"

He laughed. "Useless. Why?"

"Because Kat copied his entire laptop onto a hard drive. And there's something really big on there."

IN HAYLEY'S OFFICE, Spiller just stared at the password box, the cursor flashing inside it, like a man might inspect a broken-down car engine when he didn't know a carburetor from a crankshaft. He could click here and there, input random words, like a man might pointlessly waggle a few components under the hood, but he knew it would achieve nothing.

"Do you know anyone who could crack this?" Hayley asked.

"I'm that dodgy, am I?"

"I checked online. With the right algorithm, a decent gaming computer might be able to open a basic locked folder in maybe four days."

Spiller typed in *MurderCycle*, to no effect. "I did know someone. He'd have had this open inside a minute." He frowned at another thought, suddenly becoming aware of a shape against his thigh in his jeans pocket.

"What is it?" Hayley asked, reading his expression.

Spiller pulled out Jack's flash drive. "I wonder..."

"What?"

"Could you get me a coffee, please, Hayley? I'm exhausted. Pretty disturbed night."

She smirked. "Yeah, I imagine Sadie would do that to a man. Milk, sugar?"

"Yes, thanks." Spiller stopped leaning over the desk, and settled in Hayley's desk chair as she left the room. He stuck the drive in a USB slot and used the password off the key to open the main folder. Some of the internal folders were unnamed, so he hovered the mouse pointer over each one and viewed the details that appeared in the ghost box. The Date Created, Size, and Files.

He had checked a dozen or so, confused by most of the file names, when one set of details caught his eye. The file said *Crypto*, and Spiller mused whether this was another hidden fortune. But the Date Created was 1998, and he knew that was over ten years before Bitcoin's official first use. Perhaps the old couple had been in on the ground floor, way before the public even knew of its existence, and there were billions sitting in a crypto wallet.

He opened the folder, saw a program, and clicked to open it. The interface was basic, and a dialog box sat in the center, requesting the user to drag and drop a file or folder inside. The only other text was writ small, in the top left of the outer window box, and it said: *CRYPTOGRAPHY – PROTOTYPE – SPECIAL ACCESS PROGRAM*.

Not crypto. *Cryptography*. And exactly the program he'd hoped to find.

Spiller minimized Jack's main folder and shifted the program aside to reveal Brett's locked one. His heart was thudding as he positioned the pointer, held down the click, and dragged Brett's folder inside Jack's program. A dialog box popped up: *Decrypting. Please wait…*

"MATT, WHAT'S WRONG?"

Spiller glanced at her, but she was merely a watery shimmer of tie-dye. He wiped his eyes, but the tears would not abate. They fell like a veil, as though they needed to mercifully obliterate his sight, accompanied only by a soft sobbing that he felt would never end, because he could never unsee what he'd just seen, and he couldn't imagine how it would ever fade in his memory to the point where it might be forgotten, even for five seconds.

"Matt, what's wrong? What's happened?"

"God, no…" Then he wailed.

She looked at the computer, but the screen was dark. She reached for the button, but he grabbed her hand.

"*Don't!* Don't. Hayley, just… just don't. Leave it off."

"Did you crack Brett's folder? How?"

Spiller spoke through his weeping. "I had a program. It took about four minutes. Doesn't matter. Don't look at it."

"Jesus Christ, Matt. You're really scaring me. What did you see? Is it that bad?"

He put the heels of his palms to his eyes and rubbed furiously, like he was livid with them for allowing such images into his brain.

Hayley spoke more calmly. "Matt, I need to know. If it's that bad, I need to know. So, I'm gonna switch on the monitor and you're not gonna stop me. I've seen a lot in my time. It's okay. I'll be okay."

He shook his head and stood up. "It's not. And you won't be."

Spiller was already out of the office by the time it fully registered with her. There was a long, wheezing intake of breath, then she started to cry.

The sound of Hayley's distress faded as he left the building, and it disappeared entirely when he jumped fully clothed into the swimming pool, exhaled all his air, and descended prostrate to the bottom.

## FORTY

ON THE DOT of midnight, Bartoli arrived at Spiller's home. Spiller let him in and wandered back to the living room, leaving him to close the door. Bartoli followed and stopped in the doorway.

"Oh. Miss Woods. How you doing?"

Spiller and Sadie sat together on the sofa, thighs touching. Manny was in the armchair. Spiller took a full bottle of Michelob off the floor and swigged it straight down. Sadie was holding a tumbler of something clear, with ice. She ignored Bartoli's greeting, and took a large, clinking gulp. She tapped Spiller's empty bottle.

"You want another, Matt?"

"Definitely. Thanks."

She got up and headed out of the room, but Bartoli barred her exit.

"No more booze. Your boyfriend is coming with me. And if you don't know exactly why, I will happily fill you in."

Sadie's face was like stone. "I am getting Matt another beer, and if you don't shift your lard-ass out of my way, I will mistake you for the Taliban and stomp you into the floor. I'm pretty sure I have PTSD, so I can do that."

Bartoli thought better of it and stepped aside.

"Good choice," Sadie said, and went to the kitchen.

"One more beer, then we're leaving," Bartoli told Spiller.

"Not happening."

"I beg your pardon?" Bartoli placed his hand on his forty-five.

"You shouldn't touch your gun, Angelo. My girlfriend is extremely protective." Spiller pointed over Bartoli's shoulder.

Bartoli turned to find Sadie was levelling her Heckler and Koch at him from the kitchen doorway. "Really, Matthew?"

"Pop your gun out on the floor, mate. Nice and slow. We have things to discuss."

"You think you can pull a gun on me and get away with it? I'm a cop!"

"Gun. Floor. Now."

Bartoli obeyed.

"Sit down, Angelo."

Sadie came in with her HK and a Michelob and resumed her seat next to Spiller. She rested the gun on her thigh, with the muzzle pointing at Bartoli. Spiller thanked her and took a gulp of beer.

Bartoli looked around the room. "Where should I sit?"

Spiller nodded at Manny. "You can shift him. He won't mind."

Bartoli lifted the mannequin out of the chair and dumped him on the floor, then sat down. "What is that thing?"

"He's whatever I want him to be. In the movie, he was me. He's also been my agent."

It dawned on Bartoli. "Your mysterious pillion passenger." He looked at Sadie. "I'm guessing you think you know everything about this guy."

"Matt told me what I need to know. I know he took my ride, and everything that went down here last night. I know about his agent, and last Christmas."

"Well, that, young lady, would make you not just a fellow sociopath, but also an accessory to murder. So, what's the play here? You gonna shoot me, Matthew. Take me out to the desert?"

"No."

"You should. Because nothing's changed in the past twenty-four hours."

"The whole fucking *world* has changed in the past twenty-four hours, Angelo. You just don't know it yet."

Bartoli considered. "You're right. Things have changed. I got a gun pointing at me. So, I'm gonna double down on going after you and your dumbass girlfriend here. I will not rest. Both of you are going to jail for a very long time."

Spiller held Sadie's hand and stared into her eyes. He gave her a wink that said, *everything will be fine*. She returned a slight smile that said, *thanks, but you're wrong and you know it*. He kissed her.

Bartoli was frowning when they looked back at him.

"What is going on with you two? On the one hand, you're reacting like I can't get to you, and yet... you look like you're on the deck of the Titanic and you just realized all the lifeboats have launched."

Spiller gave his adversary a genuine smile. "What do you want from life, Angelo?"

"None of the crap that you got, that's for damn sure. I got enough to get by. A nice pension not far off. That'll do for me."

"I mean your legacy."

"I will be the man who brought down Matthew Spiller. Why are you laughing?"

Spiller adopted a straight face. "You think anyone will remember me in five years? I've done one movie and I'm unrecognizable in it. I have a TV series lined up, but that won't happen – and not because of you. Maybe, in years to come, the odd person will search YouTube for that clip of me on Mel Banaghan. Even if you did manage to send me to jail, so what? You think anyone's going to remember *your* name? You think you're getting your own Wikipedia page? You found notoriety last Christmas with my help. All those crimes you cleared up. You were on the news, in the papers. You think anyone still remembers your name now?"

Bartoli affected a bored expression. "If you're making a point, I ain't getting it. And I didn't become a cop to be famous."

"But wouldn't you like to leave a legacy? A real legacy, so your name goes into the history books? I mean, like... Mother Theresa, or Gandhi?"

Bartoli cackled. "Sure. Why the hell not? Sign me up. What do I have to do?" He shook his head as his amusement faded. "Jesus... did you just smoke some crack?"

*"What do you have to do?"* Spiller echoed. "You need to drop your vendetta against me. And Sadie. You need to leave Noah to his fate. In return, I will make you the most famous, most admired cop who ever lived."

Bartoli glanced at his gun on the floor.

Sadie shoved her HK forward along her thigh. "Or you could make a move, Detective, and then, yeah, your ass is getting buried in the desert."

Bartoli shrugged. "I'll listen. You're both certifiable kooks, but if it makes you happy, I'll listen."

Spiller stood up. "You don't need to listen, Angelo. You need to watch."

OVER THE NEXT six hours, Bartoli watched. Like any good detective, he took notes, copious notes, on a pad Spiller provided for him. Bartoli sat in the armchair, Spiller's laptop on his thighs, Spiller's headphones over his ears, keeping the sounds private, so the two people on the couch could take intermittent naps. Every so often, his eyes would drift to his forty-five on the floor, and he calculated he might even be able to reach it without waking them, but his eyes were too quickly drawn back to the computer screen. And he realized they felt safe sleeping because they knew his priorities had been remapped by the contents of the hard drive sitting on the arm of his chair, connected to the laptop by a cable.

Occasionally, one of them would wake, and they would exchange strangely empathetic looks, and Bartoli would become aware that his face was set in a rictus of revulsion. He would make a conscious effort to release the muscles behind it, only to have them tense up again the moment he focused back on the screen.

Eventually, at a little after six a.m., having dipped into a mere fraction of it, Bartoli closed the laptop and finally started to cry.

EVEN THOUGH SPILLER heard the tears, he kept his eyes shut, pretending to sleep. As catharsis went, it would be scant relief for Bartoli, but even the slightest vent of his release valve might save him from total insanity. It took five minutes for the tell-tale suppressed squeaks to give way to short sniffs and heavy sighs. When Spiller assessed that Bartoli had vaguely pulled himself together, he yawned and opened his eyes, and tapped Sadie to wake her.

"Still think I'm the bad guy?" Spiller asked.

"Comparatively? No. You think this is real?"

"You just spent six hours looking at it. What do you think?"

Bartoli nodded. Spiller stretched and got up. He indicated that Sadie could put her gun away, then retrieved Bartoli's and handed it back to him. Bartoli put it straight into his belt holster.

"Go on, then, Matthew. You're always the man with the plan. You got one now?"

"You want to get involved? Help us?"

"What choice do I have?"

"You see, that is exactly why I want you on board," Spiller said. "You don't think you have a choice. You do have a choice. But only a good person would think they don't."

"Don't suck up to me, please – I couldn't stand it. Who else knows about this?"

"Apart from the three of us, just Hayley Olsen."

Bartoli whistled. "Brett Stutz is in a lot of trouble. Does he know Hayley has it?"

"No. His newest ex, Katerina Petrova, stole his laptop, then gave it back to him. But she copied everything first."

Bartoli was visibly puzzled. "Why'd she do that? Steal his laptop."

"Because John Frears asked her to before he died."

"*Frears?* Why?"

"I'm guessing he must have heard something, seen something. Certain activities in this town are common knowledge, they're just never really talked about. Maybe it took a complete outsider to pay attention, for once. You lived in the UK, Angelo, so you'll know the name Jimmy Saville. Everyone in power knew what *he* was up to for decades."

"Probably because they were up to the same thing," Sadie said.

Bartoli's face dropped a little. "You think *Contreras* was involved?"

"No," Spiller said. "Wrong place, wrong time for her."

It clicked. "But that was why Stutz was on Mulholland that day. He was tailing Frears. Matthew, you *did* cook up that alibi for Stutz; that story about his mechanic."

"Who wants a coffee?" Spiller headed for the kitchen.

"You moron!" Bartoli said, following him. "What are you? Alibis R Us?"

Spiller kept his back to Bartoli as he set the coffee to percolate. Sadie joined them, circling her arms around Spiller's chest for comfort. He pecked her hands above his sternum.

Bartoli cursed. "Him being there that day confirms he was scared what Frears might have on him. Now, thanks to you, unless we flip the mechanic, we don't have that link."

"I didn't know about the hard drive at that point," Spiller said, turning round. "Anyway, it doesn't matter. His life is over. We have a chain of custody for the information. We have... what do the antique experts call it?"

"Provenance," Sadie said, checking the cupboards.

Spiller pointed to the correct door, and Sadie grabbed three cups and placed them out ready.

Bartoli's squinting eyes suggested he was working through the facts. "So, Katerina Petrova knows about it as well."

"No. She'd left before I cracked the password."

Bartoli laughed, ran his hands through his silver coif. "How in God's name do you know how to do that? In fact, forget about it. I don't wanna know."

"How d'you take your coffee, Detective?" Sadie asked.

"Actually, I'll skip the caffeine, I'm so tired. Matthew, do you have a bed I can borrow?"

"Sure. Upstairs, either room on the right."

"Okay, thanks. While I'm sleeping, can you go out and buy up every hard drive you can find? And order a ton of them online. We need to start backing this up, think about getting it out to some sleeper sources."

"How many?" Spiller asked.

"You're rich; hundreds. Apart from that, don't do anything 'til I wake up."

"Do we try to get Katerina onside?" Spiller asked.

Bartoli thought about it. "Better not. We can't risk anyone speaking out before we're ready to act. I'll talk to some people I know; see if I can get a team together to review everything. We can't do this on our own, there's too much to deal with."

"A team?" Spiller said.

"Some cops I knew in New York, back in the day. A couple in my department now who I trust."

"Like you trusted Contreras?"

Bartoli grimaced. "Guess you got a point. You know anyone we can trust?"

"Ethan King."

Bartoli laughed. "That guy hates your guts."

"Nope. Best buddies now. He'll be on board."

Bartoli scrutinized him, not without a touch of admiration. "How do you do it? Win people over?"

Spiller offered his beamiest grin, like he was in a toothpaste commercial.

"Don't leave the hard drive downstairs," Bartoli said. "Take it with you. Is that the only copy?"

"Hayley has one."

"And, Matthew?"

"What?"

"Having hated you for months for always being one step ahead of me…"

"More than one step, mate."

"Whatever."

Sadie gently elbowed Spiller to indicate this wasn't the time for gloating.

"*Now*, Matthew, with this… you better make sure any plan you have gets us a country mile ahead of what's just waiting to come down on our heads."

Spiller nodded. "Sleep well."

"I'm sure I won't."

## FORTY-ONE

BARTOLI WAS RIGHT. He didn't sleep well for the thirty minutes his head was on the pillow, when his exhausted mind dragged him into a ghastly dream, a greatest-hits compilation of the images he'd just witnessed.

When he did surface, it was in response to someone tapping his head with something hard.

"Okay... now, Noah, calm down, don't do anything stupid."

Noah had two guns; one of his own, which had tapped Bartoli awake, and Bartoli's holstered forty-five, which was attached to Noah's belt like a trophy. Bartoli hadn't heard anything up to that point; not Noah breaking in downstairs, nor his weapon being lifted off the bedside table.

"Got me a spare set of keys when I was here yesterday," Noah said. "Dumbass didn't even cotton on. My question to you, *Detective*, is what are you doin' here, lyin' on that son-bitch's spare bed?"

Bartoli slowly swung his legs off and sat up. "Just calm down, Noah. You don't understand what's going on. I haven't forgotten about you, but there are matters afoot that have taken precedence."

"You must think I'm dumb as a box of rocks. *Matters afoot?* You're sleepin' in his goddamn house. How'd you square that with tryin' to get me off the hook? I'm seriously meant to put my faith in you, Detective? You couldn't pour piss out of a boot with a hole in the toe and the directions on the heel."

Bartoli couldn't help but smile at the idiom.

"Laugh at me, I will have myself a conniption and you will surely die."

Bartoli wiped the smile from his face. "I'm not laughing at you, Noah. You need to give me some time. Spiller has you bang to rights. Nothing I can do about that right now. I can't discuss why I'm here. I know it looks weird. It *feels* weird, believe me, but I was too tired to drive. Listen, I can give you some money, so you can get away for a while."

"I *got* away, but there ain't no one gonna take me in now my face is everywhere. Spiller's got everyone thinkin' I tried to kill him, and I likely killed Harry Sullivan and Aiden Powers."

"Kid, I don't mean to rile you, but you did that to yourself by telling him that's what you did."

"Huh?"

"That video."

The recollection made Noah wobble like he was about to faint.

"That's gone into evidence, Noah. Same as your prints on the gun, and all around this house, *and* your threats to Spiller's daughter." Bartoli shook his head. "Poor Noah. You just had no clue the kind of man you were dealing with. You crossed a line. Any father would be protective, but Spiller is not just any father."

Noah slowly backed away and perched on a chair in the corner of the bedroom.

"Noah?"

"What?"

"If you're gonna shoot me, you better do so, because I'm getting up and I'm going downstairs to pour myself a coffee. I will be in the kitchen for ten minutes, and I suggest you leave during that time, same way you came in, but you do not take my gun with you. As things stand, I have nothing personal against you. Leave my gun, I won't say you were here. Take it, all bets are off. I will have no choice but to report it stolen."

Noah drummed his fingers. "Maybe I should just shoot you."

"Then there's no one left who believes in you."

"That gonna make a difference?"

"Honestly? I don't know." Bartoli stood up, half-expecting to get shot. "Leave my gun on the bed." He took out his wallet and emptied it, dropping five fifty-dollar bills on the bed. "It's not much, but it may help. Get yourself a haircut, Noah. Dye your hair. Give yourself a chance." Bartoli left the room and was about to take the first stair when he heard a noise, half-moan, half-growl, a mix of sorrow and frustration. It was the kind of sound he imagined might presage a gun being emptied. He halted, slowly turned around. Noah was slumped in his chair, a passable impression of Spiller's insane mannequin, like the life had been drained from him. His only movement was a slight pulsing that came from his now silent sobbing. His gun was pointing at the floor. Bartoli went back to him. "Noah, can I get my forty-five, please? I'd rather not have to explain all this. And you don't need another felony added to the list."

Noah unhooked the holster and handed it over. "Why am I in this situation? I ain't done nothin'. So, I got a bit above myself, broke his nose, said some stupid shit to his daughter."

Bartoli resisted the temptation to point out that those things amounted to more than nothing.

"I ain't goin' down without a fight, Detective. I mean that. You don't make some headway right quick, I'm gonna put Matt Spiller in the ground."

SPILLER AND SADIE could have covered more ground separately, sweeping up more hard drives from more stores, but they went together because it never occurred to them to be apart. All the while, Spiller was thinking, running through the options, trying to work out the best way to disseminate the information before it could get shut down.

Arriving at The Beverly Hills Hotel with a trunkful of electronics, Spiller had a eureka moment. He explained his idea to Sadie, who gave it the green light, but wondered if the essential players would be on board.

"I can't tell," Spiller said. "And we need to do some more checks before we even contemplate sharing this with anyone."

Sadie took his hand. "You're sure you wanna do this? Any of it?"

"I have to."

"You don't."

"This has to be done properly. If this gets buried, or passed off to someone else, it could fail. One loose cog, and the whole thing flies apart. There's too much at stake to put faith in someone I don't know."

"You put your faith in me."

He considered. "I did. And you didn't disappoint. But I lucked out, and I'm not rolling the dice again. Not on this. You can always back out, you know. I wouldn't blame you. There will be repercussions. I can't tell you how your life will go afterwards."

"*Our* life," Sadie said. "You and me, Matt."

Spiller kissed her. "You need to think hard. The life you have here… it won't carry on the same. Not if you're with me."

"I know."

"Okay. Then let's go and introduce you to the fam."

Spiller and Sadie were directed to the busy pool area, where Helen had earlier agreed to meet him. The girls were splashing about, and Helen was keeping a keen eye on them. David was the other side, talking to some guests, animatedly explaining his bandaged arm to them.

"Hey, Helen, this is Sadie, my girlfriend."

Helen stood up and smiled at her replacement. "Hello, Sadie."

"Hey, Helen. How are you enjoying LA?"

"Oh, you know… mortal threats, break-ins, shootings; much like life with this fellah back in England. Funny, you don't look crazy, so I'm assuming you either don't know too much about my ex, or you hide your insanity really well."

Spiller squirmed a little but left them to it. Despite her words, Helen was amicable enough, and Sadie was clearly taking it all in her stride, politely laughing at Helen's digs, like people overlooked barely disguised insults at dinner parties to avoid conflict.

"I guess it takes a strong woman to handle your husband," Sadie said.

Helen nodded. "It does, but this man can find anyone's breaking point, believe me."

"I realize that. Good job I have a high pain threshold. That's what tours of Iraq and Afghanistan do to a person."

Helen looked at Spiller. "This one's a keeper."

Spiller knew his ex well enough to know she was being genuine. "Yep, that's the plan."

Sadie grinned, looked back at Helen. "I hear you're a tough cookie yourself."

Helen smiled modestly.

"How's David?" Spiller asked, before he could be reprimanded for oversharing.

Helen indicated her lover across the pool, who was now peeling back the dressing to show his admirers. "The man who took a bullet for Matt Spiller? Oh, he's in his element."

Spiller diverted his attention to his daughters, who had just noticed his arrival. They both waved, and Sophie clambered out and rushed over to give him a wet hug.

Spiller growled playfully, regarding the dark patches on his jeans. "Ah, Soph! Now I look like I've peed myself."

She giggled, hugged him again, squirming against him to make it worse.

"Daddy, are you coming in?" She tried to drag him closer to the edge, as though he'd jump in fully clothed.

Spiller pulled her back and thought of the vast swathes of his body without hair, thanks to the removal of the duct tape. "Sorry, sweetie, I forgot my trunks."

Sophie noticed Sadie. "Who are you?"

"I'm a friend of your dad's."

Sophie smiled at her daddy's new friend, abandoned them in an instant, and took a running jump to re-join her sister.

"Thanks for covering all this, Matt," Helen said. "The hotel and everything."

"No worries. How long are you staying? Are you seeing the holiday out? After what happened to David?"

"Just look at him. He'll never buy another drink again. Yeah, we're staying. We've got another three weeks or so."

Spiller made a face. "Ah. Okay. So, it's probable your stay might overlap with some stuff that's about to happen."

"Like what?"

"I can't talk about it."

Helen addressed Sadie. "You know about this?"

"I do. You might wanna bring forward your return flights."

Helen sighed. "Not happening. Matt, you want to stop paying for this place, that's fine. But we're not going home because you've cocked up – *yet again*."

"He didn't," Sadie said. "But things may get a little kinetic."

"Sadie, it was nice meeting you, but I don't take orders from you. Or my husband. Never did."

"That's cool. Nice meeting you, too, Helen. Matt, I'll be in the car."

Spiller waited for Sadie to get out of earshot. "Helen, you don't need to be rude."

"No? David just got shot in your house. A bullet meant for you. I don't need strangers telling me I need to leave town. What the fuck is going on?"

Spiller shook his head. "I'll tell you when I think you should leave. But I realize I can't make you, so that would be your call."

"Are the girls in any danger?"

Spiller thought they might be, but he didn't need the vitriol that an affirmative answer would provoke. "No."

"Okay. Well, if you're not going to take a swim with your daughters, you should probably leave, because I don't really want to talk to you anymore."

Spiller acquiesced with a nod.

"And, Matt? You can settle up at reception. I'm not sure I'm comfortable being in your debt. Give the girls whatever you want, but I don't want another penny from you."

"You're not in my debt, Helen. You owe me nothing."

She stared at him. "Then I don't need your charity."

## FORTY-TWO

THE FOLLOWING WEEK was hectic. Unfortunately for Spiller's makeshift team, it wasn't a blur. While much of what they viewed was analogous, none of it was forgettable. They worked from Hayley's house, where she had increased the security personnel, and their firepower. Bartoli had taken time off work, as had Ethan King, who had been assured by Bartoli that an unprecedented promotion awaited him on the other side of all this. As the days wore on, though, Ethan began to express doubts that he even wanted to carry on in law enforcement. There was a limit to how much pain even the hardiest of cops could witness during their career, but this was an insult that wasn't diluted over thirty years. Given the involvement of John Frears in leading them to the information, Hayley had given Virginia the option of coming on board, without fully spelling out the issue, in case she declined. Once the subject had been revealed, even Virginia expressed regret at having been included.

Spiller, Sadie, Hayley, Virginia, Bartoli, and King. While a set of computers worked away night and day, copying onto hard drives, they scoured their allotted sets of data, taking notes as best they could, like a rookie legal team in a movie about the "little man" against the evil corporation. Spiller wondered whether this was his penance for past crimes; whether he was making amends and clearing the slate. Whether, in a scenario he didn't believe in, he might arrive at the pearly gates in due course, and all would be forgiven.

And all the while he was waiting for one of the headphoned individuals in Hayley's cramped office to alert him to the fact that his plan wouldn't work; that the person he'd earmarked to help them was mortally compromised.

Every so often, he would surreptitiously look up from his monitor at the others, so crucially involved in their jobs, their faces suffused in a kind of low-grade agony. Occasionally, their eyes would meet, and their expressions would mutually telegraph their sadness, before reconnecting with the task at hand.

With a son to look after, Virginia came and went throughout the week. The rest of them stayed put, sleeping over most nights in a couple of the spare rooms. None of the parties involved in *Veteran Avenue* spoke of it. It had been thoroughly relegated, and Spiller had doubts it would ever regain its prior standing in their thoughts. It was now difficult to worry about such matters, and Spiller found himself remarkably, and quite wonderfully, unperturbed about his career. His life had boiled down to that place, The House of Sempiternal Love, and he mused whether that fact held a deeper significance he'd be forced to contemplate once his sojourn there was over.

As for Sadie, he couldn't imagine being without her. Perhaps her presence in his life had burgeoned to replace the shriveling of his vacuous ambition.

With Brett Stutz in the dark about his pilfered files, they might have taken their time to perform a complete review. Weeks, months, as long as it took. What made the matter time-sensitive was Kat. She had left under a cloud, and no one knew if she'd managed to rediscover the sunshine in her life, or if it was now teeming down. If it was, would she seek shelter under a familiar roof? Hayley had seen plenty of her clients rush back to the very people who'd caused them to seek her help in the first place. Was it possible Kat might panic in her newfound isolation, return to Stutz, and confess her duplicity, just to get back in the fold?

At the end of the week, Spiller shared his plan. Either everyone was too exhausted to argue with it, or it was too brilliant to foster dissent, because it received a round of quiet nods and shrugs, and he was told to make the required call.

While Ethan went back to his family, and Virginia returned to her son, the rest of them set off for Burbank.

MEL BANAGHAN WELCOMED his visitors with a wary smile. His office at the studios had a deliberately distressed look; exposed brick and timbers in a building that wasn't built from such materials. An orange neon sign hung behind his desk, which was a slab of oak on steel legs. The sign replicated the logo of his TV show, and shelves either side displayed a bunch of oddly shaped awards.

Mel smiled at Hayley as they shook hands. "I recognize you, Miss Olsen. Not seen you in a while. You working on anything?"

"Nope. Still happily retired."

"And you are?"

"Sadie Woods."

"Are you an actress?"

"No."

Mel frowned. "I've seen you before, though, right?"

"I was Matt's driver that night he was on your show."

"Ah."

"Now we're together," Spiller said. "And Sadie's not just a driver. She's ex-military."

Mel reached to shake her hand again. "Thank you for your service, Miss Woods."

"You're welcome."

"Matt, are you okay? I hear someone took a pot-shot at you?"

"I'm fine."

Mel turned to the other visitor. "Now, you *gotta* be an actor. Were you in *The Sopranos? The Wire?*"

"I was in *Goodfellas.*"

Mel snapped his fingers. "I knew I knew your face."

"I'm kidding. Lieutenant Angelo Bartoli, LAPD Homicide."

Mel took a step back. "Homicide?" He looked at Spiller. "Matt, I know you're not right in the head, and it's your most endearing quality, but… this is getting a little freaky, even for you."

"You're not going to be sorry we're here, Mel."

"You might be," Hayley said. "You probably will be. But you need to hear us out."

"Okay," Mel said. "Everyone grab a seat."

Spiller and Hayley took the desk chairs, while Bartoli and Sadie sank into a cracked and faded leather couch that probably hadn't seen better days. Spiller opened a laptop, got it ready, and presented it to Mel, along with a set of wireless earbuds.

"What?" Mel asked. "What's this?"

"Watch," Spiller said.

Mel inserted the earbuds. Spiller played the video file, and Mel immediately recoiled in his chair, swiping the buds from his ears like they were alien bugs about to burrow deep into his brain.

"What the fuck is this? Jesus… that's… holy fuck, that's—"

"We know," Spiller said. "The whole world knows who that is."

Mel looked at the screen and grimaced, then slammed the lid shut. "Why d'you bring this shit to me? Do I look like a news anchor from *Russia Today?*"

Spiller leaned forward and opened the laptop again. "You need to watch. It's about ten minutes, a compilation we crudely put together. But there's hundreds of hours. And files galore. It's the whole nine yards, as you Yanks like to say."

"It's the whole nine *thousand* yards," Bartoli said.

Mel looked at him, puzzled. "You're a cop. Do something about it."

Bartoli stayed calm. "Watch the rest. Then if you still don't know the problem, I'll explain it to you."

Mel collected the earbuds from his desk and stuck them back in, then began watching with a horror-struck expression. Eventually, he gently closed the laptop and plucked out the earbuds. He put his hands to his face, bowed his head. He stayed like that for two minutes and no one disturbed him. Then his head snapped up, and his face was full of resentment.

"What? You want me to play this on my fucking show? Is that the idea? My show, which is *meant* to make people laugh."

Hayley smiled. "Yes. Exactly that. You think CNN is gonna show this? We need to sneak this out. It needs to be in the public domain before anyone even knows what's happening. Otherwise, it'll get buried. We don't know who's compromised."

"Detective," Mel said to Bartoli. "Come on, you're saying you can't take this up the chain?"

"I can. And maybe something comes of it. Or maybe I never hear back. Then I'm put out to pasture. I'm close, as it is. Or I get killed. Hayley's right: we need to hit hard and fast, then run like hell."

"*Run like hell?* Detective, this is my *life*. Where the hell do I run to? You think the network's gonna back me on this if I just spring it on them?"

"They'll have to," Spiller said. "They fire you, they become complicit. They'll have no choice but to stand by you."

Mel yelped a laugh. "There's *no one* gonna stand anywhere near me if I run this. They'll be too scared of catching a fucking bullet meant for me. This isn't just career-ending; this could be *life*-ending!"

Sadie stood up. "So, you're just gonna pussy-out, are you, Mel? You're going AWOL just as your country needs you? That's not gonna happen. Maybe you can *pretend* you never saw any of that, but you really think you can *forget*? You don't step up when you're supposed to, it destroys you. Whatever you decide, you're not living normal again after today – not with what you know – so you best make sure it was worth it."

Mel directed his venom at Spiller, but it was clearly a final rant borne from the frustration of having been so successfully manipulated. "Fuck you for thinking of me, Matt! Seriously. Fuck. You. I thought you put on a shitshow the last time you were here. That was nothing compared to this."

"You're in, then?" Spiller asked, smirking.

"How soon d'you want this to happen?"

"Your next show."

"*What?* I got guests lined up!"

"Cancel them."

Mel nodded. "Yeah, I should. I should cancel the lot of them; everyone I got lined up for the rest of the year. Because my show is fucking toast if I do this."

"Maybe," Spiller said, and pointed at the shelves. "Or maybe you get to sweep all of those poxy little awards into the trash and replace them with a Pulitzer. Then see what doors open up for you."

Mel pondered. "Okay. But I need to do some checks. You need to leave this with me."

Spiller handed him a hard drive. "It's all on there. And our notes and observations. Six of us have been scouring it night and day for a week."

"You're absolutely sure it's genuine?" Mel asked.

Spiller nodded. "If you know someone who can verify this kind of thing, use them, but you need to make damn sure you can trust them, and you only involve essential people on your team; people you can't do this without."

"This doesn't need to be perfect," Bartoli said. "It just needs to be powerful. It needs to set the ball rolling so it's unstoppable, so there's no shutting it down."

"No pressure, then, right?"

"And we need to get your viewing figures up," Spiller said.

"Really? I'm the most-watched talk show on TV."

"And this week you need to be the most talked-about. The network needs to go all-out promoting you."

"How do I convince them to do that?"

Spiller grinned. "You tell them that next week, you'll have me back on the show, and I'm going to be in a new TV series about John Frears, written by Hayley here, who will be on the show with John's widow, Virginia. You tell them you've got Theo Montgomery, who's not done a talk show in twenty years, and you've got the lead cop investigating the murder of John Frears, the recent attack on my life, *and* who's cracked the murder of Harry Sullivan and Aiden Powers."

*"What?"* Bartoli stood up. "That's bullshit. Unless you're gonna fess up, Matthew. Are you?"

Spiller laughed it off. "Mel, just get your network stoked, so they spend all this week shouting about your next show."

Bartoli still hated the idea. "If my bosses think I know who killed people and I'm using a talk show as a press conference, my ass is getting fired."

"Doesn't matter," Spiller said. "Means to an end. This time next month, you'll be chief of police."

Bartoli stared daggers. "I so wish you'd stayed in fucking England."

"Me, too," Mel said.

MEL INSISTED THAT Spiller wait around after the others departed. He grabbed a bottle of vodka from a mini-fridge and poured out two glasses.

"Cheers, dude. Here's to the end of my career. Thanks a bunch."

Spiller left his drink untouched. "Remember the last time I was on your show? Tell me I didn't pull in more viewers than ever before."

"More viewers is great. But you can't have viewers without a show."

"How long have you been doing your show?" Spiller asked.

"Six years. A little over."

"You miss stand-up? Saying what the hell you want, when you want? Writing your own script without anyone vetting you, so you don't offend the perma-offended wokerati?"

"Sure. But this pays better."

"Then you sold out. Literally. You sold out."

Mel downed his drink and poured another. He shrugged. "Guess so."

"You can't want to be part of the status quo after this. You had Brett on your show. You're telling me you don't want to get out in front of this? I sure as hell do. Everyone associated with him is going to be under the spotlight. That includes you, if you don't do this."

"I said I'd do it, Matt. I just wish…" He shook his head, lost for words.

"It wasn't true? Or that we didn't find the evidence? They're very different."

Mel slouched in his chair and drank some vodka. "Aren't you scared, Matt?"

Spiller thought about it. "Not really."

"Then you're even crazier than I thought. I can't even imagine how I'm gonna say the words on live TV; forget dealing with the aftermath."

"We'll work on that, Mel. Don't worry. We'll script it out. You won't have to say much, anyway. It'll speak for itself. You're just the messenger."

Mel laughed heartily. "Well, that's reassuring. You know what traditionally happens to the messenger, right?"

## FORTY-THREE

THE MOTION-ACTIVATED, solar-powered wildlife camera that Noah had secretly installed on a tree opposite Spiller's house hadn't been triggered by the thing he was hunting. It had notified him of the postman's arrival, the garbage truck, the odd stray animal, but not the homeowner himself. He'd installed it after talking to Bartoli two weeks ago. He'd purchased the device, then snuck back into Spiller's empty house, located his wi-fi password, and connected it. His cell had chirped multiple times since then, and each time had proven a dud. During the first week, he'd wondered whether Spiller had simply left town, then he'd seen the unprecedented fanfare about the forthcoming *Mel Banaghan Show*, and the crazy furor about Spiller's reappearance, like he was the second coming. It had lasted this entire week and was building to a crescendo as tonight's show drew closer by the hour. It was everywhere. On TV, across every social media channel, and sparkling down from every digital billboard across the city.

Detective Bartoli had been similarly absent for two weeks, and Noah was now getting desperate. He'd been living in a cheap motel in Hollywood that accepted cash and asked no questions, but his funds were running low. He'd burned through his own money, and the donation from Bartoli, and had pawned as much as he could easily steal from Spiller's house. He'd shaved off his hair, and had taken to wearing dark glasses everywhere he went. So far, it had worked, and the false plates on his truck were amazingly still fooling the cops, who would cruise past without a second glance.

But even if he'd had unlimited resources, his current existence wouldn't have been viable because it just wasn't any fun. He couldn't talk to people, go to the beach, try for an agent, attend auditions, or do any of the happy stuff he'd come to this city for.

Matt Spiller was the only person who could restore his old life, and tonight was the first time in two weeks he knew for certain where the scheming fuck would be.

FOLLOWING HIS WEEK of research at Hayley's house, Spiller had gone to stay with Sadie. His own home held little allure these days, tied as it was to his withered notion of how his life in LA would turn out. It was the starter home of an imposter, and after tonight, an outcast, lauded publicly, but quietly detested by the powerbrokers for the disrepute and doubt he'd inflicted. Ultimately, he imagined he would have to sell up.

It was also the place where Noah would look first, and Spiller had no doubt that he hadn't seen the last of the resentful Texan.

For now, he was just trying to calm down. There was far more at stake than last time, and he wouldn't have the false bravado of cocaine to dull his terror. As dusk drew in and the hours ticked down to midnight, he sat on Sadie's couch, holding her hand. The TV was on, but it was nothing more than background noise, a reason not to engage in the same conversation they'd had a hundred times that week. Were they doing the right thing? Always the answer was yes, and always the question resurfaced.

Suddenly, a new thought occurred, and Spiller was shocked by its absence until that moment. "Theo is going to be really put out."

Sadie nodded. "I was just thinking the same."

"He's going to be the only one on that stage who hasn't a clue what's coming."

"Can we stop him going on?"

"I don't know how, without raising a ruckus. He'll think he's being sidelined."

"Did we really need him?" Sadie asked.

"He's an extra reason to tune in. Maybe he'll attract the older crowd who'd never normally watch Mel. People who just want to know what happened to him."

"He's gonna hate us. *Veteran Avenue* was meant to be his swan song."

"It may still happen," Spiller said hopefully.

Sadie squeezed his hand, and he knew she didn't believe it, either.

"Sure you don't want me to come on with you?" she asked.

He smiled. "You don't need your beautiful face tainted by this. You'll be waiting for me, and that's all that matters."

"Shame we gotta go pick him up. That's gonna be awkward."

"Yeah, well, he did buy you a car."

THEY REACHED BURBANK at eleven-fifteen. Spiller rode up front with Sadie to avoid any backseat conversation with Theo, but the old actor seemed content with the silence, basking in the prospect of his late-life resurrection.

Bartoli was already waiting for them in the greenroom, fending off a studio assistant who was trying unsuccessfully to coax him into the makeup department.

"I'm a cop, okay? I look to you like the kinda guy who puts on powder? Ah! There you go! You can cake that asshole in makeup all day long; it's what he lives for."

"Hi, Angelo," Spiller said, entering the room. "Everything okay?"

"No. Lady, no offense, but will you please leave me alone?"

"Sir, you're gonna shine under the lights."

"Then hand out sunglasses."

The assistant gave up, and immediately swooped on a more pliable Theo, guiding him out of the room. "So wonderful to have you with us this evening, Mr Montgomery…"

Spiller sat next to Bartoli and lowered his voice. "Angelo… *tranquilo*, okay?"

"You know the week I've had? Dodging my superiors? I had to tell them I canceled tonight. They don't even know I'm here."

"Bigger picture, Angelo."

Spiller patted Bartoli's knee and stood up, just in time to give Hayley and Virginia obligatory Hollywood hugs as they arrived. With various members of Mel's team bobbing in and out, the façade had to be maintained. The women greeted Sadie, nodded at Bartoli, and sat next to each other on a two-person couch. Spiller squatted down in front of them, while Sadie perched on a hard chair by the door. He looked at her and raised his eyebrows, then subtly tapped his ribs. Sadie glanced down and zipped up her jacket to fully conceal her gun.

"How are you both?" Spiller asked the women.

"Terrible," Virginia said. "I won't be coming on stage. I'm only here for Hayley."

"Oh. No worries. You're okay, Hayley?"

Hayley leaned back, turned her face to the ceiling, and closed her eyes.

"Right." Spiller stood up, feeling like the host of a dinner party where everybody hated everybody. He went over to Sadie, laid a hand on her shoulder, and she gently inclined her cheek to touch it. "Thanks," he said to her.

AT ELEVEN-THIRTY, Mel Banaghan made an appearance, accompanied by a showrunner in a headset. Spiller could see the angst in Mel's eyes, despite the showbiz grin, and he felt sorry for the man. He was about to preside over the end of his career as he knew it. The end of a lot of other shit besides.

"Hey, everyone, welcome. Great to see you all here. Thanks for coming. We all set?"

Theo clapped his hands like a kid. "Really looking forward to it, Mel."

"Excellent. Matt, a word." He left the greenroom, leaving Spiller to follow, but it was the runner who was first out of the door, like a dog called to heel.

In the corridor, Mel and Spiller stared at him.

"You ever heard the expression *three's a crowd?*" Mel asked.

"Are you feeling all right, Mr Banaghan? You look so pale. You need a little more color on those cheeks? Want me to call makeup?"

"No. I want you to go away."

"Oh, my God, why is everyone so tense tonight? No banter, no warm-up comedian. And I have *never* seen a greenroom like that. It's like a freaking wake in there. I mean, did someone die?"

"Virginia's husband," Spiller said. "And they just found his killer, so... do us a favor and bugger off before I find a pair of scissors and start tailoring your outfit for you."

"Oh, *wow*," the runner said, as he flounced away.

"What's up, Mel?"

"*What's up?* I'm fucking terrified. What if we're wrong about this?"

"Mel, you've had people on this all week. They must think it's legit or you'd have called it off by now. Listen, if you don't break this, someone else will, and then... *no Pulitzer for you!*"

Mel smiled miserably at Spiller's impression of The Soup Nazi. "It's just..."

"I know, Mel. I get it."

Mel sucked in a big breath, then blew it out like it was rancid. "Okay, then. See you out there."

WITH A QUARTER hour to go, the showrunner appeared in the doorway of the greenroom, looking flustered.

"Sorry, folks, orders from on high. In a break from tradition, Mel wants you all on for the start of the show. I have no clue why. We're bringing on more seating now. If you'll all follow me."

Spiller, Hayley, Theo, and Bartoli got up.

The runner looked at Virginia. "Virginia, right? We need you."

"I'm not coming on."

"Oh, my God, what is happening? Are you all right? Are you ill?"

"You don't need me," Virginia said.

"But you're part of the show!"

"Oi!" Spiller called to him. "Leave her alone."

"Fine! I can't believe I left *The Late Show* for this crap. Quick now, everyone!"

The four guests filed down the corridor and out onto the darkened stage, where they took their seats as the audience began to applaud. Spiller sat closest to Mel's desk, then Hayley, Theo, and Bartoli. Spiller peered into the crowd, checking to see if any fool had managed to smuggle in some children.

"Shit!" he said, fixing on a group of four in the front row. He dashed from his seat to confront them.

"Hi, Dad," Sophie said.

"Helen, what are you doing here?"

"The girls wanted to come. It's been advertised all week, Matt; what did you expect? You didn't invite us, so I told them who I was, and we got front-row seats."

"Dad, what's wrong?" Sammy asked.

Spiller grabbed Helen's arm. "Come with me." He yanked her from her seat and took her off-stage into the wings. "Helen, I didn't invite you for a reason. You need to get the girls out of here *right now*."

"Come on, Matt, it can't be any worse than the last time you were on." She laughed.

He shook her wrist. "Tonight is going to be a whole other level of worse. You need to get the girls out of here. I swear I'll never ask you to trust me again on anything. *Please*."

Helen finally lost her amusement. "What's happening, Matt?"

Someone shouted: "Five minutes! Five minutes!"

He flared his eyes at her, clawed his fingers into her forearm.

"Okay!" she relented.

"Go and get them."

Helen disappeared, returning with David and the girls. Spiller noted the runner staring at him, but beyond caring. Spiller hurried them down the corridor and into the greenroom. He disconnected the TV monitor from the wall. He didn't even acknowledge Sadie or Virginia.

"Stay put," he told Helen, and eyed the girls for good measure. "Wait for me here. Soph, if you've got headphones, start listening to something."

Sophie looked at her mum, who nodded reassuringly, and Spiller ran back to the stage.

Mel leaned over to him. "What was that about?"

"Two minutes!"

Spiller shook his head to ward off the question, and Mel sat up straight in his chair and started practicing his best show-opening smile.

OUTSIDE THE STUDIO, beyond the perimeter of the parking lot, a Ford F150 with false plates pulled into the curb.

## FORTY-FOUR

THE LIGHTS CAME up. Mel opened his arms in a welcoming gesture and grinned like a buffoon. Spiller eyed his host and tried to emulate his fake joy. On the other side of him, Hayley was stoney-faced, Theo was beaming, and Bartoli was even more stoney-faced. It didn't matter. The audience could go ahead and be confused as hell for a minute or two. Shortly, the enigma of the strange guest expressions would pale into insignificance.

Mel waited for the applause and the whooping and whistling to subside. "Okay... okay... thank you. You're a very special audience. I mean that. You're special in ways you don't yet know, but... you will. I'm afraid you will. Because, tonight, you will bear witness to a world exclusive that will go down in history."

The audience hollered and clapped, but the sound faded quicker than normal as the majority noticed an expression they'd never before seen on Mel Banaghan's face.

Mel stopped peering into the camera and addressed his audience. He raised a finger and briefly pointed at the teleprompter that had stopped scrolling across the lens.

"I don't need that. I'm getting looks from some of my team, and I apologize to them. I'm going off-script. Rather, I'm sticking to the script, just not the one they expected."

The audience was deathly quiet.

"I'm gonna talk directly to the people in this studio because you represent the great American public. I can see your faces. I feel you. Tonight, I need to feel that human connection as I share something with you all, here and watching at home. But before I do, I need you all to do me a favor. Everyone in this audience, please take out your cellphones and start recording. I know there are signs telling you not to, but I want you to. And everyone at home, please set your DVRs or your hard drives or whatever to record. If you can't do that, please use your cellphones. Please do that now." He waited a few seconds.

"Thank you. The other thing I want you to do is, for God's sake, send your kids out of the room. That's even more important than my request that you record this show. And please don't think, *oh, it's okay, it's just Mel being a bit blue, swearing and cursing, my kids have seen this a hundred times already*. No. They haven't. And neither have you. Send them out now. If you don't, don't blame me later on." He paused again for a few seconds. "Thank you. Everyone, eyes on the wall behind me. And roll it."

A collective gasp from the audience was followed by shrieks and screams. Several people got up and ran out, gagging and retching.

Spiller heard their distress, felt their revulsion and confusion, and wept like he'd never seen any of it before.

FIVE MINUTES LATER, the compilation ended, and the audience sat in stunned silence. Their horror was too profound for tears. They had been temporarily rendered mute and immobile, and Spiller felt like he was looking out at a wall of mannequins. Slowly, he noticed people start to hold hands, hug their neighbors close.

Mel put his finger to his earpiece. "Are we still live? Okay, amazingly, we're still live. Folks, I don't know if I should apologize for this, and... if we suddenly go off the air, you'll understand why, although... all you evil cunts out there who are involved and who have the power to pull the plug on us... what's the point now? You've been outed. We've seen your faces, we've seen what you do to kids, to unwilling individuals, we've seen your satanic rituals, your perversions in all their hideous glory. We know who you are. And yes, I know about deep fakes, but we've had the country's top expert on this all week, and he swear in court that what you've just seen is genuine. No manipulation, no fakery. And bear in mind that what you've just seen is the tiny tip of a huge iceberg. You've seen five minutes out of hundreds of hours. You've seen less than one percent of the thousand faces in the more-than one terabyte of files that we possess, that were sent earlier today to several hundred addresses around the country and the world. And please go to the web address presently scrolling across the bottom of the screen, where everything has been uploaded, and you can download it all to ensure its longevity – assuming it's not hit with a denial-of-service attack in the next few minutes. But I say again to all those fucking monsters involved: it's too late. We know who you are. And it's not just videos, and it's not just recent. We have the receipts, in all forms, evidence going back to the nineteen seventies. Documents, photographs, bank statements, flightlogs. The whole kit and caboodle. And I'm sorry if this upends your belief systems, everything you've ever trusted and believed to be true. I wish none of this were true. Because governments will fall. *Our* government will definitely fucking fall. Industries will fall. Academia will fall. Religions will fall. This town we live in… that will fall. But it's better we know who these people are, because they're the ones who control our lives, and yet they are the incarnation of pure evil." Mel touched his earpiece again. "Are we still live? Amazing, we're still live. Jesus, doesn't anyone important watch this show?"

Spiller reached a hand across Mel's desk, and Mel grasped it tightly. Spiller expected the relief would imminently flood through his host to paralyze him, but he had more to say.

"If anyone's wondering why the hell I even bothered bringing guests on tonight, it's because we owe huge thanks to some of these people for revealing these horrendous, world-shattering truths. Never forget that there are good people in this world. Matt Spiller, Hayley Olsen, and Lieutenant Angelo Bartoli of the LAPD. Guys, I salute you. Most of all, though, we owe a massive debt of gratitude to the late John Frears, whose quest for the truth first sparked this whole endeavor. Finally, Matt, would you like to tell the world where this information was lurking all this time?"

"Sure. On a laptop owned by Brett Stutz."

"Brett Stutz, people. *The* Brett Stutz. Now, I should say, thus far there's no evidence in the files that Stutz himself was involved, *but…* he kept all this quiet when he could have blown the whistle, so you need to make up your own minds about him."

Belatedly, Spiller glanced at poor Theo, whose unwitting involvement seemed to have ushered in a state of suspended animation. Slowly, he became aware of Spiller's scrutiny, and he shook himself and stood up.

"I feel sick," he announced, and staggered off the stage.

"Well," Mel said. "I guess we have another forty-five minutes to fill. Anyone know any good jokes?" He addressed the camera again. "Okay, you fine people at home, I think we'll go to a commercial break now, and, uh... you might as well change the channel, because I will not be here when you get back. This is Mel Banaghan signing off for the last time. Thanks for watching. Stay safe."

THEO WANDERED IN a daze down the empty corridor, passing photographs of Mel Banaghan and his guests over the years. It seemed his face wasn't destined to join them. He'd been deceived and used, forced to watch a vile exposé in front of millions of people, and he was the only one to not receive a positive credit at the end.

A few feet ahead, the door to the ladies' restroom opened and out stepped Spiller's eldest, who held the door open for Spiller's youngest. Theo wasn't a hundred percent certain he'd nailed the relational dynamics, but he'd watched in puzzlement just before the show as Spiller had leaped from his seat to berate the mother of said kids, and he recalled Spiller telling him that he did have family back in England.

"Hey, there," he said to the older female. "Are you Matt's daughter?"

She nodded and smiled at the famous face. "Mr Montgomery, hello. That's right, I'm Sammy and this is—"

Theo's fist cut short the introductions. The girl called Sammy fell like a cut tree and didn't stir once she hit the floor. The small girl's eyes went wide, and her mouth opened, but Theo slapped her cheek and muffled her face with his leathery palm. As he started pulling her toward the exit to the parking lot, he yanked his old .357 from under his smart jacket.

OUTSIDE ON THE street beyond the perimeter fence, Noah was snoozing in his truck, equidistant between streetlamps. No one would be leaving until after the show ended at one a.m., and the stress of being a fugitive was a constant drain on his nervous energy, leaving him forever ready to fall asleep.

He tumbled out onto the road as his door was yanked open and his back-support vanished. His head hit the ground and his vision burst with stars for a moment, before he managed to focus on a strangely familiar black fellah standing over him. One hand was twisted into the abundant hair of a petrified little girl, and the other held a silver Magnum, which he pointed down at him.

"Go!" the black fellah said to him.

Noah could feel his own weapon digging into his spine, where it had popped out from his waistband, and he was loath to leave it lying on the concrete, so he just held his arms aloft.

Thankfully, the black fellah just stepped over him, hoisting the sniveling kid into the cab of the Ford, and shoving her roughly across the seat, before climbing in himself. Noah watched helplessly as his beloved truck was stolen for the second time in less than a month, and as the tailgate shrank into the darkness up the road, he finally put a name to the snarling old face.

Anticipating the imminent arrival of the cops, Noah got to his feet and ran.

THE STUDIO LIGHTS above the stage dimmed, and Spiller surveyed the audience. Some were still sitting in silence, lost in their new thoughts and their new reality; some were hugging each other; and some were filtering out, moving at half speed, as people did when they walked behind a coffin. Very few were talking. And no one was looking at Matt Spiller.

He had been forgotten. He imagined, in the unlikely event that *Man on a Murder Cycle* was released, that no one would care. Once word about this evening spread from millions to billions, it would be a long while before anyone started caring about such trivialities again, and despite his two decades pursuing fame and fortune, Spiller felt that was a step in the right direction for humankind. The world had changed tonight, and not before time.

Sadie's countenance when she rushed onstage put him in an instant, nauseating panic. She squatted down in front of him and took his hands, and he realized that this was his new girlfriend in full military mode.

"Sadie?" His voice was quivering.

She spoke calmly but quickly. "Matt, Sophie's been taken."

"What?" He gave an incongruous smile. Had she mistaken him for Liam Neeson? "What are you talking about?"

"Theo attacked Sammy and snatched Sophie. They've gone."

Spiller's mind went into overload. So much to unpack. He gawked at her. "*Sammy?* Theo took... *What?*"

"Bartoli called it in already. Sammy's got a busted face, but she'll be okay."

Spiller shot to his feet and bolted off stage toward the greenroom, leaving Sadie to follow.

The greenroom was packed and bustling. Everyone was in there, including Mel and several of his assistants. Spiller went straight to Sammy, who was still dazed, holding her head back with a napkin to a leaking nose, and showing a grimace that revealed a missing tooth.

"Sammy, what the fuck happened? Are you okay?"

Helen rounded on him. "Does she *look* okay? And Sophie's *gone!*"

"Dad..." Sammy said, but Helen wasn't finished.

"This is all your fault! You said they'd be safe! You fucking promised me!"

Spiller didn't know how to respond. He was grateful for the appearance of a couple of the studio's security guards in the doorway, but not for the message they relayed.

"No sign. Inside or outside. We're checking CCTV now."

"Dad..." Sammy said again.

"I *hate* you!" Helen told him.

Spiller found a response. "I didn't invite you, I told you to leave, and *I* wasn't looking after them. That was your job, and *his*." Spiller pointed at David.

*"Dad!"* Sammy pushed all the helping hands away from her and stood up, wobbling for a moment. She let the napkin drop to the floor

and spoke in a voice distorted by the damage Theo had inflicted. "I know where she is. I can track her."

Helen pointed at Sophie's phone on the arm of the couch. *"How?"*

Sammy ignored her mum. "I told you, Dad. After everything that happened last Christmas, I said I was looking out for her. That pendant I gave her. It's a tracking device." She pulled up an app on her phone and showed it to her dad.

"You genius," he said, took her phone and kissed her forehead. "Sadie!"

Sadie was standing right behind him. "Let's go."

"I'm coming," Helen said.

"You're not. Stay with Sammy."

"Give me the cell," Bartoli said. "I'll handle it."

"Not a chance," Spiller said.

"Where are they?"

Spiller checked the pulsing red spot on the map. "On-ramp onto Ventura, heading west."

"What's he driving?" Bartoli asked.

Sadie answered: "We brought him here, my vehicle's still outside, so... God knows. Matt. On me."

Bartoli blocked Spiller's path. "Bring him in alive."

"Sure, let's get the fucking pedo some therapy." Spiller shoved Bartoli aside and followed Sadie out into the corridor and into the parking lot.

Sadie remotely lifted the Caddy's tailgate, opened a compartment, and pulled a Heckler & Koch MR762A1 long gun out from among a bunch of other weapons and military gadgets, then handed her pistol to Spiller.

"Hang on," he said, having spotted Bartoli's Honda. He ran over to it and fired once through the side window, shattering it completely, then leaned in and grabbed the lightbox from the dashboard, unplugging it from the 12v socket.

They climbed into the Escalade, and Sadie powered the big SUV across the lot.

"So much for your auras," Spiller said to her, more harshly than he'd intended, as she screeched the vehicle onto the street and planted her foot down hard.

"I know," she said. "Sorry. I had him pegged as the kindest old man I ever met."

"We must have missed him – amongst all that data."

"Maybe he's not in there. But he obviously thought he was."

Spiller placed the lightbox on the dashboard, connected it, and set it going. "I have to get her back," he said needlessly. "This can't end badly."

"It won't. As long as he's moving, Sophie's safe."

"And if he stops?"

"We'd better make damn sure we're close. Buckle up."

## FORTY-FIVE

OUT OF INTEREST, Brett Stutz had tuned into *The Mel Banaghan Show* from his penthouse office in Century City. He'd been working late, scouring manuscripts looking for future projects. The fuss about the show over the preceding week would have piqued anyone's interest, but Stutz couldn't wait to hear what his ex-wife had cooked up with Matt Spiller. If it was that dumbass book she'd written, he would laugh himself stupid. And what the hell was that teaser about the LAPD announcing a break in a murder case on a midnight talk show? Geesh. The craziness of this city.

Since the abrupt conclusion to the show, Stutz had not felt much like laughing, and "crazy" was such an inadequate adjective, considering what he'd just witnessed.

His cellphone would not stop ringing. He hadn't bothered checking who was so keen to get in touch. Would anyone on this planet want to say anything he might possibly want to hear? Ever again?

Eventually – it felt like a lifetime but was probably no more than twenty minutes – he answered one of the calls.

"What is it, Cathy?"

The vitriol he'd seen from Cathy Zengler when anyone undermined her best-laid plans was absent in her voice. There was a mellowness that only came from complete resignation.

"Jesus. Brett… you fucked the studio, the movie, your career, your reputation. Is it true? What Matt Spiller said?"

"I had the information, but I wasn't involved."

"You know, somehow that's worse. Although, I don't believe you, and no one else will."

He wasn't sincere in his questions, but he asked them anyway: "You're a PR guru. You got any wise words of advice? How I might handle this? Spin it? What I should do now?"

*"What you should do now?"* Cathy shrieked a laugh. "Fucking kill yourself, because this is irredeemable."

"Can I turn state's evidence?" A more serious proposition.

"How? If you're not involved. Anyway, would they need it? The authorities? Sounds like they have more than enough."

"That's what I thought. So, I should kill myself."

"In your shoes, I would."

"Yeah." Stutz took one last look at the night-time cityscape, stepped forward to his balcony railing, closed his eyes as he bent at the waist, and pivoted into a literal fall from grace.

## FORTY-SIX

FORTUNATELY, THEO MONTGOMERY drove like a man who didn't like driving. He was even less keen on a high-speed pursuit. The kid currently whimpering in the darkness of the passenger footwell didn't deserve to die in a fireball. He was sorry he'd abducted her, especially as this was the daughter of a man who'd gone out of his way to help resurrect his career. At least until Matt Spiller had unwittingly dropped the curtain on that ever happening.

Theo Montgomery was beginning to think he'd done a stupid thing. He had no clue if his name was in those files. Maybe he could have left the studio that evening the same way he'd arrived, an innocent pawn in Matt Spiller's scheme to unmask the global guilty. He'd not indulged his weakness for nearly two decades, and he didn't want to leap back in with this girl. The problem was the historical nature of those files. Evidence going back to the seventies. A time when he'd been highly active. He'd picked up the taste in Vietnam. Such easy pickings over there. And it was a different time back then. They'd never really feared prosecution. Too many vested interests, too many reputations on the line. Too easy to turn a blind eye, or at least a deaf ear, to the rumors. Authorities reluctant to act for fear that the rot went too high, or because the rot at the top closed down any investigation before it could even get off the ground. And there simply wasn't the preponderance of tech back then. Now everyone had a cellphone with a video. It was all too fraught with danger.

Besides, he'd always had help from his cadre to subdue his prey. One on one, especially at his age, wasn't viable, even when it was a little kid.

Weirdly, though, he found himself veering right, onto the Hollywood Freeway, heading north, and to a location where he might find some privacy, as though he was being drawn there by a latent desire that was pushing to make itself known again.

Shortly, he took the off-ramp down to Magnolia, which cut through the center of North Hollywood Park, then took a left into the deserted parking area.

He switched off the engine and sat there for a moment, staring at the small face peering up at him in the darkness.

"It's okay," he said. "I ain't gonna hurt you."

"You hurt my sister," she moaned.

"I panicked. I was scared. Like you are now. I know you're scared, see? I'm not a monster."

"I want my mummy."

"*Ssshhhh.* It's okay. I just need time to think. I'll take you back to your mom real soon."

He didn't think that was the truth. If this kid were to be reunited with her folks, he wouldn't be the one bringing them together. Likely, at that point, he'd be dead. And Theo Montgomery understood at that moment why he'd taken her. Whether or not he was in those files, he wasn't willing to wait around for the time when someone would bleat his name to shave off a fraction of their own sentence. He couldn't live that way. The ignominy of having a bunch of news trucks outside his house, filming live as he took the walk of shame out of his own front door, handcuffed, and flanked.

"I want to go home," the kid said. "Back to England. I hate this place."

Theo took the .357 out from under his thigh, and the kid whined louder.

SADIE UNPLUGGED THE lightbox as she indicated to join the off-ramp at North Hollywood Park.

"They're still stopped," Spiller said. "Car park, far side of the road. Take a right at the end, then a quick left." His phone chirped. He answered, putting it on speaker. "What is it, Angelo?"

"We got Theo on CCTV stealing a truck."

"Doesn't matter, we know where he is."

"He had a gun. And this won't matter to you now, but it looks like it might be Noah Dalton's truck."

Spiller glanced at Sadie. "Damn. You're right, Angelo, that's for another day. Thanks for the heads-up about the gun." He ended the call before Bartoli could tell him not to do anything rash.

Sadie moved to the side of the off-ramp and stopped at the lights at the junction. "Show me the map."

"We need to hurry."

"Matt, show me."

He gave her the phone, and she nodded. "Okay. I see the lie of the land." She grabbed the scoped rifle and got out, talking to him through the window. "Budge over here. Wait for my signal. I'll call. Then drive in there and keep your headlights on. Light up his truck, then hit the lightbox. He won't be able to see it's my car. Better if he thinks it's a cop. Less personal. Chances are, he'll get out. Hopefully not with your daughter, but I can handle that."

"What do I do?" Spiller asked.

"Just what I said and nothing more. Sit tight." Sadie took off running across Magnolia, crouching as she disappeared into the park.

Twenty seconds later, he answered her call.

Spiller wanted to cover the final hundred yards in double-quick time, but he turned off Magnolia and drove sedately into position, as though he was a patrol officer routinely checking the area. He spotted the truck, and it was Noah's. It still bore the plates Sadie had swapped onto it the night they stole it. He stopped thirty feet shy of the Ford and left his engine running. He bathed the old truck in white-blue light, and he could clearly make out Theo Montgomery sitting in the driver's seat, but that was all. He wondered if Sophie was in the passenger seat, but too low to be seen. Most likely she was in the footwell. Worst-case scenario, she was lying inert in the bed of the truck, and they were already too late.

After a few seconds, he activated the dancing red and blue lights in the windshield.

Theo Montgomery quickly stepped out, holding his Magnum pointing directly at the Escalade. Oddly, Spiller felt no desire to duck. He had envisaged a scene where the muzzle of that gun was pressed against his daughter's head, and he wondered again, more frantically, if that wasn't possible because Sophie wasn't alive to be used as either a shield or a hostage.

Then he didn't need to duck, because Sadie blew out the side of the old pedo's head.

## FORTY-SEVEN

THE FOLLOWING DAY, Helen brought forward their flights, and they left Los Angeles, not even waiting around to provide the statements Bartoli had requested. What did it matter? Theo Montgomery was dead. Spiller wondered if he'd seen his girls for the final time, but he was just happy they were both still breathing, and on balance he guessed it might be best if their lives were never plagued by his toxic presence again.

The revelations he'd disseminated the night before via Mel Banaghan had gone truly global. Already people were being fired and arrested. Others with no hierarchical superior were stepping down, and some were being forcibly removed against their will. Some of those were holding their hands up, and some were fronting it out, turning their backs on the Deep State that had quietly protected them for decades, and claiming it was now out to get them. A few had already taken the coward's way out and ended their miserable existences. As for the industry of Hollywood, it was in total meltdown. And this was just the start.

In the absence of any contradictory declaration from little Sophie, Spiller and Sadie had sworn that Theo Montgomery had been a mortal threat when he was shot, aiming his weapon into the cab of the Ford, where Sophie had been cowering. It was accepted at face value because no one now cared about Theo Montgomery, and the LAPD had far bigger fish to haul in, and didn't have the resources to be second-guessing ironclad, corroborative statements.

For the next few days, Spiller and Sadie stayed with Hayley, keeping out of the limelight. After a while, the paparazzi who mistook the storytellers for the story, setting up camp outside her house on the Pacific Coast Highway, decided to move on. Virginia kept her distance, not wishing to inflict more unwelcome attention on her son, who'd suffered enough that year.

*Veteran Avenue* was put on hold. Hayley had decided she no longer wanted to be associated with the acting world, so she plumped for a literary release of the novel instead. A fierce bidding war was already underway.

Sadie gave up the lease on her apartment, and Spiller instructed a local realtor to put his house on the market, saying he would drop his keys into their office so they could take photographs. The Maserati and the Hayabusa would be left behind. Whoever bought the house could have them.

On the day they said their final farewells to Hayley, Spiller accompanied Sadie to her apartment so she could start packing her belongings, then he ventured back to his erstwhile home to collect the few items he valued. Manny was definitely coming with them.

They had decided they would head to Montana, a place called Big Timber, only because they had to pick somewhere, and one of the characters in *Veteran Avenue* had chosen that location to escape to. Mountains and fresh air, and lots of unpopulated space where they could find a refuge from the world and its woes. They would take all the cash, the gold, and the diamonds, add in the sale price of his house, his earnings from a movie that would never be seen, then work out what they would need to live a comfortable life. What they considered surplus would be divided among several charities, which were yet to be decided.

Spiller garaged the Maserati for the last time and saw with dismay that his bike was gone. He let himself into his house and swore again. More items were missing. He didn't own that much, so it wasn't hard to spot the gaps around the house. The TV, his hi-fi, some ornaments. All his bike gear was gone. He went to a kitchen drawer, and his spare keys were missing.

Noah. Damn. He'd barely given a thought to the Texan since *The Mel Banaghan Show*. Sadie had loaned him a spare semi-auto, just in case, but Spiller figured the kid had most likely gone back to Texas by now, maybe got himself a job on a ranch, working for his food and lodging in exchange for his undocumented status. At some point down the line, he'd be arrested after starting a fight in a local bar, and subsequently identified and jailed.

Spiller laid his hand on the weapon in his waistband, reassuring himself he was ready if he'd got all that wrong.

He went upstairs to pack, and quickly found his suitcase, but not in the way he'd have liked.

Halfway up, the empty blue hardshell Carlton landed on his head, crumpling him onto the steps, and tumbling him back down into the hall. Stunned, he felt for his gun, but it had fallen out. Then he was staring into the muzzle of another semi-automatic, held by someone who had not decided to flee back to his home state.

"Howdy, Matt. You miss me? I didn't miss you; I got you real good." Noah cackled at his joke. "Figured you might want your suitcase. Although I can't imagine why you'd be leavin' town when we still have unfinished business. Get up."

Spiller stood up and rubbed his head, which was swimming. "How long have you been here?"

"Since the show. Needed a place to lay low, and figured this is the last place anyone would look for me."

"You're not as daft as I thought. What do you want, Noah?"

"I want my life back. I want you to step up, admit what you done to me."

"So you can go back to acting? This town is *over*."

"You think so? You ain't changed nothin'. This time next year, it'll all be forgotten. Anyhow, I don't care about that. I just wanna go home. I called Bartoli. He's headin' over here. You're gonna admit on camera what you did. You're not the only one who can use a video to get people locked up."

Spiller shook his head. "A confession at gun point? I think that might be what they call *inadmissible*."

"Bartoli's gonna say you fessed up of your own free will. I talked to him days ago. And I called him soon as I heard you arrive. He ain't fixin' to mention any gun. You think you glow when you walk, huh? But that man detests you."

"Oh. Well, that's a bummer. I'm going to wait outside."

"You stay right there, mister."

"Hey, shoot me if you like. But I'm guessing you need me alive for your plan to work. Noah, if I'm going to prison, I'd like to take a seat at my favorite spot in the world and enjoy the view for a while."

"And where's that exactly?"

"Down by the reservoir. I go there to think sometimes. I can look out over the water and believe I'm in the middle of nowhere. You're welcome to join me."

Noah laughed. "Now you're just bein' plain facetious. I ain't lettin' you out of my sight. Not until Bartoli has you on video and in handcuffs. So, you want that to happen by the lake, I don't give two hoots. Lead the way. Just remember: if I gotta put a bullet in you and fuck myself in the process, I'll do that before I let you run. And I am a *dead shot*."

"Whatever." Spiller turned and went into the living room. He yanked open the bi-fold doors, furtively pressing the silent alarm button as he did so, and let himself out into the pool area, then headed across to the gate that opened onto the reservoir. Noah followed, wisely keeping his distance, and Spiller weaved his way down through the parched scrubland to his spot by the water. He sat on a rock, facing his foe, and smiled. "Nice here, innit?"

"You are one crazy son-bitch."

"Maybe. I don't know. This all just seems so inevitable. I've got away with so much recently, my luck was bound to run out sometime. That's all this is. Just... fate. How long before Bartoli gets here?"

"Thirty minutes," he said.

"Not putting on the blues and twos for you, then."

"*Blues and twos?* Huh?"

"English expression. Lights and siren. *Nee naw, nee naw.*"

Noah found a boulder of his own to sit on. He rested his gun arm on his thigh.

Spiller turned his face to the sun. "Do you want to hear an acting tale, Noah? You being a budding thespian."

"Hell, why not?"

Spiller looked at him. "It's a sad tale. Sure you want to hear it?"

Noah nodded. "I got nothin' better to do."

"Okay. Well, I was just starting out as an actor. Fresh out of drama school. RADA. I had a gorgeous girlfriend all the way through my three years. Jesus, we were so in love. Maybe we were naïve. Actors are at that age. And maybe they never change, who knows? Anyway, we talked about a future together, having kids, maybe coming here one day, taking Hollywood by storm. One thing we were definite about, though: that we wouldn't leave the other person behind. Whoever made it first, they'd take the other one with them. Open doors for them. We were a team. And if neither of us made it, so what? We'd still have each other. We really were that idealistic. But that's because we were soulmates. You ever had a soulmate, Noah?"

Noah shook his head.

"It's lovely. And I think I may have found another one right here in this cesspit of a town, which is so rare. Twice in one lifetime. So... we auditioned for a play together. Big production in a regional theatre. Good springboard. And we both got parts. They weren't big, but we'd be together for a few more months, and that meant everything. Couple of big names in the cast. And one I'd never heard of. Like us, fresh out of drama school. But unlike us, he went straight into the lead role. Cocky little wanker, he was. No one could understand it. He couldn't possibly have endeared himself at audition, and he was so lame at acting, but... that's life in the profession, right? It's not much of a meritocracy at times. So, we get through rehearsals, and no one likes this guy. He fancied himself, of course, and it was obvious he fancied my girlfriend, but she wasn't interested. Then the show opens. The local Press come along, and one or two nationals. And they also hate this guy. He gets slated. They like the show, they just hate him. Then one day, after a particularly harsh review, he comes in early for the evening performance and he's really drunk. The second person in that evening was my girlfriend. I had some stuff to do, so I was running late." Spiller scowled at Noah, who had physically sagged, his gun arm heavier on his thigh, the barrel pointing at the dirt. "Sorry, Noah, am I boring you?"

"Kinda."

"Then I should cut to the finale, eh? This actor rapes my girlfriend. Cops don't believe her, and I can't save her. She's destroyed. So, she kills herself. Hangs herself in his dressing room as a message that maybe she wasn't lying. Next thing I know, he's nowhere to be found. At that point, I lose the plot. I become depressed, leave the profession for a while, but I don't get any better. I *never* get any better. Couple of years later, I find out he'd been whisked away by his famous relatives, which is why he got the part in the first place. They bring him right here and they make him famous."

Noah yawned for effect. "Well, that just makes me feel lower than a gopher hole."

Spiller grinned. "You're just not getting it. Tell you what, Noah. I'm tired of waiting, so I'm going to make a move."

"Don't." Noah raised his gun.

"No, I am. Only way you stop me doing that is if we have a little contest."

Warily, Noah said, "Go on."

"You lay your gun on the ground between your feet. I make a move towards you, and if you can pick it up before I get halfway, I'll sit back down and wait for Bartoli, and I'll sing like a bird when he gets here."

Noah guffawed. "There's a good twenty-five feet between us. No one's that fast."

"Then you've got nothing to worry about."

"Shit, you just want me to shoot you. I pick up my gun, you're just gonna keep comin'."

"Then shoot me in the leg. You're a dead shot, right? If I keep coming, shoot me in the leg, then you get to lock me up *and* hurt me. It's a win-win."

Noah narrowed his eyes. "You're crazy. No way you close the distance in time."

Spiller shrugged. "Let's find out." He shifted his weight forward, like he was about to set off.

Noah shrugged back. "What the hell." He placed his gun on the ground between his boots and straightened up, placing his palms on his thighs like it was the gentlemanly thing to do.

Spiller leaned further forward, shifted one leg back to give him some spring, and placed his palms in the dirt, as though he was starting out from running blocks.

The gun in the clear plastic bag was pointing at Noah before he could even lift a palm off his jeans.

"Don't move, Noah."

"What the…?"

"Careful, Noah. I'm a dead shot, too. I was taught by the Jordanian Special Forces for a movie. I could take your earlobe clean off. But I'm not aiming at your ear. Slowly, kick your gun away from you."

Noah used the pointy toe of a boot to slide the gun out of reach.

Spiller smiled. "You should have paid attention, Noah. You should have listened to my story, rather than switching off and yawning through it. Now, focus. Think hard. Recall what I just said. Where did I say that rapist actor ended up?"

"Here. In LA."

"No. I said *right* here. In fact, you can see his house if you look over there."

Noah's gaze was pulled across the water, up the opposite bank of the reservoir. His face distorted as he looked back at Spiller. "You killed Harry Sullivan!"

"Yep. With this. I've had a little armory under this rock these past few weeks. Three guns at one point."

"You gonna shoot me?"

"I'm going to have to, aren't I? It's the only way to close the Harry Sullivan case *and* stop you coming after me. Because you're not going to stop, are you, Noah? Not until I'm dead or in prison."

"Damn straight. What else am I gonna do? You stole my life and I want it back."

"This is all your fault, Noah. I never asked you to come over and talk to me that first night. You made me your enemy. You could have stayed at your table, or you could have approached me with a little respect. I did nothing to hurt you or threaten you. This is all on you, Noah, so fucking own it."

Noah's expression altered. A look of resignation, acceptance even. "Well, at least I got my boots on. And I ain't scared. My pa would be proud. And for the record, I woulda never hurt your dau—"

Spiller sent the bullet straight through the gap between Noah's parted lips. The Texan tipped backward off his boulder, and Spiller realized this was the guiltiest he'd felt in a long time. But as with Billy, he hadn't been given much choice, and he didn't have time to dwell on it because he could hear a siren heading his way.

He prepared the scene. He picked up the spent casing, went over and placed Noah's hand inside the bag around the gun, before pulling the bag away. He pressed Noah's fingertips onto the frame and the trigger, then picked up Noah's gun and zipped it and the shell casing inside. Then he threw it far into the reservoir.

Then he sat next to Noah's body, his finger over Noah's trigger finger, and he waited.

The siren grew louder until Spiller guessed it was right outside his house. He let it cut out, gave it fifteen seconds, then fired off two bullets into the reservoir, waited five seconds, then fired a third. At that point, he scurried thirty feet away from the body and threw himself on the ground, rolling around in the dust, purposely grazing his face. A few seconds later, two officers burst through his back gate and headed down to him, weapons drawn. He held his hands up, attracting their attention, then pointed at Noah.

"I'm Matt Spiller! He just tried to kill me!"

"Is it just you?" asked the female officer. "Anyone else we need to worry about?"

"No."

"Are you hurt?"

"No. He shot at me twice, then killed himself when he heard you arrive."

The male officer cautiously approached Noah's body, then holstered his weapon when he saw the spray of cranial matter. "Sweet Jesus, what a mess." He peered at Noah's face. "No sign of any in-shoot. Looks like he put the gun in his mouth. You're sure you're okay, Mr Spiller?"

"Yes, thanks."

"You think this is related to the recent attempt on your life?"

"I know it is. It's the same fellah. Noah Dalton. Mad bastard."

"What did he want with you? He say anything?"

"Just that he wanted me dead. Like he wanted Harry Sullivan dead. And Aiden Powers. He told me he'd killed them weeks ago, but I didn't really believe him. I caught him on video saying it. I gave the detective the evidence last time. What's her name? Uh… Rainey?"

"I wouldn't know."

The female officer got on her radio, requesting assistance.

Spiller appeared to have a revelation. "You know, I bet you'll find that gun's a ballistics match to the Harry Sullivan case."

"I'm sure they'll check. You take a seat, Mr Spiller. Hopefully, they'll get you cleaned up and squared away in no time. By the way, thanks for what you did on *The Mel Banaghan Show*. You're a hero. Every cop I know says the same. You did what no cop's been able to do in fifty years. This is a different world now. A better one."

Spiller smiled. "Just doing my bit for humanity."

THIRTY MINUTES LATER, Bartoli turned up. Spiller watched him come through the back gate and stand there, surveying the scene before him. The area was busy now, different uniforms milling about. Spiller had been moved outside the cordon, marked by yellow tape that read: *Police Line – Do Not Cross. Linea de Policia – No Cruzar.* An EMS was attending to his facial injuries. He waved at Bartoli, who just closed his eyes and shook his head, then made his way down to inspect the body, which was about to be zipped up and removed. Spiller watched him ask a question of the Medical Examiner. The ME shook his head, dismissing whatever the enquiry had been. Then Bartoli spoke to the officers who'd been first on the scene, before fixing his gaze on Spiller and trudging over with a weary gait.

"What did you do, Matthew? What did you do now?"

"I'm okay now, thanks," Spiller said to the EMS, who packed her case and moved away. He shrugged at Bartoli. "I survived, Angelo."

"You think Noah deserved it?"

"*He* must have thought he did. Look what he did to himself. You're late, by the way. Noah said you were on your way ages ago."

"I was talking to your neighbors. Funny, one of them said they heard a single gunshot, then a gap of several minutes, then two shots in quick succession, then a gap of a few seconds, and another single gunshot. You told the officers Noah fired at you twice, then put the gun in his mouth. Correct?"

"That's what happened."

"So… what was that first report? The one that preceded the others by several minutes?"

"Couldn't tell you. Maybe a car backfiring."

"Sure. When was the last time you heard a car backfire?"

"Or maybe it was someone else with a gun. Lots of guns in this city, Angelo."

The two men eyed each other for several seconds.

Spiller broke the moment: "I heard you're in line for a commendation, promotion, big pay rise. For helping to crack the pedo thing. You've been in the news."

"You want me to thank you?"

"No. What I'd like is for you to leave me alone now. This thing between us… it's finished. There's nowhere left to go with it. Anyway, I'm getting out of here. Our paths won't cross again."

Bartoli thought about it. "You'll get yours. Sooner or later." Then he walked away.

## FORTY-EIGHT

THEY WERE ON the road by three o'clock, and four hours later they were on Interstate 15, the Mohave Freeway, traveling north of the Mojave National Preserve, heading for that famed gambling mecca of Las Vegas, where they planned to stop for the night. The light was already fading, and the scrubland of the desert that flanked them was beginning to lose its color and definition. Spiller had been nodding off for a while, exhausted by the day's events, and his contemplation of a second reinvention of himself in the space of eight months. He had gone from a poor taxi driver to a rich movie star to... he didn't know yet. He would still be rich, but he had no clue how he would occupy his time, and what he'd say if the people in his new town asked him what he did for a living. Perhaps he'd buy a ranch, which would make him a rancher, and who'd have believed that would have been in his stars a mere year ago?

He suddenly became aware that the Escalade was slowing down. He opened his eyes and looked at Sadie. "What's up?"

Sadie steered the vehicle off the road and stopped. She looked at him, and he saw she was holding her HK flat against her tummy, pointing his way.

"Sadie?"

"Get out, Matt."

"You're joking. After everything we've been through?"

"Get out."

Spiller had Sadie's spare gun, but it was in his gym bag on the rear seat. "You're kidding," he repeated.

"Out."

"Why?"

"Get the fuck out."

"Jesus, can I at least grab a coat from my bag? So I don't freeze my nuts off waiting for a ride back to LA?"

"You can take your overnight bag and whatever's in it. The rest stays with me."

Sadie was referring to the other bag in the trunk that contained the cash, gold, and diamonds.

"Wow," he said. "I did *not* see this coming."

"Get out."

Spiller obeyed. He opened the rear door, snatched his bag off the seat, and slammed the door closed again. The moment the Escalade began to move back onto the road, Spiller dipped into the bag and pulled out the gun. He took a wide stance and aimed at the rear glass, to the left, where he knew he'd put one through her head. He hadn't the faintest idea what had just happened, so he couldn't tell what her next move might be. Maybe she'd keep going. Or maybe she'd jump out and shoot him, having reassessed her decision to let him walk. He'd shown her how tenacious he was. Would she really risk making a mortal enemy of him?

The Escalade stopped fifteen feet away, its tail pipes clouding the cooling desert air.

Spiller had a clear line and a full magazine. He kept his aim for five seconds, then lowered his gun. He kissed his fingertips and flicked his hand forward, sending his love her way, then he turned and started walking back in the direction of Los Angeles, a hundred and fifty miles away. Behind him, he heard the engine roar and the Escalade take off, but then there was a swish from the tires as he heard it veer off the road again onto the dirt shoulder and perform a one-eighty. He heard her coming back his way, but he carried on walking. He was suddenly very tired of fighting. If this was his time, so be it.

Sadie slowed beside him, matching his pace, and lowered her window.

"Forget something?" he asked, swinging his bag over his shoulder.

"Maybe."

Spiller halted, and so did Sadie. The engine grumbled, and a car coming their way blasted its horn.

"What was all that about?" he asked. "Kicking me out?"

"I needed to know if I could really trust you."

"Not to shoot you? Dangerous game. What if I had?"

"Ballistic glass. I had it swapped for the security work."

"Oh." He laughed.

"Were you just gonna walk away from all that money in the trunk?"

"Rather than shoot you? Of course. Did I not prove myself already? Sharing my life story? Leaving a ton of money with you?"

"Did you, though? Or did you leave a *half* ton?"

Spiller clicked to her insinuation. "You looked in the other bag."

Sadie turned off the engine. "Why didn't you tell me about it?"

"Come on, Sadie. You can't say I don't trust you. I trusted you with millions."

"I know you trust me, Matt. And you're right to. You could have left the whole lot with me; I'd never have run off with a single dime. But that's not the issue, is it?"

Spiller peered at her, puzzled.

"Matt, I know you trust me. Problem is, you don't trust yourself."

He seriously thought about it; he owed her that much. Why had he withheld the news of his second haul? Had life been so crazy he'd just not got round to it? Or was he safeguarding an exit strategy?

"A lot's happened," he said, by way of defense. "I've known you less than a month. And it's been a crazy month – even by my standards."

She eyed him. "I just don't know about you."

"Don't worry about it; no one ever does. Listen, we passed a gas station two miles back, so I'm going to head there while there's still some light."

"What then?"

Spiller shrugged. "Don't know. Maybe go back to England, patch things up with my wife."

"Seriously?"

"No, I'm not that fucking deluded. I don't know, is the answer. Go back to my house, see what happens."

"You won't last a day. You know how many people want you dead after the Mel Banaghan thing?"

"Not exactly, but I imagine it's a world record."

"You're the biggest whistle-blower who ever lived. They find you, they'll make an example of you. *Pour encourager les autres*. It's suicide if you go back to LA. Maybe, just maybe, you can find a quiet spot in the wilderness, change how you look, keep a low profile."

"Yeah, and turn into old Jack, always waiting for the day when *they* come for me."

"Is that why you kept the bag a secret?" Sadie asked. "In case you ever had to run?"

Spiller smiled. "Is that the winning answer? Do you stay if I say that?"

"Is it true?"

"I honestly don't know. I do know I don't want you getting hurt on my account. So, it's probably best we do go our separate ways. It's selfish wanting you to stay. Live your best life, Sadie. You won't do that with me."

"And what if I want to stay? No matter the consequences."

Spiller glanced down the highway in the direction of Las Vegas. He did a double take, then squinted. In the distance, multiple headlights were approaching, merging into one luminosity.

"Damn. That's a lot of traffic heading our way."

"From both directions," Sadie said, staring down the highway toward LA.

Spiller looked back and forth, then at Sadie. "Speaking of consequences…"

Sadie jumped out and grabbed the HK long gun from the rear seat. She rested it through her open front window, adjusting the telescopic sight to get a better view. Then she swapped to the opposite side of the door and checked the situation coming up on her six, from the direction of Las Vegas.

"We need to get off the road," she said, looking at the nearest hills that flanked the opposite highway. As she said this, the approaching vehicles all went dark. "Matt, get in."

They both jumped back in, and Sadie set off over the median strip and the opposite lanes, powering the unlit Caddy across a small gully and into the desert with a hefty bump. She weaved between the cacti and bushes, heading for the start of the hills a thousand feet away.

"Climb in the back," she ordered. "Grab the khaki case. I got another couple of rifles in there, plus a bunch of mags and a couple of NODs."

"NODs?"

"Night vision." Sadie grinned as the hills loomed against the darkening sky.

Spiller thought her expression seemed incongruous, given their dilemma, then he remembered the unit she'd served in. "Tenth Mountain Division," he said.

"Affirmative," Sadie replied. "Whoever they are, they're in my world now."

## ACKNOWLEDGEMENTS

Thanks to my wonderful wife, Jeannifer,
and my kids, Jade, Carl, and Tina,
for their love and support.

## ABOUT THE AUTHOR

Mark Pepper lives in Manchester and has been in love with his wife, Jeannifer, since 1991. He is a RADA-trained professional actor, and the author of five novels. He spent seven years living in Spain, is a qualified secondary-school drama teacher, and was an HGV-1 driver for a while. For the past seventeen years, he has been an Intelligence Analyst, working online for various organizations in the U.S.

Printed in Dunstable, United Kingdom